# THE MIRROR SHOP

NICHOLAS BUNDOCK

ISBN 13: 9789492371706 (ebook)

ISBN 13: 9789492371690 (paperback)

Published by Amsterdam Publishers, the Netherlands

info@amsterdampublishers.com

Author's website: nicholasbundock.com

Cover design by Johnson Design. Images of mirrors courtesy of Yew Tree House Antiques, New York

Notes to the Hurrying Man by Brian Patten, published by Allen & Unwin, 1969, Copyright © Brian Patten. Reproduced by permission of the author c/o Rogers, Coleridge & Ward Ltd., 20, Powis Mews, London W11 1JN. Lines from The Sunken Garden, (London, 1917), by kind permission of the Literary Trustees of Walter de la Mare and the Society of Authors as their representative.

*Into my mirror has walked*
*A woman who will not talk*
*Of love or of its subsidiaries,*
*But who stands there*
*Pleased by her own silence.*

**Brian Patten**

# CONTENTS

# PROLOGUE

*I am a murderer. I have murdered a man.* Luke mouths the words to the cell wall. Raising his eyes, he watches the first light give colour to the window above him. From the upper right corner to the lower left it pales from burnt umber to raw sienna. He thinks of the jars of pigments in the workshop back home. He does not expect to see them again. The thought leaves him unmoved. As the light increases, the glass squares set in their iron frame grow larger while the ironwork becomes thinner. The cell, an uncertain space in darkness, now takes shape and encloses him. Not that he feels incarcerated. Far from it. He can ignore the smell of disinfectant and the half-erased obscenities on the walls and see a strange beauty in this room.

From somewhere comes an urge to shout for paper and pencil and to draw this place of rectangles and slow-moving shadows. *The French police have been so considerate*, he whispers to himself, *perhaps they will oblige. Last night they were almost apologetic when they removed the belt from my jeans*: 'We have to follow regulations, you understand.' He lowers his eyes to the navy tracksuit folded at the end of the bed where they left it. One of them had said, 'In your condition, even in August on Corsica, you may feel the cold.' Paper and pencil seems a small request. But he does not call out. To do so would disturb the stillness.

As he sits upright on the bed, no more than a mattress on a shelf projecting from the wall, his eyes drop to the floor and follow the

I

oblique shadow moving from his ankles to his legs. He cannot remember sleeping. It is growing hotter. The cell floor, below ground level, he guesses, is losing its film of damp. Yes, paper and pencil would help. He tries to remember the name of an English pointillist and minor academician who painted the effect of heat. He can see a painting of two girls by railings on a concrete promenade, their forms merging with the distant sea under an unforgiving sun. The artist's name eludes him.

What time did I arrive here? he wonders. It must have been early evening. I was happy to make a full statement. 'We will wait until the morning,' they said. That's another reason to ask for some paper: if I could write a few notes now, it would be so useful later. Writing would clear my mind. Help me explain what happened.

'No, no,' he says aloud. 'Alden was the writer, the original word man. I won't write anything. I'm not sorry I killed him. I feel no remorse. I feel nothing.'

He hears the sound of approaching feet. Perhaps they are bringing me breakfast, he thinks. I'm not hungry, but I will ask for paper and pencil so I can draw this place. I'm sure they won't refuse – they've treated me so well. When they shut the door, there was no judgmental bang, no angry twist of a key, no hammering home of a bolt. If a cell door can be closed gently, that is what they did.

The footsteps pass and fade. He is not disappointed. There is an overriding peace here now it is all over. A numbness. The events of the last two months might have happened to a stranger.

* * *

*Is it only twelve days since I last woke in this room?* In the greyness before dawn Eva watches the china animals on the windowsill assume their pale blues and greens. Ornaments from childhood, her oldest possessions, they had spoken to her, told her stories in her first bedroom. Now they seem to be asking her to review her life from those earliest years until now. *In time I will – when I am ready*, she tells them. She looks away and closes her eyes, knowing that among the small achievements and failures there had been nothing to match the intensity of the recent two-headed crisis. When had it begun? Its origins reached back many years, but was there a particular day it manifested itself – the beginning of the double loss which had changed her world? She slips back to a morning seven weeks ago.

2

# PART I

# 1

Eva frowns at the unmodernised kitchen, the elm cupboard, the chipped Belfast sink, the primitive painting of a prize ox, the stained poster of some obscure French film. But no mirror to peer into before rubbing away the night's sleep. For a dealer in mirrors, he could do with a few more in his own home.

She carries two mugs of green tea up the uneven staircase to the bedroom where she places a mug on the floor each side of the bed, slips under the covers, and casts her eyes around the room, resting them on a pitted mirror plate in a red lacquer frame. She watches its gilt decoration flicker as the sun finds a slit between the shutters. Looking down at the steady breathing of Luke's sleeping form, she wonders why she is awake before him. Isn't the normal pattern for Luke to be up and dressed and making tea before she has stirred? But then the normal pattern is for their nights together to be spent at her house on the edge of town, not here at his. Perhaps it is the change of beds which has altered her routine. Over the years how many times has she slept here? A few dozen perhaps. It's not important. So much is shared, having separate homes ten minutes apart is of no consequence. And didn't last night prove it doesn't impair fun in bed, never mind whose?

Luke rolls towards her and peppers her shoulder with half-asleep kisses. 'I'm glad you're awake.'

Eva returns a single kiss. 'Sadly, I have my first client at nine.'

Naked, she slips out of bed, walks to the window, opens the shutters and looks down at the empty street. She raises the sash window, admitting July birdsong, restrained with the approach of high summer and underscored by the harsher notes of rooks from the trees beyond the church at the end of the street. She watches a pigeon settle on a window sill of the flint tower, turns back and frowns at the room's monastic sparseness.

'Ever thought of a proper bedroom mirror?'

'I already have one.'

'Useless. It's only the blind and nuns who have to dress without one. Which do you think I am?'

'Move in with me and you can have the room next to the bathroom as a dressing room. Furnish it how you like.'

Eva raises her eyebrows, knowing the present arrangements suit them both very well. She walks to the door, unhooks her white silk dressing gown, wraps the collar round her head like a wimple, and holds it tight, with her palms together under her chin. Going to the mirror she makes an exaggerated attempt to discern a reflection of herself in the decayed bevelled plate. Slowly she turns to him and says, 'Bedroom mirror.'

Luke pretends not to notice.

Draping the dressing gown over her shoulders, she walks to the door where she lingers, running a finger over a panel. 'If you ever want to redecorate this room I'll give you a hand.'

'Come back to bed.'

'What do you call this colour? Brown? Mouse? Drab?'

'Two hundred years ago drab was a very fashionable colour.'

'Then this room wants re-drabbing.' She smiles and goes to the bathroom.

Luke stretches his arms across the headboard. That smile. After all these years the frisson of being its chosen recipient remains. He scans the room, its faded chintz wallpaper – here when he bought the place – the worn Kazak rug by the bed, the otherwise bare floorboards, the walnut chest – almost as old as the house – for clothing not hung in the spidery walk-in cupboard next to the never-used fireplace, the lone bedroom chair piled high with clothes, the William and Mary mirror. She's right, he thinks, the room *is* dreary.

He listens to the shower and imagines Eva washing her hair, not as fair as when they first met, and now helped by judicial colouring, but still the perfect frame for that smile and, he thinks, like a great frame, changes in colour and surface which come from age only make it more desirable.

Wrapped in a towel, Eva returns, carrying his shaving mirror which, with exaggerated precision, she positions on the walnut chest. Luke observes the ritual, pretending he has never before seen it. She pulls a hair dryer from her overnight bag by the chair, plugs it into the room's only socket and with her back to him sits on the edge of the bed. Switching it on, she feels one of his fingers run down her spine, accompanied by a comment she cannot catch above the whirr of the dryer. When she has finished she stands and shakes her hair. A few droplets fall on his face. Brushing his cheeks with a hand, he licks the soapy dampness from his fingers. Eva notices and smiles before putting on her make-up.

'I give in,' Luke says. 'The place is drab. We'll get out the paint brushes.'

'Not before time,' she says and begins dressing.

Luke watches, relishing the second or two when her head is covered by her navy linen dress, its plain formality adding piquancy to the moment. Living in separate homes, he suspects, fuels their excitement.

Eva enters into the spirit of the reverse striptease, pulling on the dress inch by inch before finally running her hands down her hips, awarding her voyeur with a look of coy surprise. Slipping on her shoes, she says, 'If you see any autumn crocus bulbs in the market, can you buy me a dozen?'

'Have you room for any more?'

'There's a spot by the shed which needs some end of year colour.' With a zipping of her overnight bag and another smile, she leaves the bedroom.

For several minutes Luke stares towards the window, wondering if the room would benefit from curtains. Accepting that changes are needed, he rolls out of bed, pulls on yesterday's shirt and goes down to the kitchen. He finds Eva, toast in hand, standing by the French windows, looking out into the back garden. His own slice is waiting for him on the table.

'You're so lucky with these high walls,' she says. 'Ideal for climbing roses and good barriers for weeds. My fences never quite counter the invasion of ground elder from next door.'

'Those walls out there need repair and repointing. And you have enough space for a proper vegetable plot. I have to rent an allotment.'

'But you love your allotment.'

'Come and share it with me. Sell Brick Kiln Cottage and move in here. With the spare cash buy a weekend cottage near a trout stream.'

Eva scrutinises the kitchen. 'This room would need more changes than the bedroom.' She points to a space on the wall between the cupboard and a row of iron pegs. 'A mirror there would be handy for a start.'

'I'll dig one out of the store. Which style do you want? Georgian? Deco? I've a fantastic '50s French . . .'

'You're the mirror man – I'll leave it to you. Providing it doesn't have one of those dingy pieces of glass in it – great for connoisseurs but hopeless for make-up.'

Luke strokes her hair. 'I'll find one which even disguises your roots.'

'For that you can cook tonight. My house. And *you* bring the wine.'

At 9.50am Luke steps from his front door onto the narrow pavement of Back Lane, glancing with approval at the street sign painted on a wooden board fixed to the house opposite. He recalls the recent battle fought and won against newcomers: thank God for no bright new sign and no change of name, gentrified to Church Walk. He looks up with pleasure at the irregular ridges of the old roofs, their dull red tiles in contrast to the sharp blue East Anglian sky untainted by traffic fumes. Filling his lungs, he tells himself that this is one of those mornings which validate selling the shop in Chiswick and moving – all in the face of the accountant and wiseacres who thought it madness. He approaches a dogleg separating the lower part of the street from the market place, and recalls his private myth that at some remote point in the past the thoroughfare twisted its body to protect itself from the forces of commerce.

Among the dozen stalls of Cantisham's Wednesday market he returns nods to stallholders, pausing at the plant man to buy Eva's bulbs. He buys his weekly kipper from the fish stall and looks at some farmed sea bass.

'Still catching you own?' asks the fish man.

'We're trying again on Saturday.'

Leaving the stalls, he glances up at the sundial on the imposing front of the Jodrell Arms. Ignorant of British Summer Time, it reads 9.00am. Hard to believe he has lived here for nineteen years. He turns round to

8

his shop in the corner of the market place. Difficult to remember it as the run-down ironmonger's no-one wanted to buy. Now so different from the wreck of a building viewed on that wet November afternoon in the company of an even gloomier estate agent. He looks up at the sign above the door, *LUKE BREWER ANTIQUE MIRRORS*, lowers his eyes to the bay windows either side and checks that a Venetian pier glass is far enough back to be out of the sun.

'Coffee coming up,' calls a voice as he enters.

Luke places his purchases on the desk at the far end of the showroom, settles himself in his chair and glances at a few unimportant letters until Russ, in his brown workshop coat, brings coffee and a plate of biscuits.

'Shall I put your kipper in the fridge?'

Holding the fish at arm's length, Russ disappears to the kitchen. When he returns he is nursing a large padded envelope. 'I must show you these. Keith and Michael emailed them last night. I printed them off straight away. Now here's me on the beach at Kitsilano.' One by one, he lays them down on the desk like patience cards, with the occasional verbal caption. 'They stuck that feather in my hair to make me look like a Squamish Indian . . . and that's me on Grouse Mountain. No comments about the coat – I borrowed it.'

With dutiful enthusiasm Luke says, 'Really?' or 'Good heavens', sad that his restorer enjoys a freedom with friends in Vancouver he denies himself at home. He is sure Russ has never had a partner, certainly not in England. Even Keith and Michael had been met on some other holiday.

'And that man dancing on the table is a waiter on the ferry to Victoria. And no, I didn't join in.'

'These are amazing, Russ,' says Luke, aware that in all likelihood no-one else will be shown them.

The final photograph shows Russ wearing a party hat beside an enormous Easter bunny. 'I've no idea where that one was taken,' he says, before scooping them up and returning to his gilding, a task, Luke knows, which dislikes interruptions.

\* \* \*

At 10.00am in a first floor room at the Riverside Counselling Centre Eva's first client of the day is leaving. When the door is closed she goes to her chair and makes a few brief notes about the last hour, the final session after six months' bereavement counselling. Her next appointment is half-past. Time to go down to the Centre's kitchen for a coffee, or choose from one of the many infusions most of her colleagues prefer. She decides to remain in her room, and walking to the window looks down over the city roofs dominated by the cathedral spire. The view evokes memories of another cathedral city, her childhood, her parents. Somewhere below, invisible from her window, is a world of shops, offices and traffic. In the foreground she sees her client walking away from the Centre. Watching him pause and look at the river, she remembers clients who had found a final session difficult, experiencing it as a parting of friends. Others, like the figure now walking towards Foundry Bridge, had said goodbye with a formal handshake and thanks, almost as if a business transaction had been completed. Over the years a few had suggested, 'Can we meet up sometime – a drink perhaps?' The suggestion had always been gently declined, the professional distance maintained. Apart from one occasion many years ago.

She turns away from the window, sits in her armchair and looks at the painting over the mantelpiece, a sketch in oils by Jack Butler Yeats. Beside a river two bearded anglers are in passionate debate, their animated exchange conveyed by an economy of paint: a few lines in the distance suggest hills, seven brush strokes in the foreground depict a trout. More detail, she feels, would have detracted from it. The painting was a present from Luke on her fortieth birthday. As she looks at the fishermen, imagining their conversation, she hears footsteps on the stairs. Eva opens the door so her next client can enter without knocking.

A woman in her twenties enters, slams the door behind her and with a disparaging glance towards Eva drops into the waiting armchair. Before Eva is seated her client says, 'This will be my last appointment. We're getting nowhere.'

Eva sits, registering the distress in front of her. 'Agnes, have you given yourself enough time? Perhaps, if we . . .'

'How many more of these sessions will I need?'

'It's too early to know.'

In silence Agnes fidgets in her chair, pressing the hem of her loose-worn pink shirt against her cords. 'I found this leaflet the other day which said short-term therapy amounts to about twenty sessions. I don't want to get sucked into the machine. I know someone who's been seeing a shrink twice a week for two years and she's still as mad as a box of frogs. Her latest thing is somatic counselling, whatever that is. In

Arizona. Three thousand quid's worth.' Agnes scowls. 'I suppose at that price it's got to work. Good thing she can afford it. You therapists sure know how to cater for every pocket.' Agnes looks up to the ceiling, running a hand through untidy fair hair, an inch above shoulder length. 'It does all seem a con. And a hell of a waste of time.'

'Isn't it because you were wasting time that you first came here?'

'Wasting time on men, yes.' Agnes runs her eyes along the cornice and scowls. 'God, to think last Christmas I was looking round this amazing flat in Blackheath. My boss's husband, with the fidelity record of a tom cat. Stupid or what? He could find me a better job with someone he knew, but if I wanted to start my own business that was fine – he had more than enough money to help. The day before we were going to make an offer on the place he dumped me. And he had *never* left his wife. Wasting time? Wasting my bloody life.'

'Don't you think you deserve to waste a little time on yourself now?'

With a derisive laugh, Agnes sits back in her chair.

Eva says, 'Now last week you were telling me about your first long-term relationship.'

'The Richard era. A two-year mistake.'

'When did you feel it was a mistake?'

'After a month if I'm honest.'

'Were you honest?'

'Obviously not.'

'Why do you think you continued with him?'

'I hoped things would change. I thought . . .' Agnes looks at Eva as if expecting her to complete the sentence.

Eva remains silent.

Agnes explodes. 'It's all very well for you just sitting there. I suppose you have the perfect husband, two children, a sweet cottage in the country and holidays in Umbria financed by losers like me.'

'Did you hope Richard would be the perfect partner?'

'Why do you tell me nothing about yourself? Here I am, pouring my sodding heart out, and you sit there like a block of ice. I bet your dad's a judge. I'd get more sympathy if I stopped a bag lady in the street.'

'Is it sympathy you're looking for?'

'There you go again. So smug. Miss Perfect. Miss Anonymous.'

'If it helps, no, I'm not married, I'm divorced. I have a daughter who lives in Australia. Yes, I live in a cottage. I have a long term partner, but I prefer holidays in Britain to Italy.'

Agnes stares from her chair past Eva towards the window and the sky above the city. 'I should have sussed early on that Richard was always going to use me.'

'But you did suss, surely – after the first month.'

'If you say so.'

'You said so, Agnes. And you hoped things would change.'

'Deep down I knew they wouldn't.'

'But you stayed with him.'

'I'd have stayed with the last one if he hadn't chucked me and slunk back home. I'd seen him promise other women the world, yet I still fell for it. Why do I pick them?'

'Why do you think?'

'Stop turning it back on me all the time.'

'OK, could it be a case of a certain type of person always picks you?'

'My God, you sound like my mum. Bit posher maybe but you're probably the same age.'

Being fifty-two, Eva knows this is possible. She also thinks that some therapists would explore the comment and focus on Agnes's mother. Instead she asks, 'Was there any similarity between your various boyfriends?'

'All bastards, I think.'

'And who used to make the running?'

'They would ask me out, if that's what you mean.'

'And in the early stages who was the more keen to continue the relationship?'

'Him, me, I don't know. I may have played hard to get a couple of times. My main rule was avoid the married ones. Which I did, until this last disaster.'

'Do you feel you need a boyfriend?'

'I work with a gang of women all day – OK? I sometimes like the company of a man. Is that abnormal?'

Eva wonders why Agnes is angrier today than during the preceding two sessions. 'Tell me about your work.'

'My boss designs clothes. I and the team make the design into the basis a garment we can show to the trade. Mainly children's stuff. Very exclusive. Very competitive.' She looks around the uncluttered room with its small table and three chairs. Her eyes brush past two Dufy prints on the wall, views of a harbour seen through an open window. She pauses at the oil sketch. 'The studio's nothing like this place. Swatches flying everywhere, radio on, stuff all over the floor, pressure to get it right, finish by deadlines. I'm good at what I do but in fashion forget security. We know we could all be out of work tomorrow. Not like *your* business. We *fight* to get our clients, *fight* even more to hold on to them. Yours ring up for an appointment.' She looks with contempt at Eva's dress. 'Perhaps I should become a counsellor.'

'And you have worked for the same person for seven years?'

'Since we both left art school.'

'And the affair with her husband hasn't jeopardised your relationship with her or threatened your job?'

'Not really. They have a weird marriage. She was away in the States for a lot of the time. She knew of course but never took it seriously. We still get on fine. She often confides in me as her oldest friend. I suppose I do with her, but I haven't told her I'm coming to counselling. Do counsellors ever get fired?'

'So your job, to date at least, has been secure?'

'As much as fashion ever is.' Agnes gestures round the room. 'Never been your worry, has it?'

Memories play through Eva's mind of the time, twenty years ago, when it became known she was having an affair with a client: the enquiry, the lost friendships, the move from London. 'A counsellor can have a crisis at work as much as anyone else,' she says.

'I'm sorry. Why should I get at you? It's just that . . . I think I'm scared.' Agnes becomes red-eyed.

Eva feels the atmosphere change: panic is welling up in her client. 'What are you scared of, Agnes?'

'Making another mistake.'

When Agnes has left, Eva walks to the window. Notes about the last hour must wait. Memories of her own crisis are flooding her mind with an intensity which arouses the pain felt at the time. She looks over the city roofs, breathes deeply and closes her eyes. The pain subsides. There was closure, she tells herself. It has been resolved, was resolved years ago.

She hears two of her colleagues talking in the corridor outside her room. It is a comfort to know that here she is part of a supportive group. She remembers from her London days another overheard conversation – or had they meant her to hear? 'It's all that Jungian stuff she's mad about. Just because Cranky Carl screwed one of his clients, she thinks that gives her carte blanche to do the same.' And the other colleague's comment,

'Of all people, a dealer in mirrors. Know thyself – I think not. Jung and friend Freud would have had a field day with that one.'

Eva goes to her chair to make notes. Nineteen years had proved the critics wrong. She was still with Luke. The nature of his business was immaterial.

* * *

In the workshop Russ, with a book of 22-carat gold leaf in one hand and a tip brush in the other is all concentration. Luke follows an online auction on his laptop until more coffee appears.

As Russ places a mug on the desk, Luke says, 'When you decide to retire, I'll pack up the shop.'

'My father did sixty years in all, with your granddad and later with your dad; I'll do my sixty as well.'

'Don't you sometimes miss London?'

'I've never regretted following you up here. Now I'm almost a local.'

'If you ever think you've had enough . . .'

'I'll probably die with a frame in my hand and you'll have to prise it from my rigid fingers. Just don't damage the gilding.'

A few browsers enter the shop. Two decorators call and take photos and measurements, but for the rest of the morning the showroom is silent, apart from low volume Radio 3 from Russ's workbench. Shortly after midday Luke watches the market traders pack up under a darkening sky. Within twenty minutes rain is falling. No longer competing with the sun, the mirrors assume another life. A ho-ho bird on the cresting of a chinoiserie girandole glistens, as if shaking its feathers; the carved pagodas below float in a fairy-tale world of rocks and scrollwork. Nearby, in the frame of a circular mirror, gold spheres move in orbit around their convex plate while, by the window, a decorated chair appears to move forward, as if an unseen sitter has shifted position.

Luke's eyes rest on a small gilt console table and he remembers that in a concealed drawer is a seventeenth-century needlework, discovered after the table had been bought. Walking over to it, he removes the needlework and studies its design. Faded and damaged it shows two courtly women standing in a garden of a country house, a deer park in the distance. He lays the piece on his desk and goes to his stockroom at the rear of the shop to hunt for a suitable frame. Knowing that somewhere there is a group of small stained fruitwood frames, he searches every likely box, arranged by Russ in meticulous order. Returning empty-handed to the showroom, he mutters to himself, 'I'm sure I saw them recently. Where the hell can they ...'

To Luke's surprise, stooping over the desk is a woman, examining and seemingly mesmerised by the needlework. For a few seconds she appears not to notice his presence. He finds himself rooted a few feet away, the backs of his legs touching the low bookcase of reference works on the rear wall. How, he wonders, has she entered the shop without alerting Russ who, even when engrossed in repairing an intricate carved swag, has never been known to miss the sound of the brass bell above the door? Puzzling over her presence and continuing silence, he notices that she must have been careful to wipe her feet, since there are no wet footprints on the shop's green fitted carpet.

'Without lifting her head, she asks, 'May I ... ?'

'Of course.' Luke walks to the desk.

When she lifts the needlework he notices her long, magenta pink fingernails, and as she holds it in the palms of her hands studying every detail, he tries to guess her age – difficult since her face is almost covered by a large black felt hat pulled down so that it meets a pale pink scarf wrapped several times round her neck, the ends tucked into her navy ankle-length raincoat.

'Who are they?' she asks, looking up at last.

Luke is surprised to see such deep aquamarine eyes below jet black eyebrows.

'Peace and Prosperity. Peace with the palm branch, Prosperity with the basket of fruit.'

Her eyes drop to the needlework. 'How old is it?'

'Late sixteen-hundreds. I'd almost forgotten about it until this morning. I've been hunting for a suitable frame.'

She looks up, wide-eyed. 'Is it for sale?'

Luke notices a wisp of black hair has escaped from under her hat. 'It will be, once it's framed.'

'And how much . . .' she pauses, her face halfway between a frown and a smile, '. . . approximately will it be?'

'Well, it's faded and a little frayed. Shall we say five-fifty? And if I find an old frame, another fifty. Six hundred.'

She replaces it on the desk and steps back. 'I think I might buy it. Is it rare?'

'All early needleworks are scarce. With bright colours and in good condition they can be thousands.'

'I love this for all its wear and fading. I'd like it, please. Shall I write you a cheque?' She reaches down to a large canvas bag on the floor.

Luke is struck by surprise that the sale is so simple – no 'What's your very best?' or 'How much for cash?' Is it too cheap? Russ, who is certainly listening, will, no doubt, have an opinion.

'Pay when you collect it,' Luke says. 'We'll have it ready by the end of the week.'

'I think I'm in London until next Tuesday,' she says.

'It will be waiting for you on Wednesday morning.'

She looks round the shop, her gaze resting on an overmantel mirror. Luke looks at her back. He sees her reflection in the glass. The aquamarine eyes stare back at him.

'Perhaps one day I'll buy a mirror from you,' she says. She turns to face him. 'I must give you my name and phone number.' She pulls from her bag a notebook, prints a name and phone number in large childlike writing, tears out the page and lays it on the desk.

Walking with her to the door, Luke breathes in her perfume – like a flower he cannot identify. He opens the door. This time the bell rings.

She says softly, 'Bye,' and walks across the empty market place to the baker's. He stares after her. As the church clock strikes one, he closes the door, inhaling deeply as he returns to his desk, but the perfume has disappeared with her.

'Well, she got that cheap,' says Russ from the workshop doorway.

'We've had it for years. I don't think it's even in the stock book.'

'I'll have to dose that bell with *WD40*.'

Russ picks up the piece of paper from the desk, 'Rhona Mills. Local landline number. Hasn't been in before.' He walks to the shop door and examines the bell. 'There's an Alden Mills who joined the dramatic society three months ago. New to the area. I didn't warm to him. Very dismissive that we're doing *Blithe Spirit* in the autumn.' Russ twists round the door sign to closed. 'Staying for lunch? I've an extra sandwich and there's plenty of *Guinness* in the fridge.'

Luke shakes his head. 'I've a couple of things to do at home,' he says, sensing that today he would prefer the quiet of his house to a lunch hour of town gossip with Russ.

In the kitchen of 7 Back Lane Luke heats some pasta, wondering if Eva is serious about moving in with him and reorganising the place. It had been talked about before but the conversation had always ended by one of them laughing, 'When we're both seventy.' And there was a tacit understanding that the ten minutes distance between them, if anything, had kept them together by affording a degree of independence. 'Come and live with me,' she had said when he followed her up here from London. His reply still held: 'I couldn't inflict all my junk and clutter on you.'

After removing two steaks from the freezer for dinner, he returns to the shop with the intention of phoning his accountant before going to view an auction in Newmarket. But neither task is urgent. He sits at his desk, restless. How had she – he says her name aloud – 'Rhona Mills' entered unnoticed? He considers googling her. He must know as much as possible: her address, business, husband or partner, anything on google images. But his fingers hover above the keyboard. An instinct deeper than inquisitiveness says, do nothing, you know all you need to know; cold digital information will, perversely, diminish not add to your knowledge. Hold on to your first meeting.

Again Luke recalls every detail of her visit, her voice, the perfume, her clothes, her finger nails. But why can't he remember her hands? Was she wearing a ring? Her eyes, yes. Those eyes . . . he joins Russ in the workshop. Once through the door he is in Russ's kingdom. If Russ says, 'Mix up some gesso' or 'Burnish this moulding,' he obeys as if he were an apprentice; this afternoon he is in need of distraction.

During the afternoon tea break Luke examines a William IV mirror, restored for a London dealer. 'You've excelled yourself again, Russ.'

'If I can't do it after all these years, no-one can.'

Luke turns it over. 'Not a hint of where it's been repaired. Are you performing in the Society's next production?'

'Not unless they're desperate. My acting days seem to be over.'

'But you'll be doing the scenery again, I suppose.'

'I shall try. The trouble is that towards the end of the play pictures start falling off walls, which rather goes against the grain for someone who's spent his whole life fixing chains and hooks on things to hold them up.'

'Eva and I will be in the front row to see it all.'

'Shall I box up the mirror for the carrier?'

'Let me do it. So your new member, Alden Mills, didn't like the choice of play?'

'No, but that didn't stop him offering his services as assistant director

– not that we ever have one.' Russ walks over to a tired-looking mirror, propped against the wall and lifts it on to the workbench. 'Shall I start on this next?'

Luke examines a panel on the mirror, depicting a classical scene with a chariot and ghostly shapes under layers of later gold paint. 'I'll hunt out an old piece of mirror plate for it.'

'I was thinking over lunch – I'm sure someone said his wife was a designer. But isn't everyone nowadays? Even the plumber down my road calls himself a heating designer.'

'We'll have to change your job description.'

'I'll stick to gilder and restorer, thank you.'

Luke mechanically wraps up the restored mirror, his mind far away from bubble wrap, cardboard and parcel tape.

# 2

---

They stand in silence in their waders a short way from the shore, watching their white globe-floats bob and drift on the incoming tide. It is Saturday evening.

Eva calls across the ten metres of calm sea which separate them, 'Another minute and I think I'll cast again.'

'I'm going to wait,' Luke shouts. 'I had a hint of a tug but it might be weed.'

The beach is silent, the air humid. A faint breeze brushes the marram grass on the dunes behind them but leaves the water undisturbed. Luke hears a clicking to his right and knows without looking that Eva is reeling in. He stares out to sea, recalling days when crashing waves had made fishing here impossible. When the clicking stops, he reels in his own line.

Eva calls, 'I thought I had a tug too.'

He shouts back, 'They may be following the bait.' He scans the surface. 'I can't see your float.'

They continue to reel.

'Blast it,' shouts Eva, as her float, in defiance, bounces out of the water ahead of her.

'Perhaps it pulled the bait off.'

A minute later Eva confirms that the strip of mackerel she was using for bait has gone. They wade towards each other.

'Probably the way I hooked it on,' she says.

'Shall we switch to a sand eel?'

'I'll stay with the mackerel.'

Having exchanged his soggy mackerel strip for a sand eel, Luke looks along the coastline towards Waxham. 'Most Scottish lochs we've fished haven't been this docile.'

'One of these days I'll bring a fly rod here and try to tempt the bass.'

'I'd like to see it.'

'Aunt Barbara claimed to have caught several that way.'

'She never taught you the knack?'

'No, only freshwater fishing.'

Luke surveys a deserted beach. 'The shop seems a lifetime away.'

'Ditto clients.'

With a new mackerel strip she casts again, with no great vigour, but releasing her index finger from the line with precise timing, so the weight is propelled in an almost horizontal trajectory in front of her before dropping onto the millpond surface. Next she checks that the line is not snagged on the reel, or the tip of the rod, before reeling in a few turns so that the bale arm flicks over. Luke watches in the hope his own cast will be equally precise. He brings his rod forward, eyes fixed on the sand eel, checking it remains on the hook. Bait and float drop obediently ahead of him. He too reels in a couple of turns before looking over to Eva who seems to be gazing towards the horizon, rather than at her float. He imagines her as child with her aunt by a lake in County Clare, absorbing the mysteries of fly fishing. Eva had later, with great patience, passed on these mysteries to him. The sea fishing skills he in return had shared with her seemed slight in comparison.

A flash of silver arches out of the sea about twelve metres from their floats. Luke turns his head to Eva whose brief nod indicates she also has seen it. For a minute they wait, hoping that the bass's incessant hunt for food is moving in their direction.

'Yes,' shouts Eva as her float disappears. Her rod tip bends. She begins reeling in.

Luke reels in to avoid a crossed line if the hooked fish weaves back and forth. Having waded to the beach, he lays down his rod, collects the landing net and walks towards Eva. He stands to one side of her as she reels the fish towards her. The line zig-zags as the fish fights. It remains out of view. Now it becomes more compliant and Eva reels in with less resistance, until the fish flashes out of the water a few metres away and disappears. In a moment of unguarded delight Eva allows the rod tip to point downwards. Exploiting the sudden slackness of the line, the bass veers to the right. As Eva regains the tension she reels in some more. The fish, exhausted now, gives no more than a token fight until, fully visible at last, it glides towards her.

Luke offers her the landing net.

'No, you,' she says.

On his second attempt Luke manoeuvers the net beneath the bass and lifts it from the water. They wade back to the beach where Eva removes the hook and dispatches the fish as if she had landed a trout.

'Almost two pounds,' she says, weighing it in her hands. 'More than enough for supper.'

'Shall we make it a brace?' says Luke.

They return to their rods and the tide continues its advance, forcing them back. They cast and cast again, change bait, but fail to find another bass. Eva looks towards Luke. His casting is perfunctory. Even at this distance his body language speaks of distraction. Is it tiredness? she asks. Unless there is another cause. A hundred metres away a seal's head emerges from the water. As it stares towards her she feels a pang of unease, and is glad when she and Luke are back on the beach where she watches him clean the fish at the water's edge, eyed by waiting gulls.

Walking to the van, parked in a lane on the far side of the dunes, Eva says, 'Remember the night we camped here and fished on the early morning tide?'

'Did we catch anything?'

'How can you forget? We caught three.'

'We must camp here again this summer,' he says.

Eva detects a lack of conviction in his voice.

It is almost 9.00pm when they arrive back at Eva's cottage. The old privet hedges which flank the path to the back door exude a bitter sweetness reminiscent of his childhood home. Near the door he pauses to look at a bed of dark purple daylilies interspersed with a few outrageous yellows, fluorescent in the evening light.

'Annie's suggestion,' says Eva. 'An idea filched from the irises in Monet's garden. Let yourself in and I'll lift some spuds.'

Luke unlocks the door with his own key.

While Eva goes to her vegetable garden, Luke switches on the oven and places the fish on foil in a baking tray. On her return, Eva throws on some herbs and Luke wraps the fish.

'Bubbly to celebrate, I think,' she says, producing two tinted champagne flutes. She puts on some Scott Joplin while Luke goes to the fridge for a bottle of cava. They finish it before the bass is placed in the oven and have started a second bottle before the stubborn potatoes have softened. At last, with the bass lying between them like a trophy, they drink to a successful expedition. Through the cobalt-tinted base of his glass Luke sees the eye of the fish turn blue, the one disconcerting moment in an otherwise perfect evening.

# 3

On Monday morning Luke enters the shop to hear the volume of the radio turned higher than usual. Russ hums in time with *La Fille Mal Gardée.*

'So what are you celebrating?' asks Luke over their first coffee of the day.

'I've been invited to Michael's seventieth. Eurostar and lunch in Paris.'

'Good for you, Russ. When is it?'

'October, but of course I shan't be going. I could never face the Tunnel. Worse than flying. But it's so nice to be invited. You and Eva have a good weekend?'

'We caught a bass on Saturday night. I helped weed her garden on Sunday. Today's she's away at a conference in Cambridge.'

'What's it this time – Mr. Jung again?'

'*New Directions in Cognitive Therapy.*'

'I wouldn't know what the old ones were.'

'Helping people to move away from negative thoughts about themselves.'

'Like Bing Crosby.'

'What?'

'You know the one. It's all about opting for positivity. Now, how does it go?' Russ breaks into a mocking parlando.

'I'll tell Eva to give up the talking cure and play old songs to her clients instead.'

'Got to be more fun than sobbing into a box of *Kleenex*. More coffee?'

While Russ sees to the refills in the kitchen, Luke recalls his own experiences of counselling after the break-up of a short-lived marriage. He cannot remember sobbing, only falling in love with Eva.

Russ brings in the mugs and sits on a decorated Sheraton chair.

'How's the overmantel progressing?' Luke asks.

'So far so good, but the last person who restored it slapped finger-thick gunge all over the damaged areas. Took me ages to get down to the original. Anyhow, I got it off and . . .'

It was sometime during the sixth session, Luke remembers, that he decided he didn't need counselling. He had fallen in love.

'. . . I thought the horses were missing from the chariot but it seems like they were never there. So next I thought they were being pulled by what looked like a pair of cherubs. But an hour later I discovered under all that ghastly goo they were really leaping dolphins with tiny ropes attached . . .'

Two days earlier there had been that glimpse of her in a café in Blenheim Street. She hadn't seen him, but during that sixth session he had mentioned it.

'. . . which means that the figure in the chariot which had all but disappeared must have been, as you can guess . . .'

'Neptune. Can you restore him?'

'I've got a mould I've used before, and the trident can be made from brass wire. But there's an object in the background I can't quite figure out. Some sort of sea monster . . .'

Being told she had been spotted outside the counselling environment had caught her by surprise and had elicited her natural and not her professional smile. It was a sort of victory. A first step.

'. . . or it may be another dolphin.'

'We'll have to look in the reference books.' Luke half rises from his chair with the idea of helping Russ research the mirror, but, changing his mind, sits down again. 'I'm sure you'll find similar examples.'

With a shrug Russ walks to the bookcase behind Luke's chair. For ten minutes Luke stares down the length of the shop into the market place, barely hearing the sounds from behind him of books moved and pages turned. Books had been a lifeline between sessions. He remembers how he noted whatever book he saw protruding from Eva's bag in her

Hammersmith counselling room, reading with a dealer's eyes the title on the front or spine. It became a weekly task to read whatever she was reading: when you love someone but are not yet able to act upon it, he had reasoned, what better way to feel close to her than to share a book, even at a distance?

'Found it,' calls Russ. 'I've a picture of an identical one sold in 1964. And what's missing is not another dolphin but a seahorse.' He brings the book to Luke and lays it on the desk.

Luke reads, 'Formerly at a house in King's Road, Brighton, an invoice of 1806 describes an identical pair ordered from Thomas Fentham of The Strand.' He struggles to sound as excited as the glowing Russ. 'Brilliant – a probable maker. This will make it worth more.'

'What else have we tucked away?' Russ enthuses.

'Enough to keep us going for a year or two.' Luke thinks of the four hundred unrestored mirrors in one of his barns on the edge of town, suspecting that most will still be there when Russ retires. When that day comes they can be sold off and the barn converted to houses. 'Mirrors have been good to us,' he says as Russ returns to his workshop relishing the problem of making Neptune and a seahorse. Luke hears the volume of the radio reduced to its normal level and there is no more humming from Russ, apart from a brief lapse during Widow Simone's clog dance.

When Luke returns from lunch he is surprised to find on his desk the needlework, now stretched on a board and resplendent in a pearwood frame. And by some miracle the damage has vanished. In addition, from the gentle ripples and striations in the glazing, it is clear that Russ has cut an early piece of glass to fit the frame. He turns it over and finds Russ has used old pine for the back board, even old nails to secure it. Needlework and frame seem to have lived together for centuries. He goes to the workshop.

'Russ, I didn't know you did textile repairs. We shall have to diversify.'

'It was only a few areas of cross stitch.'

'I can't even see where the damage was.'

'Nothing to it really. I don't know why those conservation ladies in their white gloves make such a to-do about five minutes' darning.'

'It certainly looks worth the money.'

'I said it was cheap.'

Luke goes to the workbench to inspect Neptune. 'Mirror's looking good too.'

'I found out over the weekend that, as we guessed, Rhona Mills is married to Alden in our drama group.'

Luke feels his face redden and stares down at the gesso sea where Russ has been adding new crests to the waves. He runs a finger along the dolphins' harness, his thoughts returning to yesterday's successful fishing trip. 'When did she say she would collect it?'

'Sometime next week.' There is a hint of 'as if you didn't know' in Russ's voice.

Luke says, 'I wonder if you say "Gee up" or "Swim on" to a dolphin.'

'I think I would say, "Don't dive",' says Russ in an admonitory tone, 'but then I can't swim.'

Luke returns to the showroom, removes a small églomisé mirror from the wall to the left of his desk and replaces it with the needlework. Standing back to admire it, he is overcome by an unaccountable restlessness and asks Russ to look after the shop for the remaining afternoon. He is in need of refuge.

Leaving the market place he walks towards the edge of town through the 1970s estate of houses and bungalows which occupy the site of the demolished Cantisham Hall, its large walled garden, now allotments, the last survivor of Victorian grandeur.

'Early in the day to see you,' growls an old man at the allotment gate.

'I need to tie up my sweet peas, Alf.'

'I remember last year seeing them in your shop window.'

'Russ says they're the best flowers to go in front of a mirror.'

Inside the walled garden Alf inspects two rows of Luke's onions. 'They look half decent,' he says.

Gratified to have the approval of the high priest of vegetables, Luke says, 'I might lift some today.'

In the Victorian hot houses where allotment holders grow tomatoes, cucumbers and optimistic lemons, Luke goes to the obsolete boiler room and finds his boots, scissors, raffia and a hoe. For half an hour he forgets about mirrors and needlework. He picks flowers from his cordon-grown sweet peas, secures new growth to the canes, cuts off laterals and tendrils, and weeds by hand, enjoying the dark soil on his fingers. Next, he hoes between rows of vegetables, pausing every few minutes to look around with pleasure at a safe world surrounded by brick walls eighteen feet high, within whose confines time obeys different rules and where the temperature is always higher than outside. As he works, his hoe releases into the air a loaminess which combines with the aroma of the low box hedge surrounding his plot. He breathes in deeply, becoming part of a place which knows nothing of emails and VAT returns. The weeding done, he lifts a few onions and leaves them on the ground to dry.

'Cup of tea?' calls Alf from a brick lean-to, once the head gardener's office.

Selecting an onion, Luke walks over to him, smelling the reek of paraffin from Alf's primus stove before he reaches the hut door. Inside, a battered kettle is attempting to whistle, as if, like its owner, it has lost a front tooth.

'Sit down, old partner,' Alf tells him.

Luke settles himself on a rickety chair cushioned with a folded corn sack and watches Alf warm a heavy brown teapot with water from the kettle, throw the water out of the door and spoon in tea leaves from an old mustard tin.

'So let's have a look,' says Alf.

Luke holds out the onion. Alf weighs it in his hand, rubs it and smells his fingers. 'Not bad,' he says. 'Probably better left in the ground a week or two longer.'

Alf pours two cups of dark tea, hands one to Luke and sits on a stool by the door. Luke sips, surprised that such a strong brew is acceptable here but not in the outside world, a confirmation of his belief that the allotments are a parallel universe.

Alf points through the doorway to an unkempt rectangle among the patchwork of neat husbandry. 'Old Maud's moved to Tudfield and it's too far for her to get here on that bike of hers. She's looking for someone to take over her plot. I could have found ten people myself by now, but it's her choice. She won't listen to advice from me. Allotment rules are rules.'

'True,' says Luke but only half agreeing as he remembers the friendships it was necessary to strike up with elderly allotment holders until, after six years, at last one of them passed on to him a plot. Alf opens a packet of ginger biscuits. At the sound of rustling paper, a grey shape camouflaged on an old blanket stirs at the end of the shed, and Alf's lurcher unfolds itself.

'I sometimes think a waiting list would be fairer,' says Luke.

'You can't control people on a waiting list.' Alf offers Luke a biscuit. 'This way we each get a chance to choose a successor.'

Without arguing Luke drinks his tea, remembering how nine years ago he initiated a change of rules to ban weedkillers and pesticides; it is too early for another revolution. The lurcher pleads for a biscuit. Alf gives him half of his own. Expecting a similar favour, the dog moves to Luke.

'Maurice, you old scrounger,' says Alf. 'Don't give him any.'

Luke obeys, smiling at the thought that Alf's adherence to allotment rules falls short of observing the ban on dogs.

'You got much more to do?' asks Alf.

'I might give everything a good watering.'

'You'd be wasting your time. It'll rain tonight.'

'You sound very certain.'

'You wait. I'm umpiring the limited over match this evening, and if we don't finish by eight, rain will finish it for us.'

Maurice salivates, a foot from Luke's uneaten biscuit.

'I'll wander up and watch you one night,' says Luke.

'Pity you don't play. We need a few more.'

'I never played much at school. We had a choice in the summer term: cricket, shooting or swimming. I chose shooting.'

'You ought to come and shoot some of the rabbits on the cricket ground. Maurice is too old now to catch them.'

'I've only ever shot targets on ranges, not animals or birds.'

'Don't let Maurice beg your biscuit. He's as fat as a seal.'

Maurice already has a tongue on Luke's biscuit. Luke gives it to him while Alf refills the pot. After a second cup Luke changes out of his boots, goes home to collect four lamb chops and walks to Eva's. When she returns from Cambridge she can sit down with a glass of wine and watch him cook dinner, complete with his own onions. But as he sits with a drink in her garden, listening out for the sound of her VW, and admiring the nodding heads of globe thistles at the back of her border, he feels a ripple of guilt that there is someone else he is more excited about seeing again. And he is annoyed with himself: how absurd to be thinking like this about a woman he cannot claim to know and with whom he has exchanged no more than a few words.

# 4

———

On Wednesday morning Luke is in the shop by 9.00am, armed with a good excuse to give Russ for his early arrival. 'The Elmans are descending later – they phoned last night. We must sort out the store room.'

'OK,' says Russ, with a look which adds, that's a new shirt you're wearing – I don't have to ask why.

In the storeroom at the rear of the shop Russ removes frames hung in neat order from wooden arms extending from the walls, and hands them to Luke who props them at random in small groups around the room. A few he leaves on the floor. After ten minutes a tidy store has been transformed into a chaos of gilded wood and glass.

Luke looks at the empty arms. 'Shall I go to the barn for some more?'

'No need,' says Russ, and he hangs an old easel from one arm and drapes a dust sheet over two more. Next he goes to the workshop and returns with a waste bin of rags and paper which he tips onto the floor and spreads around with a foot. 'Now what do they need to discover?'

'That, I think,' says Luke, pointing to a large Regency mirror. 'They'll love the leopard heads.'

'Their sort of thing,' says Russ. 'But far too obvious where it is.' He places the mirror behind some others, half covers the stack with an old curtain, steps back, adjusts the curtain, then steps back further like an artist viewing his canvas from a distance. 'They'll enjoy finding that. I can already see it flying to Connecticut.'

They half hide a few more suitable mirrors, Luke feeling that it is ridiculous for a third generation dealer to resort to such tricks. He watches Russ give the final touches to his work and by way of a signature throw an old newspaper on the floor.

'What glorious mayhem,' says Russ.

By 9.30am Luke is at his desk, Russ back with Neptune. The postman has not yet arrived, so Luke, having nothing better to occupy himself, switches on his laptop, determined that this is an ordinary working day. But before the PC has booted up he goes over to look at the needlework. Restless, he paces the shop. More than once he glances in one of the mirrors, satisfied with the look of his white open-neck shirt and black linen trousers, both crumpled to a pleasing informality. Looking in a pier glass, he is pleased that his hair is not thinning and that there is not a grey hair on his head. But as he sits down he remonstrates with himself for the stupidity of it all. At forty-eight he must be at least twenty years older than her. But does that matter? Don't thousands of couples have that age gap? No, what am I saying? he asks himself. I'm with Eva. We're happy. For some minutes he trawls online auction catalogues.

'No kipper?' asks Russ as he brings in the coffee.

'I'm hoping for more bass this week.' A pang of dishonesty: the Wednesday kipper had been forgotten, the day's routine disturbed. And he and Eva had no immediate plans to fish again. It is uncomfortable not to be truthful with Russ. He stares into the sunlit market place towards the plant stall. It is surrounded by women in bright dresses. If Rhona calls in today, what will she be wearing? Two weeks ago she was so well wrapped against the weather, hardly more than her eyes were visible. It had been enough.

Russ reads his mind. 'I hope that needlework girl isn't one of those customers who reserve something and then never set foot in the shop again.'

Ignoring a tug in his stomach, Luke summons enough nonchalance to say, 'She may be. In which case we'll up the price and sell it to someone else.'

When Russ has returned to the workshop Luke goes to the reference shelves, remembering having seen somewhere a leopard head mirror similar to his own. His hand is on the spine of Schiffer's *Mirror Book* when the shop bell rings. In one movement he spins round and stands up. He is instantly disappointed.

'Hi, Luke, good to see you. I can't believe it's been a year.' Paul Elman, in a new English tweed jacket, stretches a hand in Luke's direction.

'Paul, how are you?' It is a struggle to find a matching enthusiasm. 'And what have you done with Freda?'

'You know Freda – she's looking at every stall in the market. I left her buying a pile of locally-made wicker baskets.' Paul begins to examine the mirrors, one by one.

'I wasn't expecting you so early,' says Luke, hoping Rhona will not appear in the next thirty minutes.

'We spent last night at the golfing motel down the road.' He pauses by a mahogany mirror. 'I'm booked to play in a four-ball at two o'clock, so I had to see you early. What's trade on the fret mirror?'

'Seven.'

'Six for cash?'

'OK,' says Luke, thinking five would have been acceptable if it speeded up the visit.

As Paul pulls notes from his wallet and counts out six hundred pounds on Luke's desk, Russ appears in the workshop doorway.

'I always enjoy my first purchase of the day,' says Paul. 'It's like that first cigarette of the morning. Russ, how are you?'

'You've brought the sun with you, Mr. Elman.' Russ unhooks the fret mirror and carries it away for wrapping.

Paul continues his circuit. 'The cheval mirror?'

'Twelve fifty.'

'I like it, but I'll pass. All the young buyers want twentieth century nowadays. We're going to have to change, Luke, or we'll be dinosaurs.'

Luke assumes a sad face. 'I'm sure you're right, Paul,' he says but inwardly he smiles at the thought of the two hundred 1920s and '30s French mirrors bought cheaply by his grandfather in France after the war, and now safe in his barn, an unplanned pension fund.

The shop bell rings again. Luke twists his head, relieved to see Freda Elman. She is struggling under a pile of wicker trugs.

'A few presents solved. And one for myself.' Freda unloads her baskets and gives Luke a wet kiss on the cheek. 'Great to see you again. Now what's Paul been buying behind my back?'

'One small mirror that's being wrapped,' Paul says. 'What's your best on this, Luke?' He touches an oval Irish mirror.

Before Luke can answer Freda says, 'We don't need another of those.'

'If you say so, honey. Now Luke, what have you got tucked round the back?'

'Not much, I'm afraid. Stock's impossible to find and the auctions are hopeless.' Luke sees Russ reappear on the sidelines, ready for the game.

'Oh, come now,' says Freda, 'you must have some little treasure hidden away.'

'We're restoring an interesting Classical mirror at the moment.'

Russ ushers the Elmans to the workshop, knowing with Luke there is no chance the Elmans will buy it. Politely they admire Russ's work and with equal politeness say it's not for them.

'Sorry I've nothing else to show you,' says Luke, warmed up for the game but equally happy if Paul and Freda buy nothing more and leave.

The Elmans decide to play. Paul lays his hand on the door of the storeroom. 'Come on, sir, open up Aladdin's cave.'

'I wish it were,' says Luke, searching his desk drawers for the key, and finding it in its usual pace. Yawning, he unlocks the door.

Russ takes over, switching on the storeroom light and apologising for the dust. Luke remains in the showroom, staring out of the window, looking for Rhona, but sees only the bustle of the market and a queue waiting for the 11.00am bus to Norwich. From behind come mumblings and the sound of moving stock, but he does not turn round even when he hears Freda's voice: 'I love those leopard heads – they're tailor-made for our next show.' The bus appears, pulls up and hides the queue from his vision. A hand taps him on the back.

'I thought you said you had nothing in the store,' says Freda. 'Now what can you do on the leopard head mirror?'

'Which one is that?'

Together they go into the storeroom. Russ has now completely unveiled the mirror.

'Mrs Elman's been wondering about the Roughton Hall overmantel,' says Russ.

Freda's eyes widen. 'You mean it's got provenance?'

'We were going to restore it for a member of the family,' says Luke. 'But when we quoted a price they changed their minds and we bought it. It's got to be two thousand two hundred.'

'That's steep,' says Paul.

'We'll take it,' says Freda. 'Our restorer will fix it. The carrier will collect Friday.'

32

Luke watches Russ brush imaginary dirt from his work coat, while Freda finds an Empire picture frame which she is sure will convert to a mirror. Luke goes to his desk for the invoice book. As he opens it he notices, standing in the centre of the shop, a woman in a long white dress and straw hat. She is carrying a jute bag on which there is some writing. For an instant her face reminds him of a Copeland Parian figure which had stood on his grandmother's mantelpiece. The memory fades as the corners of her mouth move with a hint of a smile.

* * *

'I don't know what happened to me – I was so rude to you last time. I'm really sorry.'

Eva notices that today Agnes is more relaxed and that her hair has been cut and re-shaped, and the tie-back dress she is wearing is in contrast to the heavy cords worn at earlier sessions.

'You look good in that dress, Agnes. And happier too, I think.'

'I shouldn't have had a go at you.'

'You were angry. And you said you were frightened. How are you this morning?'

'I'm ... I feel ... more resigned.'

Eva waits.

'I've made up my mind,' Agnes says. 'I'm not going to make any plans for the future or rash decisions. I think I originally came to see you to get some sort of detailed course of action. But counselling's not like that, is it?'

'Not always, no. A lot of people want me to give them a blueprint which will lead to an untroubled life. Sadly, that can't be done, although sometimes we work on ways to avoid negative patterns. But it can be best to learn to wait and let things settle.'

'You remind me of when I was on holiday as a child.'

'Yes?'

Agnes looks towards the Dufy prints. 'I remember being on a beach in Cornwall. There was this rock pool full of tiny fish and minute spiral shells. I tried to scoop up the fish and pick up the shells, but I kept disturbing the sand on the bottom and clouding the water. It was infuriating until I found that if I waited and let the water clear and dipped my hand in very slowly and made my fingers like tweezers I could pick them up. But if I dug my fingers in too far, the water would cloud over again. The hard thing was waiting for it to clear.' Agnes looks towards Eva and laughs. 'Not that I'm saying men are like things in rock pools and I'm out to catch one.'

Conflicting thoughts vie in Eva's mind. Agnes's analogy is appealing but has this turnaround happened too quickly? Creative clients can be elusive. Is she fashioning a response she thinks I'll warm to? A different tack might help.

'Now you told me in your first session that both your parents are teachers.'

'My father teaches oriental languages, my mother biology.'

'And they have always been supportive of you?'

'Sort of. When I was at school they moaned about my behaviour – with some justification, no doubt. They were disappointed with my exam results, and at first they opposed my decision to go to Art School. But they came round to it. Financially I've always supported myself.'

'And you're happy with what you've achieved?'

'Yes. I'm not my own boss, but I like things as they are.'

'And having an affair with your employer's husband won't change things?'

'I can't see why.'

Eva watches Agnes's eyes drift to the window.

Agnes says, 'They have some kind of so-called open relationship. It seems to work for them. I don't think I've upset the love-apple cart.'

Eva nods in understanding, but senses an evasiveness in Agnes. I'll plunge in, Eva thinks.

'You're not envious of your employer? Her business, her name in the fashion world, even though a lot of it is your work. And she still has her husband, despite his fling with you?'

Agnes's face is scarlet. 'Envious of Rhona? God, no.'

* * *

Luke wants to speak but is aware of three pairs of eyes behind his back. He watches a smile spread over Rhona's face as she turns her head to where the needlework is hanging.

'Oh, you've framed it already,' she says, surprised and walking towards it. 'It's lovely. Thank you so much.'

Luke is certain she would have spotted it as soon as she entered the

34

shop, which was probably several minutes earlier, but the vignette of pretence is enticing. 'Thank Russ here,' he says.

Rhona studies the frame. 'And wow, Russ, you've used old wavy glass.'

'Well, I thought the needlework deserved it,' says Russ.

Luke hears Freda's voice bellow behind him, 'You never told me you do textiles, Luke.' She walks up to the needlework and forces her head in front of Rhona. 'It's so pretty. Do you have any others? We did so well with our textiles at the last show.'

'Perhaps this lady here's a dealer and might be happy to take a profit,' suggests Paul.

Russ's hand is quick to the needlework. He lifts it from its hook. 'I'll wrap this up before it disappears to America.'

'And I could never sell it,' says Rhona, smiling at Freda.

Freda forces a smile in return. 'I'm sorry – I just loved it as soon as I saw it.'

Paul turns to Rhona. 'I congratulate you on having a good eye. You know, I was in such a mirror mode today that I walked straight past it. Never saw it.'

Frowning at her husband, Freda turns to Luke. 'I guess we're finished. Cheque book, Paul.' She looks down at the desk where Russ has already prepared the invoice. She writes a cheque. 'The carrier will be in touch, Luke. It's been lovely seeing you again. Next trip you must have dinner with us.' She gives his hand a wrench. 'Love to Eva. Come on, Paul, we're behind schedule. Don't forget my shopping.' She is soon halfway across the market place.

At the door, Paul, collecting the pile of trugs, says to Luke, 'Eighteen hundred for the Irish mirror?'

'Eighteen fifty,' says Luke.

'Deal, but don't tell Freda. Send it with the others. I'll mail a cheque tonight.'

Luke closes the door and walks over to Rhona. 'Sorry to keep you waiting. I'm afraid those two tend to monopolise the shop.'

'I thought he was sweet.'

'*He*, maybe.'

'I see quite a few women similar to her in my own business.'

'Let me guess. What you do is connected with textiles?'

'Well done. I design clothes – mainly for children.'

Luke thinks she is about to say more, but she resumes her Copeland figure pose. He is desperate to break the silence.

'Do you live locally?' He feels embarrassed as soon as he has spoken.

'We moved to Ulford six months ago.'

Luke wonders which house in the tiny village is hers, but cannot bring himself to ask. The two earlier questions have somehow diminished him.

Russ arrives and hands her a parcel. 'One seventeenth-century needle work of Peace and Prosperity. I hope it brings you both.'

'You framed it beautifully,' she says.

Russ beams.

Rhona pulls out a cheque book from the depths of her jute bag. She frowns vaguely. 'How much did you say?'

'Six hundred including the framing,' says Russ.

Luke watches Rhona write the cheque with an old Parker fountain pen in large handwriting. Her signature covers almost a quarter of the cheque. He notices that the logo on her bag is a heart underneath which is written *I LOVE LITTER*. She tears out the cheque and places it on the desk. Russ hands her a receipted invoice.

Luke walks with Rhona to the door. Again, he wants to break the silence, but is at a loss. As he rests his hand on the shop door she glances at the Venetian mirror in the window.

'I'm sure we could do with a large mirror at home,' she says. 'You must give me some advice. How about tea one day?'

'That would be lovely.' Luke regrets his formal tone, but it is the best he can manage while still recovering from her appearance during the Elman's visit.

'Next week?' she says quietly. 'My diary's at home. Can I phone you tomorrow, Luke?'

'I'll look forward to it.'

Rhona hugs her parcel to herself like a child with an unopened present. 'Bye, Russ,' she calls over Luke's shoulder.

Luke turns to see Russ a few feet behind and wonders if he heard the invitation to tea.

Luke closes the shop door and looks out to the market place for a last glimpse of her. But he is disappointed. There is no sign of the white dress or straw hat. Watching a couple carry drinks to a table outside the Queen's Arms on the opposite corner of the market place, he puzzles at her unnerving ability to appear from nowhere and vanish as quickly. It is as if he has imagined her visit. He sniffs the air in search of a trace of the perfume she wore last week, but again finds it as fugitive as its owner. Perhaps she hadn't worn it today. Or perhaps he hadn't noticed it. He turns round, struggling to believe that less than a minute ago she was standing here inviting him to tea.

'In and out like a ghost that one,' Russ says. 'You'll have to tell me about her house next week. And the lowdown on her husband.'

'I shall,' Luke says, aware he too is harbouring the wish to know all about her husband, but for reasons different from Russ's. 'You were on good form this morning, Russ. I insist on buying you lunch and a pint at one o'clock.'

'That's very kind but I do have my usual sandwich.'

'Feed it to the dolphins. We deserve pie and mash.'

\* \* \*

Before her next client of the morning Eva stands by the window and allows the city roofscape to clear her mind. The vista is motionless apart from a tower crane on the horizon, its jib moving above an invisible building site. She drops her eyes to the street below and watches a woman in a '50s style dress walk in the direction of Foundry Bridge. What progress, Eva wonders, has Agnes made during the last hour? Neither of us will know yet. Heading for the city she looks so confident, so in control of her world. She watches Agnes walk past two men. One man makes a comment to the other – perhaps about Agnes – and they both burst into laughter. The ties on the back of her dress, swinging as she walks, seem like arms dismissing their gaze. When Agnes has disappeared under the lime trees, Eva moves away from the window to check her diary. Will Agnes be one of those clients who sometimes like to write between appointments? Luke had been. She still had the letters.

\* \* \*

At 1.00pm, as Russ is removing his brown work coat, Luke struggles to recall every detail of Rhona's visit – her voice, her exact words, her clothes – but already she is receding like a dream on waking. He cannot even remember where she was standing when he first noticed her. He looks down at the green carpet in the hope that it might yield some clue. At his desk he picks up Rhona's cheque and studies the tangible proof of her visit. Even better she has written his name: Luke Brewer Antique Mirrors. But there is so much more about her, unnoticed or forgotten. What shoes was she wearing? She wore a ring set with . . . what colour was the stone? Was there also a wedding ring? For a dealer with the ability to be in a room for half a minute and afterwards to recall in detail every piece of furniture, these observational failures are unforgivable. Of course there is an excuse – being caught off guard by the invasive Elmans – but he should have remembered more. And what was it about her which particularly struck him? As he and Russ walk across the market place he remembers. When she said she would phone tomorrow she used his name. She had said 'Luke' for the first time. But there was also a note in her voice. He tries to hear her say it again above the lunchtime chatter in the pub, but it has faded – the moment, the tone and she have disappeared.

# 5

Next day Luke is at the shop by 9.15am. He knows he needn't be at work so early. If customers phone in his absence, there will be no loss of business: Russ is totally reliable and there is no chance he will write down a wrong name, date or time. But today is different. As Luke sits at his desk, turning the pages of an auction catalogue, he is hit by a wave of guilt that he hasn't mentioned Rhona to Eva. But then, why should he? The invitation to tea is simply a business visit and, after all, Eva has a limited interest in shop affairs. True, most Saturday mornings she calls in for a chat and a coffee, and several times when he's been away at an auction and Russ has been on holiday, she has minded the shop, but she has never been deeply involved in the world of mirrors. Certainly she is pleased when things go well and when trade seems dead listens to what she calls 'the dealer's dirge', but she has no more interest in the business than he has in counselling, apart from his own experience. As Russ places coffee on the desk he thinks again of that Hammersmith counselling room – its dry smell, like the corner of an old library, the sage green armchairs, the cream emulsioned walls, the geometric pattern on the curtains. If only memories of Rhona were as detailed.

Russ looks down at the catalogue to a mirror in the form of two intertwined bodies. 'I'm not a great one for the '60s.' he says. 'Didn't really go for it at the time.' He points to the mirror. 'But if we had that in the window it would certainly cause a stir in town.'

'I think they'd close us down, Russ.'

'It's a very over-rated time in my opinion.' He settles into a Regency chair. 'I remember one Sunday afternoon in '67 or '68, I was wandering through St. James's Park and I heard all this angry shouting . . .'

*Why didn't I give her my mobile number? Those bloody Elmans threw me.*

'. . . well, I followed the racket up to Whitehall and there were all these marchers, shouting their way through a completely empty street, going 'Ho, Ho, Ho Chi Min.' And they were waving homemade banners at empty government buildings . . .'

*Of course she might email me – the email address is on her invoice along with the shop phone number.*

'. . . and at that moment I looked up and saw a hand draw back a curtain about three floors up. And there was this woman. She took one bored look, then disappeared behind the curtain again . . .'

*She did say, 'I'll phone tomorrow', didn't she? Or was it, 'I'll phone in a day or two?' No, definitely tomorrow. She's got to phone today.*

'Whether she was a cleaner or a member of MI5, I'll never know.'

*The question is, when?*

'And after they had all gone past it was as if nothing had happened. So I went back to the park and carried on with my walk.' Russ stands and pushes his chair to the wall as if dismissing a whole decade.

Luke says, 'Somewhere, Russ, there's a photo of you in the Chiswick shop wearing a very hippy-looking floral shirt.'

'Your father didn't approve of me wearing them for work. Made it quite clear: "Not the sort of thing our customers expect. Wear what you like weekends." I was annoyed at the time. Funny, I wouldn't be seen dead in them now, not at work anyhow.'

The phone rings. Russ looks at Luke, waiting for him to answer it. Luke wants to move his hand to take the call, but his body refuses to respond. The phone continues ringing. Russ answers it and Luke strains to hear the caller's voice.

'No, I'm afraid not,' says Russ. 'We can't possibly value a mirror over the phone. It's almost impossible even from a good photo . . . Alright, send us a good image and we'll see what we can do . . . Goodbye.'

Luke relaxes. Russ looks down at the catalogue and points to a sampler depicting a building like a doll's house surrounded by lollipop trees.

'Now I like that,' says Russ. Supposing we buy a few more needleworks? What do you think?'

'You should have kept your '60s shirts. They would sell even better.'

'They were torn up for dusters ages ago.' He returns to his gilding.

By 12.50pm there have been no more phone calls. In frustration, Luke leaves the shop and walks across the market place to the deli where he buys a pork pie. But as he returns to the shop he is convinced that the break has been a mistake and that Rhona must have phoned during his eight-minutes' absence. But on his return Russ says nothing about a caller and there is no note on the phone pad.

'Lunch in today?' asks Russ as he locks the shop door.

'The deli's new organic pies taste as good here as at home.'

'*Guinness*? I've a spare in the fridge.' Russ mutes the phone. Luke is annoyed at this but the lunchtime routine is sacrosanct. If she phones in the next hour, it will be necessary to phone her back at 2.00pm. He follows Russ into the workshop. Here Russ pulls out a small side table, removes from its drawer a tablecloth, spreads it and goes into the kitchen for plates and glasses. Luke pulls up two paint-spattered chairs and sits on one.

Russ, now without work coat, appears, tray in hand, with their lunch. He gives Luke his pork pie, sliced in four, on a plate as white as the tablecloth on which he places a mustard pot and a jar of chutney. 'Green tomato. My final batch from last year.' He places his own sandwiches and two glasses of *Guinness* on the table, sits and relaxes. 'Cheers.'

'Good health,' says Luke as Russ recounts the latest goings on of his neighbour. Luke hears details of 'her first husband' and 'her next boyfriend' but takes little notice, wondering if even now Rhona may be listening to the recorded message.

'. . . being an electrician, I suppose gave him an excuse to be round there during the daytime. But even last Sunday night . . .'

Luke tries to relax as Russ narrates the dramas of Redwell Street.

'Our Victorian semis don't have very thick dividing walls and I could tell . . .'

Luke struggles to concentrate on Russ's story, to forget Rhona, but finds his mind drifting back to an earlier experience of being a captive audience. For a moment he is sixteen and back at school in a history lesson where the voice at the blackboard explaining nineteenth century politics only makes him ponder the more vital subject of Victorian frames. Russ's animated voice summons him to the present.

'Heaven knows what will happen when her husband gets back from Dubai.'

Luke finishes his glass, looking up at the workshop clock. Twenty minutes to go.

Unhurried, Russ clears the table before bringing in, as lunchtime tradition dictates, china cups and saucers and a coffee pot. He is about to continue his saga when the peel-of-bells ringtone of his mobile calls him back to the kitchen.

'I do apologise,' says Russ, running to his phone. He closes the kitchen door behind him.

*Could Rhona be phoning Russ's mobile? No, she can't possibly have known the number. But who else? Russ never gets personal calls at the shop. A cold caller? Why close the door?*

After two minutes Luke knows it cannot be a stranger who has dared to interrupt the sacred hour, a guess confirmed by Russ's face on his return.

'Margaret's dead. Very sudden. Last family link with London. Funeral's next Wednesday. I'll have to go.'

'Russ, I'm so sorry.'

'She was the only cousin I ever got on with.'

'Have a couple of days down there. Take Monday, Tuesday and Wednesday off.'

Russ mumbles a thank you and slowly clears away the coffee things.

For an hour after lunch the phone remains silent. An eye on his computer clock, Luke occupies a few minutes with bookwork, but lacking concentration soon returns to online auction catalogues. When the search for mirrors has been exhausted, he wanders through oriental art, impressionist paintings, tin-plate toys, Judaica, fishing ephemera – anything which will provide an effective opiate against the pain of waiting. Once he is disturbed by an email alert, but it is only an advert for a seized assets auction. He moves to Continental porcelain where the elegance of a pair of Meissen figures of a suitor and lady reminds him he could do with a new pair of lightweight trousers. He goes to a favourite online site and places an order.

At 3.30pm the phone rings. He lifts the handset and presses the answer button before it can ring a second time. But his face drops when he hears the voice of the town council secretary, asking for a donation for the summer fete.

'Yes, we'll donate our usual bottle of whisky,' Luke tells him. He replaces the handset and stares at it, waiting for another call. In the next half hour a few customers come and go, but otherwise the phone and the shop remain silent. If Radio 3 is on in the workshop, the volume is so low he cannot hear it.

At 4.00pm a sombre Russ arrives with the afternoon tea, and sitting without a word in a corner of the shop, sips in silence. Luke is torn between wanting the phone to ring and longing for closing time when the torture of waiting will be over for the day. Tomorrow it may begin again but at least in an hour's time there will be respite when the shop sign is turned to closed. He carries his mug to the door and stares into the afternoon. If Rhona is not going to phone, perhaps she will call in person. On one side of the market place the greengrocer's has a small queue; on the other side youngsters on holiday have congregated around the newsagent, but there is no-one he recognises.

'Oh, I forgot to tell you . . .' says Russ.

Luke turns on his heels.

'I heard yesterday from the woman opposite me whose brother's a builder, that Rhona Mills's husband is involved in some play abroad.'

'Really?' says Luke, thinking, why the hell didn't you tell me earlier?

'Apparently Alden said it was hard to adjust to working with a local drama group. "Provincial amateurs," he called us. Hasn't been here ten minutes and wants to change everything.'

'Eva and I will be seeing some of those change-the-town fanatics at the Cantisham Society tonight. Her neighbours are giving a drinks do. They haven't been here a year and . . .'

'Don't tell me, they want to give us a heritage trail with little plaques popping up like measles everywhere. Now what could they stick outside this building?' Russ plants himself in an armchair. 'Perhaps we should invent a famous former occupant and put our own sign up. Can't you see it . . .?'

Luke nods in bored assent, knowing it is one of those afternoons when Russ, unless coaxed back to his workshop, will gossip until closing time. But today there will be no cajoling. He suspects that Russ's meanderings about commemorative plaques are less time-wasting chatter than a way of facing bereavement. He listens, looks surprised or smiles where appropriate, his eyes never leaving the phone. It remains silent.

# 6

---

'Now you're not from round here, are you?'

'No, I was brought up in Chiswick,' Luke tells a long-faced woman in an orange twin set whom he's never seen before.

'I thought you had a twang in your voice. Now, aren't you the person they call the mirror man – which I assume refers to your shop not your daily paper.'

Luke attempts affability. 'I do sell mirrors, yes. You must call in and see us.'

'Oh, I daren't in case I want to buy something. I've downsized. I've too much furniture as it is.'

'If you ever wish to sell anything...'

'Can't. Family things. Children would kill me. Now, don't you think the market place would look so much better with a couple of trees. Planes, perhaps, like a French market town?'

'That would be a revolutionary change by local standards. Arrivistes like you and me daren't suggest such things.'

'How long have you lived here?'

'Nineteen years.'

As the long face opens its mouth and lengthens, Luke spots Eva trapped in a corner. 'Do excuse me,' he says, and sidesteps his way through chattering members of the Cantisham Society to where Eva is

44

being quizzed by two well-dressed, half-drunk men delighted to have discovered she is a counsellor.

'So I guess you people find yourself in one of the biggest growth industries?' says the shorter man whose hair and blazer make Luke think of an army officer on leave.

'Do you think of counselling as an industry?' Eva asks.

'Typical shrink answer,' laughs the other man whom Luke recognises as a barrister with a second home in the town. 'Answer every question with another question.'

'I've heard the same said about lawyers,' says Luke.

Ignoring the comment, the barrister moves closer to Eva. 'Now what really interests me in your line of work is that you've probably heard every story – know every trick in the book. So . . .' He sways towards her.

Eva recoils from his winey breath.

'. . . So if you wanted, for example, to pinch another woman's husband, you would know *exactly* how to do it.'

'Or *if*,' adds the blazer, 'someone like me comes along and asks you the best way to seduce someone else's wife, you'd be able to give us a few helpful hints and guidelines.'

'I try to facilitate relationships, not undermine them.' She gives Luke a get-me-out-of-here look.

'No, what I'm saying,' persists the blazer, 'is that because you're an expert on relationships, you are – theoretically, see what I mean? – in a position to help someone who is thinking of . . .'

'Having an affair?' says Eva.

Her tone turns his face scarlet. His friend continues, 'So what advice would you give Simon here if, perish the thought, he fancies another man's wife and wants to try his luck?'

'Not the sort of advice you're looking for.'

'Oh, come on now . . . just one pearl of wisdom. I mean . . . be fair . . . is he better off staying friendly with the woman's husband, or should he point out to her what a bastard she's married to?'

'Perhaps neither,' says Luke, muscling his way between them with a force which surprises himself. 'Excuse us,' he says as Eva slips through her interrogators and heads for the open French windows.

'Thanks for the rescue,' she says as they step outside on to an immaculate lawn. 'That was a vicious elbow in the ribs you gave him.'

'My pleasure.'

'I loathe that sort of conversation. Now let's discover where my dear neighbours' ground elder is creeping through to my vegetables.'

At one end of the garden, between the fence and a summer house, is a slatted compost bin. Eva peers over it. 'Ah, the culprits.' She glances over her shoulder. 'I've tried asking them politely but this way is better.' She climbs onto the heap and with the help of a stick begins to root up ground elder, while Luke watches out for other guests. Unable to reach more weeds, she climbs out and works her way along the narrow gap between compost bin and fence. After a minute's weeding she gathers a small pile of the offending plants with their spaghetti roots and pushes them under the fence and into her own garden. 'At least I'll make sure they're properly destroyed,' she tells him. Turning round, about to manoeuvre herself back along the fence, she slips but is saved from falling by a post which takes her full weight. She grits her teeth.

Luke reaches out a hand to steady her. 'You OK?'

'I'm fine, but is my dress marked?'

'It still looks lovely.'

'Thank God.'

'Pity about the fence post though.'

Eva turns round to see that the post, partly detached from the fence, is slanting towards her garden.

Luke goes over to it and finds he is able to move it backwards and forwards with ease. 'It must have been rotten at the base. Your weight finished it off.'

'Oh hell. And it's *my* fence too. I'll have to get it fixed. Another expense.'

'I can do it – it's not a big job. Alf can get me some oak posts. Chances are a few of the others are rotten too.'

'Thanks. While you're at it I'll be able to destroy some more ground elder.'

'Maybe we should get some glyphosate to be certain.'

'What happened to your organic regime?'

'Fences are an exception.'

In the summerhouse they find half a bottle of wine left behind by another guest. When Luke has refilled their glasses, they drink and watch rain begin to fall. 'We'll down these and escape,' he says.

'Pity we can't use the side gate but my coat's in the hall.'

They slip through chattering groups of Cantisham Society members

46

towards the front door, and have almost escaped when Eva's way is barred by her earlier interrogators. 'Just one tip,' the blazer pleads.

Eva ignores them. When they are outside she looks at Luke and sighs. 'In my experience, if a man is planning an affair, he needs to be as nice about the woman's husband as possible. The more he slags the husband off, the more she is likely to defend him. But there's no way I was telling that to those pissheads.'

In Eva's kitchen Luke pours himself a whisky as she, despite the rain, goes to the garden to retrieve the uprooted ground elder for disposal. She returns shivering. Luke pours her a drink.

'Did you cultivate any new customers tonight?' she asks.

'One woman may look in sometime, but I'm not optimistic. At least you managed some furtive weeding.'

'Altogether, a successful evening.'

And I have learned that I must be nice about Alden, Luke thinks, and is immediately ashamed of the thought.

Later, when they are watching TV Eva's phone rings. Luke sits up, a voice inside him saying, *It's her at last*. But he falls back in his chair as Eva answers it and spends the next ten minutes hearing news from her daughter Helen in Sydney.

In bed that night they make love but Luke feels it is more habit than passion. Eva falls asleep, but for an hour he remains awake, staring through the window at a full moon. Stabs of guilt give way to fitful sleep. At 2am he wakes from a disturbing dream. He has rushed from Eva's house to his own where he knows the phone is ringing. But on arrival he finds the building derelict and weeds pushing through the floorboards.

He looks at Eva sleeping peacefully beside him, and recalls that she had once told him that a dream about a building can represent the dreamer's psychological state. For over an hour he fails to sleep, but there is comfort as the first grey light enters the room and he falls at last into a second, deeper sleep.

# 7

---

At 9.30am Eva is sitting in an armchair in the first floor drawing room of a Victorian house, off the Newmarket Road, in Norwich. It is the home of her supervisor Stella who is pouring coffee from a silver pot into two small cups. She places one on a quartetto table by Eva's chair, and the other on a wine table next to a many-cushioned wing armchair into which she nestles. When Stella lifts her cup Eva notices that the nails of her long fingers are painted with a red more luminescent than any colour she has ever seen.

They sit and drink in the silence of a long-established routine. 'I think a few minutes without words is a useful way to begin,' Stella had said at their first meeting, fifteen years ago. Eva had warmed to the suggestion – an approach so different from the verbal volleys of her previous supervisor in his modern office in a concrete building at the University. Eva sips the exquisite Arabica and watches Stella run her fingers down a string of turquoise beads, their colour enriched against a mauve dress, the collar of which is touched by her long silver hair. Eva is reminded of an aging Afghan hound.

Eva looks around the room whose books, bronzes and oriental rugs remind her of the Freud Museum. If Stella's possessions were swapped with the contents of Sigmund's study, she thinks, nothing would be incongruous. Three Egyptian urns on a high shelf suggest that Stella might even share the great man's love of ancient artefacts.

Stella breaks the silence in her usual tangential way. 'And how is Luke?'

'He's well. The other day he even suggested we move in together.'

'And will you?'

'Eventually, I expect.'

'And do you talk much about your work with him?'

'I tell him about almost every case. I alter a few details of course, names mainly, but I don't think he takes much interest. Years ago he loved hearing about marriage problems and cases with strong sexual issues. He used to call me his private pornographer. Less so now. Not that I ask him much about his mirrors. It's gardening and fishing where we have most in common.'

'And are the fish biting?'

'They did on our last trip.'

'Good. Now the bereavement client – how were the final sessions?'

* * *

At 9.00am Luke wakes to find a cup of cold green tea on his bedside table and a note from Eva: *You were out for the count, so I tiptoed off to work. Talk later. E. XXX. P.S. Did I exhaust you that much??!?*

As he shaves Luke realises that twice in the last fortnight Eva has been up before him. Am I getting lazy or complacent or is it my health? he asks, examining his complexion. But during the semi-rural walk to his own house, under a warm sun, his confidence returns. He relishes each step, every familiar flint and brick of the houses he passes. He enjoys peering over walls at the hollyhocks and foxgloves in traditional flowerbeds. He frowns at paved areas with box spirals and bay trees in tubs. But the silent criticism gives way to inner questioning and self-rebuke for romanticising Victorian gardens, knowing that this part of town in the nineteenth century was an area of poverty and deprivation. 'Reality, reality,' he says out loud. He makes a detour, looping down a lane so the walk home becomes double the distance. It doesn't matter if he's late at the shop – Russ will be there. He needs time to think, and walking is the best way. He remembers one of the few snippets learned at school in Latin lessons – *solvitur in ambulando*: a matter is solved by walking. And he must solve what his mind is calling *this Rhona nonsense*. Yes, nonsense it must be – unreal, a fleeting distraction. As he cuts through the churchyard with its cordoned-off wildflower areas, he is

49

determined that today he will not again be obsessed by a non-ringing phone.

Back home the house is musty, as if he has been away for more than one night. He opens some upstairs windows to let it breathe, changes his clothes, and after a quick inspection of the roses in the garden, walks to the shop, resolving yet again that this will be a normal day. From now until closing time he is a dealer and restorer of mirrors.

When the coffee has appeared Russ goes back to the workshop and returns holding a three-drawer satinwood dressing mirror which has lost some of its veneer.

'The lady who brought it in said she met you last night. "Is it worth fifty pounds?" she asked. I said we'd get back to her. She apologised that the central drawer's locked – "lost the key years ago," she told me.'

Luke examines the mirror. 'But Russ, the middle drawer's unlocked.'

'Had it open in half a minute after she'd left. Guess what I found inside?'

'A purse of guineas? A gold ring?'

'All the missing veneer. I can have the lot stuck back by lunchtime.'

'Do you think I have a twang in my voice?'

'No. Why?'

'Oh, something this woman said to me last night. I think we'll give her the fifty pounds and say that if we do well with it once it's restored, we'll give a donation to the Cantisham Society.'

'How badly did she annoy you last night?'

'She has this idea that the market place needs a couple of plane trees.'

'Perhaps she should move to France.' Russ, mirror in hand, returns to the workshop.

The phone rings. Aware of new resolve, Luke moves a slow hand to it. 'This is W J Haulage about the Elman shipment ...'

Having dealt with the carrier, Luke relaxes in his chair. Levelheadedness has returned. A few steamy fumes of scotch glue drift from the workshop. The smell of a working day is reassuring. He is in control of his life; perhaps the morning walk has released a few endorphins and bestowed some equilibrium.

\* \* \*

'Now what have we overlooked?' asks Stella.

Eva smiles at the question, always asked towards the end of their meetings, and reflects on her recent cases. In the silence she feels that it is during the moments they do not speak that the real work of supervision is conducted. She looks out of the half-open window behind Stella's head. Wisteria leaves cover the upper three panes. Two months ago racemes of almost the same colour as Stella's dress had hung from the climber. Now the flowers had long gone and it needed its summer pruning. 'I think we've touched on all the case issues.'

'No other matters?'

'I don't think so. Only . . .'

'Yes?'

'In a recent counselling session I found myself reliving the emotions I felt when I had to leave London. I was unnerved.'

'Did something in the session trigger this?'

'The client was directing her anger at me – quite personally – which I thought useful, but it did strike an old wound which I thought had healed.'

'Healed, perhaps. But don't the shadows of emotional wounds always remain? And we who are mad enough to be therapists are often in situations where the shadows seem to come alive.'

'It was uncomfortable.'

'How are things now?'

'The pain was short-lived. The following session she apologised for her outburst and I think we're now making progress.'

'The old shadows can become useful tools. Now when do you start your mini-sabbatical?'

'At the end of the month. But it's only until November, and in August I'm reading a paper to a study group in Birmingham.'

Stella rises from her chair. 'Now come downstairs and look at my lilies. They're being attacked at night by some invisible creature and I need your advice.'

\* \* \*

Mid-morning Luke is standing in the centre of the shop among two couples and three children. The adults are taking varying degrees of interest in the stock, the children are eating ice creams. A sale is unlikely, but since they have opted for his shop and not the coast on such a hot day, there may be a chance of some business. None materialises and as soon as they have left the shop Russ emerges from his workshop, rag in hand, and removes children's finger marks, real or imagined, from every low surface. Why does he do it? thinks Luke. It's so unnecessary and . . . No, it's part of the shop routine. Today is a normal day and Russ must follow his normal patterns.

Other callers enter and leave, and he sells a decorated washstand. Normality restored, he goes home for a lunchtime sandwich. Sitting in his kitchen, he watches clouds build from the south and the sunlight shrink from the walled garden. With its disappearance his confidence fades. He is trapped, as if the morning's routine, rather than imparting stability, has only served to remind him that he is caught in dull mundanities of his own making. He shivers and goes upstairs for a sweater. On his return he looks at the angling reports in the local paper. The bass have moved along the coast in large numbers towards Cromer. Perhaps he and Eva should have another fishing trip. He considers texting her but hesitates. Through the kitchen window he watches a heavy summer shower, ideal for garden and allotment, fall and pass over, leaving on the lawn raindrops which sparkle in the returning sun. The shower seems also to have refreshed his mind, but as soon as he returns to the market place a malaise descends. The sight of the shop front with his name over it makes him shudder. It is as if he is looking at his own gravestone, recording a safe, uneventful life. His work, once seen as a challenge to be seized and enjoyed, has now become a monotonous routine. Shocked at the realisation, he halts, staring up at the hotel sundial. Below are the words *Time is short*. They tell him that his world has become too comfortable and without any prospect of change. Even thoughts about dawn fishing in the North Sea, with all its unpredictability, no longer excite him.

As Luke approaches the shop an urgent-looking Russ opens the door. 'You haven't forgotten about tomorrow's auction at Tudfield, have you? It starts at nine and the viewing's only this afternoon.'

Retracing his footsteps along Back Lane and down an alley to his garage, Luke is glad of an escape from the shop. But driving to Tudfield, the sight of mauve tufted vetch and acid yellow ragwort on the verge of the country road induce a sadness: it is the third week of July; midsummer is over. In many fields barley and wheat have already been harvested. The cycle of seasons is turning but his own life is stationary, fixed in an unchanging, colourless routine. There should be some pleasure in driving to view this auction, one of the few remaining which has no online catalogue. Once he would have felt the excitement of the chance of a bargain. Today it is a duty which would have been forgotten but for Russ's reminder.

Despite the auctioneer's poor advertising, the village hall car park is so packed he is forced to leave his van a hundred metres up the road. Walking to the hall he recognises the vehicles of other local dealers and habitués of salerooms. Members of both categories are rooting around the outside lots spread on the paved area near the hall's front door. He inspects the unrestored pine furniture, battered armchairs, garden tools, flower pots and miscellaneous boxes of garage and shed detritus. He is drawn to a pair of Victorian terracotta garden urns, but closer inspection reveals cracks and losses. Inside, the furniture on offer is stacked around the walls, while at the far end smaller items are untidily spread on grubby white sheets on trestle tables. Luke says hello to the porter and joins the shuffle of viewers. There are only two mirrors which might be worth bidding on. Both are large, nineteenth century and plain but with the gilding in fair condition. One retains its original glass, the other is terminally cracked. Habit suggests he should buy them. Restoring them is an easy task for Russ. There are plenty of spare mirror plates in store which could be cut to the size of the cracked plate. The likely hammer price would leave plenty of room for profit. But today he doesn't care.

A semi-retired Norwich dealer appears at his side. 'Your sort of gear this, isn't it, Brewie?'

'Was, Len, was. I've enough restoration projects for two lifetimes as it is.'

'You'll still buy them, I bet.'

Luke looks round the room and sees four Georgian chests of drawers and a set of eight Regency chairs. 'A few lots for you furniture boys, I see.'

'Nothing to get excited over. The business has changed.'

'So why are you here?'

'Same reason as you. Always have done. Can't change now.' Len shrugs and stalks off.

Luke looks at him move from chest to chest, a man governed by ingrained habit, not choice. Have I become like that? he wonders.

Turning to leave, Luke is confronted by a pair of wide blue eyes.

'Luke, hi,' she says, almost sings, and rests a hand on his arm.

Luke feels his earlier resolve drain away.

'I was going to phone you when I got back home,' Rhona says. 'Now what about tea on Sunday afternoon? You'll be able to see how much we need a mirror.'

For a moment Luke envisages himself flaked out in an armchair at home on Sunday afternoon, exhausted after a morning's gardening at Eva's and her usual large 1.00pm lunch. 'That would be lovely,' he says.

'Shall we say four o'clock? Doesn't that sound wonderfully old-fashioned? It's a pity I don't know how to make scones. You couldn't look at a plan chest I was thinking of buying, could you? I'm worried there might be some awful damage I haven't spotted.'

Rhona leads him to a corner of the hall where a black-painted plan chest is almost hidden behind an assortment of canvas golf bags. A heap of Second World War uniforms is piled on top. Luke checks that each of its nine drawers runs smoothly. Having examined the top and sides, he hauls it forward to see if the back is sound.

'Looks fine,' he says. 'It's in two halves, so it shouldn't be difficult to move.' He notices that she is wearing a light blue cotton shirt over jeans. Her jet black hair is tied back with a diaphanous floral scarf. He tells himself, remember these details.

'How wide do you think it is?' she asks.

Again he runs his eye over it. 'Forty inches. And in every dimension. It's almost an exact cube.'

'Don't you have to measure? How clever. What do you think I might have to pay?'

He notes that her lipstick is almost the same colour as her socks and that there is the tiniest gap between two of her lower teeth. 'You might get it for twenty. You may have to pay a hundred. But I'm only guessing.' Two of her shirt buttons are open and the top of her black bra is visible.

'I've never bid at an auction before. I think I'll be too nervous. I may have to get Alden to do it for me.'

Luke wants to say, 'I'll bid for you,' but some inner force, perhaps the wish not to appear to rival Alden, restrains him. 'I'm sure you'll manage,' he says.

Again she rests a hand on his arm. 'You're so kind. Now I'm definitely going to dig out my recipe books and find out about scones.' She looks down the length of the room towards a woman who is waving at her. 'That's my lift – I must dash.' She sways forward as if about to kiss him or perhaps expecting Luke to kiss her. Taken by surprise he doesn't move and Rhona melts into the hall.

As he drives home he recalls what she was wearing, reciting each item like a mantra: jeans, light blue cotton shirt, pink socks, black bra, floral scarf – silk perhaps – around her head. Only the colour of her shoes escapes him. He remembers the tiny gap between her teeth, the suggestion of a parting kiss, and above all her eyes, the blue eyes. But was she wearing a ring? What is her height? These details are uncertain. And yet he knew the size of the plan chest at a glance and even now recalls the exact shape of its wooden handles. Should he attend tomorrow's auction? She is sure to be there. He needs no excuse: the dusty world of the country auction with its dealers' rings, intrigue and poker faces is home territory. No, he is seeing her on Sunday; to see her before would somehow devalue that visit. He is forty-eight, not fifteen in Chiswick High Street, stealing glimpses of the girl in the florist's who worked on Saturdays; buying flowers for no-one in particular, simply for an excuse to see her, when she was the one person he wanted to give them to but was too scared to say anything.

# PART II

# 8
---

As Luke drives to Ulford, the oak trees along the familiar road seem to have grown or moved position, and as he passes a barn he is certain he has never seen before, he wonders, how can a road I've travelled a thousand times have altered so much? A mile later a telephone box at the crossroads before the Ulford turn seems to have sprung up overnight among the faded green cow parsley, heavy with seeds, which cover the roadside. And yet, since it is the famous K6 model, it must have stood there bright red and obvious for God knows how long. Curious too that the seven mile journey at a speed dictated by narrow rural roads has been quicker than expected.

It is 3.50pm when he arrives at Ulford church. He pulls in at a makeshift layby and cuts the engine. Under the eaves of the church, house-martins dart to and fro, almost invisible against the flint wall. He looks at a late Gothic window and notices a rectangular panel of medieval fragments leaded among later clear glass quarries. In the church where his grandmother's funeral had taken place there had been a similar group of remnants in a window. He can still remember the inscription, *Gather up the fragments*. He had thought at the time that this described his own work – gathering often damaged mirrors, long-removed from their original settings, and finding a new home for them. The church in front of him, without a house in sight is perhaps itself a remnant, almost the last survivor of an earlier Ulford which had later been rebuilt half a mile down the road. Was Rhona's house part of the original village? He looks down the lane on the right, the junction half-hidden by the bushes and ash trees in the churchyard. It is still too soon to drive down there.

He closes his eyes and listens to birdsong, but can hear Eva's comment over lunch: 'A customer on a Sunday afternoon? Isn't that a bit of an imposition?' His reply, 'A sale's a sale,' was weak, a deception. 'Shall we meet up at the Queen's Arms for pub grub at seven?' he had added. Luke opens his eyes and checks the time. Another minute and he can go. As he watches the light sparkle on a small lancet window of the church, a voice inside him says, *Let's get this nonsense over*, but it fails to prevent his heart racing as he restarts the engine and turns down the lane under the ash trees. Soon it becomes a rough track, tarmacked but narrow, divided by a central ridge of grass. The lane continues downhill for a hundred metres, levelling at a bend from which he catches a glimpse of a building behind a beech hedge. This must be the house. He slows as the beech hedge gives way to a farmyard entrance with an open five bar gate on which is a sign, Saffold Farm. Driving in, he finds himself in a gravel yard and parks near a blue Citroen estate. From under it a white cat stares at him with suspicion. The yard is silent. To his right is the rear of the house, about 1800, he guesses, and with a single back door. Ahead is a converted barn – a studio? To his left a larger barn is in need of repair. Turning round he sees an overgrown paddock with sycamores beyond. The unmown grass and trees are motionless in the still afternoon.

He walks to the door, counting four windows on the ground floor and five dormer windows above, suggesting bedrooms with low ceilings. He gives the heavy iron knocker a double strike. A few sparrows fly out from a clematis on the wall. There is no sound from inside. Waiting, he looks either side at flower beds planted with French lavender. Around the door trails an old rose, a few soft pink flowers enjoying the afternoon sun on the west-facing wall. He wonders if he should knock again, and even if he has arrived at the wrong time, or if Rhona's vagueness has allowed her to forget the appointment, but he continues to wait. Turning around, he sees the cat fixing him with eyes reserved for uninvited callers. He looks away and towards the barn conversion where a modern doorway has been built into its original arched entrance, now mostly bricked-in. On each side are flower beds planted with herbs; a mauve creeping thyme spreads over the brick path which leads to the door.

He knocks again and is encouraged to find the cat at his feet, as if expecting to enter. The sound of footsteps proves the animal correct. As Rhona opens the door he sees a curious object glitters and sway in a dark passageway.

'Luke, this is lovely,' she says and gives him a hug, her hair touching his right cheek. He feels awkward. His hands fall on her waist. There is no kiss and she moves back, smiling and resting her hands on his forearms as if greeting an old friend. She says nothing but hunches her shoulders, excited. At that moment the cat crashes through their feet into the house.

'That's Rambo. He lacks all the graces cats are meant to be blessed with.'

'I never knew this house was here – it's so secluded.'

'That's why we bought it. I wanted somewhere to work where it would be almost impossible for people to drop by. Come through. Mind your head on the low beam. I hung those beads on it to warn people of the danger. Not that it stops Alden from bruising his head ten times a day.'

The passageway leads past an open door. Luke steals a look and sees a large kitchen, cupboards and worktops all in white, whose clean modern lines make no concessions to the old farmhouse. The exception is a well-worn York stone floor. As Rhona walks ahead, Luke registers her yellow dress, almost ankle length and printed with small red flowers. He notices too her tanned feet and ankles – she is barefoot– and her bright green toenails. He also catches her perfume, unmistakeably the same as she wore in the shop on her first visit. She leads him into a small room at the front of the house.

'The old couple who lived here before us called it the parlour. We've kept the name.' She turns round with a faraway look. 'Parlour always reminds me of a cosy room in a Beatrix Potter story.' She points to one of a pair of armchairs facing the fireplace and goes to a window and adjusts the catch from half to fully open.

Luke absorbs the room. Here, unlike the kitchen, the cottage style has been allowed full sway: chintz curtains, a faded Donegal carpet on the Norfolk pamments, printed linen loose covers on the armchairs, a small oak side table between them, a third armchair in a corner, watercolours of rural scenes on the walls, Staffordshire figures of the four seasons on the mantelpiece. On the chimney breast a modern landscape in oils seems out of place. A vase of sweet williams stands in the hearth. As Rhona moves away from the window he sees a small

Pembroke table level with the sill and covered with a white tablecloth on which is a tray with two floral-pattern side plates and two cups and saucers. Rhona sits on a stool by the fireplace, her legs stretched out in front of her.

'Alden's out somewhere this afternoon,' she says.

Luke suspects she has followed his eyes and seen him note only two cups.

'Just as well really,' she says. 'He takes no interest in mirrors, or any other furniture for that matter. Even the room at the other end of the house which he pretentiously calls the library, he furnished with a mindless mixture of chipboard shelves and heavy carved bookcases. He resents the fact that I use a corner as my own office. The only room he has given any thought to is the kitchen which he designed himself. He's so proud of it. I think it's like a mausoleum and I'm very happy to let him bury himself in it, since he does all the cooking. In fact he was a little miffed this morning when I said I was going to do some baking.'

It occurs to Luke that she has not explained that Alden is her husband or partner, but assumes he knows.

'I do love your shop,' she says. 'Nestled in the corner of the market place as if it's been there for ever.'

'Only nineteen years, I'm afraid. I bought it when I moved up from Chiswick.'

'Really? How interesting. I used to pass through Chiswick when I was a student. I shared a flat in Fulham but loved taking a bus down to Kew to draw the gardens.'

'Probably the 27 or 391.'

'Was it? I'm hopeless with anything to do with figures.'

There is a hint of Cinderella about her, he thinks – barefoot by the fireplace. But the nail varnish and yellow dress belie the comparison. He imagines her as a black and white photograph until, after a few moments, the colours re-emerge. There follows a silence, perhaps half a minute – he's not sure – but it is not uneasy; in her presence he is comfortable to say nothing. If he were to leave this instant, the afternoon would have been perfect. It is an unfamiliar feeling, painful to bear if he gives it thought. His eyes move to the mantelpiece and the Staffordshire seasons. It is a relief to be drawn back to the known world of the old, but his eyes return to her.

'Pretty, aren't they?' she says. 'My granny gave them to me when I was twenty-one. I think they even have the maker's name on them somewhere. I can't remember who.'

'James Neale?'

'You know I think it is. How clever of you.'

'Not really. I'm a third generation dealer and the business has never been restricted to mirrors.'

A breeze from the front garden ruffles the curtains. Rhona rises effortlessly from her stool. Smiling, she waves in the direction of the painting on the chimney breast. 'That's where I'd like a mirror.' Slipping from the room she says, 'While I find the kettle, have a think what would suit it best.'

Looking at the wall above the mantelpiece Luke wonders whether she is in the least concerned whether she has a mirror or not: it is all a gentle game, but one to be relished. He walks over to the window, inhales the warm summer air and looks at the garden, brutally formal, he thinks, with a lawn divided into four by a cross-shaped gravel path. A rosebed in the centre of each quarter is planted with a single dark red standard rose, all in full bloom. To complete the rigid design, a terracotta urn planted with glaring red pelargoniums stands at the intersection. Luke hears a noise beside him and sees Rambo jump up and station himself on the sill, one eye to the window, the other to the room.

Luke returns to his armchair, determined to commit every detail to memory. There will be no difficulty in remembering Rhona's yellow dress, but even the smallest detail of the parlour must not be forgotten, down to the mouldings of the woodwork and the tone of the off-white walls. Since all these objects are part of Rhona's life, he must become familiar with them, make them his own. It is a pleasing room, unobtrusively decorated: the skirting board and picture rail have been newly painted, but the old dark green paint on the door has been retained, its surface around the lock rubbed to the bare wood by generations of hands. The design of the fire surround is understated, its bullseye corners small and delicate, the cream paint original. Any mirror above it must be equally restrained. He stands and looks at the painting it would replace. With its rocks, olive trees and a distant glint of a cornflower sea, it must surely be a Mediterranean landscape, but it has no title or signature – a work of some quality but not helped by a cheap frame.

'It's nice, I think, but sort of in the wrong place.' Rhona is carrying a tray with a teapot and milk jug, a plate of scones, butter and jam. She places the tray on the Pembroke table and raises a warning finger at Rambo. 'It's Alden's painting, a present from Lynton, but I think it would look better in his library.'

Luke wants to ask more about Alden: what if anything is his work? Does he work from home? How long have they been together? Who is this Lynton? But this is not the moment. In the fullness of time he will learn everything. Didn't Eva once say that in her work questions are sometimes best asked sparingly? Of course, this is not a counselling room, but the afternoon's dynamics awake memories of one.

Rhona claps her hands. 'Now come and try a scone. I bought some cream but I'm afraid Rambo got there first.'

When he has returned to his chair with his tea, he watches Rhona settle into the armchair next to his, her plate and cup sharing the same small table. The silence between them is disturbed only by a meadow brown butterfly which drifts through the window and drops on her shoulder, its wings spreading on the pale red flowers of her dress. Motionless, Rhona looks at it from the corner of an eye.

'Oh dear,' she says quietly, 'if it's looking for nectar it's going to be disappointed.'

'Perhaps,' Luke finds himself lowering his voice, 'it's attracted by the colours. Who wouldn't be?'

The meadow brown moves towards the fireplace and flutters above the sweet williams before landing on them.

'I may have the ideal mirror for this room,' Luke says. 'It's rectangular with a delicate gilt surround, partly worn back to the gesso.'

Rhona is listening attentively, but he hears another conversation conducted beneath this talk of furnishings. 'It's in my store,' he says. 'I can't remember if the plate is original or not. I could bring it across and let you see how it looks.'

'Luke, that sounds divine. On dark evenings I shall be able to light candles in front of it. I bet your house is full of beautiful things.'

Luke describes his house and explains he lives on his own, at which a look of surprise from Rhona leads him to describe his relationship with Eva.

Rhona raises her fingers to make inverted commas. 'A psychotherapist for a partner?'

For an instant Luke is offended to hear Eva ridiculed, but Rhona's eyes make all things forgivable. 'She trained as a psychotherapist but is happy to be called a counsellor. I think some of her colleagues regard her as a bit of a maverick.'

'Do you think you will ever live under the same roof?'

'We joke about the possibility, but it seems very distant.'

'What a happy arrangement,' she says. 'My own life is not so tidy.'

Luke wants to know more about her private life, but contents himself with the thought that her need of a mirror has given him an excellent excuse for a second visit.

The meadow brown returns to her dress, this time resting on her knee.

'It must like that pattern,' says Luke. 'I think I agree.'

'This is one of my old art school efforts,' she says. 'Everybody else was obsessed with blacks and whites, so I thought I'd do something different.'

The butterfly ascends towards the open window.

'I'd love to see some of your current designs.'

'I'll give you the studio tour later. Tell me, Luke, what do you do when you're not working?'

'I enjoy fishing. I like French films and music of the '50s and '60s. And I have an allotment.'

'Alden promised me some homegrown vegetables this summer, but he spent all his time making that suburban garden in the front and never got beyond digging out a vegetable plot the size of a handkerchief which remains unplanted.'

'A garden can take years to be established.' Luke is aware that by defending Alden he is following Eva's advice to a would-be adulterer, albeit a light-hearted comment after a conversation with a fool – 'Don't criticize the husband.'

'You're too kind,' says Rhona. She goes to the kitchen to refill the teapot.

Luke leans back in his chair and knows he is falling in love with her. An inner voice says, *It is hopeless, ridiculous. She is merely flattering you.* And he feels guilty about betraying Eva. Doubly so, since he is using skills she has taught him to his own advantage. But, he thinks, hasn't life been too safe for too long? Rhona makes me feel so alive. She gives me a new energy. The voice says, *She is flirting with you – that's all. She's been cruel about her husband; she may be cruel to you.*

*Yes, I know she is flirting with me,* he tells the voice, *but why not enjoy the moment, the excitement that someone twenty years younger is happy to be*

*in my company, to confide with me about her partner? But isn't it deeper?*
*There is an electric charge between us – unspoken, hidden beneath talk of*
*trivia, but felt most keenly in the silences. This unseen Alden of the hi-tech*
*kitchen may be an obstacle, but the charge makes all things possible.*

Rhona returns from the kitchen and refills his cup. 'I've been trying to imagine you on your allotment,' she says. 'I didn't know there were any in Cantisham.'

'They're hidden inside a large Victorian walled garden.'

'How magical. I love allotments. As a child I used to look at them from the train window and make up all sorts of stories about the animals which crept in at night.'

'We don't encourage the animals.'

'There's no end of rabbits in our orchard. Alden wants to bring in the pest control men, but they always look so mean, don't they?'

Luke wants to say 'The pests are pretty damn mean too,' but says instead, 'I bet Rambo hunts the young ones.'

'Yes, but that's nature and somehow forgivable. And it diverts him from stalking birds and that I don't like. A few weeks ago he ate a baby swallow. How he found it I dread to think. Alden just laughed. I was so angry with him.'

Luke almost says that he too would be angry, but looking at Rambo says in a Mr. Jinx voice, 'One swallow doesn't make a summer but it does make a very tasty meal.'

Rhona frowns. 'You're as bad as Alden.'

Luke thinks this is a reprimand until he sees the corners of her mouth quiver and she laughs.

Jumping up, she says, 'Come and see the studio.'

Luke follows her out into the passageway, shooting a glance down the hallway towards a door which must be a second kitchen door. Further on is another door – to a dining room perhaps – and a staircase at the far end. Alden's library must be one of two rooms on the other side of the hallway. It is important to know the geography of this house. Since Rhona, for all her vagueness, her lovely this and wonderful that, misses nothing, he is determined to be equally astute. With an eye trained since childhood to see and remember detail, it would not normally be a difficult task. But the last twelve days have shown that extra diligence is required in the face of her disconcerting ability to impair his powers of observation. He will be vigilant. Nothing will be overlooked. At the same time there are rules. It would certainly be unacceptable to go online and search every possible detail about her, her business, her husband, their house. Such cold inquiry would destroy the mystique.

They are almost at the studio door, when a motor bike snarls down the lane and into the yard with no audible reduction in speed. It comes to a gravel-spraying halt a few feet in front of them. A man in black leathers kills the engine, climbs off a Triumph Thunderbird, kicks down the side stand, pulls off his gauntlets and removes a black helmet, revealing a mass of untidy dark brown hair. Luke decides that some women would perhaps call him ruggedly handsome, were it not for the pale, bony hands.

'Might have a problem with the tappets,' says the biker.

Rhona raises her eyebrows and turns to Luke. 'Like we're interested,' she says.

The comment is unheard or ignored. 'Bloody good machine though. And it's almost thirty years old. Anyway, hi, you two.' He slaps his gauntlets down on the seat.

Looking at the white fingers, Luke imagines them touching Rhona.

'Luke, this is Alden,' says Rhona.

Alden extends his right hand. Luke shakes it, noticing a tuft of grey hair to one side of Alden's head.

'Luke's come for a chat about mirrors,' Rhona tells him.

'My grandfather clipped me round the ear once for not calling them looking-glasses.'

'He was a sweet old boy but a little bit of a snob,' says Rhona.

Luke springs to the grandfather's defence. 'A lot of that generation called them glasses. They used to come into the London shop. My restorer called them the Alice band, as in *Through the Looking-Glass*.'

'Perhaps they were right,' says Alden. 'Certainly *Alice Through the Overmantel Mirror* doesn't have quite the same ring about it. On the other hand,' he continues, 'to take another case . . .'

'He's in lecturing mode,' says Rhona.

'On the other hand,' insists Alden, 'Mirror, mirror, on the wall sounds much better than looking-glass, looking-glass et cetera. And it would be too much for a driving instructor to ask you to look into your rear view looking-glass.'

'He's the original word man,' mocks Rhona.

'This word man must get back to JB,' says Alden, striding towards the door of the house.

Luke wants to ask who JB is and why Alden must get back to him.

But on the principle that it may be to his advantage not to ask what it is assumed he already knows, he says nothing and has a memory of the first day at his detested school, surrounded by people bigger than himself who knew what a wapper was, what the second bell meant, what it was to be given a blue paper and a host of other incomprehensibles. A system of mentors had been introduced a term before he left, too late to have helped him. He had soon discovered that the best policy was don't ask questions; nor would he do so this afternoon.

Rhona leads him to the door of the studio, pointing at the herb beds and saying, 'Not Alden's work – much too irregular.' Having opened the door, she places a hand on the small of his back and guides him in ahead of her.

His first impression is of a fashion boutique after an act of sustained and mindless vandalism. Parts of garments, rags, strips of cloth, swatches, drawings and various bladed instruments are spread at random on long tables and flow onto the floor. On a rail a line of dresses are rough-seamed, unfinished tatters, as if the vandal in a fit of conscience has attempted to reassemble them.

'We seldom complete anything here,' Rhona explains. 'This is an ideas factory. People buy my outline designs and have them made up in factories in India and China.'

Luke begins to discern order in the apparent crime scene. Only then does he look about the building and appreciate how new windows in the south wall, and lime-washed timbers have given a space and light unguessed from the red brick exterior.

At one end is a modern mezzanine. 'Storage area,' Rhona tells him. She turns and points to the other end dominated by a long drawing board covered with jars of pencils, pens and paints. 'My workspace where the ideas take shape.'

Luke's eyes rest on drawings for children's clothes based on 1930s gangsters.

'Our biggest customers at the moment are in the US. Rich kids' parties have to be themed. If the shops want the Mob look for kiddies, we supply it. Alden, of course, is quite cynical: "Spend money on designer clothes for your brats to compensate for the fact that you never talk or read to them." Mind you, he doesn't object to taking their money.'

She pulls out some drafts of designs based on Russian national costume.

'This is the latest venture. I'm doing a range for a new children's boutique in Moscow.' She leads him by the arm to the tables and shows him part of a child's costume – whether for a boy or girl he can't decide – with jacket and trousers covered with small applied fishes and shells. 'The sea is always a popular theme,' she says. 'And anything which touches on green issues. Alden often questions what the carbon footprint of the final garment might be. Designed here using foreign fabrics, made up in the Far East, shipped to New York, LA or wherever. But I do things for the home market too.'

She takes Luke's hand and leads him to the far wall and lifts up a length of silk spread over a piece of furniture. 'And here's my new plan chest – in use already.' She pulls open a lower drawer. Luke notices the contours of her body through the yellow dress. She extracts more drawings and spreads them on top of the chest. 'Old ideas,' she says. 'Medieval, Spanish, The Nutcracker, whatever the dear children, or rather their mothers, want for their next party. And usually, like their mothers, they'll wear it only once and ... '

Luke, only half listening, finds he cannot move his eyes from the line of Rhona's spine and her hair falling abandoned about her shoulders as she bends over.

'... and we also do a more down-the-line range for high street stores. In some parts of England ...'

He wants to touch it, to feel its softness and weight in his hands. Too soon she turns round.

'You must have quite a workforce,' he says.

'Five. I had sixteen in London.' She points to two photos above the plan chest. 'On the right – that's us – a couple of years after I started the business.'

Luke looks at a group of women in a studio, Rhona standing in the centre with her arms round those nearest to her. In the background he can make out Alden's head. Luke considers asking about Alden's role in the business, but Rhona anticipates the question.

'Alden insisted he was in the photo, being a sleeping partner. That's his sister in front of him – Moira.'

Luke looks at a tall woman with close-cropped hair.

'She's the third shareholder – a working partner in those days, but now, mercifully, more dormant than Alden after marrying a hedge fund manager. This can come down now.' She removes the photo and slips it into the top drawer of the plan chest. 'It's not good to keep looking back.'

Luke looks at the other photograph, Rhona and four women standing outside Saffold Farm.

'That's us now,' Rhona says. 'A much smaller team. I was expanding too quickly in London. Now I concentrate on the upper end of the market. Higher risks but greater rewards.'

Luke wants to ask if Alden has a job apart from his sleeping partnership, but says instead, 'I've a customer who runs a hedge fund. When he talks to me about his work and million pound deals my mirrors seem like throwaway baubles.'

'My sister-in-law calls my business a cottage industry which is slightly annoying.' Rhona waves her arm around the room. 'Designs which leave this *cottage industry* find their way to at least twenty countries. Lowering her voice, she says, 'I certainly earn far more than her brother. He says he's quite happy I'm the main breadwinner, but I'm not sure if I really believe him.'

Again Luke wonders about Alden's work, but says nothing as Rhona returns to the plan chest. She opens a drawer and shows him a small design based on a peasant costume. 'I promised Lynton's grand-daughter, Phoebe, I'd give her one of my drawings.'

Luke notices in the drawer a photograph of a group of children.

'My second family. An orphanage we sponsor in India. Each year a percentage of our profits go to them. In the textile world child labour is rife, and I can't control where my designs end up or which factories produce the end product.' She picks up the photograph and lays it on the plan chest. 'I try to make a small difference. Alden calls it tokenism and gets annoyed when I call them my children.' She closes the drawer. 'We don't have any of our own – fortunately.'

Luke hears a wistfulness in her voice and sees her look towards a worktable next to the plan chest and study a dress design. 'Excuse me a moment.'

Rhona takes up a pencil, scribbles some notes on the design, unpins three pieces of floral-printed cotton from the dress and rearranges their position.

Luke marvels at the sudden transformation of the garment into a dress now more colourful, vivacious.

'Work never stops in this cottage industry,' she says. 'Let's go back indoors.'

As she leads Luke into the yard, he wonders if it is time for him to leave. The afternoon has been so electric he wants to quit while the current is live. To outstay such a welcome would be unthinkable. But she pre-empts him. 'Now you must come and see where I've hung that fabulous needlework.'

Back in the house she leads him through one of the doors he saw closed in the hallway.

'We call this the snug,' she tells him. 'A bit pubby I know, but again it's what the old owners used to call it'.

Snug it is, Luke thinks: two sofas, a TV, coffee table, a small fireplace over which is a portrait of Rhona with sea-green hair.

'A brief phase at Art School,' she says. 'The painter's quite famous now as a shoe designer.'

On one side of the fireplace in an alcove and above an old oak chest of drawers hangs the needlework. 'The perfect place,' says Luke.

Rhona smiles back, motionless, again the Parian figure. After a few moments' silence she spins round and points to the other alcove where the wall is bare. 'If you could find me another needlework for here . . .'

Alden bursts through the door. 'That drip Connor has let me down and can't come to Santa Marta.' He turns to Luke. 'Don't fancy a week in Corsica do you? Flight and expenses paid for light duties?' The leathers have been exchanged for baggy green cords complete with fishtail waistband and yellow braces worn over a white T-shirt.

'Alden, I'm sure Luke hasn't the faintest idea what you're talking about.'

Alden drops onto one of the sofas, stretches his body full length, throws back his arms, brings his hands together behind his head, and closes his eyes.

Rhona touches Luke's arm and they sit on the other sofa.

'Lynton,' begins a weary Alden, 'you know, Lynton Travers the artist, come August will have been living in Santa Marta for sixty years.'

'It's a tiny village in the mountains,' Rhona says.

'Unscarred by tourism.' adds Alden.

'But there is a hotel and a café,' says Rhona, 'and the village has mobile network.'

'It's unspoilt,' says Alden. 'I wanted to mark the anniversary in some appropriate way. There's going to be a retrospective exhibition of his work but that's in Paris and not until next year. A London gallery wanted to put a show on, but Lynton is having none of it – he fell out with the art establishment years ago. I had long discussions with some old friends of his . . .'

Luke searches his memory for the name Travers but finds nothing. Perhaps Russ has heard of him.

'Now, as it happens, the village square has this amazing flight of steps leading up to the main door of the church. The interior is a ruin – what's left is now a gallery – but the exterior walls survive, and the paved area in front of the door and the steps below are a great space for an outdoor play. So what better way, I thought, of celebrating the anniversary than producing a play in his honour. My first thought was that it had to be Shakespeare – a Mediterranean setting, set partly on an island. There was only one play I could choose of course.'

In an uneasy silence, Luke realises he is expected to guess the chosen play.

'In the shadow of war, like much of Lynton's life,' says Alden. 'Come on.'

'Alden wanted to put on *Othello*,' says Rhona and yawns.

Alden frowns. 'That was my *original* choice. But when I broached the idea to Lynton, he was uneasy about it. "I've seen enough tragedy and violence in my life," he told me. "I don't need any more." And as ever Lynton was right.'

Rhona turns to Luke. 'Alden's always rather lionised Lynton,' she says.

'Nonsense,' says Alden. 'Ten years ago a university friend introduced me to him . . . '

'A girlfriend,' says Rhona.

'An *old* girlfriend. But ever since Lynton and I have remained friends.'

'But you're *always* saying what an inspiration he is, how he changed your life – showed you that art, whether painting or writing,' she turns to Luke, 'or even my humble rag trade,' she fixes on Alden, 'is the most fulfilling thing in life.'

'He inspires me.'

'And, darling, we await with eagerness your great play or biography.'

Luke sees Alden's fair skin turn beetroot. It is time to rescue the maligned husband. 'So which play is to replace *Othello*?'

Alden lowers his feet from sofa to floor and extends his right arm, '*Peter Pan*.'

Luke feels he should make a response to this changed choice of play, but before he is able Rhona says, 'At least it's not heavy with deep meaning.'

'Not at all,' says Alden. 'In fact it's been argued that *Peter Pan* was influenced by Shakespeare. One could, for example, compare Tinkerbell with Puck in *The Dream*. Added to that ... '

'Here we go again,' says Rhona. 'As far as I'm concerned it will be much more fun than boring old Shakespeare.'

Alden looks up to the ceiling in disdain.

'Oh, darling, that look would be perfect for Captain Hook.'

Alden looks down at the floor while Rhona attempts to suppress a laugh, a failed effort which Luke finds irresistible.

Ignoring her, Alden raises his eyes towards the central '50s lampshade. 'The choice of *Peter Pan* was Mathilde's. She saw it as a child and has always wanted to see it again.'

'Mathilde is Lynton's lovely French wife,' says Rhona.

'Two drama students,' says Alden, 'and a professional dancer, are taking the leads. Other friends, amateurs but gifted, complete the cast. I'm directing and playing the pirate Starkey. Unfortunately, an old friend who was to play Smee has cried off. Added to that I'm still short of a pirate who was to double as prompter.'

'It's a farce before it's started,' says Rhona.

'You should speak to Russ, my restorer,' says Luke. 'In fact you may have met him at the local drama society.'

Alden lowers his eyes. 'Russ? Oh, yes. Not sure if we exactly hit it off.' In sudden excitement he raises his arms. 'Why don't you both come? Have a part each. Russ would make a good Smee, and as pirate Cecco, you'll only have three lines, apart from joining in with the pirate song.'

'I'm not sure,' says Luke.

'Close the shop for a week or two like they do in Paris in summer. Make it a working holiday. I'll pay for the flights and hire car and your accommodation will be free. I'll show you some photos of Santa Marta. It's a great place.' He leaps off his sofa and leaves the room as if Luke has already agreed.

'Don't let him twist your arm,' says Rhona. 'And don't get taken in by all his theatre talk. You wouldn't guess he's a solicitor would you?'

'I thought he was a writer.'

'God, no. Probate solicitor. On and off. He's opted for locum work so he can spend more time on his creative ambitions.' Rhona looks to the door and says quietly, 'Never mention the legal thing to him. It earns him money but he's embarrassed he has to do it. Mind you, it was his decision to read Law at university and then train with some London firm.

Deep down I'm sure he would have rather done English or Drama Studies.'

Savouring the confidences, Luke allows himself a question: 'Have you been to this Corsican village?'

'Five times. It's very pretty, but it might best be visited without Alden.'

'Where do you stay?'

'A wonderful old house – Les Puits. It has seven bedrooms and has never been modernised. It was where Lynton lived before he restored the abbot's house, which is where he lives now. Some of the rooms at the back overlook . . .'

'Look at these,' says Alden entering the room holding a photo album. He sits on the arm of the sofa next to Luke, and turns a few pages. 'Here's the centre of Santa Marta. Isn't it wonderful? There's the old church. Here are some of the other houses.'

Luke sees photos of stone buildings with green shutters, pine-covered hillsides and a river running through a rocky gorge. Pretty, he thinks, but almost anybody's holiday snaps. At the end of the album is a large photo of an old man at his easel in a studio.

'Lynton,' says Alden. 'The old monastic buildings next to his house are now accommodation and a large studio for his summer school students. They are providing most of my cast and set-builders. Beautiful isn't it? Have I tempted you to join us?'

'You can't expect an instant reply,' says Rhona. 'Anyhow I'm sure Luke needs to speak to his partner first and also to Russ.'

'That's fine.' Alden is back on the opposite sofa. 'All three of you can be my guests.'

'I can't promise anything,' says Luke, 'until I've spoken with Eva. As for Russ – at such short notice . . .'

'Your Russ would be great for Smee. Oldish, balding, a little rotund – he's made for the part.'

Luke feels his left hand squeezed by Rhona. 'I think it could be fun. Why don't you mull it over?'

Luke looks at her, knowing he couldn't refuse those blue eyes if she suggested leaving for Corsica that afternoon. 'What are the exact dates?'

Alden answers for her. 'We'll be over there from the fourteenth. We only have a week for rehearsals. The play's on Saturday the twenty-second. Why don't you fly out a couple of days beforehand and stay for as long as you like? It doesn't matter if you miss the first rehearsals. Let me know as soon as you can.'

Alden stands and Luke finds himself standing too, Rhona next to him.

'Of course,' Luke says, aware that this is the moment to leave.

As he walks from the back door to his van he commits to memory the number of the blue Citroen. Before he climbs into the driver's seat Rhona hugs him and gives him a very gentle but protracted kiss on the cheek, followed by the lightest touch of her lips on his. Luke wonders if Alden has seen this from the back door of the house. And if he cares.

Driving from Saffold Farm he tells himself that the idea of closing the shop for a week or more is ridiculous. And anyway, Eva is at a conference in mid-August. But before he has reached the top of the lane he asks himself, who draws up the holiday schedules? And if Eva is away . . . Before he passes the church his mind is made up.

Luke looks at his left hand on the steering wheel. When Rhona squeezed it there was a message in her touch which had nothing to do with Alden's production. And the message was underlined by the kiss. His head is awhirl. Too much has happened. He is elated. He is also driving too fast. He can still feel Rhona next to him on the sofa, giggling as she mocks Alden. He can see the curve of her spine, smell her. *And* those moments of silence. Best of all the silence. He and Eva could sit in a room and not speak, had done many times, usually reading in her cottage, or the silence of fishing. But silence, doing nothing at all and still feeling they were living to the full – had that ever happened? I hate these comparisons, he tells himself. But I can't help drawing them. No, they draw themselves. His van almost collides with an oncoming Volvo. The two vehicles swerve up their respective roadside banks to avoid a crash. The Volvo driver mouths obscenities at him. Luke knows he is at fault and raises a pacifying hand.

The other driver opens his window, 'Tired of living, are you?' he shouts.

Luke shouts back, 'Sorry,' and drives on. The near miss hasn't cooled his excitement. On the outskirts of Cantisham he looks at his watch. Not yet time to meet Eva, but the prospect of an empty house is unbearable. He pulls up at the Woodcutters, a dreary pub on the edge of town which, he suspects, owes its survival to the big screen in the bar. He hasn't been in since a first visit years ago; today it deserves another chance. A blackboard outside reads *TV – Bayern Munich v Norwich. Relive the day.* It is only when he climbs from the van that he sees a card on the passenger seat. Handwritten it says *Rhona* with a large *X* and a mobile number. He kisses it and places the card in a back pocket.

Inside the stuffy bar Luke finds a dozen locals. One calls out to him from a table, 'Didn't know you were a City supporter.' It is Alf, with a half empty pint in front of him and Maurice asleep at his feet. Neither he nor anyone else in the pub is taking more than a passing interest in the match.

'Drink up and I'll get you another,' says Luke. They watch football and talk vegetables and fence posts, but Luke feels that part of himself has not left the sublime comfort of the parlour at Saffold Farm. More than once he checks that the card is still in his pocket.

* * *

'You? Watching football in the Woodcutters? I can't believe it.' Eva laughs. They are in the Queen's Arms, braving the new chef's Thai Special. Luke has said nothing about his visit to Saffold Farm. 'I knew Alf would be there, and there was some allotment business to discuss.' The facts are half true but Luke knows he is approaching the point when he will have to be honest with Eva about Rhona, or he will be entering a world of lies and deception. Perhaps he is already there.

'And this afternoon's customer?' asks Eva. 'Did you make a sale?'

'Yes, a very satisfactory day. Now tell me about your afternoon.'

'I fell asleep doing the crossword and didn't wake until four. Gave the house its token weekend clean. Made myself do half an hour's weeding. And in the pub – did you cheer when the goals were scored?'

'You have to enter into the spirit of The Woodcutters.' This again, he knows is approaching a lie, having arrived at the pub as the second half of the game was starting, by which time he had missed all the goals in the match. Afterwards, there had been replays, but . . . Eva deserves to be told about everything before further duplicity.

'Busy week ahead of you?' he asks.

'No,' she frowns. 'You've known for ages I've run down the workload before my mini-sabbatical.'

'Oh, of course.'

'Luke, what's the matter? You seem distracted.'

'Sorry. Guess I'm tired. The beer in the pub didn't help.'

'And maybe you shouldn't see customers on a Sunday.'

'Perhaps not,' he says, knowing he would see Rhona on any day, at any hour of her choosing.

'What was this customer like?'

'Boring couple on the edge of town, but as long as they spend money with us . . .'

After the pub, as usual on a Sunday night, they go their separate ways, Eva towards Brick Kiln Cottage, Luke towards Back Lane. As soon as he is in the door of Number 7, he rushes to his diary in the kitchen, turns to the pages of August and confirms, as he suspected, that the month is free of appointments. But the four days, 19 – 22, each has a pencilled note, *Eva in Birmingham*. He smiles, knowing he can invite Eva to Corsica in the confidence that she will refuse. He does not believe in Fate but some power is on his side. And there is no need yet for Eva to know about Rhona. But another voice says to him, *What exactly is between you and Rhona? You talked. There was silence. There was an innocent goodbye kiss. Nothing more.* He almost believes it.

Before going to bed he googles Lynton Travers and makes some notes: Born in England. At the age of eight was in the Basque country with his Communist father when the Civil War broke out. Father fought against Franco. Young Lynton remained in Spain and sometimes ran messages in the mountains for the Communists. Both returned to England during the Second World War. Art School, early success, clashes with the critical establishment about his return to traditional subjects. Move to Santa Marta where he was instrumental in restoring a derelict village. Former monastery now the home of a summer school.

Again resisting the temptation to find out more about Rhona, he searches online for the stage version of *Peter Pan*.

# 9

---

Restoring Rhona's mirror is a sacred ritual, each part of which must be carried out with the utmost devotion to detail. Even the drive to the storage barn on the edge of town at 7.00am on Monday is no workaday task. And his head, since waking, has been abuzz with thoughts about the future. A 5am plan was to phone Rhona's mobile number as early as reasonably possible – he must hear her voice again. But a simple phone-call is insufficient; there must be a pretext other than, 'Thanks for a great afternoon,' or some such platitude. Far preferable to be able to say, 'I've found that mirror I mentioned – shall I bring it over?'

He arrives at the barn earlier than any of the tenants of the light industrial units, beating even the wood-turner, normally at work by 7.30am. Unlocking the main gates and parking near his barn, by far the biggest building of the complex, he entertains more thoughts of the future, of plans for converting the barn into a house with an entrance and garden not affected by the units. With so much space, so many outbuildings, if Rhona ever needed a new studio . . . The conversion plans, like Russ's retirement date had remained a distant prospect, but now . . .

Inside, he walks down one of the rows of mirrors stored on pallets in bays, according to size and date, many bought years before he was born, including the frame destined for Rhona's parlour. He removes its cardboard and paper covering, his fingers trembling. It is exactly as he remembers: a simple 1820s design, its water gilding worn in places with the bole exposed, giving it, to his mind, the charm of natural ageing which no amount of deliberate distressing could ever replicate. He is certain she will love it.

Now the second stage of the ritual. Since it is without a mirror plate, a suitable glass to be cut to size must be selected from stock. The loose plates are stored at the far end of the barn. There can be no compromise in quality. Rhona must have Vauxhall glass of the period, not a thicker Victorian plate. The search begins. Half an hour passes, he hears the wood-turner's van arrive, another vehicle pulls into the yard, he hears the sounds of power tools from the units, but the desired glass eludes him. He continues to hunt, certain that somewhere there will be the perfect piece, with wear equal to the frame but not so worn that its days of reflecting are over.

In the dim light of the barn he imagines Rhona looking into it as she walks past, or sitting at night in a room lit only by the candles in front of it. He sees himself sitting there with her. By which time Alden would somehow have disappeared from her life. That is a certainty.

At last, the elusive plate. He lifts it, but at the same time two large eyes look up at him from the floor. The glass moves in his hands. He almost drops it. The eyes, oval and silver, too big for a mouse or rat, stare at him. He freezes before realising that they are two pools of mercury which must have bled from this or another old mirror plate. He relaxes, smiling at the thought that if Health and Safety officers knew about this store, they would issue orders for its immediate closure.

He places Rhona's mirror plate safe on a palette. With a knife blade he sweeps the eyes into a jam jar, feeling lucky not to have dropped the precious plate and now to be clearing up its razor-edged shards.

The remainder of Monday and all Tuesday, in Russ's absence, is spent carrying out minor restoration to the frame's woodwork and gilding. On a rushed commercial job, he and Russ might have employed quicker techniques, but this mirror demands the best of which he is capable. No modern wood adhesive can be used; instead, traditional scotch glue that needs to dry overnight. Time-consuming, but short-cuts are unthinkable. Gesso and boulle also demand time, but for this task hours will not be counted.

At 9.00am on Wednesday he turns the shop sign to open. Outside, the market goes about its unhurried business, but in the shop it doesn't matter if there's none – serious, casual, trade or private – only the task in hand. Strange, as ever, to be here without Russ, and difficult to recall when Russ last took a few unscheduled days off. Tomorrow, on his return, there will no doubt be a full account of the funeral.

Luke stares at the mirror plate. But now it is more than a mirror; it has become a talisman which, handled in the correct way, will produce the desired result. He opens his tool box and removes his diamond glass cutter. To use Russ's is unthinkable - under workshop law cutters are one-man tools. He measures, makes marks, measures again, positions the ruler. Now he must concentrate on the line down which he draws the diamond, make himself forget that she will see this object almost every day of her life, pause in front of it, look at her reflection and see those eyes return their blue gaze. For a minute he must not think about her, certainly not look in the mirror at himself; the workshop is a place of frames and edges, not reflected faces.

He scores along the length of the mirror plate. Lifting it a few inches, he taps the back with a steel rod. The score line deepens. With pliers he snaps off the unwanted margin and places it to one side, pleased that his hand on the diamond remains steady after years of reliance on Russ. Turning the mirror ninety degrees, he lowers it back onto the black rubber mat which covers the workbench and repeats the procedure along its width.

The offcuts are retained with the others. Narrow, impractical-looking strips, they may have a use in a future job. He returns the pliers to their clip on the wall among the other communal tools, and his diamond cutter to his own small tool box. Having moved the glass to another table, he vacuums the work surface, removing any tiny splinters which might damage frame or fingers. Only when the frame is laid face down on the workbench and the mirror plate is fitted into the rebate, does he return to the thought that this mirror is Rhona's. More than that, he has decided it will be a gift to her.

\* \* \*

Eva sits in silence in her counselling room. It is a day of intermittent sun and racing clouds. The sound of a sudden gust of wind emphasises rather than diminishes the peace. In the armchair opposite Agnes sits relaxed, wearing a pale blue cotton dress and black sandals with straps of a Stella nail varnish red. If she is wearing any make-up, it is so subtle Eva cannot detect it.

'You are looking very well,' Eva tells her.

'I feel it.'

'Compared with two weeks' ago, you seem much more in control.'

'I think I am. But occasionally I have . . . they're like small shocks pulling me up.'

'What sort of pulling up?'

'They seem to be getting at me.'

'They?'

'Two voices.'

'What are they saying?'

'Conflicting messages. But both talk at the same time.'

'Tell me about them.'

'The louder one tells me how stupid I was in trusting a creep like Alden. Of course, I know now I was stupid, but the voice says, "You still don't know how bloody idiotic you've been." It wants to rub it in.'

'And the other voice?'

'He – or is it she? – quietly suggests that there's a chance – just possibly, against all common sense – Alden and I may still get things together. A hundred to one, a thousand to one chance, but still possible. I don't want to hear this message either, but it nags at me all the same, hard on the heels of the other. I'm not going mad, am I?'

'Not in the least. Finishing a relationship is not so different from a bereavement. Something dear to us has ended – a life, a love. Part of us accepts the fact, but the loss can take many months to make itself felt. We want to go back in time to when things were different. In the case of a death, this is of course impossible. With a lover . . .' Eva pauses.

Agnes continues for her, 'We remember the good times, imagine they could be repeated.'

'So when you have these shocks . . . voices, what do you do?'

'I try to ignore them, get on with my work. Luckily they don't come very often.'

'Ignore them so they go away?'

'I guess so, but . . .'

'They haven't quite gone yet?'

'Not quite.'

'No?'

Agnes draws herself up in her chair. 'I suppose I become aware of them, whatever they are, about twice a day.'

Eva decides Agnes is attractive, but not in any usual or obvious way. Much of her charm is in her voice, a confidence tempered with a hint of vulnerability. 'Instead of ignoring them, have you tried talking to them?'

Agnes frowns. 'How do you mean?'

'Supposing, for a moment, I was the voice of reprimand. Would that be OK?'

'Why not?'

Eva sits up and pictures herself as her old English teacher, Miss Forbes, a harridan who believed literature was to be read and analysed, not delighted in. 'Agnes, you have no inkling how incredibly imbecilic you have been, carrying on with someone you knew would let you down.' Eva raises her nose in the air, brushes the back of her head with a hand, picturing Miss Forbes touching her bun of white hair. Agnes is visibly shocked. Will she retreat or confront me? wonders Eva in a silence, broken by, 'Well, what have you got to say for yourself?'

Agnes goes for confrontation. 'I know I was stupid. Right? And you don't have to tell me again. OK?'

For a moment Eva wishes she had been able to talk back like this to Miss Forbes. She now relaxes into her chair, the harridan dismissed, and says quietly, 'Of course, you may get back with him. Give yourself time and you may find that . . .'

'No way,' snaps Agnes.

'You don't know for sure. Many happy relationships are founded on the most inauspicious of beginnings.'

'I don't want a happy relationship with him.'

'You were happy once.'

'Cloud cuckoo land.'

'It sometimes felt like cloud nine.'

Agnes pauses. 'Get lost,' she says, shifting her feet and looking away.

Very quietly Eva says, 'It may seem like a million to one chance you could be happy with him. But think, most people meet their partners as a result of those sorts of odds.'

'I've already met him, been to bed with him, regret it. Now it's over.'

'Is it?'

'Yes.'

'Are you certain?'

'Piss off.'

They both laugh.

Agnes eases herself back into her armchair. 'So ignoring's not the way. I've got to answer them back. OK?'

'It might help. We'll have to see.'

Eva glances up at the fishermen, pauses, looks at Agnes. 'And at work? Everything's fine?'

'Yes, and Rhona's always very good to me. She lets me choose my hours, which is why I can come here most Wednesday mornings. She knows I will always work weekends if there's a panic. And she's even offered to lend me, interest free, the money for a deposit to buy my own place, if I ever decide not to rent.'

'And you don't find her presence makes you think about her husband?'

'No, he's hardly involved with the business and I seldom see him, thank God. *And* Rhona seems to have found some other guy.' Agnes looks up at one of the Dufy prints. 'Do you think it's really possible for people to live together and have a so-called open relationship?'

'It can mean quite the opposite.'

'You mean not being open with each other.'

'It may come to that.'

'So open relationships are a bad idea?'

'Different arrangements work for different people. Some couples seem to thrive on secrecy and intrigue. Others have an unspoken rule that mistresses and boyfriends are permitted providing that children, property and reputations aren't damaged.'

'Do what you like but don't frighten the horses.'

'Something like that.'

'But in your counselling experience, how many open relationships are successful?'

'Any answer I give you would be misleading. I tend only to see relationships in crisis. What matters to us now is whether you are affected by whatever relationship exists between your employer and her husband.'

'I'm sure I'm not. In fact I seem to benefit from her good moods when she's got some other man on the horizon.'

Eva smiles.

'I haven't met her latest. Apparently he's some mirror dealer. She bought a piece of needlework from him the other day.'

Eva feels the blood drain from her head.

It is 10.30am. Luke needs his coffee. There has been no Russ today to bring it to him promptly, followed later by the offer of a refill. In the kitchen he makes himself a strong pot with the Ethiopian organic coffee Russ always buys, and carries it to the workshop where all is ready.

On an electric hotplate a double chamber glue pot is at a gentle simmer. Beside it are a dozen small pine glue blocks, rectangular and chamfered, which will hold the plate into the rebate of the frame. One by one, he takes a block, brushes some glue on two sides and rubs it to and fro along the face of the rebate adjacent to the mirror plate. When, as the glue spreads and strengthens, he feels resistance between block and rebate, he leaves it in place. At the same time he ensures that the blocks touch but do not press hard against the back of the glass. Any surplus glue he wipes off with a damp cloth. It is a satisfying task, but once completed, he is glad to remove the glue pot from the heat from where its smell has permeated the whole shop, smothering even the aroma of Russ's coffee.

Luke looks at the back panel standing to one side on the floor. It can be screwed on when the blocks are dry, a task no doubt Russ will carry out first thing in the morning. Not that it matters. The main work is done. Rhona can be phoned tomorrow morning and the mirror can be shown to her whenever she wishes.

* * *

Averting eye contact with Agnes, Eva looks up to the painting whose brushstrokes are moving uncontrolled about the canvas.

*Mirror dealer. Luke? An affair? Surely not? But how many mirror dealers can there be? I must move the conversation on elsewhere. Luke? Can't believe it. Find out more from Agnes. No – Professionalism. Conflict of interests. Ignore, ignore. Twenty minutes left. The anglers are staring at me. Put this on hold. Agnes is not aware of anything. Yes, put on hold. And move on. Luke? No, impossible. Change direction. Too late – Agnes is talking...*

'...to my surprise Rhona insisted on giving me the full details on Monday morning. She dragged me into the orchard during our coffee break, sat me down on a deck chair and bared her soul. Like she's using me as her in-house counsellor. For most of the time I sat there in silence and let her warble on.' Agnes laughs, 'Do you know, in the last few weeks I think I must have picked up some of your listening skills.'

*How many mirror dealers do I know? Only one, but in a twenty, forty mile radius there must be others.*

Eva hears herself say, 'The effects of counselling are bound to impinge on your inter-personal relationships.'

*Where did I get that word 'impinge' from? I never use it. Must regain control.*

Agnes says, 'My first reaction was to tell her I've heard it all before. Last time it was the happily-married schoolteacher. The time before it was the clarinettist. Then there was the orthopaedic surgeon. Before that the Polish art student. Loads of others. Now we have the mirror dealer from up the road. But I yawned and looked through the branches and up at the sky and listened to the old, familiar story. She's rather pleased that this one's not married.'

*Up the road, up the road. Which road? In a previous session I'm sure I noted that her workplace is not far from Cantisham. Can't remember precisely where. In the country somewhere, yes. But where? Can't remember the name of the village. Will it be in my notes? And Luke is not married. Take a deep breath. Stabbing. My stomach.*

Eva says, 'Do you feel that this role as Rhona's confidante will impede your own progress?' The knife stabs again.

Agnes looks away in thought.

*How long has it been going on? Or has it just started? Agnes is speaking again.*

'. . . and there was a time I might have been unduly influenced by her. Not now though. Not any longer. I remember once when we were in London . . .'

*Can't continue with her as a client. Recommend another counsellor. But up the road? Up the road? I need to know. Agnes has stopped speaking. Has she asked a question? Or have I missed some vital point relating to Rhona and Luke. Must find out more. Find out where Rhona's work is. Not directly.*

Eva says, 'I'm not sure how helpful it is looking back at Rhona's various entanglements. It may be that you are lucky living here in the city and not closer to her.'

Agnes looks puzzled. 'I was sort of thinking of renting a cottage nearer work. Are you saying that I shouldn't?'

'No, all I suggested,' says Eva, 'is that you may like to think about how near you want to live to an employer who might be very demanding on your emotional resources. Sometimes physical distance is important.'

In silence Agnes reflects on the comment.

Eva feels sick – sick about the possibility of Luke having an affair with Rhona, sick that she is steering the conversation towards an answer to the important question of where exactly Rhona lives. Sick that she has ceased to be a counsellor and is now in forbidden territory. A voice from many years ago is talking of client abuse.

'I needn't live in Ulford itself. There are several nearby villages where I could rent or buy a property.'

Eva recoils. *Ulford. Ulford, up the road from Cantisham.* The blade in her stomach twists again. *It must be Luke. Can't continue with this client.*

'Agnes, you are really sounding so much more positive about things compared with two weeks ago. Now we had planned two more sessions and if necessary, resuming when I return from my break. However, I feel so much progress has made, we should perhaps have just one more session next week. How do you feel about that?'

Without apparent thought Agnes says, 'I'm in your hands. A couple of weeks ago I almost walked out and you helped me to see that I should stay. Now, if you think we've reached the point when only one more session is needed, that's fine. I trust your judgement.'

Eva wonders whether there isn't a hint of glibness in Agnes's tone. 'OK,' she says, 'Let's look towards next week as a final session. Of course, if at any time some issue arises which means you want to resume our meetings, all you have to do is phone the Centre. I'm officially having a break in two weeks' time until the end of October but I only plan to be away from home for a few days, so I could always find time to see you. Or, if needs be, you could make an appointment with one of my colleagues. How does that sound?'

Agnes cocks her head to one side, rests a finger on her chin and thinks for a moment. 'Fine,' she says.

'Next week we can explore how you think you've progressed since your counselling began. Also, how you will feel about not coming here on Wednesday mornings. Some clients . . .'

'I know how I'll feel. I shall miss seeing you.' Agnes scans her surroundings. 'And I shall miss this room too.' She looks at the fishermen. 'Especially that picture.'

Alone, waiting for her next client, Eva looks again at the oil sketch. The colours are now motionless and the angler no longer stares at her.

She wishes that in her bag there was a packet of Gitanes, given up for twenty years, often missed and now craved. Or a drink. A large gin. Scotch. Anything. To hell with the discipline of making some notes about the last hour. 'Planning an affair . . . apparently he's a mirror dealer.' Those are all the notes which matter and they're not likely to be forgotten. But Luke? Surely not.

Eva stands and paces the room. I must be rational, she thinks. What has been suggested is a planned affair. Rhona is clearly a schemer whose marriage survives despite or because of infidelity. Perhaps what she told Agnes is a fantasy, a dream, a half-baked plan which will have no chance of success. Luke is too sensible. He would never fall for such a game. But if the affair has started, would she know? She has been a counsellor long enough to know the answer to that. And what can she do about it? She and Luke aren't married. They don't live together . . . but hasn't she always accepted that they were as close – closer – than many couples who did and certainly closer than a friends-with-benefits arrangement. No, she can't believe it. She goes to the window and looks down on the street below. A few cars pass, a woman is taking an obese alsatian for a reluctant walk, two swans drift by on the river. On the horizon the boom of the crane moves very slowly, then stops, like a clockwork toy winding down. No, she must not be disturbed by some comments from a client. Her trust in Luke could never be that fragile. She must prepare herself for her next client.

Eva turns back into the room. I shall do nothing but note Agnes's comments, she tells herself. I shall certainly not confront Luke or start spying on him, like some of the jealous women I have seen over the years. I shall mention this to Stella of course – she is sure to have some wisdom to share. Apart from that, life continues as normal.

She hears footsteps in the corridor outside. As her next client settles in the armchair, Eva realises that in the next hour Luke is of far greater concern to her.

* * *

Luke sits at his desk turning the pages of the local paper. But now even the sea fishing reports hold little interest. He is restless, aware of a new energy. He wishes there was more practical, humdrum work to be done in the shop to absorb the hours. A customer would be welcome, even a timewaster. None appears. At 1pm he flips the shop sign round to closed and with no intention of opening again today, sets out for the allotments. It is lunchtime but he has no appetite.

Beyond the allotment gate he is at ease; the old walls are more than a physical protection. He walks to Alf's hut and to his relief Alf is not there. Nor does there seem to be any other allotment holder at work this afternoon.

Having changed into his gardening boots, he inspects his onions and lifts them all, laying them on the soil to dry. Glad of the opportunity to be alone, he examines, one by one, the other allotments, making comparisons with his own vegetables before returning to his own plot. Here he ties the latest growth on his sweet peas, hoes the carrots, tracks down and disposes of a snail near his courgettes and gives everything a thorough watering. The allotment, exuding a smell of wet soil, seems to thank him. When all is in order, he goes to one of the hothouses and sits back on a kitchen chair, his feet resting on an old earthenware celery forcer. Warm and comfortable, the air heavy with the fragrance of tomato plants, it is silent here, apart from the sound of a bee searching the glass roof for an escape hole. Closing his eyes, he wonders what Rhona is doing this afternoon, what she is wearing. For some minutes he is next to her in the parlour, talking of butterflies and mirrors but enjoying a deeper conversation beneath the spoken words. He feels so close to her here. Such feelings could never be enjoyed in the shop, but this walled world has its own laws of time and space which make all things possible.

The bee is no longer buzzing. Perhaps it has found an escape. He does not open his eyes, but begins to reflect on his life, reviewing the years one by one. Falling asleep he slips back to schooldays, travelling in an army truck on the way to Bisley for shooting practice. He drifts to another rifle range close to a lake. Wandering off during the afternoon's programme, he finds himself at the water's edge, watching the sun play on the surface. Close to the bank, almost at his feet, a sluggish carp swims among water lilies while gunfire echoes in the distance.

\* \* \*

As soon as her client has left, the pain in Eva's stomach returns, not a stab, but a prolonged ache. She stares out of the window and over the Norwich rooftops as if looking for some sign of encouragement. It would be so good to see Stella today. Perhaps she should phone. An emergency appointment? No, that would be desperation stakes. But she *is* desperate. 'Must talk to someone,' she says aloud. 'But who?' She turns away from the window and walks into the centre of the room and stares at the Jack Yeats painting. 'Annie. Yes, garden fanatic Annie,' she says to the fishermen. She drops into the client's armchair relieved to have made a decision.

Within fifteen minutes of a phone call to her friend, Eva is driving out of the city. As north-west Norwich gives way to fields and woodland her earlier panic subsides enough to allow her to see that it is a perfect summer's afternoon. But the realisation is immediately followed by a sense of unreality. Can this be happening to me? Am I really about to visit a friend to discuss the possibility of my partner's infidelity? Luke and this designer woman? It's impossible. No, Agnes must be mistaken. And didn't Agnes say that Rhona had bought a needlework? Does Luke deal in needleworks? I've never seen one in the shop. By the time she has turned off the A140 she is convinced that there has been some misunderstanding which has left her or Agnes or both with a false impression. Driving along the narrow road, the verges a mass of thistledown, it is hard to imagine any disturbance in her well-ordered world.

She pulls up outside the smallholding to be greeted by Annie's Jack Russell. On leaving the car she bends down to pat the dog but finds she has no enthusiasm for pleasantries. Seeing Annie, all smiles, coming out of the house, Eva realises that this is not going to be an easy visit.

'Drinks outside?' Annie suggests. 'Village shop white – I think I live on it.'

Eva follows her to the garden at the rear of the house where a narrow lawn overlooks a gentle slope laid out in terraces, alternating flowers and vegetables. At the side of the lawn is a small summer house with open double doors. Inside are two chairs and a table where a bottle and glasses are waiting. While Annie eases out the cork and fills the glasses, Eva admires the ordered and weed-free terraces.

'How is it that all your plants are further ahead than mine?' Eva asks.

'The south-facing slope helps.' Annie takes a deep drink. 'Eva, is everything OK? When you phoned earlier, I thought I detected an uneasy tone . . . not like you?'

'I had a client this morning who totally unnerved me.'

'Threatened you?'

'Not physically or even verbally – nothing like that. It was what she said.'

'Isn't that an occupational hazard in your line of work?'

'It can be. Sometimes a comment throws you into self-doubt, undermines your confidence.' Eva finds herself struggling to be open.

'I couldn't have your job. How's the peach tree I gave you?'

'Despite the peach curl, I had a great crop.'

'It's not Luke, is it?'

'Luke's fine. I think.'

'You only *think* Luke's alright?'

'This client of mine, a woman, was going on about infidelities.' Eva pauses and plays with the stem of her glass. No, she can't bring herself to tell Annie everything. At least, not yet. 'And I began wondering about Luke . . .' She downs some wine.

Puzzled, Annie looks at her. Suddenly she jumps to her feet. 'Eva, you've obviously been upset by whatever nutty cow you've been trying to help. I'm certain you and Luke are the same couple you always have been. At least you see more of him than I see of Phil and you don't even live in the same house. Now come and look at this new variety of chard I've been growing and forget whatever's bugging you.'

They walk down the path between the terraced beds, arm in arm, glasses in hand.

'What do you call it,' Annie continues, 'when one of your clients starts unloading their stuff on you and odd things happen? Trans-something?'

'Transference and countertransference,' mumbles Eva, hoping to avoid a discussion on the dynamics of counselling.

'Well, I bet that's the answer. Nothing wine or gardening can't cure.' She bends down at the end of a row of deep green leaves on blood red stems and picks two. 'Have a bite of this.'

Eva chews on the chard, nodding in appreciation. Annie looks at her knowingly. 'Listen, Phil's often away for weeks on end in developing countries. Of course I used to wonder exactly what he gets up to in his spare time where sex is cheap and readily on offer. And I still occasionally wonder. But what is the point dwelling on it?' She laughs, 'And to date there have been no STDs. More to my worry is when he volunteers to help in the garden. Try this other variety.' She points to another row of chard, a paler shade of green. 'I asked him to weed out an infestation of green alkanet earlier in the year and he goes and digs up all the young foxgloves on my semi-wild bed. You'd think an agronomist would know the difference.'

'I definitely prefer the other variety,' says Eva mid-mouthful.

'Whatever your misguided fears about Luke, at least he would know his digitalis from his pentaglottis.'

'I always let a few alkanets remain at the end of the garden. The bees seem to like them.'

'Have you any evidence Luke is having an affair?'

Eva is taken back by Annie's bluntness. They have reached the bottom of the slope where a semi-wild bed covers the whole width of the garden. 'No, not really,' she says, knowing she is being elusive.

Annie touches her arm, 'Come inside and have some lunch.'

Eva points to a group of plants at the rear of the bed. 'Look, you still have a few foxgloves left,' she says.

'There you are: men are sometimes not total disasters.'

As they turn back Eva feels miffed that Annie's world appears so trouble-free. They walk up the slope, pausing at the dwarf beans, the celeriac and a row of lettuces, one of which Annie pulls up.

By the time they have retrieved the bottle from the summer house Eva is determined to say no more about Luke. It is Stella she needs to speak to and as soon as possible. After lunch she makes an excuse and leaves.

'Keep in touch and don't worry,' Annie shouts as Eva starts the car.

'Thanks,' Eva shouts back, longing for the first quiet field entrance where she can stop and make a phone-call. A mile down the road she turns onto a concrete sugar beet pad and phones Stella. After a few rings she hears Stella's recorded message. Frustrated, she ends the call, stares across the field and listens to an invisible skylark. A mistake to have visited Annie, she thinks, but at least the visit has shown how important it is to see Stella. She rings the number again and again hears the message. This time she leaves her own. 'Stella, it's Eva. Can you phone please? I'd like to see you. Soon, if possible. It's urgent. It's about . . . if you could phone today I'd be grateful. Thanks.' She ends the call and the pain in her stomach subsides. As soon as she is back home she changes into gardening clothes and forces herself to do some weeding, her mobile and landline phones on a stool beside her.

After half an hour she gives way to the afternoon sun and lies down on a blanket in the shade of the laurel. She would welcome sleep but Agnes's voice replays itself again and again, 'Apparently he's some mirror dealer.' She opens her eyes and looks up at the canopy of leaves where the ten syllables seem to echo among the mesh of branches. Without thinking, she grabs her mobile and phones the shop. After six rings, she hears, 'This is Luke Brewer Mirrors. We are sorry no-one can take your call. Please leave . . .' She rings off and phones his house. Another recorded message. She tries the shop again, but hears the same message. Is he busy with a customer? she wonders. Often he leaves the phone for Russ to answer, but with Russ away has he really let it ring? Or is he in the back room searching for some long lost frame? She dials his mobile but is told the number is unavailable. In a mind heavy with suspicion she forms a vivid picture of Rhona from the details supplied by Agnes, only now she pictures Luke with her. No, I'm not going there, she counsels herself and falls back on the blanket.

She breathes deeply and tries to relax. A minute later her mobile rings. She seizes it.

'Luke, where have you been?'

'Eva, this is Stella. I'm returning your call.'

'Oh, I'm sorry, I was expecting . . . Yes . . . I wondered if I could see you as soon as possible.'

'Of course. I'm in London at the moment, but I'm back tonight. Can you wait until tomorrow?'

'Yes, tomorrow would be great.'

'Ten o'clock?'

'Yes, thanks.'

'Eva?'

'Yes.'

'I don't mind burning midnight oil if you'd prefer.'

'No, tomorrow is fine.'

'I look forward to seeing you.'

The few words with Stella, the appointment made, are a palliative. In a spirit of partial release she returns to the house and five minutes later is walking towards the town centre, telling herself she needs to buy some bread. As soon as she enters the market place she looks across to the shop, squinting in an attempt to tell at a distance if the shop sign says open or closed. But a few steps later, she sees him walking to the shop door from the other corner of the market place.

'Luke!' she calls out.

He waits for her at the door.

92

'You've caught me red-handed . . . or rather black-handed,' he says, showing her his soil-encrusted fingers. He kisses her.

'You've been on the allotment?' Eva tries to hide her relief.

'Skiving from work, I'm afraid. But at lunchtime I thought, why should I be a slave to the business? Russ would be ashamed of me.'

'Dinner at mine as usual? I walked in to buy a loaf.'

'I'll come back with you. Let me set the alarm and pick up my mobile'

Eva follows him into the shop, reprimanding herself for unfounded suspicions. 'Was Alf at the allotments today?'

'Not when I arrived, and you won't believe it but after a spot of weeding I dozed off in one of the hothouses and didn't wake up until that old flea bag Maurice started licking me when Alf turned up to pick some tomatoes. And he's got those fence posts for you. I'll pick them up and put them in for you at the weekend' He rubs his eyes. 'I'd have slept for another hour but for that wretched mongrel.'

'I shall definitely be reporting you to Russ first thing tomorrow,' Eva says, deciding she believes him. On the way home she wonders if she should steer the conversation to needlework, but walking with him along the familiar roads to the edge of town, greeting acquaintances, pausing for a few words with a neighbour, she feels that her world is so normal and trouble-free that she must dismiss the idea as a poisonous compound of jealousy and paranoia.

# 10

'It was a very moving service,' says Russ as he brings in the coffee. 'Family and all the old guard were there – those of us who're still alive that is. And St. Jude's was as lovely as ever, with clouds of incense to see Margaret off. Now you've got to have one of these biscuits. They come from a new Italian deli on Chiswick High Road which years ago used to be . . .'

'Brewer & Son Mirrors.'

'You would hardly recognise the old place. It's sad, in a way, going back. And it's all so smart round there now, with the pavements crammed with posh mothers or their nannies behind designer push chairs. You did mean me to fix the back on that mirror you've been working on, didn't you?'

'It was my occupational therapy in your absence. Screwed on OK, did it?'

'Have a look.'

They go to the workshop where Russ lifts the mirror up onto the workbench.

With less enthusiasm than he feels, Luke says, 'I cobbled it together when you were away. I may have a customer for it.'

'Best bit of cobbling I've ever seen. I'll have to look to my laurels.'

Russ stands the mirror on the floor and they return to the showroom.

'Most of the old shops have gone,' says Russ. 'It's depressing, but

some of the pubs have improved no end. I was treated to sup
Swan last night . . . '

Luke sits back and listens to a course by course descrip
pub's cuisine, relieved Russ is not going to quiz him about the
destination of the mirror. It will no doubt be a two cup report, but
afterwards he will make some excuse for leaving the shop, go home and
make the phone-call.

* * *

Eva sips her coffee and looks up at Stella's Egyptian urns, relaxing into
the security the room always gives her. Yesterday, when she had phoned,
she had pictured herself pulling into Stella's driveway, dashing from her
car and throwing herself into Stella's arms as soon as the front door was
opened. It had not been like that. Driving to the city, she had found that
the mere thought of Stella's company dispelled much of her agony, and
by the time she had parked, walked slowly to the door and pressed the
white enamel bell button, desperation had receded.

She looks towards Stella, sitting opposite in her wing chair, exotic in
a red and blue dress with floral embroidered belt. When Eva lowers her
eyes she sees Stella is not looking at her but towards a vase of faded
anemones on the stone hearth. In the silence, each time their eyes meet
Eva feels her problem is somehow diminished. And wasn't last night
with Luke, supper and bed, so comfortable, so normal, that yesterday's
panic may have been a foolish, self-inflicted over-reaction?

After a few minutes Stella places her cup on the octagonal wine table
beside her chair. 'Those flowers are like favourite shoes. They're at their
best the day before they fall apart?'

'You can guess why I wanted to see you.'

'Guessing usually gets in the way of listening.'

'Yesterday I saw my client Agnes.'

Stella sits back, occasionally stroking the left arm of her chair with
long scarlet-tipped fingers, as Eva recounts yesterday's session with
Agnes. Eva omits nothing but pauses once as if about to cry. No tears
appear. 'Was I wise in telling her that next week would be our last
appointment?' she asks, at last feeling a tear on a cheek.

Stella rises from her chair, walks to Eva and places a hand on her
shoulder and rubs it. 'My dear, dear, Eva, what an ordeal you have
suffered.'

Through tears Eva says, 'I felt like killing Luke – if it's true.'

Eva feels Stella take one of her hands and gently squeeze it before returning to her own chair.

'Shall we explore that 'if'?' says Stella.

'How can we?'

'Well, it might be worth considering whether Agnes knew exactly what she was doing?'

'You mean she might have been telling me a pack of lies, making the whole thing up?' Eva looks away and finds herself staring at a bronze dog.

'It is a possibility. Didn't she recently say to you, when she was upset, "You're just like my mother"?'

'She did, yes.'

'And might she possibly be angry with you like a child is angry with a parent?'

'I think we'd moved beyond that stage. Agnes had even apologised for earlier outbursts.'

'Isn't anger sometimes like an incoming tide? Only, instead of seconds between each breaker, with anger there can be days?'

'And we never know whether or not the biggest breaker is yet to come.'

'Exactly. So perhaps, between sessions, Agnes felt another wave of anger towards her parent figure. And like a child she wants to hurt you. The small child may, in uncontrolled anger smash her mother's favourite piece of china, but a grown-up child may be more subtle. Agnes may have discovered that your partner is a mirror dealer and now she wants to use this knowledge to punish you. If this is so, perhaps you and your client have further to go.'

Eva frowns. 'No, I'm certain she was telling me what she believed to be true.'

'Very well, but I had to mention this possibility.' Stella leans forward, arches her hands and brings them together, reminding Eva of a cluster of berries.

'Now, have you been unprofessional?' Stella continues. 'Perhaps.' She shrugs and the berries disappear. 'Forgivable and no harm, I suspect, to your client. I think you are wise to have one final session with her. And you have suggested another counsellor. That's good. But you want to talk about Luke, don't you, not standards of professionalism?'

'I called on a friend yesterday, but I couldn't bring myself to open up to her. She knew there was a problem and that I was holding back. I was disingenuous.'

'If she's a true friend she'll understand. Tell me, Eva, are you surprised with yourself that you haven't made Luke aware of what you've been told?'

Eva sits up in her chair, tense. 'It did occur to me to confront him, but it felt like making an accusation on flimsy hearsay. I didn't want to be like those clients I see who suspect a partner of cheating and make all manner of wild assumptions.'

'But you were angry?'

'I was upset, but I didn't see how bringing the matter up with Luke would help things.'

'Don't you suggest to your clients that it might be helpful to discuss things with their partners if there are uncertainties?'

'Almost always, yes.'

Stella smiles. 'So why haven't you done the same?'

Eva frowns. 'I suppose I thought we were different.'

'In what way different?'

'We don't live together, we've never seriously talked about doing so or getting married.' She shifts in her chair. 'I suppose there is a tacit understanding that we each allow the other certain freedoms.'

'Including the freedom to have affairs?'

'The problem's never arisen.'

'Do you love him?'

'Of course I love him.'

Running the fingers of her right hand through her hair, Stella stands, rearranges the cushions in her chair, walks to the window and looks out into the garden. It seems to Eva a long time before she turns round. When she does she points to the empty chair.

'Now, Eva, sit in my chair.'

Eva stands, walks over and lowers herself into Stella's chair, but is ill at ease, a usurper.

Eva is about to turn to the window when Stella says, 'Look at the chair you've vacated. Imagine you are still sitting there.'

Eva looks at the tub armchair and absorbs the unfamiliar view of the room. She does not recall ever having noticed two miniature silhouettes on the wall behind where she usually sits.

'Now imagine yourself there.'

Eva struggles to picture herself opposite.

Stella says softly, 'What do you want to say to that person?'

'I want to say . . .' She hesitates. 'I want to say, "Don't be so sad. Everything will . . .".' She finds herself unable to continue. Eva closes her eyes and shakes her head.

'Everything will be alright?' says Stella's distant voice.

'Yes,' Eva looks up and Stella is at her side. Eva begins to get up but Stella rests a hand on her shoulder.

'No, stay there. Otherwise it will become like musical chairs.'

Stella settles herself opposite Eva and claps her hands with a grin. 'Time for a story, I think,' she says.

Eva relaxes, wondering where Stella is leading her.

'Once upon time,' says Stella, 'a long time ago, I had a client, a woman, a lady in the old-fashioned sense. Let's call her Esther. Now Esther had an inkling her husband was having an affair. There were hints, suggestions. Nothing definite or confirmed, but a suspicion – maybe a little more than a suspicion. Esther came to me in a very distressed state. She was about thirty. And at that time I wasn't much older. You won't be surprised to hear that at some point I asked her whether she had voiced her disquiet to her husband. Emphatically she said no and wouldn't entertain the idea. On one occasion I suggested she really ought to consider talking about her worries to her husband, but she was quite adamant. I can still hear her saying, "I'm not sure if that's the sort of thing one does".'

Eva smiles and is about to make a comment, but Stella says, 'No, wait, there's more to come. I don't know if I still have my notes about the case, and I can't remember exactly what I wrote, but I certainly thought, typical English upper class reserve and inability to express her emotions – it's a wonder she came to a counsellor in the first place. Or some such stereotypical reaction. Well, as it happened, Esther and husband lived in a very large house, a minor stately home you might say. And Esther decided to move from the large bedroom she shared with her husband to another of the many bedrooms and in a different wing of the house. I think she gave him some excuse – his snoring or to be nearer the children, something like that. She certainly didn't say, "I think I need more space," or whatever the equivalent was in those days. She continued seeing me for many months, always worried, and very upset when suspicions became supported by facts. Yes, her husband was having an affair, and with a woman she regarded as a friend. I was very worried for her. I strongly suggested that she at least consider talking to her husband about it, but she refused. She lost weight, her GP supplied sleeping pills, then some other medication. And I was worried not only for her but for her children. At one session she talked only about suicide. If ever there was an example of somebody who should have communicated with her partner this was it. And finally it happened.'

'She took her own life?'

'No. One morning she found a note on the kitchen notice board – that had become the default method of communication. It read, *The stupid thing with her is over. If you could* . . . ? That was all – a few dots and a question mark. No explanation and no apology apart from the word *stupid* and no asking for forgiveness apart from the enigmatic *If you could* . . . ?'

'What happened next?'

'Esther came to me for one more session. And she spent the best part of an hour thanking me for listening to her for months on end while she was, as she put it, "ignoring every damn bit of advice you gave me." I pointed out that giving advice was not what I was there for, but she simply said, unconvincingly, "I know, I know." And I never saw her again, but she always sends me a Christmas card from herself and her husband with *Love and thanks* written on it.'

'It must have helped living in a very large house. Leading separate lives in a small flat would be more difficult. And wasn't your client risking her sanity, maybe her life, on the chance, some would say slim chance, on their staying together?'

'Exactly. But, for her, this – what shall we say? – aristocratic disdain for soul-baring actually worked. Or to put it another way, sharing one's feelings with one's partner in times of crisis is usually helpful, but not necessarily always.'

'But had she done so,' Eva insists, 'she might have saved herself months of agony, and the affair might have ended quicker.'

'It might have done, but we don't know for certain. She made her own decision and I have to respect it.'

'In her situation I'm sure I would have . . .' Eva pauses, scrutinising Stella. 'You've told me all this, haven't you, because you think I'm in an Esther position? Luke and I are as good as living in the same large house where we have the advantage of a wing each – separate bedrooms whenever we want them. But are you saying I should follow your Esther's example and say nothing?'

'I never gave Esther direct advice, nor would I do so to you. I simply throw the possibility into the pile of options. Some counsellors wouldn't allow it near the pile. We sometimes fall back on the occupational clichés: 'Get in touch with your feelings; share them with your partner.' Our profession has its aphorisms and correctnesses, but you are sensible enough to take a broader view.'

Eva looks up at the ceiling and runs her eye along the delicate plasterwork. 'Luke was very passionate last night,' she says softly.

Stella tilts her head a fraction to one side.

Eva averts her eyes and looks towards the anemones. 'Oh,' she says, closing her eyes and dropping her head. 'Some things can be at their best the moment before they fall apart.'

* * *

For the second time in a week Luke is impatient to escape the shop. He feels he has been force-fed each mouthful of Russ's supper at the Swan, down to the last crumb of artisan bread.

'I must collect some papers from home,' he tells Russ during a long-awaited pause in a protracted coffee break, and not waiting to see if Russ raises his eyebrows, walks to the door as casually as the excitement coursing through his body will permit.

The phone-call to Rhona must be made from home where he will be alone, away from the ears of Russ. Of course he could stand in one corner of the market place and use his mobile, but to do so would be cheap and unworthy. He needs to be away from the workaday centre of town, and undisturbed in the seclusion and comfort of 7 Back Lane. Here, not a word she says will be drowned by a passing lorry, and it will be possible to focus on her voice, to remember each phrase and intonation. And when I speak I must be relaxed, he tells himself as he approaches the front door. This must have the appearance of a business phone-call, although she, as much as I, knows that the transaction is far deeper than a conversation about a mirror.

Inside the house he is nervous and begins composing the exact words he will say to her. He even contemplates making some notes in large letters to have in front of his eyes as he makes the call. The absurdity is soon dismissed, but only to make way for another: which is the best room from which to phone her? Where will he be most relaxed? For the last few days he has envisaged phoning her while sitting in the kitchen and staring into the peace of the garden. But with the phone in his hands, the sight of starlings strutting the paths and the grating call of others on the garage roof makes him reject the idea. Now the front room seems preferable.

A ripple of guilt hits him as he enters and sees on a table a DVD of the film *Gervaise*, untouched since he and Eva sat in this room and watched it. How many evenings, how many old Continental movies have we enjoyed here over the years? he wonders. The question has a ring of finality.

Luke sits back in one of the two Edwardian leather chairs and removes from his pocket the slip of paper with Rhona's name and mobile number. Again he looks at the hastily scrawled note, its black ink written with a fountain pen in a large script, the figure nine formed with two cursive strokes like a large lower case *g* written by a child. The two lines of the kiss bisect each other exactly. He looks up at the Carolean silvered mirror hanging incongruously on the wall above the TV screen, stares into the grey, decayed mirror plate and for the first time wonders when on Sunday afternoon Rhona had had the opportunity to scribble this note. She was not out of his sight for a moment after Alden appeared and as far as he can remember, from the time he arrived at Saffold Farm he was continuously with her, apart from those few minutes when he was left alone in the parlour while she prepared tea. That was when she probably wrote it. If not, she must have written it before he arrived. He sits up and looks out of the window on his left into the empty street, wondering which alternative is true. Uncertain, he turns his head to a film poster of *Theodora*, the eponymous empress dancing provocatively as chariots race in the background. The note may not have been a last minute afterthought on her part, he tells himself. The realisation sends a new surge of excitement through him. At the same time it imparts a new confidence. He dials her number and waits, his eyes drifting to the figure of Monsieur Hulot on a poster of Jacques Tatti's *Trafic*.

'Hello-o,' answers Rhona, half singing.

'Rhona, it's Luke, I . . .'

'How lovely. I did so enjoy seeing you on Sunday. I'm really sorry Alden was so rude.'

'I've dug out a mirror which may suit your parlour.' He fixes his eyes on the blank TV screen and tries to sound relaxed. 'I could bring it over some time.'

'How exciting. You're a star. I'm in London right now, but I'll be back tonight. What about tomorrow? I can't wait to see it. Is eleven o'clock a good time? My gang have got the day off, so we won't be interrupted.'

'Eleven is perfect.'

'Any more thoughts about joining us in Santa Marta?'

'I'm having a word with Russ this afternoon.'

'Do try and come. With or without him.'

* * *

Eva grips the arms of the wing chair. 'The rat,' she says.

'You cannot be certain,' cautions Stella.

'If it's true I would . . .' Eva scowls at the anemones.

'What would you do?'

'If I were twenty years younger I would smash every mirror in his shop.'

'But now?'

'I'd break the ones in his house. He's more attached to those.'

'Will you?'

'No. No, what does it achieve? Of course, over the years I've sometimes thought he might meet someone else. We've none of the usual ties – children, a millstone of a mortgage and . . .' Eva looks up at Stella for a moment. 'You don't think this is the past catching up with me, do you? Get into a relationship with a client and inevitably, sooner or later . . .'

'You've been with Luke longer than many relationships survive.'

'Perhaps in my case the sooner or later has happened much, much later.'

'Would it help to revisit the time you and Luke first got together?'

'No, not now. I'm too upset.'

'I don't want to be a cracked vinyl record, but you still cannot be one hundred per cent certain anything is awry.'

'No, but I'm one hundred per cent suspicious.'

'How will you be with him when you see him next?'

'I don't know. I've really no idea.' Eva repositions herself among the cushions, too many for comfort. 'We're meant to be meeting for supper in the pub tonight and I'm not sure if I can face it.'

'And if he did have an affair and it didn't last, would you want him back. Or, to ask an old-fashioned question, is he worth fighting for?'

'I don't know.'

Stella nods. After a long silence, she reaches for her diary. 'Come and see me after the weekend. How about Tuesday? Come after work. Shall we say seven? That way we can talk for as long as we wish. And perhaps you can stay for supper.'

'I'd like that.'

* * *

Luke throws the phone on the other armchair, takes a deep breath, springs out of his seat, punches the air in triumph, claps his hands and raises his two arms to the window in a victory salute. Now for a celebratory drink. Champagne would be great. There's a case in the cellar but why trundle down the narrow steps and get covered in dust? There'll be a bottle of something in the kitchen. The elm cupboard in the kitchen reveals several bottles of red wine, gin and an unopened bottle of vodka – not the usual drink of choice but today is not an ordinary day. He pours himself a large measure, adds a splash of tonic and goes into the garden.

Alone outside, raising his glass to the neighbouring roofs, he is hit by another pang of conscience, remembering that vodka is Helen's favourite drink? How will she feel if he and Eva split? When she was growing up, hadn't he been as much a parent to her as her own father? 'Oh, hell. To whatever,' he says to the sky and downs most of the drink. At the end of the garden he sits on a wooden bench under the fig tree. Starlings return to one of the gravel paths; they no longer annoy him. When the time is right I will tell Eva, he thinks. It will be hard but it's not as if we're married. Maybe we'll remain close. Doubting this last thought, he frowns and drinks a few last drops of vodka. And now for Russ, he tells himself. I'll be a better listener this afternoon, even ask for more details about his return to Chiswick. At the correct moment I'll raise the possibility of Corsica.

About to leave the house, he is hit by elation as he passes the front room. It is as if Rhona's voice on the telephone has lingered here. He stands in the doorway and hears her say, 'I did so enjoy seeing you on Sunday.' Walking to the shop he wonders if there has ever been a day when he has felt so alive.

* * *

At midday Eva returns to Brick Kiln Cottage with every intention of gardening herself into mental equilibrium. The strategy has been successful when facing minor problems in the past; perhaps it will help now. She will work for an hour, stop for a sandwich, work through the afternoon. First task, to prune the laurel branches which have grown so much that they are stealing light from the irises. Next it will be necessary to check again for any reappearance of ground elder. Maybe, after these and a dozen other jobs, a sufficient reserve of emotional strength will have been built up in order to face Luke tonight. She is pulling on her gardening clothes, wondering if saying nothing to Luke is the best policy – the Esther strategy – when the phone rings. It is Annie.

'Eva, you free later? We're having a girls' night out to Cromer flicks. Want to join us? Fish and chips afterwards.'

'What's the film?

'Choice of two. We could either see . . .'

'Yes, of course I'll join you. Don't tell me what's on. I'll go along with whatever you choose.'

She replaces the phone with the pleasure of reprieve. Seeing Luke has been avoided – at least for a day.

* * *

As soon as Luke opens the front door a grinning Russ appears from the workshop.

'Guess what's gone,' he says, waving an arm around the shop.

Luke looks around, wondering what has been sold, a search made harder by the fact that Russ, after the sale, has rearranged much of the remaining stock. The old game, he thinks, but today, to humour him, I will play along until closing time. Standing in the centre of the shop, he casts his eyes around the walls and the floor. From his vantage point he can see into the workshop. With a quick glance he checks that Russ has not taken it upon himself to sell the only item of stock which has any importance. No, Rhona's mirror is still there.

'I can see everything's moved, Russ, but I can't for the life of me see what's missing.'

'You must do. Surely.'

'No.'

'Sometimes I think a customer could steal a six foot pier glass and you wouldn't know it had gone.'

'That's why you're so vital to the business, Russ. Give me a clue.'

'Definitely not.'

'Is it mirror or furniture?'

'You tell me.'

Luke realises that the missing item is a large Regency oval mirror which this morning had been hanging over the bookcase, but which now has been cunningly replaced with a slightly smaller oval mirror from the store room. Nevertheless, he will continue guessing until at least lunchtime.

'I'll get there, Russ. Give me a minute or two.'

'Shout when you've worked it out.' Russ goes back to the workshop, reappearing a second later to scoop away the invoice book from the desk. 'No cheating.'

At 1.00pm Russ reappears. 'I think I've beaten you this time.'

'I'm not giving up yet. I'll go and buy a pork pie to stimulate the brain cells.' He leaves the shop, buys the pie and two cans of *Guinness* and returns to find the workshop prepared for lunch in the usual meticulous way. Since the guessing game will not be permitted for the next hour, alternative tactics are required to sustain Russ's good mood. 'So tell me again about the changes in Chiswick High Street,' he says. 'Are there any market stalls left?'

'I think the big Sainsbury's has had its impact. Mind you, a few stalls do a roaring trade on its doorstep. I bought some dahlias there for the church. What you wouldn't recognise . . .'

Luke eats his pie slowly and makes an effort to listen. Patience is needed: after lunch, when shop business can resume, Corsica can be broached.

'Of course Hogarth's statue is still there and the Town Hall and the Old Pack Horse on the corner, but it's the plague of new eating places which surprised me . . .'

*I shall have to ask Russ to say nothing to Eva, at least not for the moment – that shouldn't be a problem, but after today there will be no turning back. The moment Russ is informed, a critical line will have been crossed. I am not daunted by this, only aware of its gravity. And I am certain that Russ who, without ever being unfriendly towards Eva, has always been suspicious of the world of counselling, will be loyal enough to support any decision I make.*

'. . . and down Devonshire Road of all places there are at least four restaurants. It's a different world now. And my old house in Kingswood Road, so I'm told, was sold last year for over a million. Not that I regret moving, mind. I've got no-one to leave my house to whether it's worth a million or twopence.'

At 1.55pm Russ clears the table and neatly folds the tablecloth. When he reappears from the kitchen he is once again in his work coat. Meanwhile Luke has turned the shop sign to open and seated himself at his desk. Before Russ can resume repairs to a walnut dressing mirror, Luke turns towards the workshop. 'Russ, can you spare a moment so we can talk about the summer?'

With a quizzical look Russ makes himself comfortable on a Sheraton chair.

'Russ, I'm planning a radical departure from our normal routine this summer. It means closing the shop for a week in August. The business can certainly stand it, and of course it will be paid extra holiday for you.'

Luke looks to see if Russ's face betrays any reaction to this suggestion. There is none.

'Now the reason for this is that I've been invited – in fact you and I have both been invited – to join Alden and Rhona Mills for a week in Corsica, helping with a one night production of a play. Flights and accommodation will be paid for. What do you say?'

Russ frowns and takes a deep breath. Luke is certain the response will be negative.

'Which play?'

'*Peter Pan*. It will be performed in a small village in the mountains, miles away from the tourist centres.'

'I thought something was going on.'

'How d'you mean?'

'Well . . . you and Rhona.'

There is a frown on Russ's face.

'Nothing is going on, but . . .'

Russ's frown breaks into a smile. Luke takes it as a good sign. 'Was it that obvious?'

'Well, I've known you all your life. And I suppose that mirror in there with twelve hours faultless work on it is heading in her direction too.'

'I'm delivering it tomorrow. I've said nothing about this to Eva.'

Russ holds up his hand. 'That's none of my business. Now I shall have to give some thought to this holiday plan. It's all very sudden.' With that he returns to the workshop and immerses himself in a cushion mirror's loose veneer. Luke remains at his desk pretending to be busy with online catalogues. He even prints out a few pages to enforce the impression. Of course, he encourages himself, it doesn't matter if Russ joins me or not, but the invitation was for the two of us and from Rhona as much as Alden and it would be a pity to disappoint her. When the shop phone rings he seizes the handset hoping it is not Rhona cancelling the meeting. It is Eva.

'Change of plans for tonight. Out of the blue Annie has invited me to join her and some of the girls for a cinema trip. Couldn't say no. Hope you don't mind.'

'Not at all. Enjoy the evening.' He sits back, pleased at the prospect of an evening alone to compose his thoughts. In twenty hours' time he will be with Rhona.

During the afternoon tea break nothing more is said about Corsica. Luke absorbs himself in the crossword in the local paper, while Russ stands by the door looking out into the market place. The uneasy silence suggests to Luke that there is little chance Russ will be joining him. It is not until 5.00pm that Russ gives any indication of his thoughts. As he switches off the lights in the workshop he says casually, 'I suppose I'd better blow the dust off my panama hat.'

With equal composure Luke says, 'Have you heard of an artist called Lynton Travers?'

'No. There was an architect, Martin Travers, but no Lynton I've heard of. Why?'

'He's a friend of Alden's and lives out there. This performance is in his honour.'

As they leave the shop Russ strokes his chin and says, 'I wonder how they'll do the flying scenes in an open air production. It was the large oval mirror, by the way – as I'm sure you've already noticed.'

## 11

---

E va brushes through a rail of women's jeans in the discount store. If she is to find a suitable pair, they will almost certainly be in the men's section, but hope or habit makes her start here. She moves to the next rail, in an attempt with each hanger moved, garment rejected, to dismiss the canker of suspicion. A deep breath, eyes closed. It was Annie's advice, quietly given last night, before the film, 'Don't look so sad. Go to the city tomorrow and buy some clothes. It may not cure what's dragging you down, but it sure as hell will help, even if this film doesn't.' But watching a comedy at the Regal turned out to be a panacea. And the four of them had laughed so much in the Albion afterwards that they had attracted frowns and a murmur of 'ladettes' from a morose regular. Since the youngest of them was thirty-eight, this was the ultimate compliment and the cause of more hysterics. The emotional high had not receded overnight. Eva opens her eyes. Rhona was not going to ruin her life. From now on hers was the Esther strategy.

The women's jeans prove as hopeless as ever and she walks towards the steps of the first floor men's clothes, on the way passing the rails of dresses. Again from habit she lingers, brushing aside each dress, hanger by hanger.

A head on the other side of the rail looks up. 'Eva, hi. What a surprise.'

It is Agnes.

Eva freezes. The shopping trip was devised as an escape from the unthinkable, not a reminder of Rhona.

'Hello, Agnes. We both obviously have a nose for a bargain.' She moves along the rail, knowing that to meet a client between sessions is best avoided: the encounter ends here.

Agnes also moves along the rail. 'I'm so glad to bump into you,' she says. 'I was going to phone to see if we could meet before our last session.'

Eva looks at a light cotton floral dress she has unhooked from the rail. 'I think we should wait until next week. And this is hardly an ideal place to talk.'

'Why don't we go for a coffee? There's a great place up the road.'

'Agnes, that's very kind, but we should keep our meetings on a professional basis. And this morning I have shopping to do.'

'That dress will crease like tissue paper, you know.'

'Don't be offended but it's really for the best.' She returns the dress to the rail.

Agnes reaches forward, straightens the dress and slowly says, 'I know about Luke and Rhona. I didn't on Wednesday morning, but since then I've learned.'

The blade twists in Eva's stomach. 'Agnes, I don't want to know,' but the moving blade tells her she needs to hear everything. She unhooks another dress.

'That's no good either. See, you've creased the material just by holding it. Come on, the coffee shop's only two minutes away.'

Eva looks down and sees she has gripped the shoulder of the dress so tightly that it has lost its shape. She throws it on top of the rail and turns to walk away, but her feet will not move. The Esther strategy does not cover this situation. She knows she should say, 'Please phone or wait for next week's appointment,' and not lingering walk out of the shop. Instead, she hangs the dress back on the rail and says, 'Very well. Coffee.'

They leave the store and cross a road in silence, only broken by Eva at the top of a narrow street. 'Most counsellors wouldn't do this.'

'I guess you're not like most counsellors.'

'More stupid, I suspect.'

To Eva's relief the coffee shop is empty.

Agnes insists on paying. 'I'm in your debt – this is the least I can do.'

They carry their drinks to a secluded back room. Eva sits down, forcing herself to admit that, now she has slipped away from a professional persona, she is glad to be here. But she will not show it. Not yet.

'I was going to phone for a chat, says Agnes. It's like, well, when Rhona told me on Monday about her latest guy, she didn't mention his name, but back at work on Wednesday afternoon I had to pay a bill from the business cheque book – it's one of my jobs when she's away. And I was a few stubs into the book and there it was in her writing: Luke Brewer – needlework. I knew exactly where the shop was, since I usually drive through Cantisham on my way to work, but I'd never been inside. So with Rhona away, I left work at four-thirty, hoping to discover what this new man in her life looked like. Inquisitive, I admit, but with Rhona it does help to keep an eye on the details of her emotional games. However, when I reached the market place, much to my annoyance the mirror shop was closed. But I was sitting in my car saying, "Serve you right for being a nosey bitch," when this man appears. And a second later you dash up to meet him and give him a kiss. Well, I'm like open-mouthed as the two of you go into the shop, reappear a minute later, walk off to the baker's, then disappear arm in arm down a side street.'

Eva winces as the blade, now ice cold, turns again.

Agnes continues in a hushed voice. 'I thought you were distracted during our session on Wednesday morning. Now I know why. I didn't realise I'd dropped a bombshell.'

Eva's eyes fall to the table while her hand involuntarily moves her cup round in its saucer but does not lift it. Neither woman speaks until Eva looks up.

'I am really sorry for you,' says Agnes. 'You've helped me so much, you don't deserve this.' Nervous, she gulps her coffee.

Eva places her elbows on the table, rests her head in her hands and sways from side to side, aware that part of her life is slipping away, until she feels a hand on her wrist, stroking it. After a few moments the hand grips her tightly. 'I would like to help you,' Agnes says gently, followed by a firm, 'Now, drink that up.'

Without thinking, Eva obeys. 'I thought, I hoped,' she says, 'that there might have been some mistake, a confusion. I thought . . .'

'I've been there. No end of times. You cannot, don't want to accept the hell-awful truth.'

'But Luke? Why?'

'You've not met Rhona.'

Eva wants to cry. 'This place is claustrophobic. Let's go somewhere else,' she says, getting up and pushing her chair aside. It falls over. She leaves it. Agnes follows. At the café door Eva is lost. The city has become a foreign place. She stares up and down the road. The sunshine is oppressive. Agnes takes her arm and guides her, steering her along a narrow street. Eva does not know where she is or where they are going, only that it is a hill, quieter than the road behind them. All she can see is a replay of Wednesday night at her house. She feels sick.

At the top of the hill she is aware of a church tower, parked cars, a moving taxi. There are shops nearby and a few pedestrians. She does not recognise the street.

Agnes leads her round a corner. 'In here.' She leads Eva through an open churchyard gate. 'It should be open. And empty.'

Eva allows herself to be guided along the stone path and through the church porch to the door. The interior is spacious, darker and cooler. She shivers. Agnes pulls a black cardigan from her bag and hanging it over Eva's shoulders leads her to an aisle, ushering her into a pew.

Secure now, Eva sees that, thanks to a stone pillar, she is invisible from the main door. And it is safe enough to cry.

When she can speak, she says, 'I have needed to do this for two days. I was on the point of tears when I talked to my supervisor yesterday morning but . . .'

'Counselling room tears can't beat the real thing. I should know – I'm the bloody expert.'

Eva looks up and sees a strength in Agnes unnoticed until now. She notices that on the middle finger of Agnes's left hand is a ring set with a red stone. Eva stares at it, Agnes follows her eyes.

'Garnet, my birthstone,' Agnes says. 'I'm an Aries. What are you?'

'Taurus. I've an emerald ring Luke gave me.'

For a minute Agnes holds her hand. 'Are you practical, like Taureans are supposed to be?'

'I am in the garden.'

'I'd love to see it. Is Luke a gardener?'

'Yes, but we don't live together. We've been with each other for almost twenty years, but have always had our own homes.'

'Does that make all this easier?'

'Right now, no.'

'What will you do?'

'Yesterday I thought that if he did have an affair I would do nothing. Today I want to kick open his shop door and tell him to go to hell.'

Agnes takes her by the arm. 'Look, I don't know anything about you and Luke, but I do know about Rhona, and I guarantee that the affair – and that's what it is – won't last. No way. I've seen it so many times. God, it's because of the last one that I got tied up with Alden. For a time I was sure their marriage was dead in the water. He thought so too. But oh no, back they came together again, brimming with forgiveness for each other.' Agnes pauses. Somewhere to the front of the church a door opens, followed by the sound of voices.

'Never mind them,' says Eva.

'You see the whole point of their affairs is that they persuade themselves they really have found that God-sent new partner. But it never happens. She's always saying, "Alden's one hundred per cent actor, even if bad actor." But the truth is, Rhona is also an actor, only she's better at it. This Luke thing won't last. I guarantee it.'

'You sound very certain.'

'Listen, if you've been with him for years, you'd be a fool to allow Rhona of all people to split you up. And you're in a stronger position than any of the partners of Rhona's other men.'

'Why?'

'Because doubt and uncertainty are the real killers if you think you're being cheated on – worse than betrayal in my experience. They set fire to the imagination and you torture yourself.'

'I've started that already.'

'But you don't need to. I shall be able to tell you exactly what is going on between them. Times, dates, places, if anything is happening. You'll still be hurt, but you won't be helpless. We can phone, we can meet. And I can tell you now, I bet my life that they won't be together at Christmas.'

There are more voices at the east end of the church. Eva says, 'Perhaps you should speak to Luke and warn him off.'

'I've tried that once or twice with Rhona's other guys. It's always too late. My advice is to tell yourself Luke has an illness, not fatal, but with a maximum duration of six months.'

Eva opens her mouth to reply but a soprano voice from the chancel fills the church. It is not an interruption. She looks at Agnes and sees that she too finds the voice curiously comforting. They listen until the first soprano is joined by a second. But the rehearsal soon breaks off to allow a discussion between the singers.

Agnes says, 'If you don't wait for Luke, you will have let Rhona ruin both your lives. You can prevent that.'

The singing begins again, this time without a break.

'This is wonderful,' whispers Agnes.

Eva closes her eyes, focused only on the music.

\* \* \*

Luke sits in his van outside the shop. Behind him the mirror, well-wrapped and covered in a blanket, is securely tied to the bulkhead. Russ lingers by the open shop door as Luke plugs in his iPod, searches for a song to match his elation and settles on Sylvie Vartan's *Irrésistiblement*. He turns up the volume and sees Russ grimace as he lowers the windows.

For the first few miles of his drive to Saffold Farm, he is at one with the music, singing along with the chorus. But the peace of the country lanes, the rich greenness of the hedgerows, a backdrop to swathes of bending seed-heads, induce reflection and he turns it off. He must gather his thoughts, become at one with this idyllic morning.

But the gentle weather cannot prevent a rising apprehension. Sunday was so sublime, can it ever be repeated? Of course, if conversation becomes uneasy there is always the mirror to discuss, to move, to hold in position above the mantelpiece. Its presence behind him in the van gives confidence. On arriving at Ulford church he pulls into the layby opposite. A superstition dictates that since waiting here for a few minutes on Sunday was the precursor of a magical afternoon, good luck will follow if he waits here again. He looks across to the church. The view is unchanged since Sunday, except for a poster on the noticeboard, advertising a fete. Three sparrows fly down from the roof of the church porch. It is a good omen: he once restored a mirror which showed Aphrodite descending to earth on a throne drawn by sparrows. He checks his watch. Noon exactly. Before he restarts the engine he tells himself, I will remember every detail of this afternoon, not only what she is wearing and every word she says, but every stress, every pause, every subtle change of tone. Instinct tells him that however wonderful the first visit, this visit will surpass it. But a minute later, as he pulls into the yard at Saffold Farm and parks exactly where he parked on Sunday, he sees Alden in long khaki shorts and red T-shirt striding towards him.

Alden glad-hands him. 'God, I could do with a vehicle like this on Corsica. It reminds me of the old camper van some friends and I bought to go bumming round Europe when we were twenty. I can still remember the punctures: one on the Simplon Pass and one in a sunflower field a hundred miles west of Istanbul. Now, is it a yes for the play?'

'It's a double yes, but I'm not sure about Eva.' He takes a step towards the front door, hoping to see Rhona appear.

Alden slaps a hand on Luke's back. 'That's terrific. Let's talk about it in the garden before my beautiful wife appears.'

Luke is pleased to detect some irony in Alden's last three words.

As they enter the house Alden says, 'She had to spend an extra night in The Smoke and didn't get back until an hour ago, so she's soaking off London in the bath. I'm under orders to apologise on her behalf and find you a drink.'

In the kitchen Alden pulls two bottles from the fridge. 'Beer OK?'

'Great,' says Luke, the hope gone of a quiet glass of wine with Rhona. He thinks he can hear footsteps upstairs and the sound of running water.

With the speed of a bartender Alden opens the bottles, using a device hidden below a gleaming work surface. 'Don't need glasses, do we?'

Before Luke can say he hates drinking from bottles, Alden leads him to the passage in the centre of the house and out through the front door into the formal rose garden. In one partially shaded corner near the hedge are two old garden chairs with stencilled cushions. As he sits, Luke is uneasy, a feeling worsened when Alden pulls up his chair so they are face to face.

'Here's to the play,' announces Alden, lifting his bottle.

'The play,' echoes Luke with less enthusiasm.

'Have you ever seen a production?'

'Only the Disney version. I read some of the play online the other night.'

'Good. There's some advantage in coming fresh to it. You don't have preconceived ideas. Of course, it is a children's play, but there's a load of stuff beneath the text which goes much deeper.'

'So your job as director is to bring out all the levels.'

'No, the trick is loyalty to the text. It's all there in the words.'

And perhaps the silence between words, thinks Luke, looking up to the first floor of the house and wondering if the bathroom is on this side of the building. Since the sounds from upstairs which he heard on entering seemed immediately above the kitchen, he doubts it.

'Tell me,' says Alden bending forward, 'as someone fresh to it, what struck you about the play?'

Luke hesitates. It is like being back at school. 'I found the stage directions rather long.'

'Some dramatists love that. Bernard Shaw was the worst of course. Banging the socialist drum with those interminable introductions. The great pity of it is . . .'

Thinking he can see a movement in one of the first floor rooms immediately above the front door, Luke lifts his beer and slowly drinks so he can sneak a second look up to a small window whose curtains have a '50s oak leaf design in black. Bedroom or dressing room? he wonders.

'. . . so why not shut up and give us the play? Now, what do you think is really going on in *Peter Pan*?'

'I suppose it's all about a power struggle,' suggests Luke, aware that he hasn't yet finished reading the prescribed text.

'Yes, but whose struggle?'

'Over who rules the island – Peter Pan or the Pirates.'

'Yes, but isn't it much more. Have Peter and the Lost Boys power enough to survive without grown-ups? Where did Peter get his magic powers from? And deep down . . .'

Luke sees another movement at the upper window.

'. . . what happens in the play itself?' demands Alden.

'The pirates get their comeuppance. A hint of a love interest between Peter and Wendy.' He takes a swig of beer and another furtive look towards the window.

Alden waves an arm. 'All well and good, but what's the *real message* of the play?'

Luke looks towards the hedge by the lane for inspiration, the afternoon sinking into discomfort.

'Alden, stop bullying Luke,' comes a voice from the front door. 'I could hear you from the bedroom.'

Luke turns round to see Rhona walking towards him in a red dress, shaking wet hair in the sunlight. Ignoring Alden, she gives Luke a hug and with the hand away from Alden's vision gives Luke a gentle, double pinch on the back.

Rhona turns to Alden. 'You should have been a prosecuting barrister, not a probate solicitor.'

Alden ignores her. 'The essence of the play is that . . .'

'Oh do shut it,' says Rhona. 'Luke has come about a mirror. You can bang on about your theories another time.'

'More later,' says Alden to Luke, rising from his chair. 'Anyhow, I have to go and see a mechanic now.' He places a hand on Luke's shoulder. 'Great to have you on board.' With an insouciant, 'See you,' in Rhona's direction he stalks off.

'I'm sorry about him giving you the third degree about this bloody play,' she says, looking at Luke's almost full bottle. 'We'll give him five minutes to get his leathers on and disappear, so I can see your mirror in peace.' Sitting down in Alden's chair, she crosses her legs, lounges back and takes a deep, contented breath.

'I've had two days of hell in London,' she says. 'Successful from a business point of view, but the only thing which has kept me going is the thought of you, your mirror, this chair and this garden. And now I know you're coming to Santa Marta, that will make it seem like a holiday not an Alden drama trip.' She shuts her eyes.

In the silence Luke tries to relax, but Rhona's wordless proximity is almost unbearable. He is glad when they are disturbed by birdsong from the hedge.

'That's a greenfinch, isn't it?' says Rhona.

'Very good,' says Luke. 'I can see there's a country girl hiding under the London business woman.'

Rhona opens her eyes. 'Not really. I've a CD of birdsong I play occasionally. It has an accompanying leaflet saying which bird is which.' She runs her fingers through her drying hair. 'But I suppose you know your willow warblers from your yellow hammers.'

* * *

In St. Giles's church the rehearsal continues to the pleasure of its audience of two. When it is over Eva and Agnes listen as the echoes of the voices resound in the Gothic interior. After some moments of silence, the noise of conversation elsewhere in the church allows them to speak.

'I don't want to talk any more about Luke and Rhona,' says Eva. 'The singing has somehow reduced their importance.'

'Shall we move on to a pub?'

'I'd love to know what that music was.'

'Let's ask the singers.'

They go to the front of the church, but the singers have gone. On their way out, however, Agnes points to a notice in the porch: *Monteverdi's Vespers and the Salve Regina for two sopranos, Sunday 9th August.*

Eva says, 'I might come back and hear them.'

'I'd join you,' says Agnes, 'but I'm looking at a house to rent. How about the Micawber Tavern?'

At the foot of the hill near the pub Eva stops, looks up and down the road, frowns and turns to Agnes. 'I don't remember walking up here.'

'You were pretty spaced out. I must have given you a hell of shock by the clothes rail.'

'You did and it took a few minutes to hit home.'

'You look better now.'

At the bar Eva buys a G & T for herself and a lager for Agnes. The background chatter of a dozen other people in the pub provides a security which Eva welcomes. 'Cheers and thanks,' she says. 'But I'm not sure I'm happy about you becoming my spy on someone I love.'

'Oh, I shan't be spying. I'll simply be keeping my eyes open in the general run of things. And if you want to meet up with me for a chat, that's fine.'

Eva looks around the pub – its painted black beams, its line of real ale beer pumps, the guest beers blackboard, a city clientele – knowing she has never before been here; she also realises that she has entered a world very different from the one where she is comfortable.

'Of course,' says Agnes, if you want to take scissors to Luke's suits or scratch Rhona's eyes out, feel free, but don't kill her or I'll be out of a job.'

Eva smiles. 'I had thought about that.'

'Killing Rhona?'

'No, cutting up his clothes.'

'That's the sort of drama Rhona would love. It would stir her up to design a dozen new children's ranges. And they would be fantastic, believe me.'

'I would quite like to meet her.'

'Socially or as a client?'

'I was thinking socially, but in the counselling room it could be interesting. Sadly, already having a personal connection, that wouldn't be ethical.'

'Do you still think it's unethical meeting me?'

'You ceased to be a client when we walked to the coffee shop. Now you are . . .'

'One of your therapeutic successes?'

'I was going to say a friend.'

Agnes raises her glass. 'Therapy and friendship.'

'Why not?'

'You will have to stop asking so many questions if our friendship's going to last.'

They clink glasses and lower them to the table. Agnes rests her chin on her right hand. 'A weird coincidence, us meeting in the discount store. I hadn't been there for months.'

'Nor me.'

'You don't seem surprised.'

'I'm not. It sometimes happens in the counselling process. Unaccountable coincidences occur – synchronicity.'

'Like the song by the *Police*?'

'We Jungians smiled when we heard it.'

'My elder brother was always playing it. Do you believe in that stuff?'

'Even my most sceptical colleagues struggle to explain it.'

Agnes sips her drink and sighs. 'God, are all your clients as rude as I was to you?'

'Some make you seem very polite.'

'Your father's *not* a judge, is he?'

'He wasn't, no. Both my parents are dead.'

'Now I feel really bad. Two weeks ago I was so angry.'

'I'm glad you felt safe enough to express it.'

* * *

The growl and roar of Alden's Triumph revving up and rocketing out of the yard brings a grateful smile to Rhona's face. As the sound fades in the distance, leaving the garden silent, she says, 'And now the mirror – I'm so excited.'

Leading Luke back through the house, she pauses in the passageway and points into the kitchen, its surfaces spotless and free of clutter. 'Like an operating theatre isn't it? Is your kitchen like this?'

'Not quite.'

'I bet it isn't. I hate kitchen units. I hate the very word unit – reminds me of a regiment of soldiers. Alden should have been in an army legal department. Do you have kitchen units?'

'No,' says Luke, knowing that if he did he would have them all ripped out by midnight.

In the yard Luke opens the back doors of his van, climbs in and unties the mirror.

'Do unwrap it here,' insists Rhona. 'I can't wait to see it.' She steps up onto the van beside him.

Luke removes three layers of Russ's neat bubblewrap.

As soon as the first corner is revealed Rhona says eagerly, 'I love it, I love it,' and when the whole mirror is revealed she sits crosslegged on the floor at the back of the van and stares at it, enchanted. 'I know before we take it in, it will be perfect.'

'Don't get your dress dirty. My van isn't . . .'

She jumps up and hugs him, saying in his ear, 'You know what I think of hygenic surfaces.'

For an instant Luke considers kissing her, but to do so would spoil the excitement that he is being seduced. 'Shall I carry it into the house?'

'Yes, yes, yes,' she says with an enthusiasm which assures him how right it was to let her set the pace. Instinct says there will be a time, a place, circumstances of her choosing when there will be so much more than this playful flirting.

As they walk across the yard, Rhona leading the way, he notices some black marks on her dress where she sat on the van floor. These, with the dusty soles of her bare feet, give her a déshabillé allure he finds irresistible.

He holds the mirror tight, again noticing in the cool interior of the house how her perfume hovers in the still air. It is as if all his life from birth, through education to the world of dealing and restoring has been focused, without his knowing, on this afternoon. In the parlour, Rhona, deft as a cat burglar, sweeps away the pottery figures on the mantelpiece, lays them on an armchair, and unhooks the painting so Luke can position the mirror. As he hoped, he finds that the old wood screw, well-fixed into the wall and far more than was needed to support the painting, is in the precise position for the chain on the back of the mirror.

Rhona moves to the far side of the room. Before Luke can join her she says, 'It looks like it's always been there. How do you work such magic?'

'It was simply waiting for years in my store for the perfect room.'

'I would like to think it was here originally. Does that ever happen – do mirrors sometimes find their way home after years of absence.'

'I have known it to occur. Russ always says furniture has a mind of its own and knows which house it wants to go to.'

'That's the sort of thing Lynton says. How much do I owe you?'

'I would like it to be a gift. Russ and I are going to be your guests for a week. The least I could do . . .'

'Oh, Luke, I couldn't possibly.'

'Please take it. I've never given a mirror to anyone before. I can think of no better occasion to start.'

'Luke, you're too generous. I must think up some surprise for you in return, although it could never be as wonderful as this. Now wait for me in the garden while I find some wine and glasses – I won't ask you to drink out of a bottle.'

While waiting for her, Luke stretches out his legs and tries to relax as much as the slatted wood chair and thin cushion permit. Unseen in the hedge the greenfinch begins its speed-drill song.

'Let's move out of the shade,' calls Rhona from the door. Still shoeless, she is carrying a tartan rug beneath a tray with a bottle of rosé and two pink-stemmed glasses.

'Could you?' she signals to him.

He takes the tray from her and watches her spread the rug with an elegant sweep of her arms onto the sunny square of lawn beneath the parlour window. Luke places the tray to one side of the rug

'Why Alden loves sitting in the shade I can't imagine,' she says. 'The English summer is short enough as it is.' She drops to her knees, fills two glasses and lies down on her side. 'It's probably all to do with Lynton who often paints outside but always in the shade. But this is England, not the Mediterranean.'

Luke lies down beside her. She gives him a glass. When their eyes meet he is about to ask about Lynton, but has no need.

Rhona shuts her eyes. 'Lynton is a landscape and portrait painter who settled in Corsica around 1950. Alden thinks he's some sort of unsung hero. He has plans for a biography of him and is halfway through writing a play about his early life. And all this while Lynton simply wants to live quietly, paint quietly and teach.' She opens her eyes, takes her glass and sips, replaces it on the tray and rests a hand on Luke's arm. 'In fact it's Alden who's chasing celebrity status.'

'How exactly did they . . . ?'

'While he was at university reading Law, Alden met a girl who was part of a gang of about twenty who used to descend on Lynton's place in the summer. She persuaded Alden to join them. Free accommodation in a Corsican mountain village and near a wonderful river for swimming and not far from the sea – which student wouldn't want to go? Alden immediately found Lynton an inspiration and wished he could be like him – even tried his hand at painting for a time.' She smiles wistfully. 'With sadly limited success. I guess deep down Alden likes him because for over sixty years Lynton's been an independent spirit and a self-imposed exile which is, I suppose, what Alden would like to be himself, if he could break out of his mould. Anyhow, their friendship remained long after Alden's old girlfriend had faded from the scene. More wine?'

Rhona stretches an arm to the bottle and refills their glasses. When she lies down again she is closer to him. 'You'll enjoy meeting Mathilde. She's much younger than Lynton and is sometimes as much his nurse as his wife.'

Luke watches Rhona sip her wine and place her glass on the lawn where a small patch arrests her attention. Craning her neck to look closer, she stares in puzzlement at the grass. 'What is that tiny plant with those sweet ears and pink stem?'

Luke moves closer to her and examines it. 'Its nicest name is angel's tears.'

'That's wonderful. I've never thought of an angel crying.'

'It can make *gardener's* cry. It's also called mind your own business.'

'Oh dear, is it a weed?'

'One of the worst for a lawn I'm afraid. It's very invasive.'

'How do I get rid of it?'

'Lawn weedkillers are no good. Some people would dig out this area of grass, destroy any roots and resow.'

Rhona traces her finger along the lawn, slowly turning her back on him until she is prone. 'It seems quite a large patch,' she says, extending her arm towards the house.

Luke looks at the curves of her body, clearly delineated through her thin dress. 'It probably invaded the lawn from the walls. It's a weed which loves old brickwork.' He can see she is braless.

'You're right,' she says. 'There's some on the row of bricks nearest the ground. It looks so harmless, nestled in the old mortar.'

'It doesn't pay to be too sentimental.' His eyes are on the line of her dress, tight on her hips. He can see no waistline of underwear.

Too quickly she turns back towards him. 'I shall have to improve my gardening skills – under your instructions.' She looks up. 'Oh dear, it's clouding over.'

Rhona quickly finishes her glass of wine. When, following her lead, Luke has finished his, she lays her hand on his left wrist and slowly stands, in a gesture of reassurance, perhaps promise. 'Let's have another look at your wonderful mirror.'

* * *

Eva drinks the last of her gin and tonic and brings down her glass hard on its mat. 'Do you think the affair has started?'

'I doubt it. That's not Rhona's way. She loves a gentle intrigue at first. And the less interested the man is, the more she enjoys it. I've seen the most attractive guys try to chat her up at a party. They get nowhere. No, Rhona likes the gradual build-up. The occasional hint, the oblique suggestion. It's second nature to her. No, it's first nature. She was born that way. The Rhona Courting Ritual. There ought to be a wildlife programme about it.'

A ghost of a smile passes over Eva's face.

'That's better,' assures Agnes. 'In a few months' time it will be over, Luke will be a little hurt, but not irreparably. You'll have to pick up the pieces, but they'll all stick together again. And with a touch of anger and some domestic TLC everything will return to normal.' She finishes her drink. 'Would I make a good counsellor?'

'I'm in no position to say. God, I want to meet this woman.'

'I'm sure you will.'

'What do you mean?'

'Rhona loves to confront her competition.' Agnes picks up both glasses. 'I'll buy the next round.'

'Only tonic for me – I'm driving – but put it in this glass. At least there'll be a whiff of spirit.'

Eva watches Agnes go to the bar, reflecting how strange but refreshing to have discovered someone so much younger as a confidante. When Agnes returns Eva says, 'Tell me about your house-hunting.'

'I'm fed up with sharing a place here in the city. And the landlord's fed up with us too. So it's galvanised me into renting my own place. I'm looking at a cottage tonight. Rhona says I should think about buying, since prices are still on the rise.'

'She sounds like a shrewd business woman.'

'No flies on her when money's involved. But she gives the impression of knowing nothing about it. God, I shouldn't have slagged her off so much to you – after all she did offer to give me an interest free loan if I ever need a deposit.'

'I wouldn't say you slagged her off. It seems the two of you have a good mutual understanding.'

'Well, I suppose it's not every woman who'd be faintly amused if she found out an employee was shagging her husband.'

'It's certainly not the response I normally hear in the counselling room.'

'God, you crack me up – "the response I normally hear".'

'I'm afraid it takes more than one gin for me totally to lose my professional persona.'

'I'd like to see you after half a dozen.'

Eva thinks back to the raucous night with Annie and the girls. That had been an escape, perhaps an unconscious denial that years of undisturbed happiness were now under threat. She chokes on her tonic. With effort she manages to hold back tears. 'I'm sorry, I suddenly thought about Luke and Rhona and what they might be planning. And here we are chatting.'

'It'll be like this for a time. Sudden stabs of pain. Out of nowhere. I expect you tell your clients that.'

'Yes.'

'But your strength is you haven't lost him. Unless you decide to give him the heave-ho. You simply have to wait. It's not like a bereavement. Or me trying to get over my latest mistake. Now, I shall phone you every day. In fact twice – morning and evening.'

'You don't need to. I'm sure . . .'

'The least I can do is to spare you from the hell of not knowing. All you have to say when you answer is, "I'm good, thanks" and end the call. But I bet you don't.'

'OK, but not at weekends. The chances are he'll be around and we won't be able to talk. And he may even answer the phone.'

'Monday first thing then.'

Eva sips her tonic, searching for a lingering tang of gin. 'How will I survive this?'

'A day at a time.'

'Can I change my mind? Could you put a shot of gin in this?'

'Of course.' Agnes takes Eva's glass and pauses. 'How did you meet Luke?'

'Bring me the drink and I'll tell you.'

* * *

In the parlour Rhona sinks into one of the armchairs by the fireplace. Luke sits in the other. In silence they look at the mirror. He is transported back to the magic of Sunday's visit. So strong is the feeling that the intervening days seem like an illusion, but after a minute, the presence of the mirror and the absence of sweet williams dispel the fantasy.

Rhona follows his eyes. 'Would a small vase of flowers look good in front of the mirror between the figures?'

'I shall always think of this room with flowers in the fireplace, but they would look fine in front of the mirror, especially sweet peas.'

'I suppose it's too late to plant some.'

'Yes, but I'll bring you some. I grow them myself.'

'Is there anything you can't do?'

'I can't act.'

'Don't worry about it. I shall enjoy finding you a costume.'

They drink and look at the mirror and occasionally at each other until Rambo appears at the open window and jumps onto the arm of Rhona's chair. It is an interruption which indicates the visit is at its end.

'I must get back to the shop.'

'Won't you stay for a sandwich?'

'I would love to, but a vestige of duty tells me there's work to do.' It is hardly true but Sunday proved that there is a precise moment to leave, whatever the temptation to linger.

'You're right, dearheart – duty calls me too – I have a work programme to draw up for my team when I'm away.'

As he stands, Rhona stretches out a weary arm so he can help her to her feet. When they are in the passageway near the kitchen Rhona asks, 'Is your own house full of lovely things?'

'A few.'

'I should love to see them,' she says confidentially, as if Alden's units have ears.

'Come over any time.'

'I'd love to. Sadly, I'm very busy in the studio. And Alden's got some of his friends staying. Let me phone. I may even think of a surprise for you.'

When they have walked out into the yard and are standing by the van, she hugs him, slowly moving her head so she can kiss him on the lips. Luke holds her and kisses her in return for several ecstatic seconds. Simultaneously their heads move back and they release the hold.

'Damn next week's work,' she teases.

As he starts the engine, she waves goodbye. Through his wing mirror he sees she is still waving as he drives out of the yard. His heart pounds, countless thoughts racing in his mind. He is already living with her – her house, his house, it doesn't matter. When she splits from Alden there will no doubt be some division of assets, but there is more than enough in the Brewer coffers to buy half of Saffold Farm if need be. No, early days for such thoughts, he tells himself. Right now enjoy each moment. But on the other hand, what is the point of starting out on a journey without a map? She may want to move back to London. That possibility too is not insuperable. As for that pedagogic twerp on the Triumph, he can exit down stage right, swigging from a bottle. So great is his elation that half a mile from Saffold Farm, he pulls off the road into a field entrance and cuts the engine. Is it possible they have kissed? He can still feel the gentle, then firmer pressure of her lips on his. He looks into the rear view mirror for some trace of lipstick, and is sad to find none. And they kissed on her initiative. A doubting voice, like a dark creature perched on his shoulder, tells him that a hug and a quick kiss on the lips signifies nothing. *You've been holed up too long in a small market town*, it tells him. *That's how she says goodbye to everyone – at least everyone except her pompous husband. And perhaps she addresses all her acquaintances with the word 'dearheart'.*

'Does it matter, does it matter?' he says aloud to the creature by his ear. 'She wants to meet up again.'

\* \* \*

'So you had an affair with a client,' says Agnes. 'That's got be more serious than going to a pub with one.'

'Luke's counselling had ended before we met up socially. But he was a former client and there is a strict professional code . . . '

'I don't see it. He was no longer your client. You were both free agents.'

Lowering her voice, Eva says, 'The therapist-client relationship must have boundaries.'

'No need to whisper. Do you think those guys over there care about codes of conduct.'

Eva looks towards the bar. A sun-tanned man is describing a friend's wedding in Barcelona. 'Chaos or what? The Spanish celebrant couldn't even pronounce the name of the bride.'

Agnes takes Eva's hand. 'Look, my cousin married her doctor. They had to be discreet for over a year. She changed doctors. He moved to another practice. Got quietly married. No fuss. And they're very happy.'

'Luke and I tried to be secretive. But two of my colleagues found out about us and took great delight in making my life hell. And my ex-husband rather enjoyed my predicament.'

'What was he like?'

'Mark was a modern languages teacher when I married him. A good one too. But he always had a wish to do something less cerebral. And then he met a girl who was starting her own interiors business and . . .'

Eva finds it painful to continue. She is relieved to hear guffaws from the bar and the raconteur's ear-piercing bellow. 'What's more the best man was too drunk to read his speech, and a bridesmaid had to read it for him. Now there was this joke . . .'

Agnes says, 'And so Mark swapped the blackboard and French lessons for expensive paints and curtain-making.'

'Pretty much.'

'I suppose she was much younger.'

'Twenty-two. Mark and I were in our early thirties.'

'And your daughter lived with you?'

'Yes. Mark made a token effort at parenthood, but we moved up here and Luke was more of a father. Helen only saw Mark once or twice a year.'

Agnes finishes her lager. 'I guess this Rhona nonsense digs up all the bad stuff when you and Mark split up.'

'No. It was too long ago. A different life.'

A salvo of guffaws explodes from the bar.

'Look,' says Eva, 'can we go back to the café?'

* * *

It is 1.30pm as Luke approaches Cantisham. Not hungry, he can't face the lunchtime shop or the silence of 7 Back Lane. On the outskirts of town the superstition reasserts itself that he should, as far as possible, follow Sunday's pattern. Since on Sunday he dropped in at the Woodcutters and met up with Alf, perhaps it is propitious to go there again. On the other hand, Alf always has lunch at home and will not be at the pub. The superstition is not straightforward: which is more important, the place or the person? After some mental casuistry, he decides on the person and drives round to Alf's house, a Victorian railway cottage near the long-closed station. And there is a conscience-salving excuse for the visit – Eva's fence posts.

'Want some tea, old partner?' asks Alf at the door.

Luke follows him into the dark kitchen. As his eyes adjust he sees the crockery, old magazines, seed trays and jars of growing cress which cover the table. Both kitchen chairs have pairs of boots on them. Shelves around the room are heavy with homemade pickles and preserves. The floor is spread with newspapers which look in need of their weekly or monthly change. In a corner above an ancient radio is a dusty photo of a family member in First World War uniform. Seeing Alf's shaving mug and razor standing in a grimy sink, he recalls old Maud's description of the room, 'a dead mouse away from squalor.' But today he loves every unswept corner. The kitchen is all things Alden would hate.

'Sit you down there,' Alf tells him, pointing to a shapeless armchair already occupied by Maurice.

Luke takes a step forward and glances towards Maurice who, understanding the protocol, vacates the chair, shakes dust from his coat, and coils onto a blanket under the table. Alf brings over two mugs of tea, hands one to Luke, removes a pair of boots from one of the kitchen chairs and settles down.

'Suppose you've come for them fence posts. They're in the back yard. Were the old ones set in concrete?'

'Looked like it.'

'I can let you have a few spiked sleeves to drive through the old holes. When you doing the job?'

'Sunday, I thought.'

'Good plan. There won't be any rain until about Tuesday. You eaten?'

'No, I've been out delivering a mirror. I don't have much of an appetite.'

'Rubbish.' Alf gets to his feet. 'You've got to eat in the middle of the day. You're one of them who eats dinner at night, aren't you? Night-time's for drinking – ask the vegetables.' He pulls out a thick-cut loaf from a chipped enamel bread bin.

At the sight of Alf's dirt-encrusted hands Luke searches for an excuse to avoid the sandwich, until he pictures Alden's slender, white fingers. 'That's very good of you, Alf.'

Between slices of bread Alf layers Cos lettuce leaves, cress pulled from a jar, two thick rectangles of Cheddar, a coating of homemade chutney and more lettuce leaves. He is about to pass it to Luke when as an afterthought he takes it back to the table, selects a jar of pickled onions from a shelf and forks one onto the side of the plate. 'Set you up for the afternoon that will. You want to get down to your allotment later. Looks like some bug's been having a nibble at your runners.'

The uncut sandwich in front of him seems to Luke like a small handmade brick, complete with the thumb imprint of its maker, but lifting it with two hands he is determined to enjoy it down to the last bite of acidic onion. 'Shall I give them an organic spray?' Luke asks.

'Don't waste your money. Nothing a dousing with soap and water won't cure.'

To Luke's surprise the first mouthful of sandwich encourages his appetite, which he takes as confirmation that his decision to come here and not to the Woodcutters was well-judged. When he has finished his sandwich and after a refill of strong tea, all obligations to superstition honoured, he knows the next meeting with Rhona will be favourable. Meanwhile, day-to-day life can resume. When he and Alf have loaded the fence posts and spikes into the van, Luke drives away, warmed to the prospect of some DIY work in Eva's garden: it won't ease his conscience, but at least it will occupy a day when he cannot see Rhona.

# 12

—————

'If I hadn't known he was embarking on an affair, I think by now I would have guessed,' Eva tells Agnes.

As promised, Agnes has phoned first thing Monday morning – first thing by Agnes's reckoning being 7am. For Eva, wide awake since the early hours, it is not too soon. She looks out into her garden where a blackbird sounds its warning notes. 'We went to an exhibition opening on Friday night,' she tells Agnes, 'but instead of the usual Indian meal afterwards he had booked a table at a new restaurant on the coast about ten times as expensive.'

'So it's not all bad.'

'I'd prefer an honest curry to phony lavishness.'

'And the weekend?'

'The Saturday routine. Walk up to the shop mid-morning. Chat about nothing to Luke and Russ – that's his restorer. The trouble is that chatting about nothing is avoiding everything. It's a game and I hate it.' She watches the blackbird, silent now, dart into the laurel bush.

'So tell him what you know. You'll feel good for five minutes. And however he reacts, you'll spend the next few months wishing you'd kept your gob shut.'

'I wish I could talk to my clients like that.'

'Perhaps you should. Look, I guarantee the whole thing will be over by the end of the year.'

'Didn't someone say that in 1914?'

'That was a new sort of war. This is Rhona playing the same old game.'

'By the end of the year?'

'At the latest. Might even be before September Fashion Week. And she's abroad with Alden for the second half of August – I'm going with them. No way it will last. If it's even started.'

'But it might be six months?'

'I thought you were good at being patient.'

'I am with clients. This is different.'

'Did he spend Saturday night with you?'

'Yes, but he was all in, having started taking down part of my garden fence after work. He just managed to stay awake for supper, but a stubborn fence post had totally knackered him, so he was asleep almost before he got into bed. Looking at him lying there, dead to the world, I didn't know whether to feel sorry for him or smother him with a pillow.'

'Which did you do?'

'I had to keep him alive to finish the fence. He crawled back to his own home Sunday evening.'

'Did you go to the concert?'

'Concert?'

'In the church. Monteverdi.'

'I forgot about it. Anyhow, I had to see my fence finished.'

'Great. You sound in charge. I'll phone again tonight, by which time I will have spoken to Rhona. Any news and I'll fill you in.' Agnes rings off.

Eva stares at her phone. 'Land line . . . life line,' she says to it, and looks out again to the garden where the blackbird is now on the lawn stabbing at a worm.

\* \* \*

'Yo ho, yo ho, the pirate life,
The flag of skull and bones.'

It is 10.00am Monday. Luke gently closes the shop door.

'A merry hour, a hempen rope,
And hey for Davy Jones!'

'Morning, Russ. You're an impressive baritone.'

'I'm trying to enter into the pirate spirit. Alden phoned me last night to tell me how he sees the role. I've booked our flights. Southampton to Bastia – couldn't find anything better. Coffee?'

'I'll book a taxi and hotel for the night before. 'Expensive, but since Alden's paying the air fares and car hire I don't mind treating ourselves.'

Luke follows Russ into the kitchen. 'I still haven't spoken to Eva about Corsica.'

'Or about Rhona,' Russ murmurs into the *cafetière*.

'I'll tell her today. About Corsica, that is.'

'It's none of my business, but in my limited observation of these matters, the sooner the better seems the best policy.'

'You're right, of course.'

Humming *yo hos*, Russ pours the coffee. Luke notices a copy of the play on the workbench. 'Do you know all your lines?'

'Those which Alden hasn't cut.'

'Shall I run through them with you?'

'OK, but I'll simply say them. No expression. Definitely no actions.'

In the shop Russ sits on his usual chair where, cued by Luke, he continues unfalteringly through each scene as edited by Alden.

At the end Luke applauds. 'Word perfect, Russ.'

'I may be now, but put me in a costume and tie a sword round my waist and I'll forget the lot.'

'I'm sure you won't. So what else did Alden have to say?'

'He mentioned that some of the cast are staying with him this week.'

'I wonder which ones.'

'A few of the main roles apparently: Peter, Wendy, Hook and Tinkerbell who's going to be a dancer, not the old-fashioned light darting around the set. Years ago I saw a production where . . .'

Luke pretends to listen, but thinks only of how to break the news to Eva. When Russ pauses to drink the last drop of cold coffee Luke says, 'Am I being a bastard, Russ?'

'It's not as if you're married.' Russ is less convincing than in his role as Smee.

'I'll tell her about Corsica this afternoon. She's at home this morning. It may not be the whole truth but it's all I can manage for the moment.'

Russ raises his eyebrows.

'No, Russ. Nothing much has happened between me and Rhona. Look, I'm trying . . .'

'I understand.' Russ carries the empty mugs to the kitchen.

* * *

Eva, already exhausted by the day, makes a half-hearted effort to attend to some domestic bills, when the phone rings. She seizes the handset.

'Eva, this is Agnes. I'm at work. I can't talk long. I'm on my mobile. I've slipped out from the studio. A minute ago Rhona told me something you've got to know. Luke apparently has agreed to join her and Alden in Corsica in August.'

'What?'

'Alden's producing a play out there. Luke's agreed to help out.'

'I don't believe it.'

'It's an amateur production. *Peter Pan*.'

'You're joking. What the hell's going on?'

'I'll phone again tonight when I know more.'

'Don't bother. I'm going straight round to the shop to find out what he's up to.'

'Don't. Please don't.'

'Why not? I saw him Friday night, on Saturday, on Sunday. He said nothing about it. Now I'm going to have it out with him.'

'That would be a mistake.'

'Why?'

'First, it won't make any difference. Second, they'll soon work out we know each other, and you'll lose the upper hand. Third, an argument between you and Luke is precisely what Rhona would love.'

'So what am I meant to do?'

'Nothing. Be glad you know what's happening. And if he really is joining us in Corsica, I'll be on the spot to know if anything's going on. I'll keep in touch with you and you'll always be ahead of the game.'

'I feel ten moves behind.'

'No, you're not. Believe me. I've got to go now, but I'll phone tonight. Meanwhile, be strong and don't do anything stupid.'

Agnes rings off. Eva remains in her chair staring at the handset. No, Luke must be confronted once and for all. She taps in the first four digits of the number, hesitates, winces and cancels the call. Perhaps Agnes is right. 'I cannot get you out of my head,' she says quietly to an unseen Rhona, 'but you will not win. Nor will you reduce me to helplessness.' Her eyes turn to the utility bill crumpled in her hand.

* * *

Standing near the shop door, Luke surveys the market place: the hotel, two private houses, pub, the other shops. He sighs at the thought he knows all the proprietors – even the names of the three people queuing at the greengrocer's. 'And they all know my name,' he says aloud. 'How did I become a provincial shopkeeper?' Recoiling at the admission, he turns round to face Russ holding a restored fret mirror.

'You're hardly a shopkeeper,' Russ says. 'Not like Barry over there with his ironmongery and overpriced turps. Where shall I hang this?'

'Sorry, I was mumbling to myself.'

'I do it all the time as I work, but you never hear it above the sound of the radio. The mirror?'

'Anywhere you can find wall space. Do you ever miss London?'

'Not on the evidence of my last visit.' Russ walks to the back wall of the shop.

'You don't feel trapped in this small market town?'

'You can get trapped in London.' Russ hangs the mirror.

Luke sits in the centre of the shop on a Hepplewhite chair. 'You've never had my dilemma, have you?'

Russ leans against the marble top of a console table. 'I did go through that involvement with Derek.'

'Who?' Luke sits up at the revelation.

'Didn't I ever mention him? The picture restorer in Nassau Street.'

'I don't remember.'

'It's water long under the bridge now. We went to a few concerts together and things might have moved on, even though this was the early '60s when so much was illegal. What I didn't know was that there was someone else, a wealthy architect.' Russ looks up in silence at the newly-hung mirror. 'Let's just say I was glad to extricate myself. But it taught me that triangles can be tricky.'

'I'm in more than a triangle. There are four of us involved and two are married.' Luke stands up. 'Any more of that coffee? And if there's a drop of Scotch in the kitchen cupboard . . .'

While Russ is out of the room Luke paces the room, looking at his stock with displeasure. The business has become a trap. Why continue it? There's enough money in the pot to survive. The phone interrupts his thoughts.

'Hello,' he snarls at the headset.

'Luke,' says Alden, 'we'd be delighted if you and Russ could join us for dinner on Wednesday. Short notice I know, but there are some of the cast I'd like you to meet, and do bring . . .'

Luke hears Rhona's voice in the background say, 'Eva'.

'Eva,' echoes Alden. 'We'd love to meet her.'

'That's very kind. Let me have a word with Russ.'

Luke bursts into the kitchen. 'Russ, it's Alden on the phone inviting you, me and Eva to dinner on Wednesday. What the hell shall I tell him?'

'Accept of course,' says Russ without looking up from the bottle of uncorked *Talisker*. 'It might make things so much easier all round.' He pours a generous measure into each of the mugs in front of him.

Before they have sat down in the showroom Luke looks out into the market place. 'My God, Russ, it's Eva. Coming this way. What shall I say to her?'

Without answering, Russ scurries to the workshop. Luke goes to the door.

'Darling, how strange, I was about to phone you.' He kisses her. 'Coffee for Eva,' Luke shouts towards the workshop.

'You know, you sometimes treat Russ like a servant.'

Luke detects a hint of reproof in her voice.

'You're right – which is partly why I was going to phone.' Luke points her to Russ's chair and says quietly, 'Russ works far too hard, so a few days ago when a newcomer in his drama group raised the possibility of a trip to Corsica for an amateur production of *Peter Pan*, I told him to seize the opportunity – 'Take an extra holiday, you deserve it.' And when I discovered the dates overlap with your week in Birmingham, I jokingly said to Russ, 'No chance of me joining you, is there?' And I thought no more of it until Russ tells me this morning that it's all fixed up. It rather took me by surprise.'

'I should think so. Will you go?'

'I think I might. You're away. The shop's quiet in August. It could be fun.'

'Who is this newcomer to Russ's drama group?'

'Alden Mills. Typical amateur enthusiast. A solicitor who'd rather be an actor. His wife bought a mirror from us recently.'

Russ appears at the workshop doorway. 'Coffee?'

Eva feels an urgent need to check out these facts with Agnes. The story seems to have two versions. Not quite contradictory but somehow .

.. 'So Russ, what are you scheming for Luke? You're not trying to turn him into an actor are you?'

'I'm hoping he'll be close at hand to prompt me every time I blank.'

'I shall have to meet this Alden and his wife. It's not everyone who could make you close the shop for a week.'

'You'll soon have a chance,' says Luke. 'Alden phoned half an hour ago inviting you and me and Russ to dinner on Wednesday. We're not busy, are we?'

'I must check my diary,' says Eva, thinking, *try keeping me away.*

* * *

As soon as Eva has left the shop, she texts Agnes: *Phone asap. Things have happened.* Before she has reached home she receives a reply: *At work. Difficult. R. in room. Will phone 6.*

Back home Eva wonders how she can possibly fill the day until 6.00pm. There is only one way. She pulls on some old clothes and goes into the garden. Finding a hoe and a fork, she walks to the far end and looks beyond the hawthorn hedge to the adjoining meadow where bullocks are grazing. Turning back to an uncultivated patch, she sees alkanets which seem to have sprung up overnight. Annie is right: they too easily take over. She sets about uprooting them, surprised at the depth of their cordlike white roots. Although partially shaded by the horse chestnut in next door's garden, she soon runs with perspiration, and in need of less strenuous activity, moves to the vegetables where she hoes the rows of leeks and parsnips. But today the task lacks its usual pleasure. Vegetables have always been grown to be shared with Luke. For how much longer? Two hours later, when there are no more weeds with which to drive out thoughts of Rhona, she surveys her work. She wants to be proud of this cherished, well-designed, productive garden; today it is no more than a diversion. By the back door she kicks off her gardening boots and goes in for a shower. Afterwards, in dressing gown, slumped in an armchair, she attempts to give full concentration to a pile of seed catalogues, in a losing battle against sleep.

A subconscious clock wakes her at 5.50pm, lifting her from a dream of her childhood bedroom on the outskirts of Worcester with its view over the Malvern Hills. Before she is fully awake her mobile rings.

'So what's happened?' Agnes asks.

'Luke's told me about his trip to Corsica. Apparently it was only finalised today.'

'That's not what Rhona told me.'

'I called into the shop to have it out with him, but it seems Russ is the one who's arranged things.'

'That's not the impression I got.'

'Who do I believe? Luke or Rhona?'

'At this stage,' says Agnes slowly, 'neither of them.'

'Some comfort that is.'

'No, don't say that. You are still ahead of them and I shall continue to relay to you everything Rhona says.'

'You don't suppose, do you, that a lot of this is in Rhona's head? I mean she may think she's lined Luke up, but in point of fact Luke believes he's simply joining Russ for a few days abroad.'

'It's possible. Theoretically. With Rhona the boundary between fantasy and reality can be very blurred.'

'I can't wait until Wednesday night.'

'Why Wednesday?'

'Hasn't Rhona told you?'

'Told me what?'

'Luke and I are having dinner with them.'

'First I've heard.'

'She didn't mention it?'

'No, but then she was so excited about Luke going to Corsica . . .'

'I'm dying to meet her.'

'Be warned, she'll be absolutely charming.'

'Won't you be there?'

'I haven't been invited. Shall I phone tomorrow?'

'Only if there are developments. We don't need to speak until after the dinner party – unless I'm desperate. Can I phone you on Thursday?'

'Ring at eleven-thirty. I'll make sure I'm out of the studio. By that time I will have heard Rhona's account of the evening. We can compare notes. Now remember, if you need to call me before then, do so. I know what you're going through.'

Assured, Eva hangs up. Perhaps, perhaps, she tells herself, the affair to date has been conducted only in Rhona's head. If this is true, Luke has been judged and found guilty without cause. Has she allowed unfounded suspicions to go viral in her mind? By the time she is ready to leave the house for supper at Luke's, she is determined that she will suspend all doubt until at least Wednesday night. And as she walks towards Back Lane she feels she is not alone: Agnes is at hand to supply facts and down-to-earth advice, while tomorrow's appointment with Stella will no doubt produce its own insights and wisdom.

# 13

Mid-morning on Tuesday Luke, holding a wrapped cartouche mirror, opens the shop door so a customer can leave. As the summer heat strikes his face he looks up into the clear sky before, with some reluctance, he closes the door, walks to his desk and places a cheque in the top drawer. It has been a satisfactory morning following a good night. In the last twenty-four hours he has regained control of his life. The supper he and Eva enjoyed at his house was the pleasure it had always been, as was the night he spent at her cottage. And they had lingered over breakfast as they always did on days when she had no early client. And she showed, he thought, no hint of suspicion. But then, why should she? He has spent many hours fantasising about Rhona but what in fact has happened between the two of them apart from a single innocent kiss? As for fantasies, who doesn't fantasise? And in the world of reality a mirror has been sold and a cheque will be paid into the bank at lunchtime. True, tomorrow's dinner appointment may be awkward, but surely the very transparency of it will be only for the good.

He sits at his desk and searches online for a map of Santa Marta. He is zooming into the Corsican mountains when the ringing phone provides the first annoyance in a trouble-free day.

'Hello,' he answers curtly.

'Luke, hi. Have I phoned at a bad time?' It is Rhona.

'Not at all. Right now I'm staring at a map of Corsica.'

'Santa Marta is so small it's probably not even marked. Look, I'm really sorry Alden sprung that invitation on you. He hardly discussed it with me before he phoned you. But all the same I'm so glad all three of you can come. Meanwhile, have you a spare hour this evening? I'd like to take you somewhere.'

Luke smiles in the knowledge that tonight Eva is seeing Stella. 'No, I'm sure I'm doing nothing.'

'Wonderful. Can we go in my car? I can be outside your shop at seven-thirty.'

'This is very mysterious.'

'I thought you liked mysteries. I'll see you this evening.'

Luke is not sure whether Russ has overheard the conversation or not. He doesn't care.

* * *

Prompt as ever Eva rings Stella's doorbell, waits and looks at the green and maroon trumpets of the Nepalese lilies either side of the doorstep.

'You see, your cure for them worked,' are Stella's first words as she opens the door.

'Those colours are so soft I think I shall buy some for myself. I tend to overdose on my Casablancas.'

'Go ahead upstairs and I'll find some wine – not the least advantage of an evening appointment.'

Waiting in her usual chair in Stella's drawing room, Eva realises that yesterday's gardening and the afternoon's shopping in a stifling Norwich have exhausted her. And, of course, worry. In the early evening light the room's atmosphere is different from other visits here, always in the morning or afternoon. Apart from the unfamiliar angles of shadows, the room, always a place of quiet, has assumed a stillness, as if the furnishings have been moved to induce tranquility. But every chair and table is in its familiar place, the only discernible difference from her last visit being that the vase by the hearth now contains pink and mauve stocks. Eva closes her eyes and inhales the scent.

She opens her eyes to see Stella placing a glass of white wine on the table beside her. Stella leaves the bottle by the stocks, sits and raises her own glass in a silent toast. They both drink and as ever remain wordless for several minutes. Wanting the silence broken – there is so much to say – Eva is content to focus on the summer dress in the chair opposite.

Stella's hands rest on her lap so that her red fingernails are absorbed by the dress's abstract design. Eva watches her readjust one of her cushions, a signal that the time for talking has at last arrived.

'Luke is having . . .' Eva falters. 'I am almost certain Luke is embarking on an affair. I know because . . . I've a broken a cardinal rule. I've been in contact with my client, Agnes – on a social basis.'

Stella remains silent.

'We met by chance in a shop. I wasn't assertive enough to prevent a conversation. Since our last counselling session she has discovered that the new man in her employer's life is Luke.'

Eva recounts to Stella her conversations with Agnes, in café and church and later on the phone. Stella, listens, once or twice rolling a finger on one of the beads of her necklace. Eva, determined to omit nothing, snatches gulps of wine as she talks. Stella leaves her own glass untouched on its octagonal table.

Eva concludes, 'I know you only told me about your client Esther to give me a possible course of action, but that is the path I shall take. There will be no confrontation.'

* * *

In his garden Luke, his head awhirl, paces the lawn, his heart hammering in his chest. The accumulated sun of the day radiates from the old brick walls around him, as he struggles to accept that soon he is to meet with Rhona, and at her suggestion. It is a reality, not a dreamed-up hope of a middle-aged man. But the question remains which has plagued him every minute of the last seven hours, nagged away when he was trying to distract himself by helping Russ with gilding, stayed with him during a lunch hour at the allotment, pressed itself on his brain during an unbearably long afternoon in a hot shop. And now. Where does she plan to go? A pub? A restaurant? An exhibition? Not to her house, surely? Isn't Alden there with his guests? Or has Alden taken them out for the evening, leaving the house free for Rhona? This is the most enticing option – Rhona and he alone at Saffold Farm. But hadn't she said, 'Have you a spare hour?' Didn't that imply a short visit? Foolish to speculate – perhaps she merely wants one of the mirrors moved? No, surely, she would have said so, wouldn't she?

He drops onto an iron bench at the end of the garden where he notices some petunias wilting in a border. He goes to find a watering can, but halfway to the back door forgets about the flowers, asking himself, why go, wherever it is, in her car? He walks back to the bench. No, the mention of an hour must definitely rule out a restaurant . . . unless Rhona, for whom vagueness is a leitmotif, is being vague about time. He notices the flowers again and makes another attempt to find a watering can.

Walking back towards the end of the garden, carrying a full can of water, he wonders what he should wear for the evening. He goes indoors and settles for jeans and a green check shirt, and having little faith in the weather, even on the hottest day of the year, throws a Guernsey sweater around his shoulders. Again he wonders if they will be going to a pub or restaurant. Not that he feels hungry, even though he hasn't eaten since lunchtime when up at the allotments Alf had once again forced on him a doorstep sandwich.

At 7.15pm he locks the house and walks back to the shop. In the forecourt of the Queen's Arms half a dozen tables are packed with drinkers, and at the hotel opposite customers from the bar have flowed out to the benches in the market place. By his shop there is no-one and no car parked. He does not remember waiting here before, not for any reason. Standing in the doorway, a feeling of alienation descends: he is an outsider in his own town, by his own building. He checks his watch, looks to his right, the direction from which he expects her car, sees nothing and turns round, a newcomer to Cantisham, a visitor seeing this shop for the first time.

He hears a car approaching the market place and in a tremor of excitement jumps forward. But it is not blue, not Rhona's Citroen. He drops back to the doorway, where the evening light is striking its glazed upper panels. He looks at his reflection and straightens his shirt collar, embarrassed to feel like one of the local boys who hang around the market place on Friday nights, out to impress the girls. Another car approaches from Rhona's direction.

* * *

For some time after Eva has finished speaking Stella says nothing, but Eva reads in her face an understanding devoid of criticism or reprimand.

Business-like, Stella says, 'So you have settled on a strategy regarding Luke?'

'I have. I almost discarded it. I'm glad I didn't.'

Stella runs her fingers along her necklace. 'You had planned a final session with Agnes and you have pointed out to her that this is no longer ethical. You had already suggested she might like to see one of your colleagues. This being so, you have no reason to feel bad about developing a friendship with her.'

'But surely it goes against so much we are taught. Contact with clients outside the counselling environment should be avoided. Apart from Luke, I have never before struck up a friendship with a client. Even when he was my client, I ceased to be his counsellor before we had a relationship. This didn't prevent my colleagues in London making life impossible for me, but certainly, since then, I have adhered to the rule. And if I see a former client in the street and they walk past – perhaps they don't even recognise me – for me that's a sign I've done a good job. I've helped them. I'm no longer needed.'

'That can be the case. It may even be the norm.' Stella smiles, shrugs, picks up her glass and downs half of it. 'In human relationships outright generalisations are seldom possible, and there is nothing necessarily unprofessional about your meeting Agnes. Now whether it is wise or helpful for Agnes to be your ears and eyes, this is a different matter. Have you thought about her own motives?'

Eva relaxes, her professionalism not a matter for censure. She says, 'I remember you once spoke to me about some clients wanting to hurt a counsellor. If this is true of Agnes, I suppose she could be relishing my predicament. No, I think she genuinely wants to help.'

'There is another possibility.'

'Yes?'

'Agnes, having been, as it were, in your care for some time, the child to your parent, is now relishing the chance to reverse the roles. To be your equal.'

'Is that an issue?'

'Not necessarily, especially if you are aware of the possibility.'

'I really think Agnes believes she is helping me. After all, her advice that I should not go storming into Luke's shop and have a showdown is not so different from what your Esther counselled herself to do in similar circumstances. I certainly don't think Agnes is on a power trip. Now it's me who needs some help and she finds herself in the position to give it.'

'Will you continue to see her?'

'Her phone calls certainly help. What would you advise? As a friend?'

'As a friend I would say, if you feel uneasy about her phone calls or meeting her, simply say you don't need them. If, on the other hand, you sleep better at night having talked to her, continue. It's better than insomnia or pills. Some more wine?' Stella rises from her chair and refills both glasses. Before she resumes her seat she says, 'One great lesson you seem to have learned already: what Rhona tells Agnes is not necessarily true, or at least not the whole truth. And to discern the truth from the embroidery is probably impossible. So you will never totally dispel your doubts.'

'I'm learning to live with that, but it will be a relief to meet Rhona. We're having dinner there tomorrow.'

\* \* \*

It is a Citroen. Luke checks the number plate before he looks towards the driver. Yes, it is her car. He raises his eyes to see Rhona behind the wheel. She waves and pulls up by the shop.

As he opens the passenger door she says, 'Luke, how wonderful you could join me at such short notice,' and squeezing his right arm with an inscrutable look, bends towards him so he thinks she might kiss him. But she presses the play button of the CD player and *Magical Mystery Tour* begins to play. 'You'll have to guess where we're going,' she says.

'I've been trying to all day, but a trip lasting about an hour defeated me.'

'Did I say an hour? Well, maybe an hour or two. Unless you have to get back home.'

'No, no, I'm free all evening.'

As the possibilities of a restaurant, pub or exhibition reassert themselves, Luke looks at Rhona's clothes for a clue, but her rust denim dress, with floral buttons at the front and her brown leather shoes tell him nothing. As they leave town on the Norwich Road a city destination suggests itself, but soon they turn off on a side road and head north.

'Still guessing?' she smiles.

'I've ruled out the city. Any clues?'

'Not until the next piece of music.'

When *Magical Mystery Tour* is over, she ejects the disc and inserts another, reducing the volume to inaudibility with a look which says, you'll have to be patient.

Luke relaxes into his seat. It occurs to him that he must have been driven by Eva hundreds of times, but it was never like this. He no longer wonders where they are going or how long the journey will be: this drive can last a lifetime.

'Have your guests arrived?' he asks as they stop at the junction to a main road.

'Not arrived – taken over. I've been hiding myself in the studio while they talk, argue, have mini-rehearsals, drink endless coffee. Alden becomes a different creature on these occasions. The full actor-manager-director side of him takes over. A man possessed. And he becomes ridiculously extravagant. Tonight he's taken them off by taxi to some gastro-pub. I could have gone with them but . . . now I mustn't miss my next turning.'

Rhona drives slowly, looking for a side road. When she decides she has found it, she says, 'Soon be there,' and turns up the volume.

Luke is surprised to hear a song thrush singing its repertoire. A harsher sound, perhaps a magpie, is discernible in the background. Finally, a wren.

'Thrush, magpie, wren. You see I'm learning,' says Rhona.

'I'm impressed . . . so this evening is about birdsong?'

'Maybe.'

'And I have to guess which one.'

'If you think you can. Of course I may not tell you if you get it right.'

'That's not fair.'

'Yes it is. I want it to be a surprise.'

The wren gives way to the impatient click-click of a starling.

'*Sturnus vulgaris*,' says Rhona triumphantly.

'You have been doing your homework.'

'Alden's always using Latin phrases, so I thought, what the hell, I'll learn a few and drop them on him from time to time.'

'I know. You're going to take me to hear some nightingales.'

'I'm not telling.'

'Yes, nightingales it is, but I have to tell you they're more common on the heathland towards the coast.'

Rhona slows and parks on the verge under some trees. 'We have to walk now,' she says.

Listening for birdsong, Luke leaves the car, his sweater draped over his shoulders. He hears nothing. 'I give up,' he says.

'Down this path,' she orders, striding ahead.

Luke joins her on a baked mud track, hard under foot and dappled by shadows as the evening sun filters through overhanging branches. After a few hundred metres the track forks. One way leads to rough open ground. The other, where Rhona leads him, winds under oak trees. For some minutes, they walk in silence, picking their way among a network of deep-rutted paths where the dusty sweet smell of dry leaves stirs childhood memories. To their left Luke can make out a field. At one point the path swings towards it, allowing him to see swallows skim over the bending heads of wheat. It is the only sign of wildlife. He looks at Rhona. She smiles and shakes her head.

Now the track becomes wider and flatter. They walk side by side. Narrowing, the track becomes a path, sloping uphill and away from the field. Rhona slips her arm through Luke's. A thrush flies in front of them and disappears into some bushes. Luke hesitates and turns to Rhona. Again she shakes her head. He enjoys the silence. In it he realises that neither at Saffold Farm, nor in the shop, nor this evening, has she asked him more than a couple of questions about his life – never the veiled inquisition from new customers, or from fellow guests at local dinner parties, out to fit him into a sociological box. And he is surprised that he himself, naturally inquisitive, has no wish to ask her similar questions: where were you brought up, are your parents alive? Of course, he has learned a little about her without asking questions and has spoken about himself without questions from her, but all has been incidental to a another dialogue which transcends such trivia.

As they continue he feels her arm tighten on his. They are so close her hair occasionally brushes his right ear. He wants to stop and hug her, but this walk and its uncertain destination are more important. At the top of the slope the woodland thins and the path turns ninety degrees to the right. Soon they are away from the trees and at the edge of a heath. Another wood, of pines and oaks, is to their left. Luke can see at the far end of the heath the slow movement of grazing cattle, but otherwise the landscape is still and silent. There is no wind and here, away from the shadow of trees, the air is warmer. It is a place, he thinks, where we might hear a nightingale. But there is no sound.

'Isn't this heavenly?' Rhona says, dropping her left hand to hold his.

At that moment the silence is broken by a far-off sound, perhaps a lawnmower. They stand still, but after several seconds the noise stops.

Rhona turns and takes Luke's other hand. 'Did you hear it?' she asks.

'The two-stroke engine?'

Rhona looks at him mysteriously. At that moment the sound returns. Luke realises that this is what they came to hear and immediately understands. Moving close to her, he whispers in her ear, 'A nightjar? How did you know they were here?'

'One of my team brought me here yesterday. Isn't it magical?'

Failing to see the bird, they listen to its intermittent call drifting across the wide expanse of heath from an indiscernible direction.

'I've only heard them once before,' says Luke. 'I must have been about twelve.'

'Did you ever see one?'

'Sadly, no.'

'We did last night but only a fleeting glimpse – a dark shape moving from a low tree on the heath towards the woods.'

For several more minutes they look across the heath and along the line of trees at the edge, but see nothing. And the sound does not recur.

'Let's move on,' says Rhona, pulling Luke by the hand. The path, now flanked by low gorse bushes, rises slightly until they arrive at an outcrop of trees, an intrusion on the heath.

'It's near here we saw it,' she tells him.

Halting to survey the heath, they see no movement apart from a few small moths above the gorse, and hear no sounds above the background hum of insects. The nightjar remains silent and invisible. Rhona looks disappointed.

'Never mind not seeing one,' he says. 'To hear it was the greatest treat. As I waited for you by the shop I had no idea . . .'

'Look,' says Rhona pointing back down the path.

A ragged silhouette in erratic flight moves from the woods to the heath, dances midair and darts back into the trees. A few moments later it reappears and repeats the sortie. Further down, another nightjar follows the same pattern. For several minutes they watch.

'Strange, aren't they?' says Rhona. 'Primeval, not really birds at all. More like Jurassic creatures evolution forgot about.' She takes his hand again. 'Shall we walk across the heath? It would be a pity to go back along the path and disturb them.'

They walk down a small track on tinder dry turf, occasionally turning back to watch the birds. A little further on, she steps off the path and walks to a patch of short grass surrounded by bracken. When she turns round Luke thinks she is about to speak, but in silence she lowers herself to the ground and sits, leaning back. Luke sits beside her. He wants to hold her in his arms but does no more than reach out a hand and brush some strands of hair from one side of her face, aware that his heart is pounding.

Rhona leans back a little more and closes her eyes. 'Kiss me,' she says.

He gently kisses her, feeling her fingers run through his hair. Her perfume in the evening air is overpowering.

Her hands drop to his shoulders and untie the arms of the sweater draped around them. Pulling him closer, she whispers, 'Luke, make love to me.'

* * *

Stella places her right elbow on the arm of her chair and rests her chin on the back of her hand. The posture reminds Eva of Rodin's *Thinker*.

'Into the lion's den,' says Stella.

'The lioness's, and I'm apprehensive about it. I shall be more spy than guest, looking out for signs of what may be going on.'

'That client of mine we called Esther had many such social occasions. At first she drove herself to distraction trying to see if her husband and the other woman were exchanging furtive glances. And if she decided they were not, she wondered if they were deliberately ignoring each other. In the end she learned that she felt strongest when she avoided any such mind-rending suspicion.'

Eva grimaces and finishes her wine.

'Hard,' I know, Stella continues, 'but you don't have to continue along this road. I only told you about Esther as an example of a possible course of action. If you wish to speak frankly to Luke, that may still be the best route for you.'

'I'll wait until after tomorrow evening.'

Stella rises from her chair. 'Help yourself to some more wine. I must see how our chicken is progressing.'

While Stella is out of the room, Eva fills her glass and waits, asking herself if she is strong enough to follow the Esther strategy, and if Stella was wise in first mentioning it. She looks at the familiar furnishings of the room, the Egyptian urns, the unfashionable clutter of mahogany and heavily patterned cushions, curtains and carpets, wondering whether Stella's counselling is as defunct as her taste in interior design. But as she settles into her chair she finds the room now replaces her misgivings with a strength and security which counters self-doubt and renews her confidence in her supervisor. This is a safe place where she cannot be paralysed by thoughts about Luke or Rhona or questions of professionalism. But it also forces the question what she would do if Stella retired, moved away or died. She walks to the window. Maybe she herself should take on supervisory work. Were she to do so, the model of Stella would be a good one to follow. Perhaps that is where the future lies.

She lifts up the smallest of the Egyptian urns and runs a finger over its rough surface.

'About 1400 BC,' says Stella from the doorway. 'My grandfather was an archaeologist. I keep them in his memory.'

Eva glances up at the others, one of which has a cover in the form of a jackal's head.

'No, don't worry,' smiles Stella, 'his ashes aren't inside. He's buried in Alexandria. I think dinner is ready.' Eva replaces the urn and follows Stella downstairs.

* * *

Luke looks at Rhona's hair spread over his right arm, and reaching with his left hand to his sweater eases it under her head. She lies beside him, her legs resting across his. Their shoes and his jeans are on the grass by their feet. She is still wearing her denim dress, unbuttoned. The rhythm of her breathing suggests she is asleep. He does not know how long they have lain there; he has remained awake for an indefinite time during which thought has been suspended. Now, despite some inner resistance, it reasserts itself, informing him that this is the first time he has ever truly made love. Whatever the pleasures shared with Eva, they have never been of this order.

He feels Rhona's breath, slow and deep, against his body. Yes, she must be asleep. He remembers that for a few seconds he had been worried, afraid of disappointing her, but she had looked at him and widened her eyes in a smile beneath which all his anxiety had evaporated. As she stirs and snuggles close to him, he is determined to spend the rest of his life with her. He remembers her look as she opened her eyes and stared down on him before she moved off him and lay at his side from where she has hardly moved. It was a look which assured him that she felt the same way.

Rhona stretches her right arm across his chest and grasps his left shoulder. 'Don't ever leave me Luke. Help me get away from that monster Alden.'

'I'll do anything in my power for you.'

She opens her eyes and looks up at him. 'I think you're at an impasse too, aren't you, Luke?'

'But I'm not married. Fortunately.'

'I'm glad you're not, but I think you might have entered a cul-de-sac the day you fell for your therapist.'

Luke hears a voice in his mind, *Our years together have proved* . . . but he says, 'I now know you're right.'

'Will it be hard breaking up from her?'

'It will be for her.'

Rhona sits up and kisses him. 'Perhaps you should not have gone to a therapist in the first place.'

She kisses him again, and begins buttoning her dress. 'It is the one thing I agree with Lynton and Alden about. Psychotherapy and counselling are minefields best avoided. And for creative people they can be fatal. Not in the sense that they will kill you, but worse, your creativity – your soul – will be strangled.'

'Have I wasted half my life?'

Rhona waves a hand across his face. 'No, stupid, nothing's wasted now that you and I have met.'

'I wish I'd met you ten years ago.'

'I was eighteen and unbearable. You would have hated me.'

They laugh and hug and Luke feels her cold arms. He puts his Guernsey on her and straightens some of her hair ruffled by the neck of the sweater.

'I've never worn one of these before,' she says. 'It makes me feel like a fisherman's daughter in a Victorian painting.'

'I think it suits you.'

They stand and look at the brick red sky in the west. When they turn they see the dull glow of the waning moon above the opposite side of the heath.

'A C for Corsica,' she says. 'The moon wants you to be there with me.'

149

'Shall we wander back while we have light?'

'Yes, I expect by now even the nightjars have gone to bed.'

But at the edge of the heath, near the trees, they see against the darkening sky a nightjar's ungainly shape as it flies from cover.

'They've stayed up especially for us,' says Luke.

Hand in hand, on their way back to the car, they stop near the edge of the woods to view the sunset across the wheat field.

'We must be careful not to look too much at each other tomorrow night,' Rhona says.

'I shall find it hard not to.'

Rhona gently slaps his arm. 'You must behave.'

'Trust me, I shall.'

'This evening may have made it harder for us to play innocent.'

'Had we not made love, the problem tomorrow night would have been not looking at you. Now the problem is not looking at you and giggling.'

Simultaneously they burst into laughter.

'Race you back to the car,' she says and starts sprinting ahead.

Luke, surprised how fast she can run, fails to catch up with her before they reach the verge where the car is parked.

'You won,' Luke says, out of breath.

'Shall we call it a tie?' she says as she settles herself into the driver's seat. 'I did have a better start. But you do get a prize.' She opens the glove compartment and hands Luke a red envelope. From its size and feel he guesses it is a CD.

'You probably already have it,' she says. 'I ordered it online and wasn't certain which one to choose.'

Luke opens the envelope. 'Françoise Hardy's first album. How thoughtful. Thank you. I have the 1962 vinyl but not the CD.'

'Put it on.'

Rhona starts the car and they drive away from beneath the trees as Françoise Hardy sings *Tous les garçons et les filles.*

In Cantisham Luke directs her to Back Lane.

'So this is your den,' she says at the door of number seven.

'Can you risk seeing inside?' he asks.

Rhona raises her eyebrows.

'No, Eva's in Norwich or back at her cottage.'

Rhona looks up and down the street. 'It is so lovely here, the church at one end and that intriguing bend round to the market at the other. I would like to paint it. And all this is your house? Seventeen hundred and something?'

'Mainly Queen Anne. I think the cellar's older.'

'I bet you have some lovely wine.'

'A little.'

'Alden really regrets Saffold Farm has no cellar. He talks of digging one. Of course he never will.'

In the hallway she hugs him until, opening her eyes, she gazes in amazement at a blue lacquer and gilded corner cupboard with a mirrored door. She steps towards it. 'This is like looking back into history,' she says. 'Where did you find it?'

'It was my mother's.'

'Your mother's dead?'

'Both my parents died when I was in my twenties.'

'I'm so sorry,' she says, as if the loss were recent. 'What's through this door?' She steps into the study.

Rhona smiles at the film posters. 'Ah, your man cave. I love *Theodora*, although that emperor on the throne looks disturbingly like Alden.' She sinks into an armchair. 'To think,' she says, 'a few weeks ago I walked into your shop and said to myself, lovely mirrors but what a serious old stick of a proprietor. And I thought for a moment Russ was your gay partner. Now I know different.'

'I should hope so. Mind you, I thought this extraordinary girl in the large hat, apart from being amazingly lovely, had an unapproachable mystery about her. I still don't know how you could enter the shop without being heard and later vanish like mist. I thought I could never hope to get close to you.'

'You were quite close this evening.'

'Yes, but I feel you will always retain some of that mystery. How can you appear and disappear like magic?'

Rhona hugs him. 'We enchantresses can't give away our secrets.'

'Have you eaten tonight?'

'I raided some of the cheese Alden bought for dinner tomorrow and made a sandwich. He was livid. He always prepares things well in advance and unknowingly I had robbed him of the most expensive of three French cheeses he had bought for his soufflés. 'You've forced me to adapt my recipe,' he shouted and stormed out of the house.'

'I shall look forward to whatever he gives us,' Luke says, with as much sincerity as he can muster.

'Luke, darling, do stop being so nice about him. He's a brute and I want to be with you, not him. In fact I would love to live in this house.' She brings her hands together as if in prayer. 'If you would have me.'

'Move in whenever you wish.'

'I'm afraid there would be boring money problems. I might have to sell Saffold Farm and find new premises for work.'

'I own some barns on the outskirts of town. I converted them into commercial units. Several are at least the size of your studio.'

Eva follows him when he goes to the kitchen to find some wine. While he is extracting the cork, she goes to the French windows.

When he brings her a glass of Vouvray she says, looking out to the garden, 'This is so secluded.'

Luke switches off the kitchen light to allow her a clearer view. She sips her wine. Slowly she turns at him, 'This would be so safe for children.'

Back in the study, each in an armchair, she says. 'After tomorrow evening we have nine nights apart and the next day you'll be on your way to join me. I shall be beside myself waiting for you.'

'I'm dying to see the village.'

'It is so beautiful. What I love is a dawn drive to the river for a swim before the sun gets hot. I'm usually the only one awake that early. You'll have to join me.'

'I'm afraid I'm not a strong swimmer.'

'Oh, I'm so pleased. Nor am I. I can't stand people who power off freestyle towards the horizon while I'm still splashing in the shallows. Alden, of course, was in the university swimming team.'

When she leaves she offers to give Luke back his sweater.

'Keep it,' he tells her. 'I feel it's yours now.'

'I shall treasure it. A reminder of a perfect evening. And a perfect beginning.'

# 14

On Wednesday afternoon at the Riverside Counselling Centre, Eva leaves a partners' meeting and goes to her room, reflecting that the business discussed during the last hour had been routine, uncontroversial, so different from equivalent meetings in London shortly after Luke had ceased to be a client and became her lover. She watches an old woman on the riverbank throw breadcrumbs to a growing rabble of mallards, and smiles, remembering that one of her most vehement critics had, within the last twelve years, married and divorced, while she and Luke were still together. A seagull muscles its way among the mallards. The woman tries with varying success to throw only to the ducks. Eva looks up to the city roofs and feels a new strength: Rhona was not going to come between them.

Looking out from her room, she relishes the thought that she will have no more clients until late autumn. In the distance the crane is motionless. To its left she makes out part of the tower of St. Giles. Only last Friday, she thinks, I was there, cowering behind a pillar, distraught, Agnes beside me. Hearing, across the rooftops the sonorous bell of the City Hall clock, followed by a higher pitched bell from near the cathedral, she feels the need for reflection; the Counselling Centre is not the place in which to do it.

Making her way down to the river, she crosses Bishop's Bridge. There is a welcome peace here on the edge of the cathedral precincts. She looks to her left at a row of neat Victorian terraced houses. She has often imagined living here, if she were forced to move from the country. Today, for the first time the fantasy is replaced by the practical question, and why not, in a few years' time, why not? Where Luke might fit into this possibility she is not certain.

She passes alongside the high wall opposite the medieval Great Hospital, turns the corner near the law courts and walks up towards the city centre. Passing the Erpingham gate with its view of the west end of the cathedral, she is reminded of childhood walks in her home city, while a little further on, the bust of Edith Cavell makes her recall the statue of Elgar looking down to the Worcester porcelain museum. Why, she asks herself, has the past resurfaced so much these last two weeks? She walks to a nearby restaurant, finds a secluded corner seat, orders a sandwich and a lager, and returns to thoughts about Luke and Rhona. Intuition tells her a crisis is imminent. Instinct tells her that she must buy a new dress for this evening's dinner.

At 7.30pm as Eva wraps mauve tissue paper around a dozen dark red echinaceas cut from her garden, she sees Luke's van appear in the lane outside her house. Throwing a shawl round her shoulders, she lingers for a final look at herself in the hall mirror.

'That's one hell of a little black number,' says Luke when he appears at the kitchen door.

'And a hell of a big number on the price tag.'

'Didn't you manage to knock them down?'

'Always the dealer.' She hands Luke her car keys. 'You can be my chauffeur,' she says.

'Shoes new too?' he asks, looking at her shiny black high heels.

'Almost as expensive,' she says, feeling she can face anything the evening throws at her.

In the car, she relaxes and looks at Luke. An old green linen suit and well-worn tan loafers do not indicate any special effort to dress for tonight. It seems impossible that he might be involved with some other woman, let alone the one she is about to meet. 'What's this Rhona like?'

'She's bought a couple of things from the shop, so she must be alright.'

'Pretty?'

'Not a stunner.' He looks at the dress again. 'Certainly not a knock-out.'

'Any children?'

'I don't think so.'

At Saffold Farm Luke pulls into the yard where Russ's old Rover is parked in a corner. He climbs out and opens the door for Eva. Standing on the gravel, she surveys the back of the house, admiring the roses.

Eva looks towards the converted barn. 'I wonder if that's her studio.'

'Probably.'

They walk to the door, Eva absorbing as much of the side of the house as she can. Luke, resisting an impulse to open the door and walk in, extends a slow hand to the knocker and gives it two tentative strikes. From inside comes the noise of raised voices. Russ's distinctive laugh can be heard above them.

Eva looks at Luke. 'Sounds like he's a glass or two ahead of us already. Knock louder.'

Luke obeys, glad to seem unfamiliar with the house and its ways. The door is opened by an elfin, fair-haired girl of about twenty, wearing a gypsy dress with raggedy hem. My God, thinks Eva, if this is Rhona ...

'Hi, I'm Louise,' she drawls. 'They all call me Lou. They put me on door duty. You must be Eva and Luke. The others are in the parlour. Come in, but watch the low beam.'

They follow her into the house. In the passageway Luke sees Rhona coming towards them, wearing a simple grey dress, her hair is tied up in a knot. His immediate impression is that she would pass for a Victorian governess were it not for a French jet necklace and matching earrings.

'Eva, Luke, how lovely of you to join us.'

Eva gives her the flowers. 'From my garden.'

'They're beautiful. How clever you are. My fingers are so ungreen you wouldn't believe.' She kisses Eva. 'I love that dress. Tell me all about it later.' Turning to Luke she gives him the most formal of kisses, holding the flowers between their bodies.

'I'm going to find these a vase immediately. Lou, darling, show these guys into the parlour.'

They follow the gypsy dress into the front room. Before Eva can give a second thought to Rhona she finds her hand being wrenched by Alden.

'Great of you both to come,' he says. 'You've met Lou – Tinkerbell – and you know Russ better than I do.' He points to Russ, in alpaca jacket, white shirt and paisley tie, who gives a shoulder height wave to Luke and Eva. 'And these are Josh and Felix,' says Alden, pointing to the occupants of armchairs by a wall, both in jeans and T-shirts. 'An English Peter Pan and an African-American Hook, both violent in their different ways. Typecasting I suppose.'

Josh and Felix say, 'Hi.'

'And I'm Cassie – Wendy,' says a red-haired American girl who is sitting on one of the arms of Josh's chair.

'Feistier than the original,' says Alden. 'We may need to . . .'

'It's the modern way of playing her,' says Cassie.

Luke looks uneasily around the parlour, disliking the way the furniture has been moved since his first visit – a violation of his memories of that afternoon. He checks that the mirror is still exactly as he hung it and that the pottery figures on the mantelpiece are in place.

'Bubbly OK?' asks Alden, going to the table by the window where three bottles are in ice buckets. He lifts one up. '*Veuve Cliquot*. Lynton's favourite. And mine.' He fills two glasses.

'Who's Lynton?' Eva asks Luke.

'The old boy whose place we'll be staying at.'

Alden overhears. 'Old boy? He may be almost ninety but he was half wondering whether he shouldn't take a part in the play himself.' He gives Eva and Luke flutes of champagne, and seeing Louise has no glass says, 'Are you sure you won't have just a small one?'

Louise shakes her head. 'Dancers tend to drink less than actors: our profession has to be more disciplined.'

'Not that you can compare ballet and drama,' says Alden. 'Dance doesn't have to be text-based.'

Louise stares hard at him. 'Dance is more about feelings than words, Alden, which makes it closer to the truth. If truth counts.'

'Truth to the text matters.'

'Well, I'm glad I haven't a speaking part.'

'Which is why you'll be the most wonderful Tinkerbell: your dancing will say more than any of us can express in our lines.'

'Oh, don't be so smarmy, Alden. I much prefer you when you're being argumentative.'

'For an anti-words woman you use them very well. I'm off to inspect the meat. At least that doesn't insult me.' Alden heads for the door, pausing to give Louise a placatory kiss. She responds with such excessive distaste that Eva decides they are almost certainly having an affair.

'I'm kinda glad I'm a painter and I'll be spending most of my time up at the school,' says Cassie. 'Winding up Alden is fun, but like exhausting.'

'He enjoys it really,' says Felix.

'The only trouble is,' laughs Cassie, 'we all enjoy it a lot more. And he may bang on about the text, but he's as good as rewritten the whole work.'

Rhona enters, looking around at the hilarity. 'I bet all this is at Alden's expense. I'm ashamed of you.' A frown changes to a smile. 'You should know by now that mocking him is strictly my domain.' She walks over to Eva. 'Please come and join us in Corsica. The boys will so outnumber us girls you would be doing me a huge favour.'

'I'm giving a paper in Birmingham in ten days' time.'

'Can't you send it to them?'

'Sadly, they'll want to see me in the flesh, ask questions and drag me into a seminar before they tear me apart.'

'Then I insist you come out another time. We usually go for a few days in the autumn.' Rhona looks across the room. 'Felix,' she calls out, 'could you find my glass and hand round the nibblies?'

In a softer voice Rhona says to Eva, 'They're all very nice but so young. You have to tell them to do everything. I shall feel like a summer camp organiser. Now, on the couple of occasions I've been to the mirror shop I've only seen Luke or Russ, so I guess you're not involved in the business.'

'No, I'm a counsellor.'

'Really? You'd be ideal for Santa Marta. All those egos knocking against each other. You'd have a full-time job. Are you certain you can't join us?'

Eva shakes her head, trying to square the amiable, level-headed woman next to her, with Agnes's scheming vamp: if it is all a pretence, it is far more successful than the Alden-Louise act. But maybe after she has had a few drinks . . .

'Now where did you find this fantastic dress?' Rhona lifts one of the ties and runs the fabric between a thumb and forefinger.

Eva looks at Rhona's eyes, suspecting that in this tactile proximity there is far more than talk about fashion.

Releasing the tie, Rhona steps back. 'I bet it's not English. German?'

'Well guessed.'

'Not at all – it's my business.'

'And do you work from here?'

'We converted the barn into a studio. Would you like a look?'

Two high-pitched laughs fill the room. Eva sees that Russ and Louise are sharing a joke. She also notices that Luke, boredom on his face, is listening to Felix.

'Yes I'd love to,' Eva says, wondering for a moment if she should suggest that Luke join them; it might be instructive to see them together – the kiss when they arrived revealed nothing. But the ploy is too obvious. Wait and observe must be the policy.

Luke notices Eva and Rhona move towards the door and panics, but as Rhona ushers Eva through the door, she looks towards him with a fear-allaying smile which, he is certain, no-one else in the room has noticed.

Rhona strides across the yard to the studio and opens the door, but waits until Eva is on the threshold before switching on the lights.

Eva blinks at the textile mayhem in front of her. 'It's like entering a kaleidoscope.'

'This is where I try to make a living.'

Eva picks up a strip of printed cotton from the floor.

'The remains of a '30s dress. I've been reusing the design for a top.'

'It's all so . . .'

'Untidy? That's what people always say when they come here.'

'I was going to say exciting. Has Luke seen this?'

'I tend not to bring men in here. They find it boring.'

'It's very different from his own workshop. Now that is tidy.'

'Come and see these children's clothes I've been working on.'

Rhona leads Eva to a corner where half-finished Russian costumes are spread out on a workbench.

Eva holds up an embroidered shirt. 'I love this.'

'I've tried to combine traditional and modern. It's for a Moscow boutique. Let me show you a girl's outfit.' Rhona whisks through a rail of half-finished garments.

Eva watches her nimble fingers and wonders if a matching deceit is at work in her head.

Rhona finds a girl's outfit and places it on the worktop. Eva examines the headdress. 'Do you have children?' she asks.

'One daughter, but she's far too old for this.'

'Does she take after you or Luke?'

'Me a little. Not Luke. Helen was from a previous relationship. Does this headdress have a special name?'

'A Russian word I can never remember. My team's always reminding me, but it's no good: languages were never my strong point.'

Eva walks over to the rail. 'Do you have any finished garments?'

'Almost none. We simply produce ideas for other people to manufacture. Occasionally I'm sent a finished product as a present.'

'So you don't see the fruits of your labours?'

'Not often. Unless in a magazine. The real results are in the bank balance.'

Eva runs her eyes over the workbenches. 'How many people do you have working for you?'

'Five.' Rhona points to a photo on a wall. 'There we all are.'

Eva walks up to the photo and sees Rhona and four women, arms round each other's shoulders, standing outside the studio door. Agnes is not among them.

'It was taken the day we moved here by my right-hand girl, Agnes.'

Eva has a disturbing feeling that Rhona is reading her mind. In the glass of the frame she catches Rhona's eyes and turns round. 'Did you always want to be in fashion?'

'Heavens, no. I originally wanted to paint. In fact it was my painting which got me into art school.'

'I would love to see some.'

'I'm not sure if I have any here. Unless there's a scrap or two in the plan chest.'

Rhona leads Eva to the far corner of the studio, crouches down and pulls out the bottom drawer of a plan chest. Eva looks down at the dark hair in front of her, assessing how far it would fall if its ivory clip were released. And has Luke touched that hair? Or the nape below with that small mole an inch above the top of her dress?

'Here're a few.' Rhona stands up, clears a space on top of the chest and spreads out six drawings of figures. 'They were all copied from Dutch old masters.'

'They're exquisite, especially the folds in the clothing. You ought to frame them.'

'It took me ages to realise that my interest was in the garments not the people.'

'But the figures are beautifully drawn.'

'No, I can see hundreds of mistakes. Look, that arm is all over the place.'

'I still like it.'

'You're very kind. Please take it. Does Luke do framing?'

'I think I can persuade him.'

'Shall I find you a cardboard tube?' asks Rhona. 'If you leave it on a table in the house, one of the gang is bound to spill wine on it.' Rhona takes the drawing from Eva and goes to a low cupboard below a window. Eva, following her, looks out into the orchard where she counts a dozen rabbits feeding beneath the trees.

'Too many of the little creatures, I'm afraid,' says Rhona, standing. 'I'm told I shouldn't be sentimental about them.' She places a cardboard tube on the nearest workbench, neatly rolls up the drawing, slots it in and hands it to Eva.

'There're a lot of potential suppers out there,' says Eva.

'That's what Alden says. He's longing to make paella from his own rabbits, but I won't let him.'

'How did you meet Alden?'

Rhona indicates two rush-seated chairs by the window. Eva places the tube on top of the cupboard and sits down. As Rhona moves her chair so they are facing each other, Eva wonders what Agnes would make of this studio *tête-à-tête*.

'After I left art school, before I started my business, I took any bit job I could find, art evening classes included. One September Alden turned up to learn to paint. Having met Lynton a few weeks earlier, he returned to England with the idea that he too could be an artist. Ridiculous or what?'

'Not completely. I've had several clients who've had projected ambitions. They meet someone who impresses them and they want to be like them. And it's quite common for a client towards the end of their counselling to become convinced that to be a counsellor is their true vocation. Sometimes it can be. Usually it isn't.'

'With Alden it definitely wasn't. Of course, on Alden's next visit to Corsica, Lynton was very kind about his efforts, and gently suggested that he should spend more time drawing. But true to form Alden wanted to get stuck in with the palette knife as quickly as possible. The message sunk in eventually, and now Alden satisfies his artistic urges with writing and producing.'

'Does he help with the business?'

'You're joking. He's clueless about fashion and textiles. He works as a locum solicitor. He isn't very proud of it, because he still nurses his writing hopes.'

'Surely law is more lucrative than writing?'

'A year ago he got fifty pounds for a short story in some obscure magazine and he spent more than that celebrating. How did you meet Luke?'

'After the break-up of his marriage he was my client. The counselling ended and we began to meet socially. It was a very difficult time.'

Eva sees Rhona's eyes widen at this revelation – whether genuine or feigned surprise she can't decide.

'How beautifully romantic,' says Rhona.

'That's not what my colleagues at work thought.'

'They were probably envious.'

'There's a code of conduct about relationships with clients. It blew up in such a way it was best for me to leave. So we moved up here.'

'I think that's wonderful. And Luke's lovely. If you ever want to swap him for Alden . . .'

Eva attempts to smile.

Rhona jumps to her feet. 'Enough of this nonsense. Alden will be furious if we're late for his soufflés.'

As Eva walks ahead to the door, she feels a tap on her shoulder.

'Don't forget your drawing.' Rhona hands the cardboard tube to Eva. 'I wouldn't have blamed you for leaving it behind.'

'I would have blamed myself – it's a very kind present.'

As they enter the house they see the others leaving the parlour.

'Oh, there you are,' calls Russ to Eva. 'We were about to send out a search party.'

Luke, last to emerge, finds Rhona at his side. She whispers in his ear, 'You've never been into the studio. OK?'

For a moment he is taken back by this sudden confidence. He turns his head to her but finds she is already weaving her way through the others. In the dining room Luke sees a large circular table covered in a linen cloth and laid with silver cutlery around a central bowl of garden roses.

'Now sit wherever you like,' says Rhona, 'and none of this boy, girl, boy, girl silliness.'

'Anyhow, you can't do it with a five and a four,' says Russ.

Last in, Luke finds a chair between Cassie and Josh. Glad not to be next to Rhona, he also knows that around a circular table it may be hard not to catch her eye. He watches her slip in on Josh's left, a proximity which makes the chance of eye contact as minimal as the table's shape allows.

Eva sits near the door, next to a chair left vacant for Alden. Felix, on her other side, fills her glass from one of the three opened bottles of white wine on the table. 'Aren't round tables fun?' he says. 'And we can always have a séance afterwards. I wonder if Alden's got a ouija board.'

'Definitely not,' says Alden, entering and now wearing a blue and white striped apron. He carries two trays of soufflés in large ramekin dishes on plates. He places the trays on the table, one either side of the roses. 'It's playing with fire. Lynton's nephew was a good artist until he dabbled with ouijahs. After that he never painted again.' He returns to the kitchen.

'That rules out tonight's entertainment,' says Felix.

'We'd better grab these before they sink,' says Rhona, taking a ramekin for herself. 'That would be a crime worse than dabbling in magic.'

'Oh dear,' says Louise, 'can we risk *Peter Pan*?'

'*Peter Pan* is about white magic,' says a voice behind a basket of home-baked rolls.' Alden places the basket on the table. 'Unlike *Macbeth* which can be plagued by accidents.'

'What about *Blithe Spirit* which we're doing in the autumn?' asks Russ. 'I mean, it's all about a séance and an angry poltergeist.'

'Comedies don't count,' says Alden, removing his apron, hanging it over the dining room door and sitting down.

'This is delicious,' says Eva. 'Walnut, parmesan . . . and some other cheese?'

Alden beams, mid-mouthful, 'Mathilde gave me the recipe.'

Eva is about to ask who Mathilde is when Rhona helps her out.

'Mathilde is Lynton's wife.'

Eva looks around the table and sees Luke listening to Russ who is talking quietly to Louise about *Blithe Spirit*.

'. . . and your dress would look wonderful on Madame Arcati. Mind you, the lady we've got lined up for her would have to lose a stone or three. Added to that . . .'

As Eva notes that there has been no eye contact yet between Luke and Rhona, Alden turns to her.

'Somebody said you're a psychotherapist. Have you always practiced in Norfolk?'

'No, I trained and started work in London,' Eva says, wondering for a moment if it was Luke or Russ who mentioned her profession to him. Or Rhona?

At great speed Alden finishes his soufflé. 'A lot of work but gone in a minute,' he smiles. 'I'm afraid I'm very suspicious of psychotherapists. I always think that had the great creative minds submitted to therapy, they wouldn't have produced anything.'

Eva realises that all other conversations have stopped.

'It's the creases in our minds which make us create,' continues Alden. 'Iron them out and we can't paint or write anything.'

'I don't see my work as ironing out,' says Eva. 'More of helping people feel comfortable with whatever creases they have.'

'Ah, but when you're comfortable, can you create? Would Van Gogh have left us those marvellous sunflowers and irises had he been comfortable?'

'Psychotherapy might have prevented his suicide. He then might have given us many more paintings.'

'Or he might have died a sad old man, never having lifted his brush for the second half of his life.' Alden gets up from the table and goes to the kitchen. At the door he turns round. 'And there is a theory that Van Gogh was murdered.'

Rhona catches Eva's eye. 'I apologise. The troubled creative mind is one of his favourite hobby-horses.'

'Good soufflé though,' says Felix, standing to clear the nine empty dishes.

'Maybe his true vocation is cooking,' says Cassie.

'That's just as well,' says Rhona. 'I'm hopeless in the kitchen.' She leans forward to Luke. 'Do you think we could do with a mirror on that far wall?'

Pleased that Rhona is no longer appearing to ignore him, Luke looks towards the boarded-up fireplace and its modest surround. 'Maybe an understated mirror would stand well on the mantel shelf.' He turns to his right. 'What do you think, Russ?'

Russ eyes the wall up and down. 'Yes, as long as it's simple and square.'

'Like Alden,' says Louise.

'Naughty, naughty,' says Russ, gently slapping her wrist. 'If you're not careful we won't get our next course, let alone pudding.'

'Perhaps you and Russ could look out something suitable,' says Rhona.

Luke again stares at the empty wall in front of him. 'It would certainly make the room look larger.'

If this is all an act, thinks Eva, Rhona – and Luke as well – are playing it all with great skill. Is it somehow too convincing?

Felix appears with a pile of warmed dinner plates, followed by Alden carrying two stuffed and rolled loins of pork. As Felix returns to the kitchen, Alden looks around for a compliment.

'How exquisitely sliced,' says Eva. 'My efforts always seem to lose shape when I take the string off the meat.'

Alden begins to serve. 'The secret is not to have a stuffing which is too crumbly.'

Felix brings in dishes of potatoes dauphinoise and savoy cabbage. When he sits down Eva asks, 'Will this be your first trip to Santa Marta?'

'Yes,' he says quietly, 'but I'm beginning to wonder if I shouldn't have taken up an offer to do the Edinburgh Fringe. But Corsica has guaranteed sun, and Alden's paying me better.'

'So you're a professional actor?'

'I hope to be. Is psychotherapy the same as counselling?'

'People argue over the differences, but the aim is pretty much the same.'

'A friend of mine needed counselling after a week of psychodrama. When I was offered a similar course I turned it down.'

'Very wise,' says Alden, as he appears between them to fill their glasses. 'I lost my first girlfriend because of psychodrama.'

All eyes focus in his direction. He enjoys the moment of silence.

'Well, let's hear the details,' insists Louise.

'Not the psychodrama story, please, Alden,' says Rhona.

The protest, Eva decides, is as much encouragement as restraint.

Alden gives a shrug of indecision.

'Come on,' says Felix, 'You're obviously dying to tell us.'

'OK,' says Alden and returns to his seat where he knocks back half a glass of wine. 'Many years ago . . . long, long before I met the beautiful Rhona . . .'

'Yeah, yeah, yeah,' says Rhona.

'Do you want me continue?'

'Out with it,' says Cassie.

'In those sad and half-forgotten days, I had a girlfriend who was at drama school, and she once had a weeklong course of psychodrama, during which she . . .'

'What was her name, Alden?' asks Cassie.

'. . . during *Lynette's* week she would come home every night with stories of soul-searching, delving into the subconscious and even dancing naked in a half-lit room with her fellow students. The leader, enabler, or whatever she called him, was this hoary old therapist called Neville, and every night it was Neville said this and Neville told us that and Neville's really fantastic. And so profound were the insights gained from her journey of self-discovery that she assured me it would do me good if I went on a similar course.'

'Sounds as if it would have been up your street,' says Louise.

Alden ignores the comment. 'And being a cooperative sort of guy, I went along with her and said, "Well, book me into a course if you think it's so wonderful." And the next day she comes back, having paid for me to have a weekend in Devon with the same psycho-guru who had clearly impressed her so much.' Alden bolts a mouthful of pork.

'And you actually went?' asks Cassie.

'Of course. But for some reason Neville and I didn't exactly hit it off.'

'Perhaps you didn't look so good naked,' says Felix.

'No, even before anyone took their shoes off for the obligatory sit-in-a-circle soul-baring, I thought, this man is a total prat, and worse than that, a control freak.'

'Takes one to know one,' says Cassie.

Alden gives his plate a sardonic smile. 'Well, it has to be said, the course I'd been booked on wasn't the heavy duty psychodrama stuff Lynette had enjoyed. My weekend was what Neville called in-depth group work. And the first two hours were taken up by everybody sharing the miseries of their lives, past or present. For some reason I was the only one who had nothing to contribute.'

'Clearly, a happy childhood, free of repression,' says Eva. She looks towards Luke whose auction-room face reveals nothing.

'So I sat there,' Alden continues, 'listening, but without anything to add to the pots of agony bubbling around me. On the whole nobody seemed to notice me until the first session the following day. Here I must say that official bedtime hadn't been until 3am. I suspect the idea was to grind down even the most resistant reserve. At any rate, the procedure was to find a corner of the rambling old house where the course was held, and get your head down as best you could.'

'I'm sure there were plenty of cushions,' says Russ.

'I've never seen so many. Dozens to hug, weep into and, in the case of one angry Danish girl, punch the hell out of. At any rate my chosen place of repose was a corner of a conservatory which I thought I had for myself. Here I make my big mistake.'

'You woke up in the night and peed on a rare orchid?' says Josh.

'Much worse. I snored. And unbeknown to me someone else was sleeping, or rather trying to sleep, in another corner, hidden by a fruiting vine.'

'The angry Danish girl?' says Josh.

'No, it turned out to be an otherwise mild-mannered civil engineer. But in the morning, at the first session after the herbal tea and nut bar which passed for breakfast, he laid into me with such abuse for disturbing his sleep that you would have thought I had tried to garotte him during the night with a trailing plant.'

'Why didn't he go off to a quieter room?' asks Russ.

'Too simple. He was obviously relishing the chance to have a go at someone in public. Now, in the course of his tirade, this engineer points out that there is a custom at these weekends that anyone who snores must sleep in the adjacent barn conversion. I now twig that most of this lot have been to these madhouse parties before, and are fully conversant with the snoring regulation. To give the guru Neville his due, he does tell everyone that this is my first weekend and I had probably not read the notes at the bottom of the timetable pinned up in the kitchen.'

'Always read the small print,' says Russ.

Eva looks towards Luke, wondering if around the table there is information she herself is failing to read.

'So,' continues Alden, 'with suitable humility I say sorry to the red-eyed engineer. But that makes it worse. Everybody questions the sincerity of my apology. Mind you, I do have to say there may have been a trace of a smile on my face as I said it.'

'What did you expect?' says Josh.

'Not what followed. Neville, who has clearly been noting my twelve hours non-contribution to the gathering, turns from being sympathetic and singles me out for special treatment. "Why do you resent us all?" asks Neville. "But I don't," I tell him. "I sense a lot of anger in you, Alden," he tells me. Well, I admit that up to that point I didn't feel much either way, but the way he called me Al-den, emphasising the second syllable really got my goat. I told him I couldn't see much point in the weekend, but I was happy to bash on until the end of the final session at six o'clock, even if I didn't have much to say. In response, he silently gets up and lies down in the centre of the circle. "Al-den, come and lie down on top of me," he says. And I see this ring of smiling eyes encouraging me to do as he says because it will do me good.'

'Lie on him?' asks Cassie. 'I take it you still had clothes on.'

'I never removed more than my shoes. Back to my edifying weekend – one girl gets to her feet and holds my hand, as if she's a sponsor in some evangelical convention. It was like they were all going to sing *Shall we gather at the river?* if I stepped into the middle.'

'And did you?' asks Louise?

'No, I simply asked Neville very quietly why he wanted me to lie on him. Perfectly reasonable, I thought. Wrong again, it transpires. "Please trust me, Al-den," says a voice from the carpet. And at the same time my sponsor squeezes my right hand.'

'Was she pretty?' asks Louise.

'I can't remember, but I tell Neville that lying on top of men for no apparent reason isn't my usual style. And at that a bearded man takes hold of my other hand. I can recall his limp fingers. But I stay firmly where I am in the seated circle.'

'Party pooper,' says Cassie.

'They all certainly thought so, since I was ignored for the rest of the morning. Which suited me fine.' Alden swallows some more food and a glassful of wine. 'But over the frugal salad lunch Neville appears at my side and says, "We really must address that anger, Al-den." I'm about to argue the point but since I look like losing the last whole grain roll, I politely smile at him, concentrate all my energy and think to myself, *If I've got a load of anger, Neville, I give it all to you, matey – deal with it.* Curiously, I felt a weight lifted from me. Elated, I headed for the hippy bread.'

'Did he ever tell you why he did want you to lie on top of him?' asks Russ.

'No, but later Lynette said it was to make me feel that Neville was as vulnerable as me, or some such psychobabble.'

'And the naked dancing?' asks Louise.

'That was at the end of the day. One or two of them couldn't get their kit off quick enough. Some did a half-strip. The music chosen for the occasion was *A Whiter Shade of Pale*, which seemed a bit passé, although Neville was probably trapped in the '60s.'

'But how did that make you lose your girlfriend?' asks Cassie.

'Apparently the girl who took my right hand was a friend of Lynette's and at drama school with her. She gave Lynette a hug by hug account of the whole weekend and my alleged non-cooperation. Lynette was deeply appalled and wanted me to go back to Neville for one-to-one counselling. I refused of course. I think what finally broke us up was my telling her that I had deposited a heavy load of supposed anger on Neville himself.' Alden turns to Eva. 'You see my first experience of therapy may well have been my last.'

'Not everyone would find such groups helpful,' says Eva. 'I certainly wouldn't myself.' She looks around the table, again detecting no eye contact between Luke and Rhona.

'At any rate, Lynette and I split up and I heard only one more thing about Neville.'

'He'd got off with Lynette?' says Cassie.

'No, he jumped off the Severn Bridge, and that was the end of him.'

'He clearly couldn't bear the burden of your anger,' says Louise.

Alden gets up from his seat. 'I would like to think so.' With a malevolent smile he leaves for the kitchen. For some moments the room is silent.

Over peach crumble and dessert wine Eva decides she has been part of a well-rehearsed performance, the room's only certainty the faultless food.

Furthest from the dining room door, Luke is the last to leave for coffee in the parlour. In the passageway he feels a tap on his shoulder and hears Rhona's lowered voice, 'Isn't he an ogre? He really believes he sent that Neville to his death, through some destructive power of thought. Sometimes he really scares me. I'll phone early tomorrow?' The reassurance tells him that the whole evening is part of an Alden-centred world soon to be exploded.

Oiling his guests with *Braulio* digestif, Alden tries to persuade them to play charades but Felix puts on some jazz and turns up the volume. Luke, sitting next to Eva in almost the same position where, on his first visit, he sat next to Rhona, is uneasy, alienated in a room redolent with the memory of being alone with her.

'Was that mirror one of yours?' asks Eva.

'Yes. Fits in well, doesn't it?'

'Like it's always been there.'

'That's the look we go for.'

'You dealers and your looks.' She regrets the acerbic tone.

As he finishes his coffee Luke sees Eva yawn. It is a welcome signal. After thanks and goodbyes and a bear hug each from Alden, they are seen out by Rhona who gives them each a kiss and reminds Eva to take her present with her.

As Luke drives out of the yard, Eva says, 'And you're spending a week with that lot in Corsica?'

'Mad, I know, but Russ will enjoy it.'

'A strange evening.'

'Good food though.'

'It was all part of the performance. Dinner and theatre often go together.' She is tempted to add, 'Alden is clearly having an affair with Lou,' but disinclined to point out the Mills's marital fault lines, asks, 'Have you seen Rhona's studio? I found it fascinating.'

'Fashion's not my thing. I expect Russ would love to see it.'

At Brick Kiln Cottage Eva asks, 'Will you come in for a nightcap?'

'Thanks, but I'm way over the limit as it is.'

Alone in her kitchen Eva sits down, stares at the table top and lets the evening flow over her head. There is no gain in repeating to herself each word spoken by Rhona to her, or to Luke, or searching for the truth behind appearances. But it is difficult not to rid her head of Rhona's voice, 'And Luke's lovely. If you ever want to swap him . . .' Maybe I've already lost him, she thinks. No, too much wine has made me maudlin. I simply do not know what *is* going on. If anything. Seizing the cardboard tube, she walks across the room and tossing it into the broom cupboard gains a moment of satisfaction.

# 15

By mid-morning Thursday Rhona has not phoned. Worried, Luke
sits at his desk in the shop. It is well beyond the point, he thinks,
which can possibly be called 'early'. And yet the whispered 'I'll phone
early tomorrow,' had been definite, emphatic and entirely her
suggestion, a promise which dissuades him from phoning her himself.
So far their relationship has been at her bidding, in her time, and total
bliss; there will be no conscious pursuit by him now to threaten it. Of
course, he thinks, if there were some wise counsellor at my elbow – he
imagines one of Eva's male colleagues – I would no doubt be asked, *Isn't
everything on her terms? You have known her only three weeks – is that a long
enough period in which to make major decisions about your future?* But I am
not in a counselling room, he reassures himself. 'Stuff your cold advice,'
he whispers to the imaginary counsellor, and banishes the image. No,
after last night, perhaps first thing for Rhona could be 11.00am. God
knows when she got to bed. It was different for Eva and me – we
left early.

'Coffee,' says Russ's hungover voice as a mug is placed on the desk.

'How much longer did you stay last night?'

'Let me put it like this: I shall leave any glass-cutting until after
lunch.'

'A good evening then.'

'Which I'm paying for now. I should have left with you and Eva.'

'What did we miss?'

'Alden got his way with the charades.'

'I'm sure you were very good at it.'

'Nobody guessed my *Waiting for Godot*, but I'm not sure if that was my bad acting or the drunk audience.'

'Did Rhona join in?'

'No, very sensibly by this time she'd gone to bed.'

* * *

On Thursday morning Eva revises her paper, *When Therapies Conflict*, to be given in Birmingham. It is so much easier to work on it now there are no clients' appointments in her diary, no case notes to write up. But despite this, despite having slept well, the shadow of Luke and Rhona hangs over her. Every few minutes she looks at the kitchen clock or her watch.

At last Agnes phones.

'Eva, hi, are you busy?'

'No. Tell me everything.'

'Rhona led me out to the orchard at coffee time this morning. I was certain she had some great revelation in the offing. Well, she began in her usual roundabout way by telling me about the dinner party. She really liked meeting you by the way.'

'I bet she did.'

'No, she seemed genuinely pleased you liked her drawings. And I've never known her to give one away before. Loads of people ask and she's always like, 'No, I'm so sorry, I need them for reference.' So you really made an impression.'

'Why am I not flattered?'

'I gather Alden was on good form.'

'He certainly likes his audience. But I thought Rhona was encouraging him.'

'She always does – while pretending not to of course. Did you spy anything going on between her and Luke?'

'Only that it was somehow all too normal, as if rehearsed. In fact the whole evening was a performance.'

'Those dos always are. Nowadays I'm happy to avoid them. Well, Rhona was building up to the nitty-gritty when Alden comes striding through the apple trees asking where the car keys are – he's taken all his mates to Cambridge today for lunch and a punt before he shoves them onto the London train. And what with all the searching and arguing who had them last, that was the end of what was shaping up for a good heart to heart.'

'Right now I'm trying hard to distract myself from thinking about her and Luke.'

'And you won't have to after tomorrow. You'll have Luke for yourself for a week. After we arrive in Corsica I'll phone you with any news. Now when I get back you must come over and see my new place – I'm moving in this afternoon.'

'I look forward to it.'

Eva replaces the handset, her confidence returning. Isn't this the first day of her mini-sabbatical? Despite Luke and Rhona – if there really is a Luke and Rhona – a small celebration is called for, perhaps a visit to a few garden centres, the purchase of some plants, and an opportunity to disperse or forget the shadows over her life.

* * *

Around noon Luke goes to the window and looks across the market place, remembering Rhona's first visit to the shop: the unheard entry, her invisibility after leaving, her transient perfume. And how, he asks himself, has she retained that elusiveness, even after they have become lovers? He returns to his desk to check his mobile in case by some technological quirk she has left a message without its bleeping. As he frowns at the empty inbox the ringtone sounds.

'Luke, darling, you've probably given up on me.'

'Of course not. Your guests must have exhausted you.'

'Oh, it's not them so much – I leave them to Alden – it's sorting out the business so I can be away for a fortnight. It's been sapping all my energy this week . . . well, not *quite* all. But now at last everything's in order. The team have been working overtime, and I've given them the afternoon off. I did so enjoy meeting Eva last night. I think we behaved very well, didn't we?'

'Impeccably.'

'When we were in the studio I half suspected she had an inkling about us, but there's nothing we can do.'

'Did we give ourselves away?'

'No, but I suspect she has razor instincts.'

Luke's stomach tightens. 'She said nothing to me.'

'Don't worry, all will be well, and even better if you come over this afternoon. Alden and the gang have already left for Cambridge with talk of punting. Late afternoon he'll take them to the station. Is two o'clock OK?'

'Let me look at my diary,' he teases. 'I have three customers to see after lunch, a mirror to deliver to a supermodel at two, a dental appointment at two-thirty. But I think I can reschedule. Two o'clock it is.'

With hours of doubt blown away by a minute's phone-call Luke calls out, 'Russ, I'll be at the allotment for the next hour.'

Leaving the market place, he tells himself, *In a couple of hours and I'll see her again.* It is too long. But once inside the walls of the old garden he is closer to her. The vegetables and flowers, the higher temperature of the sheltered, secret world and the absence of people make him feel her unseen presence.

Gardening boots on, he waters his tomatoes and courgettes, thins a row of carrots, weeds the celeriac and wonders where his life will be when he starts to lift them as the frosts begin. Finally, he ties up his sweet peas, removes tendrils and laterals, and cuts eighteen long-stemmed blooms for Rhona. Placing them in a jar of water in the shade, he goes into the hothouse and sits on a bench. The minutes pass unnoticed. Someone has left a copy of the local paper, open at a half-completed crossword, a biro on top. He answers a few clues until from nowhere Maurice's head appears on his lap. He strokes the dog's head before a whistle from outside calls the mongrel away and it bounds away in search of Alf.

Later Luke walks down to Alf's hut.

'Could you keep an eye on my stuff from next Thursday for a week?' Luke asks. 'I shall be on holiday.'

'Leave it me. Nothing will die.'

'If you want to pick anything ...'

'I will, don't you worry. Going anywhere interesting?'

'Corsica.'

'Eva going with you?'

'Not this time. She's got work commitments.'

Before returning to the shop, Luke goes home with his sweet peas and places them on the stone floor of the hallway. At he joins Russ whose hangover, he is pleased to discover, does not interfere with the customary lunchtime gossip which absorbs almost an hour of waiting.

At 2.oopm he turns off the engine of the van and the voice of Françoise Hardy on his new CD, and walks from his van to the back door of Saffold Farm. There is a deep silence in the yard, no breeze or birdsong and no sign of Rambo on the lookout for strangers. Has he made some mistake with the time? Will Alden appear and see the accusing flowers in his hand? As he strikes the knocker he notices that the door is ajar. He waits but hears no sound from inside. Mystified, he again lays his hand on the iron loop. Before he can strike it he hears a window being opened above him.

'Come on up,' calls Rhona.

He looks up to see the window being closed. Intrigued, he enters the house. In the passageway he notices that the kitchen door is open. Peering inside, he sees a glass vase on a worktop. He walks over to it, fills it with water at the sink and arranges the flowers. He is tempted to leave them here as an act of defiance in Alden's world of stainless steel and granite, but decides to carry them to the parlour and place them on the mantelpiece in front of the mirror. Rhona can find them later.

Walking up the bare pine boards of the narrow staircase, he is so enthralled at exploring an unfamiliar part of the house that when he reaches the passageway at the top, his usually dependable sense of direction fails him. Deciding at last that the room from which she called must be entered by one of two doors either side of a large print of Albert Bridge, he hesitates between the two. He looks down at the wedges of light below the doors in the hope of seeing a moving shadow, but there is nothing.

'Where are you?' calls Rhona.

When he enters he finds himself in what must be a spare bedroom, sparsely furnished with a double bed, a chair and a pine chest of drawers. A single watercolour of a harbour hangs on a wall. There is no sign of Rhona; she must be in the other room. But as he is about to leave he notices a slight movement under a deep-quilted eiderdown and a tell-tale wisp of dark hair on a pillow.

'Found you,' he says.

Rhona's head emerges. 'I haven't a stitch on. Climb in. I have a confession to make.'

Luke quickly strips, slips under the bed clothes and lies beside her, almost without body contact.

'So what have you been up to?' he asks.

'When the gang left I changed all the bedding. So we're now between clean sheets, but I seem to have lost some pillow cases. This was Lou's room and I'm afraid these are her pillows.' She turns towards him and breathes in deeply. 'You can probably detect a trace of her scent.'

'Is that all you have to confess?'

'So far, yes. Can you forgive me?'

'Well, it is a serious lapse in housekeeping.'

'How can I make amends?

'I'll rack my brains.'

'Unless the punishment is in the crime.'

'In what way?'

'You may feel you are in bed with two girls, not one, and I have to compete for your attention.'

'I'm sure you never need to compete.'

* * *

The best of celebrations, thinks Eva, as she places two newly-bought pots of agapanthus in the porch. When she has watered them she places on the table some bread, cheese and homegrown salad leaves, along with a chilled can of lager to toast her mini-sabbatical. As an afterthought she checks her landline messages. There is only one. It comes as a body blow.

'Eva, this is Sister Cyra. Your aunt is not at all well. We've had to transfer her from her flat to the nursing wing. She keeps mentioning your name, over and over. If there's some way you can come to see her, I think it might be for the best.'

Eva clutches the phone to her stomach and stabs the repeat button, this time noting that the message was left at 11.50am. And for the last three hours, she accuses herself, I've been idling my way round garden centres. I must go to her. Now.

She immediately phones St. Anthony's Retirement Home, Corofin, waiting a seemingly interminable time for an answer. Finally she is put through to the soft Filipina voice of Sister Lourdes. 'Miss McKelvey is a little more alert this morning. We were worried about her during the night. She didn't say much when we admitted her, apart from mentioning your name again and again. At the moment she's still sleeping.'

'Would you tell her when she wakes that I'm on my way. I'll catch the next plane.'

'We'll have a room ready for you, if you wish to stay with us.'

'I'll be with you tonight. It may be quite late.'

Eva launches herself into a frenzy of online flight searches, and manages to find a last minute seat on an evening flight from Stansted to Shannon. She then phones the conference organiser in Birmingham to cancel her lecture, offering to email it. When the call is over, the blade again twists inside her: hadn't Rhona, last night, for different reasons, suggested sending the lecture? It is as if Rhona, in some inexplicable way, has now engineered this bitter reality. Eva throws some clothes into a case, knowing that, whatever there is between Rhona and Luke, she must phone him. She dials his mobile, but receives only his messaging service. Annoyed, she phones the shop.

'He's out this afternoon – seeing a customer, I think,' Russ tells her.

The thought that the customer might be Rhona occurs to her but is of small importance. 'Would you tell him that my aunt is unwell and I'm on the next plane to Ireland. If he could water my plants – there are some new agapanthus in the porch – I'd be grateful.'

'Can I help? Where are you flying from? I can close the shop and drive you to the airport myself.'

'Thanks but I've ordered a taxi.'

* * *

'Luke, the flowers. That was very sneaky of you.' Rhona, in a white dressing gown, brings in two glasses of white wine, sets them on the table between the armchairs facing the fireplace in the parlour, settles herself into one and stares at the mantelpiece. 'And being in front of your mirror we get double the number. You grew them yourself?'

'On my allotment.'

'You must take me there one day.'

'It's my escape from the world.'

'How intriguing.'

Rambo, appearing at the window, jumps into the room.

'All we need now is a butterfly,' says Luke.

'I think they prefer a floral dress to this white bath robe.' She touches the towelling fabric in a way which, Luke feels, could entice through the open window every insect in the garden.

Rhona drinks deeply, stands, and strokes his head before lowering her hand to grip his left shoulder. 'I'll phone you every day from Santa

Marta. You know what Alden often says? "All creatures are sad after sex." Only he likes to quote it in Latin. I don't think that's true, do you?'

'I've never been so happy.'

'I've an envelope for you with detailed directions how to find the village. Alden insists that you approach us over a mountain pass, almost a track, not via the sensible road. I'm not sure if I agree with him. It does make a spectacular approach to the village, but it scares me and the hairpin bends as you come down make it too dangerous for the driver to look at the amazing views. Please take care, Luke.'

'Russ can be my eyes.'

Around 4.30pm Luke drives away from Saffold Farm, watching a waving Rhona through his nearside wing mirror. As he moves up the lane he is aware of taking her with him. For the first mile she is sitting next to him and he can feel her breath close to him. But on the outskirts of Cantisham, the sight of pedestrians and passing cars diminish her presence until she fades from the passenger seat. Already he misses her.

He parks outside the shop, planning to assist at the workbench for half an hour. But Russ is at the door before he can enter.

'Message from Eva. Her aunt's very poorly. She's on her way to Ireland.'

'Has she left?'

'Over two hours ago. She tried your mobile, but . . .'

'Where's she flying from?'

'She didn't say, but she'll phone you from Shannon.'

'I wish I'd been . . .'

'She asks if you can water the plants, indoors and out.'

Without entering the shop, Luke drives straight to Brick Kiln Cottage. Having let himself in with his own key, he looks at the notepad by the phone for clues about her flight plans. He finds none and phones her mobile, but it is unavailable. He waters the plants on the windowsill, goes to the garden and inspects the vegetables. At the end of the garden he notices some bindweed, fetches a spade and digs out as much as he can find. The task feels less an act of kindness than a penance for his time at Saffold Farm. The exertion in the sun tires him but fails to ease his conscience.

Back inside the house, he carries a glass of water through to her sitting room and sinks into the sofa. The cottage is silent. At the window to his left, a branch of a climbing rose brushes the glass, a sound which intensifies the stillness. He stares at the wood burning stove and remembers helping to fit it, making the register plate himself. In front of the hearth is a Turkish rug which Eva bought at an auction they attended together. On the windowsill is a photograph of Helen, Eva and himself on Helen's graduation day. Despite the warm day, the room feels cold, adding to his unease, as if the house is telling him he no longer belongs here. Resisting the suggestion, he looks up to the painting on the chimney breast, an impressionistic scene of grazing cattle, a present from him the Christmas after she had moved here. He quickly stands, goes upstairs to the landing where he opens a window for ventilation. He takes a deep breath and returns downstairs. It is not until he locks the cottage door behind him that he exhales and breathes in the air of the garden.

At home that evening, waiting for Eva's call, he decides he must join her in Ireland. If Barbara is dying he must be there. Eva may be in Corofin for days, perhaps several weeks, and he must be at her side. He will leave at first light tomorrow and drive to Holyhead. And he will take the van – it may be useful later. And Eva may need more clothes than she managed to cram into a suitcase. Russ can go to Corsica without him. When Rhona phones tomorrow he will explain. That will be the hardest part, but she will understand. Online he goes through ferry times from Holyhead to Dun Laoghaire and makes calculations of distances and driving times. The journey can easily be done in a day; two years ago he and Eva had driven home from Corofin in well under twenty hours. He will be with her late tomorrow. Arrangements can be made for keeping an eye on her cottage. He is packing his own suitcase when Eva phones.

'I won't hear of it,' she insists above the noise of Shannon airport. 'I have all I need. You and Russ must have your holiday.'

'My things are packed. I'll leave before dawn.'

'Nonsense.'

'What extra clothes of yours shall I bring?'

'I've everything I need.'

'You don't know how long you'll be over there.'

'Barbara may make a quick recovery. We've had false alarms before. I might be back in a few days. Now I must find a taxi.'

'All the same, I'm more than happy to join you.'

'And I'll be more than happy if you can ask Annie to keep an eye on my garden. I'll email you tomorrow.'

'Give Barbara my love.'

Eva's phone cuts out and Luke stares at the half-packed suitcase.

Surely Eva cannot be clear-headed after such a fraught day? Perhaps he should ignore her wishes, seize a few hours' sleep and leave for Ireland. He continues packing and carries the suitcase downstairs. At the foot of the stairs he looks through the open study door. He can hear Rhona's voice when she walked in, 'Ah, your man cave.' If he is to go to Ireland he must phone her. Russ too.

In the kitchen he dials Russ's number. There is no reply. He leaves no message. He will phone again later. Should he now phone Rhona? Vacillating, he stares into the garden. There is weeding and dead-heading to be done, and a hundred other tasks demanding attention in Eva's garden. He phones Annie.

# PART III

# 16

In the subdued light of Barbara's room Eva sits at the bedside. When she first entered, the head on the pillow seemed to belong to another patient, and she had wanted to ask the nurse if she had been shown to the right room. It was only after some moments of shock that she had accepted that this frail woman with thin hair, life registered by the occasional quiver at the lips, was her aunt. The forehead on which she had pressed a kiss had felt like cold parchment. She thinks back to her last visit, in March, to the old but active, alert, woman with the rounded face beneath thick grey hair, who had joked outrageously about her neighbours in the other flats.

Eva looks around the room, its small wardrobe, chest of drawers and bedside table, so different from the flat in the residential wing where Barbara had crammed the possessions of a lifetime into a comfortable but confined space. On the table a shaft of light through the green curtains catches a silver photograph frame which a member of staff must have brought from the flat to the nursing room. Eva studies it. Taken, she guesses, in the 1930s, it shows Barbara standing between her parents in the garden of the family house in Limerick. Returning it to the table, she notices a painting of the same house propped against the wall on top of the chest, but not quite in the centre, and she remembers the exact place where, until recently, it hung in Barbara's flat. Walking over to it, she adjusts its position and returns to her chair. Strange, she thinks, how people are defined by the objects around them, and sometimes with the advance of years by fewer and fewer. 'What things define me?' she says aloud.

After twelve hours of travel there is a profound peace. Part of her is still driving to Stanstead, checking in, boarding and flying, travelling by taxi through the late evening along the main roads to Fountain Cross before taking the R476 to Corofin. In the silence of the room the journey recedes. After half an hour Barbara's breathing becomes more audible. It is an encouraging sound. Again Eva thinks back to her last visit here. Was it only four months ago? It seems much longer. Then, Barbara had enjoyed long, slow walks around the gardens with the aid of a walking frame. And one afternoon she had insisted on being pushed in a wheelchair for over a mile, talking all the while and never content with a mere 'Good morning' to any passer-by.

A nurse enters. 'You must get some sleep yourself now, dear. It's been a long day for you.'

With some reluctance Eva lifts herself from her chair, bends over the bed and kisses her aunt. As she leaves the room the nurse says, 'She's very weak but you'll be able to have a chat with her in the morning.'

Eva goes to her room on the ground floor. It has a wardrobe and chest identical to those in Barbara's room, but its en suite shower room and drinks-making tray bring to mind a *Travelodge*, which is, she thinks, what St. Anthony's has now become for her aunt. Unpacking, she realises Luke was right – she could do with more clothes for what is an open-ended visit, but dog tired she decides this minor worry can wait until morning.

She falls asleep playing through mental pictures of her many visits to Barbara, first at her house, later at her flat here at St. Anthony's, the fishing trips to Lough Corrib, the outings to Galway and Coole . . . the flow of images is briefly interrupted by a picture of Luke and the dinner party yesterday evening, but her thoughts move to a springtime walk with Barbara in the garden where they paused at a clump of narcissi.

In the morning she is woken by a knock on the door, followed by the appearance of one of the kitchen staff.

'It's eight o'clock, darling, and your aunt is as bright as a button. Now matron has given me strict instructions that you're not to go galloping upstairs before I've seen you eat a proper breakfast.' She raises a finger. 'Now take your time. There's no reason to rush.'

Eva's first instinct, despite her orders, is to run up and see Barbara, but the tone of admonition restrains her and she lies in bed, blankly staring at a print of the Burren. Turning her head, she becomes aware that last night she failed to draw the curtains. For some further minutes she looks out into the garden and beyond its stone wall into the County Clare countryside, acutely aware how different this place is from the ordered arable flatness of East Anglia. Ten minutes later, as she walks to the kitchen, she passes two residents in the corridor, both of whom greet her and seem ready for a chat. But not yet at one with the rhythms of St. Anthony's, she smiles and heads towards the obligatory breakfast.

At a small table in a bay window of the dining room, a huge plateful is placed in front of her. It reminds her of one of the many breakfasts she and Luke had enjoyed in the fishing lodge at Rutland Water. Again she wonders about him and Rhona, but cannot allow such thoughts to figure high in her emotional priorities. It is difficult enough today eating alone, when all her meals at St. Anthony's have previously been with Barbara, either in her flat or more recently in this same room with other residents. Luke had often accompanied her – Luke who now, she realizes, has receded in her life. She feels the loss, but it is a distant sadness which has been overtaken by a preparedness for a greater bereavement. She looks out to the formal front garden. It is divided by a gravel drive leading to the front door. The side nearer her is a rectangular lawn edged with standard roses. In the centre, a stone pedestal supports a bronze portrait bust of the founder. The opposite lawn is pegged out for croquet. If one has to end one's day in care, she thinks, St. Anthony's is no bad choice.

'Eva. Eva, they said you were coming,' are Barbara's first faltering words. As they exchange a kiss and a hug, Eva is shocked at her aunt's fragility.

'I flew over as soon as I heard. I'm sorry to find you so unwell.'

'Don't be sorry. I know how things are.' Barbara's voice regains some of its familiar strength, and a glint appears in her eyes. 'As we say, I'm ready to be reeled in.'

'Please don't talk like that.'

'Why not? I've heard so many people here ask, "Am I dying?" and here I am lucky enough not to need to ask. I know, Eva, I know.'

Eva feels tears in her eyes, and takes Barbara's hand.

Barbara in her turn grips Eva with a firmness she finds surprising.

'You must be happy for me,' says Barbara. 'I'm quite ready, you know. Now give me your news.'

'Helen is still enjoying Sydney. We spoke the other day . . .'

Eva, watching Barbara close her eyes, continues with updates on work, garden and fishing, omitting any reference to her doubts about Luke, until Barbara relaxes her grip. It seems she has fallen asleep. But the grip tightens and Barbara opens her eyes.

'You haven't mentioned your mirror man.'

'Haven't I?' Barbara mustn't be burdened with Luke and Rhona.

'The cancer hasn't got to my brain yet. What's wrong between the two of you?'

'Things are a little difficult. In fact . . .'

'The fact is it's a wonder you and he have lasted so long. I've never said so before, but now . . . well, there won't be another chance.'

Barbara moves her right hand towards Eva as if she would like to hold it, but cannot find enough strength. Eva takes it in her own. In silence they exchange smiles.

After a minutes Barbara closes her eyes. 'I suppose it's another woman,' she says.

Too upset to speak Eva squeezes Barbara's hand.

Luke's not a bad man,' says Barbara, 'but all those years ago wasn't he the stick you beat Mark with for leaving you? You were more upset at the time than you knew – far too angry to fall in love with anyone.'

That's not true, thinks Eva – the drugs have affected her reason.

'It was a long time ago,' Eva says and feels Barbara's fingers tighten.

'There you were – Mark runs off with a pretty young thing about to start her own interiors shop, and you are suddenly with Luke, king of the mirrors, three generations ahead of her in a similar line of work. You couldn't have hurt them more with a shillelagh.'

Eva wants to protest but feels Barbara's fingers loosen, as if the outburst has weakened her.

A nurse says, 'She's sleeping again.'

For a minute Eva describes yesterday's journey, finding her voice has hushed with the slow acceptance that this is not a visit to a sick woman but a vigil of uncertain duration.

Two hours later Eva leaves the room to allow a doctor to make an examination. In the matron's office he tells them, 'There is an obstruction in the kidneys. We could admit her to hospital for investigations and perhaps surgery, but I wouldn't recommend it.'

'The change of environment and any procedure would be too much for her,' adds the matron.' My advice is that she should remain here.'

'How long,' asks Eva, 'do you . . . ?'

The doctor and matron exchange glances. 'Mentally she is very tough,' says the matron, 'and you've seen how she has her lucid moments, but she tires quickly. She's in no pain, thanks to the morphine patches. But the prognosis? A few days.'

\* \* \*

Through heavy rain Luke walks to the shop. Any dutiful notions that he should follow Eva to Ireland have been subsumed by the thought that today Rhona flies to Corsica – already she is in the air. He stops abruptly, repeating the three words. Hasn't she always been "in the air" – ethereal, elusive? Of course she is physical, practical, but isn't there a thread in her her, the most loveable part, which is always just out of reach – furtive as the angel's tears in the clefts of the brickwork? He consoles himself with the knowledge that this evening she will phone him. How he will bear the six days before he will see her again he has no idea.

Mid-morning in the shop Russ insists on an unnecessary run-through of Smee's lines. Word perfect, he now gives them more dramatic emphasis, at one point forgetting his workplace *sotto voce*, much to the bewilderment of a customer entering the shop. Luke is amused – like himself, Russ, for his own reasons, is eager to be in Santa Marta.

At 5.00pm in steady drizzle, Luke walks to Eva's cottage. It should not be a long visit: her greenhouse tomatoes will need watering, but after the rain the garden can be left for a day or two. Looking through the glass door of the porch and seeing some letters lying on the floor beneath the letterbox, he lets himself in and leaves them on the kitchen table.

Despite the open landing window, the cottage feels airless and oppressive, as if it begrudges him oxygen. It also has an atmosphere of disturbing unfamiliarity, so strong that he is reminded of houses visited when asked by a local solicitor to carry out a probate valuation of contents. He feels he should be searching for overlooked rarities. And yet he knows this cottage well, is familiar with every item of its furnishings. Here there is no forgotten Chelsea plate at the back of a cupboard, no silver coffee pot black with neglect in a sideboard, no seventeenth-century wine glass hiding among empty *Kilner* jars in the larder. He goes upstairs to open another window.

In Eva's bedroom the open wardrobe doors and clothes flung on the bed speak of her hurried departure. He surveys the room, as familiar as his own bedroom. Two of his books are on his side of the double bed, and in the wardrobe he can see a line of his shirts. He clears a space on the bed and sits down, head in hands. When he looks up he notices the row of china rabbits Eva collected as a child. Various costume necklaces are draped around their necks. The largest has bangles hanging from its blue ears. Between the rabbits is an assortment of pots of cream. The domestic untidiness is both reassuring and disturbing. Doesn't he belong here, not in Rhona's world? For a second he sees every object at Saffold Farm as a prop in a drama written and acted out by Rhona and Alden, where even a spontaneous word or action seems, on reflection, to have been scripted. Yet yesterday afternoon was sheer magic, and the thought of hearing her voice again this evening is almost unbearably thrilling. He gathers his shirts from the rail and the books from the bedside table.

At home that evening he reads an email from Eva: *Barbara very weak. She may have only a few days. Thanks for your offer to come over here – and for the watering. I can manage things here. X E.*

He welcomes the matter-of-fact tone; a more effusive message might have been painful. He replies in similar vein.

It is almost midnight when at last Rhona calls. 'Luke, Luke, Luke, I'm missing you millions,' she says. 'We left before it was barely light this morning. Drove to Heathrow. Flight to Paris. Change. Flight to Figari. And Alden was impossible. Always fretting we'd be late. Why aren't you out here? It's usually so lovely. But without you . . .'

Luke hears a series of kisses. 'Here summer disappeared with you,' he says. He describes his day and Eva's departure to Ireland.

'If you feel you should be over there supporting her, of course I would understand,' she says. 'It would be awful not to see you, but you must do what is best. And never mind this stupid play – I'm already sick of it.'

Luke hears a long sigh.

'But Luke, darling Luke,' she says, 'I'm hoping against selfish hope that by some magic turn of events you'll soon be with me.'

'Russ and I are both definitely coming. We'll be with you late afternoon Thursday.'

* * *

For Eva the weekend sees no change in her aunt's condition. In the mornings Barbara is able to drink a little and exchange a few words, but any hope of a conversation has faded with the old woman's strength.

On Sunday, after an institutional roast dinner in the residents' dining room, Eva is about to return to the bedside, when a nurse says, 'You must look after yourself, dear. Now go for a walk and enjoy the air, or we'll be treating you for mental exhaustion.'

Without protest Eva obeys, but to leave St. Anthony's is like an act of truancy. At the top of the drive she looks back, worried, towards Barbara's room. With sad reluctance, she turns and continues with her walk, with a plan to visit the museum in the old St. Catherine's church. But a burst of sun changes her mind and slinging her coat over her shoulder she heads for Lake Inchiquin. It is a walk she has enjoyed before. The last time was in March – she remembers comparing the stone built houses, walls and wild flowers to their very different equivalents at home. But today she finds herself recalling her first visit here when she was twelve. Her parents had seen her onto the ferry. Barbara had met her at Dun Laoghaire and driven them in her ancient green Singer Estate to Naas where they had stopped for tea. Then on to her house on the Ennis road. She retained vivid memories of its clutter of furnishings brought from the much larger Limerick home she had never known, but felt she knew well from Barbara's fund of anecdotes and the photograph albums in the bottom drawer of her mahogany bureau.

Pausing to examine an unfamiliar fern on the verge, she asks herself, why am I reflecting so much on the past? Is it Barbara's critical condition, or my relationship with Luke, or a combination of the two? Is the unconscious asking me to review my life, to prepare for loss, to face the need for change?

Walking from the road down to the lake, the present reasserts itself. Nothing seems to have changed here since earlier visits. But now it looks uncared for. A rowing boat on the stones near the water's edge is in need of repair and a coat of varnish. Close to this spot, on that first visit, Barbara had placed a rod in her hands and taught her the basics of casting. Later, she and Barbara had fished here from a boat, and it was here she had first seen her aunt land a brown trout. The following year, on this lake at night, she herself had caught her first fish. Are there still trout here? she wonders, looking out over the still surface. To her right she looks at a modern house standing on a promontory but seeming to hang over the lake. She can hear her aunt's disparaging voice, 'It should never have been built.'

Eva looks out towards the island, hoping she might see a fish rise. The surface remains undisturbed. Walking on she sees a dead fish lying on the grey stones. Close inspection shows it to be a small pike which, she suspects, had been caught by a disappointed trout fisherman and not returned to the water. The sight depresses her. There is a beauty here, but it is not the lake of her memories.

\* \* \*

Each evening Luke receives a short email from Eva, telling him that there is no change in Barbara's condition. Each night he waits in his study for Rhona's call. Their conversations are never long enough. On Tuesday she ends the call with an abrupt, 'Alden's coming. Must go. Love you.' He had wanted to tell her about Russ's latest rehearsals in the shop, annoying at first but soon a cause of hilarity. And he was going to mention his plan to go fishing the following morning to relieve the pain of her absence.

At 3am on Wednesday Luke drives into the empty car park at the top of the cliffs at Overstrand, pulls on his waders and checks his fishing gear before making his way down the steep path to the beach. In one hand he holds his rod, in the other a heavy water-filled container of sand eels with its battery-powered aerator. As far as he can see, east towards Sidestrand and Mundesley and west towards Cromer, the beach is deserted. He meets only a fox scavenging near the bend at the bottom. It looks up, startled, suspicious, then darts ahead, losing itself in the scrub of its own cliffside path, but leaving behind a foul odour which lingers in the air. Apart from birds feeding near the water's edge on the incoming tide, the coast is silent and still. On the horizon he can make out the yellow lights of boats, but in the greyness before sunrise it is impossible to tell how big they are or how distant. He stands on the beach and looks out to sea, knowing that in one direction there is no land before the Arctic Circle. Far away, in a different direction, near another sea, Rhona is waiting.

He trudges over the shingle in the direction of the dull outline of Cromer Pier, and having passed all the breakwaters, halts at a favourite spot where he and Eva had sometimes fished. Will we ever do so again? he wonders, looking up to the cliffs, unstable masses of geology in slow surrender to the sea. A recent landslip has exposed an acrid black silt which is leaching to the beach, a wound in the coastline. As he walks away from the foot of the cliffs towards the sea, the cries of the feeding birds become louder, but when he approaches they rise and move away from him further along the shore. He wades into a sea less calm than at Waxham two and a half weeks ago, but the breakers are gentle, negotiable. Under his feet the shingle is uneven.

Having checked that his sand eel is secure on the hook, he casts. The line snags. He loses balance and falls. Salt water fills his mouth. Gasping, he tries to stand. Water is filling his waders. In panic he pulls himself above the surface. At last on his feet, he finds he is still holding his rod. His hand is in pain. He sees his right knuckle is bleeding. It must have struck a stone when he fell. He staggers to the shore, each step wrested from the damp weights round his legs. On the beach he removes his waders, pouring out the sea water. He removes his wet socks and wrings them out. For some time he sits on the shingle, looking over the leaden sea which had almost claimed him. The sun rises and the outline of the pier becomes sharper. Out to sea a crab boat appears, moving parallel with the coast. He carries the container of sand eels to the water's edge and releases them. Walking back to his van, he does not dwell on the morning's failures. His thoughts are only on Rhona.

# 17

---

'Come on, give it some beans,' says a man in the seat behind Russ, as the plane accelerates for take-off.

Luke looks out through the porthole on his left, then to his right at Russ, head in a book but eyes closed, as the plane lifts above the runway.

'Up, up and hooray,' sings the unseen passenger.

Russ winces, his lips atremble as if uttering a prayer. Luke wants to ask, 'If you're like this now, what are you like on one of your flights to Canada?' but decides not to disturb a suspended animation, so different from yesterday's backseat chatter in the taxi on their way to Southampton.

The plane gains height and turns south, the cabin crew begin their sales and Russ steels himself to look towards the porthole before quickly returning to his paperback. Luke smiles; now is clearly not the time to resume conversation. It is only later, when the captain announces that they are skirting Paris that Russ looks up. White-faced, not risking a view of the clouds, he glances at Luke.

'I can't abide looking out of the window,' says Russ. 'Especially if I see the wing wobbling up and down. I know it's meant to, but it still scares the life out of me.'

Luke closes the porthole shutter.

Russ's colour is restored when Luke buys him a coffee, but in turbulence some is spilt on his red and white Hawaiian shirt. Twenty minutes later, in further turbulence, he drops into feigned sleep, punctuated by more mouthed prayers.

Luke reopens the shutter and gazes down at the clouds, relishing the freedom of being hundreds of miles from home, the shop, customers, and . . . Eva – the name seems to have attached itself to the list by mistake, as if someone else has added it. He wants to delete it. How can he be glad to be away from her, when he should be at her side in Ireland? He eases his conscience by recalling her words to him in her last email: *Enjoy yourselves and don't waste money phoning. I'll see the photos when you get back.*

As he looks at the mosaic of browns and greens below, the feeling of release from all things familiar reasserts itself without qualification. Rhona – it is so long since they were together. Their phone calls have always been too short, the shadow of a relationship. Above the drone of the jet engines he can hear her voice. He tries to recapture the moment when, sitting with her in the parlour, he wondered if her presence would summon a butterfly. He closes his eyes. He sees her hand on her white towelling robe. He feels her stroke his head.

As soon as the plane touches ground Russ closes his book and with relief takes in the view of Bastia airport. Disembarking, he is quick down the steps. He looks up in gratitude and smiles as he inhales a heat shimmering with aviation fuel. As they trail through arrivals and are waved through passport control Luke, unable to keep up, loses him among other passengers, only rejoining him at the baggage carousel.

'This always reminds me of some mechanical giant vomiting indigestible food,' says Russ. 'And my case is always last through its epiglottises – is that the plural?'

'Ask Alden. He'll know.' Luke finds himself echoing Rhona's disparaging tone.

With retrieved luggage and after a search for the car hire desk and a longer search the car itself, they head out of the airport. Luke is at the wheel of the Peugeot 207. Russ clutches a Michelin map and Alden's directions.

On the N198, before they switch on the aircon, Russ leans through the window. 'Just smell the maquis,' he says. 'The guide book was right.'

'I bet it will be even more pungent when we leave the coast road,' says Luke. On the horizon to their right he makes out the silhouettes of mountains.

'Aren't those cork oaks?' says Russ, pointing. 'This reminds me of Majorca.' He launches into an account of a past holiday.

Luke barely listens to Russ's story of losing his wallet in Palma. He throws occasional glances past Russ's head. Somewhere among the mountains is Santa Marta. And Rhona.

'Don't you agree?' asks Russ.

'Sorry, I was concentrating on the road.'

'Always keep wallet and passport with you.'

'Of course. When do we turn off?'

'Not until Solenzara. I'll tell you when. Now my favourite trip that holiday was to Pollença . . .'

Luke's mind returns to Rhona until Russ directs him to the D268 where the sharp bends of the mountain road demand full concentration. Russ is now silent.

\* \* \*

Late morning on Thursday, at the bedside Eva watches Barbara open her eyes, dull at first, but within a minute alert, like embers rekindled.

'I want you to do one final thing for me,' Barbara says.

'Of course. Anything.'

'You haven't brought your rod with you, I suppose.'

'I dashed over here with no more than a suitcase.'

'Never mind. If you go down to my flat you'll find one.'

'You want me to go fishing?'

'I want to see you cast one last time. Go out onto the lawn down there and I'll watch you from the window.'

'You want to see me rod in hand?'

'With line and fly as well.'

Eva looks out of the window towards the front garden.

'Now move my bed round a little and I'll see you perfectly.'

Eva moves the bed a few inches to give Barbara a clear view. 'Give me five minutes.'

Before going down to Barbara's flat Eva calls into the matron's office and explains Barbara's request.

'That solves a mystery,' says the matron. 'In the night she was mumbling incomprehensibly about you and fishing. We thought it might be delirium.'

'No-one will mind if they see a strange woman dry casting on the lawn?'

'I doubt if anyone here will give it a second thought.'

In the flat Eva is disturbed by the sight of familiar furnishings, somehow different now that Barbara is not among them. It is as if each chair, table and picture is in a state of waiting. Above a desk, a rectangle on a wall, a shade lighter than its surround, marks the place where the painting of the Limerick house had hung. She drops onto the sofa, unable to suppress the thought that on her aunt's behalf she is saying goodbye to these furnishings. Her eyes rest on a Victorian bookcase filled with rows of books on angling and gardening. Three rod bags are propped up against one end. She wants to set about her duty but the atmosphere in the flat compels her to remain seated. She looks at the desk chair which speaks of its owner through the wear on the upholstered seat and arms. The cushion, covered with old Aubusson tapestry, is shaped and frayed by years of use. When she dies, thinks Eva, this chair will also lose its spirit.

She forces herself towards the three rods. Although following Barbara's instructions, to untie their canvas bags is an intrusion, but as soon as she handles them she is aware that this is a duty which must be performed with due respect. Having laid them on the floor, she selects the newest. In a fishing bag hanging in the kitchen she finds a reel with line. A fly line and leader are still attached. Deciding that there is enough space in the flat for the task, she slots the two parts of the rod together and threads the line. Examining the contents of two pouches of flies in the fishing bag, she sees that some of them have rusted hooks or are dishevelled beyond recognition. As she stares at the bright-coloured rows of hair, feather and fur in front of her, she hears Barbara telling her as a child, 'Any colour as long as it's black.' Eva pulls out a zulu fly which, with its black body obeys the old adage, but with its red tail should make it visible on the grass for herself, if not for Barbara. She ties it on, and with a pair of nail scissors from the bedroom cuts off the loose end from the knot. Having checked that the knot is tight, she slips the scissors into the back pocket of her jeans.

Duty overcoming a sense of the absurd, Eva leaves the flat and walks to the lawn, positioning herself where, she judges, Barbara can see her. Her calculation is confirmed when, looking up, she sees the matron's head appear at the window, followed by a thumbs up. Eva looks around the front garden, glad no-one else is in sight. She stands to one side of the founder's bust and targets the far end of the lawn. It takes time to adjust to the unfamiliar rod, but after letting out what seems to be sufficient line, she finally lets the fly drop. It falls about three metres short of the intended spot. Eva frowns, flicks up the line and drawing out some more backing, casts again. Once again, the zulu falls short, and the third cast is no better. The fourth is effortless, and the fly drops at the very edge of the lawn. Eva turns round and looks up to the window. This time she sees the matron extend her hands in front of her and applaud. Eva lays the rod on the lawn and goes to join them.

'Did you see me?' Eva asks as she enters Barbara's room where the bed has now been moved back and the matron has left.

'I did, and you have remembered everything I taught you.'

Eva sits down on the bedside chair.

'Apart from one thing,' continues Barbara. 'Never leave your rod where someone might tread on it. You don't want one of these old fools round here standing on it and breaking the tip. Now go and put it away.'

Glad to see Barbara returned to her familiar self, Eva goes back to the lawn and reels in the zulu which bounces towards her like a tiny, obedient pet. She lifts it and cuts it off the line. As she dismantles the rod, the two pieces part with the familiar sound of rushing air. She has a sudden memory of holding a flag at a girl guide parade when she was eleven. Afterwards, taking the pieces of the pole apart, one end had come out of its tubular brass socket with a similar noise. Wondering why this distant memory of another ritual had resurfaced, she walks back to the building.

In the flat, with a sad finality, she replaces the rod in its canvas bag and returns reel and fly pouch to the bag on the kitchen door. Before leaving, she sits at Barbara's desk, looking at the clutter of objects on its ink-stained green leather top. There are two millefiori paper weights she remembers from an early age. She lifts one up to her eyes and stares into the flowerheads imagining, as she did years ago, that she is a diver above a coral reef. Before leaving, she pauses by a small blanket box near the door. Kneeling down, she lifts the lid and inhales the smell of camphor wood, unsurprised at her desire to renew yet another childhood pleasure. Inside the box are old newspapers and postcards. Quickly she closes the lid. There will be a time to examine the contents. Not today.

When Eva returns to Barbara she finds her tired, as if the simple act of looking through a window has exhausted her. In silence Eva sits with her until lunchtime when she helps feed her, but Barbara takes only a few mouthfuls. Eva reaches for the glass of water.

'At least have a drink,' Eva tells her.

'Not yet. I am ready you know.'

'I understand.'

'Do you?' Barbara pauses and only with effort continues speaking. 'Everything is in order. I've left all of it to you. This place has taken a slice of the cake, but there's still plenty left and I want you to enjoy it.' She struggles to take a breath. Rasping, she says 'The sister has some final instructions, but don't bother with those until the time comes.' Barbara's head sinks back on her pillow. She closes her eyes.

\* \* \*

After Luke has negotiated twenty kilometres of steep ascent, skirting the Solenzara river, Russ announces, 'At the next bend we take the road on the left. Alden's note says, *Ignore the road signs.*'

Through thick woodland, Luke turns down a side road, uneasy as they pass a *Route Barrée* sign. He lowers a window and is struck by the smell of the maquis. They follow a series of signs prohibiting lorries and coaches and giving warnings of falling rocks. The road, potholed and badly surfaced, rises steeply. Near the top of an incline is another, much larger, *Route Barrée* sign.

'Are you certain this is the right road?' Luke asks.

'Alden says in his notes that we are to forget the signs and keep going. Worth it for the views, even if it's longer than the other way. Personally I think we should have ignored him, but there's no turning back now.'

Near what seems to be the highest point of their climb, the road, barely more than a track, disappears in a clearing among pine trees. Since the main road they have not seen another vehicle. Luke stops the car. He and Russ look at each other, bewildered by the remote place where Alden's directions have left them stranded. Towering over them on the left is a forbidding rock face. Above its knuckle-bone summit a bird of prey hovers, a black line against a pale blue sky. Apart from a whisp of breeze, the clearing is silent.

'Over there,' says Russ, pointing to a gap between the pines. 'Alden says that near the top the road almost peters out. This must be it.'

Unconvinced, Luke restarts the engine and cautiously moves over the rough ground. As they near the trees he sees, in an opening, a partly tarmacked track and bumps his way towards it. After about two hundred metres the track becomes a road which dips through a dense forest before climbing again, with sheer drops first on one side of the road, then the other. Russ, in pointed silence, clutches his seat. Levelling, the road continues through a gorge, the rock face almost vertical on each side. There are no passing places. Luke dreads an oncoming vehicle. To his relief there is none. After a few minutes they arrive at a sharp bend beyond which the road widens. Open-mouthed, he stops the car. In front of them the mountains fall down through forests of pine and oak. In the far distance there is a glimmer of sea. At intervals the zigzagging road is discernible in spectacular descent before being lost among a range of lower mountains. There is no building in sight. The view is flanked by walls of rock rising out from the trees and with vegetation diminishing towards jagged peaks. The summits to their left glow yellow in the afternoon sun. Luke struggles to accept that a few hours earlier they had been at Bastia airport whose noise and concrete have now receded to a distant past, old memories of another holiday.

'Somewhere down there must be Santa Marta,' says Russ.

'Perhaps they have the binoculars trained on us.'

'If I were Alden I'd be thankful we've made it this far.'

'We'll take a different route when we return. I couldn't do this again. Shall we stretch our legs before heading down?'

For a few minutes they stand by the car to absorb the view and inhale the aromatic mix of pine and mountain herbs.

The descent proves longer than they had judged from the summit, but the road, despite its twists and variable widths, has fewer potholes than its counterpart on the ascent. The danger is not so much the occasional steep drop at the edge, but fallen branches which have partly blocked the road. On a hairpin bend, they are halted by a stubborn goat, hind legs rooted to the road and front legs on a bank, its head pulling at tufts of grass. At a junction, a kilometre further on, they see a signpost. One arm points to Zonza. It seems more a walker's path than a road. The other arm indicates Santa Marta.

'So it does exist,' says Russ.

'Could you doubt Alden?'

Russ opens his eyes wide and looks towards the sky.

It is the top of the church tower which they see first, pinkish brown where it is struck by the sun, an arched upper chamber without louvres or bell. For a minute it disappears among trees, but soon reappears above the rooftops of a village in a natural bowl almost completely surrounded by mountains. Before they enter the village the road ceases to be tarmac, and they rumble over a surface of rough flags and cobbles until arriving at the corner of a square. Stone bollards prevent vehicles from entering. On three sides of the square are buildings. The partly ruined church is in one corner. The fourth side is rough ground. It borders a gulley with woodland beyond.

'La Place des Pèlerins. And that must be the summer school,' says Russ, pointing to a large heavily-restored building on their right. 'And beyond the terrace next to it must be Lynton's house. The church, what remains of it, is next door. Alden's notes say Les Puits is at the lower end of the square.'

Luke drives down a back road behind a range of buildings, all clearly of great age but like the summer school converted to their present use. One is now a small hotel, another a restaurant. Further down, beyond a car park, they see a sign forbidding vehicles. 'Ignore it,' says Russ. 'We park beside Les Puits.'

As they round a right-angle bend at the end of the road, Russ directs Luke through a wide entrance between gateposts topped with weathered stone balls and into a yard dominated by an ancient olive tree. There are no other cars. To their left is a large granite house of three floors, all of whose irregularly-placed windows have dark green shutters. A massive arched double door is closed, but a smaller door to one side is half open. *Les Puits* is carved into one of its stone jambs. Luke parks beyond the tree by a wall covered in flowers of morning glory.

Before they are out of the car the small door opens and Rhona appears in a long-sleeved white linen dress and red sandals which match her fingernails, her hair tied in a messy bun. Beaming and lifting both arms in welcome, she runs towards them. For a moment Luke is too excited to move from his seat and Russ is first out of the car. Rhona greets him with a hug and kisses him on each cheek.

'You look lovely,' says Russ. 'I would say you look like you've stepped out of a Venetian painting, but I won't, since not everyone would take that as a compliment.'

As soon as Luke steps out of the car Rhona gives him a prolonged hug. 'I've missed you so much, I've done nothing but count down the hours before you join me. The others have gone off to Bonifacio today for a boat trip and I've been glad of some peace, away from all their madness.' When they have kissed she says, 'Now tell me about your journey. I always worry when Alden gets people to drive over the mountains on that impossible road.'

'There was a moment when we thought it had vanished.'

'He took me that way on my first visit. To scare me, I think.'

'It terrified us,' says Russ.

'I've said I'll never do it again.' She turns to Luke and says softly, 'Mind you, if it were just you and me and you insisted . . . Come and see the house.'

Inside, Luke and Russ stand in the cool of a large stone-paved hallway and blink as they adjust to the dark interior. There is no furniture apart from a rustic bench and a painting of a saint holding a book. Russ examines its gilt frame.

'Home from home,' says Luke.

'This used to be the old monastery's guest house,' says Rhona. 'Lynton moved here when it was the only habitable house in a deserted village. Mathilde hung that painting as a gesture towards the house's origins. After he rebuilt the old monastery buildings, they kept this for friends to use at a nominal rent.' She sees Russ examining the bench. 'Alden says that's made of solid walnut.'

'Well, I hate to disagree,' says Russ, 'but I'm sure it's chestnut.'

'Oh, do tell Alden that – he hates to be corrected.' Rhona throws open another door.

Russ and Luke find themselves looking into an internal courtyard, half of which is covered by a vine shading a large refectory table and a dozen rush-seated chairs. The far wall is cloistered. Beyond its central arch Luke sees a door, partly open, through which La Place des Pèlerins is visible. Dotted about the courtyard are earthenware pots of herbs. In one corner is a stone well.

Rhona bends and runs her fingers through some stems of basil. 'Herbs are doubly fragrant here. This is where we eat in the evenings.'

'And if it rains?' asks Russ.

'The basil smells even better,' she laughs. 'And we can eat in the kitchen. Follow me.'

She walks back across the courtyard, pausing to point at a large green lizard high on a wall, before leading them back into the house to a kitchen with a single tap above a stone sink under the room's only window. On the sill stand pots of marjoram. The only furnishings are an old food cupboard, a small fridge and odd chairs round a kitchen table on which is a jar of white flowers whose scent fills the room.

'Not many mod cons, I'm afraid,' she says. 'And no hot water, but we do have an electric kettle. The tap water's fine to drink, but the water from the well is fantastic. There used to be another well outside but that's been filled in.' She points to a jug on the table. 'Felix has taken it upon himself to keep the jug topped up. He's the only one of us who enjoys winding the bucket up and down.' She pours them each a glass. 'Now don't look for the bathroom because there isn't one, but we do have a shower – only cold of course. But there are, amazingly, two loos.'

When they have each finished a second glass of water, she says, 'Let me show you your rooms.'

At the top of a stone staircase on the first floor Rhona shows Russ to a small room with his name chalked on the pine door. 'You have a view of the stream – quite dry at this time of year – and the old stone bridge, and if you strain your neck you can see the church. The tower's the only old bit. What's left of the interior is now a gallery for the school.'

Leaving Russ in his room, Rhona leads Luke up a wooden staircase to the second floor. On the landing she opens a plank door on which, as with Russ's room, his name is chalked in Rhona's writing. Inside the bedroom she goes to a window, draws back the white curtains and pushes open the shutters. 'You get a great view of the mountains.' Together they gaze through the window.

'My favourite time here is early morning, before everyone is up, and before holiday-makers arrive. It's the best time for a swim.'

'Can I join you?'

'I insist on it. We'll tiptoe out at six. Now, over here . . .' She goes to a small window on the opposite side. 'Here you can look down on the courtyard and listen to any late-night gossip.' She points to a window with half-open shutters. 'That's my . . . our room. Thankfully, Alden and I have single beds.' She takes hold of his hand and gently pushes him onto the bed and sits beside him. 'It's only the thought of you joining me which has kept me sane. But to be away from Alden right now I'd settle for a Blackpool boarding house, as long as I could share it with you.' She kisses him passionately, runs her fingers through his hair, then strokes the shoulder of his navy shirt. 'I thought this was linen but it isn't, is it?'

'Hemp.'

'Really? Can we put it to another use?'

'The label says, *This fabric cannot be smoked.*'

'If ever a warning were a challenge . . .' She kisses him. 'I had this nightmare when you were away that you were drowning.'

'I almost did.'

'No.' She grasps his arms. 'What happened?'

'Yesterday, early in the morning, I was bass fishing. I lost my footing, wading near the shore.'

She grips him tighter.

'I was under the water. My boots were filling, weighing me down. I had to fight to stand.'

'Poor darling. But how did I know?' She brushes his forehead. 'Do you believe in telepathy?'

'When I reached the shore I thought of you.'

'Thank God you're safe.'

In the cool of the shuttered room her perfume has gained a muskiness he has not sensed before. He is desperate to make love but knows this is not the time.

'We'd better find Russ,' she says. 'I'll make us some proper drinks before the hordes return.'

As they go downstairs she says, 'I've been drinking gallons of white wine spritzers, but the others stick to beer, or some local aperitif mixed with fruit juice which I can't stand. I'm surprised Alden drinks the stuff, but since Lynton likes a glass at lunchtime, I suppose that makes it acceptable.'

'I look forward to meeting Lynton.'

'You'll see him tomorrow.'

In the stone-flagged kitchen Luke and Russ sit and chat with Rhona, enjoying spritzers and slices of almond cake, until the tranquility of the house is disturbed by the sound of two cars entering the yard, followed by the slamming of doors and loud voices.

'Russ, Luke, great to have you here,' says a tanned and perspiring Alden in long white shorts and white seersucker shirt. He pumps their hands. 'How d'you like the road over the mountains? Amazing views, aren't they?' He picks up the jug of water and drinks from it.

'Where the road ends near the top was a challenge,' says Luke.

'It deters all but the most doughty and protects us from through traffic.'

The others, familiar from the dinner at Saffold Farm pile into the kitchen, greeting Luke and Russ with the sort of hugs which, Luke thinks, might be reserved for long-lost friends, not people they have met only once. In the mêlée, he watches Rhona slip away.

'I'm Agnes,' says a girl in baggy yellow shorts and orange shirt. 'I'm helping Rhona with the wardrobe.'

'We call her the head prefect,' laughs Felix.

'So watch your behaviour,' says Josh.

'Ignore them,' says Agnes. 'I do.' She looks Luke and Russ up and down. 'I think the costumes we've got for you will fit. You can try them on later.'

Luke returns to his room and lies on the bed. Closing his eyes, he recovers from the journey. Slowly, he is aware of a preternatural stillness in the house, undisturbed even by the sounds of movement and voices elsewhere in the building. Has he ever, even in the seclusion of his own home experienced this degree of quiet? Perhaps, in the old greenhouse at the allotments, there have occasionally been hints of it but here the feeling is so much deeper, as if Les Puits is making him part of itself. He must explore.

The rooms near his, by the names on the doors, are occupied by Felix and Josh, but round a corner at the end of the corridor is a brown-painted door on which is pinned a notice: *STORE – PRIVATE*. The two words ignite in him the inveterate inquisitiveness of the dealer. He tries the handle but the door is locked. He looks both ways along the empty corridor before running his fingers along the head of the door frame where he feels only dust on its thick moulding. Noticing that the architrave has partly moved away from the wall, he again runs his fingers along, this time probing with his fingertips the cavity between architrave and wall, a hope rewarded by the feel of a key tucked in the recess. It proves impossible to prise out with fingers alone, but with the help of his car key he lifts it from its hiding place. From its age and rust he suspects the door lock might have changed since the key was hidden, but despite these doubts he inserts it through the door's iron escutcheon. Repeated attempts fail to turn the lock. Perhaps his suspicions were correct and it is the wrong key. Or the lock is too rusty. Risking more force he makes a further attempt. This time the key turns and with such ease that he imagines some unknown helper on the other side of the door has oiled the lock for him, an impression reinforced when without noise the door swings opens. He removes the key and enters. The imagined assistant has not materialised and he finds himself in what seems to be a windowless room, but as his eyes adjust he sees blades of dusty light stealing through a small shuttered arch on his right. There is no sign of an electric light or a switch on the walls near the door. After a final look over his shoulder, he pushes the door until it is almost closed, leaving only a small gap through which a faint light seeps from the corridor.

The floor is a clutter of cardboard boxes, piled two or three high, through which there is barely space to move towards the window, or to the wall on his left. Where the walls are visible there are patches of decayed plaster. Opening the box closest to hand, he finds it packed with books. He removes a few and reads their titles, all crime novels by Gaston Leroux and Georges Simenon. To handle them is to be accused of trespass. He moves to another box near the centre of the room. It is full of art books and catalogues of old exhibitions. He pulls out a Matisse exhibition catalogue of 1910 and thumbs through it, wondering about its value. He replaces it with care on a pile of other catalogues of equal rarity. The remaining boxes contain only old curtains and kitchen ware.

Moving to the window he stares through a chink in the shutters and finds he overlooks the courtyard where he sees Alden, standing near the well with Louise. She has exchanged the shorts he remembers her wearing in the kitchen for a salmon pink dress. They are deep in conversation, but he cannot hear their voices. Louise rests a hand on Alden's forearm and leads him away from the well and out of vision.

Turning away from the window, he notices on the opposite wall a faint glimmer from an object almost totally hidden behind plastic crates. Moving to them he sees they are full of old shoes. Behind them he finds the single side of a small tabernacle frame. He lifts it and examines its gilding and back. Replacing it, he notices a double cupboard fitted into the far end of the wall. Stepping over a heap of old rugs, he opens the door to see that half the cupboard has shelves heavy with old tins of paint. In the right-hand unshelved cupboard are some worn-out hand tools, but in front of a long bundle strapped in canvas he finds the three companion sides of the frame wrapped in torn brown paper. He smiles, wondering whether a little dealing might be combined with the holiday. He crouches and inspects their condition. Pleased to find there is little damage, he rewraps them with care. He is about to investigate the canvas bundle when he hears sounds from the corridor, perhaps footsteps. He freezes. The footsteps pass by. When all is silent he closes the cupboard. Careful to make no noise as he negotiates the piles of boxes, he moves to the door and looks out into the corridor. It is empty. He steps out, locks the door and replaces the key where he found it.

As he returns to his room he imagines a conversation with Lynton, and sees himself driving from Les Puits in a week's time, the four sides of the broken frame neatly packed in the top of his case, along perhaps with the rare catalogues. But as he sits on his bed he hears Eva's words on the way to dinner at Saffold Farm, 'Always the dealer,' and remembers a tone in her voice, unregistered until now. It was less joking than critical. Perhaps she already knew about him and Rhona.

# 18

When the evening rehearsal is about to begin Luke stands by the well, script in hand, nervous. Not yet in total shade, the courtyard is a reservoir of heat. He is encouraged by the fact that few of the others are carrying scripts – a sign perhaps that they have no need of his prompting. Felix and Josh, shirtless, push the table back against a wall to make an acting space. Louise, wearing a diaphanous dress over a bikini, is flexing and stretching. Luke looks towards the opposite corner. Russ, now in khaki shorts, is going through his lines with Agnes.

'Odd couple, aren't they?'

Luke sees Rhona beside him, placing a large jug of iced water and some plastic beakers on a flagstone. 'Ban on alcohol until after rehearsals,' she says.

'Still appearing from nowhere?'

'Shall I stop it?'

'Please don't.'

Rhona again looks towards Russ and Agnes. 'Russ has a new friend.'

'Agnes gave me an odd look when she introduced herself. Does she know about us?'

'Yes, but it doesn't matter – she's discreet and she can't stand Alden.'

'Where is the great director?'

'In the kitchen, slicing local salami and talking to Matthew. That's the guy who's doing the lighting and special effects. Sensibly, he's booked in at the hotel.'

A dozen cast members Luke has not seen before enter the courtyard. Cassie is with them. The brilliant designs of their tops and shorts make Russ's Hawaiian shirt look dreary.

Rhona squeezes Luke's arm. 'The rest of the contingent from the summer school. They went to Ajaccio last weekend and cleaned up on *Desigual*. I'll introduce you.'

Luke is exchanging handshakes and asking who plays which part when from the centre of the courtyard Alden silences everyone with a clap of his hands. 'Act Two. Straight into the Lost Boys – no need to rehearse the mermaid dance.'

Rhona and Agnes disappear towards the kitchen, pausing to talk to a man Luke assumes is Matthew. Bald-headed, wearing loose denims and carrying a Panama hat, he stands to one side scribbling notes in a small leather-bound notebook.

Half an eye on Russ for whom stagecraft is second nature, Luke follows the other pirates, joining in the thunderous *yo hos* and finding Felix's visceral Hook a terrifying experience at close quarters. He is glad of his early exit and a word-perfect cast who leave him blissfully unwanted for most of the act.

Before Act Three Matthew, quietly-spoken with a Yorkshire accent, introduces himself to Luke, then to Russ with whom he strikes an immediate rapport. When the play permits, Russ gravitates towards him.

As the rehearsal progresses, Luke's eyes are focused more on the kitchen door and he wonders if it will be noticed if he slips away. But increasingly he finds himself drawn into the play. Josh's Peter is impressively mercurial, while Lou's Tinkerbell is both cunning and flirty, using her supple limbs and balletic skills in an uninhibited attempt to seduce Peter. She leaps in delight when Wendy is struck by Tootles's arrow, and performs a jubilant dance when the pirates appear with the captured and bound Tiger Lily, played by a French student, Thérèse. Luke hopes that there will be a break in rehearsal after Act Three but Alden calls out, 'Straight into Act Four.'

'We must have a drink first,' says Josh.

'But you had time for that when you were offstage,' shouts Alden.

'Hey, chill out, man,' calls Felix.

'Two minutes,' orders Alden.

Felix, Cassie, Josh and Louise talk quietly to each other as they pour themselves some water. Luke cannot hear their conversation, but suspects some conspiracy against Alden.

Agnes appears during the break with velvet coats for Luke and Russ. Luke's fits perfectly. Russ's is too tight. 'I'll let that out. Now you needn't wear them until the dress rehearsal,' she says, and walks over to the actor playing Michael, Dan, a sculpture student from Boston who kisses her as she helps him pull on a voluminous nightshirt.

The cast race through the fourth act.

'Slow up. Take this seriously,' shouts Alden.

'Hey, Alden, this *is* meant to be light-hearted,' says Cassie.

'But not a farce,' says Alden. 'Tinkerbell almost dying is a poignant moment.'

The remainder of the rehearsal continues almost without interruption. Peter's 'And now to rescue Wendy' signals not only the end of the act but also supper time. The summer school contingent, apart from Cassie, leave for their own canteen, while Josh grabs one end of the table, Felix the other, initiating a scramble to set supper – clearly a routine which over the last few days has established itself.

Within five minutes bread, olives and various dips are on the table, with bottles of beer and wine in large pottery jugs. Luke sits between Russ and Cassie, looking out towards the middle of the courtyard. When Rhona and Agnes appear, they sit together at the end of the table. A little later Alden approaches the table with three enormous bowls of pasta, two with salami, one with shellfish. Bowls of salad follow. Alden sits himself opposite Luke and Russ, a position which, Luke guesses, allows him to be part of any of the animated conversations already echoing round the courtyard.

Above the noise Russ shouts, 'To our hosts.'

After a clinking of glasses, Russ says to Luke, 'We could be back at Saffold Farm.'

Only, there is no Eva, thinks Luke, as he allows himself to catch Rhona's eye. She blows him a discreet kiss. He thinks Agnes saw it, but doesn't care. He watches Alden slowly dominate the banter and provoke repartie with all-comers.

Mid-supper, Josh asks Felix, 'Is *Peter Pan* just as popular your side of the pond?'

'Pretty much,' says Felix.

'Who first called the Atlantic a pond, I wonder?' says Louise.

'Some twentieth-century executive, I suppose,' says Felix. 'When air travel had shrunk the distance.'

'You're years out,' says Cassie. 'It goes back at least to the 1800s.'

'For example?' asks Alden.

'Any number of American writers.'

'For example?'

The table is hushed.

'Too many to name.'

'Name me one.'

Cassie reddens. She claws her hair in desperate thought and looks down at the pine boards of the table, as if a name might write itself on the weathered surface.

Opposite, Alden is triumphant. 'Can I encourage your memory with a small bet?'

'I don't want to take your money,' she says nervously.

'We could bet something else.'

'What are you after, Alden?' says Josh.

'He wants her body,' says Felix in a stage whisper.

'Make it a round hundred euros,' says Josh.

Cassie scowls at Josh, says nothing and again fixes her eyes on the table top.

'A hundred euros it is,' says Alden. 'I think my money's safe.'

The smugness on Alden's face makes Luke want to say to Cassie, 'take your time, I'll cover your bet.' Luke looks round the table. Rhona's stare says, don't get involved.

Alden looks up at the vine. 'As my tutor at Oxford always said, "Never state facts when you can't give your sources".'

Cassie slowly raises her head and looks Alden in the face. 'Harriet Beecher Stowe. In the introduction to the novel *Dred*. 1850s.'

Alden opens his mouth but remains speechless.

'Seems like Cassie's just won a hundred euros,' says Felix.

'I'd like to check the book,' says Alden.

Cassie stretches a hand across to Alden. 'Want to make it two hundred. It will be there. Definitely. In the text.'

Alden looks at her unblinking green eyes. 'OK, you win,' he says.

The table is all smiles, followed by guffaws. Alden smiles last, but sardonically, unable to laugh, as slowly he realises that the whole conversation from pond to *Dred* has been orchestrated, leading him to lose a hundred euros. With difficulty he affects some good humour. 'You bastards are better actors than I thought.'

'And we'll be even better come Saturday night,' says Cassie.

They continue eating, the table talk fuelled by free-flowing alcohol, but Alden has lost his bravado. As Josh is telling a joke, a loud bang echoes round the courtyard, followed two seconds later by another. Luke and Russ exchange startled looks. Luke is certain they were rifle shots, but to his amazement no-one else is concerned.

'Only the locals having a go at the wild boar,' Alden tells him. 'The season started a few days ago. You'll hear the odd bang, but it's mainly dawn and dusk – Santa Marta's version of the reveille and last post.'

'So we might get noises off during the performance?' says Russ.

'Hopefully not. Lynton spread the word that we'd appreciate some peace during the play. Even better, they'll all be in the audience.'

'How many are you expecting?' asks Russ.

'Two hundred plus. A couple of coach parties are coming, one from Porto-Vecchio.'

At around 10.00pm Luke sees Rhona and Agnes leave the table. A few minutes later he gets to his feet. 'Alden, you must excuse me. The drive over the mountains sapped all my energy.'

'But wasn't it worth it? Ten o'clock tomorrow. Straight into the final act.'

Luke goes to his room, finds a towel, locates the primitive shower on the floor below, and spends the briefest time possible beneath its begrudging nozzle. Returning to his room, he finds Rhona on his bed, naked.

'How tired are you?' she says.

Luke turns his head towards the window through which voices can be heard.

'Forget about them,' she says. 'And Alden's far more interested in Louise than me and you.'

As he undresses Luke notices three purple-brown oval bruises on her left forearm.

'Alden,' she says. Then louder, 'It's always bloody Alden.'

'He punched you?'

'He probably wanted to. These are just his finger marks where he gripped me.' She turns her arm and Luke sees a circular mark much larger than the others. 'His thumb,' she says.

'He's insane. Was he angry about us?' Luke lies beside her.

'It's not about us. He got to bed late two nights ago. I was deeply asleep. The smell of the drink on him woke me before he slammed the door and kicked his shoes across the floor. He was obviously too drunk to realise what he was repeating aloud, "The cow, the little cow." I knew immediately he had had some argument with Louise. It was her he was swearing about. I pretended I was still asleep. He was soon dead to the world, snoring like a pig. I barely slept myself. When I crept out of bed, he grabbed me by the arm. "Where the hell you going?" he snarled. I think he was still drunk, and probably thought I was Louise. His eyes were half closed. I banged my fist on his arm to make him release me. At first it had no effect, but he slowly relaxed his hold. When his eyes fully opened he looked daggers, not because of me,' she rests a hand on Luke's, 'or us, but because I wasn't the woman he'd been dreaming of.'

Luke looks again at her arm. 'It's like you've been bitten by a dog.'

'A mad one.' She throws back her head. 'But what are a few bruises if they get me away from him. And the good news is that they patched up the tiff yesterday.'

'I saw them earlier in the courtyard – the best of friends.'

'They're more than that. They have plans to shack up together in London or Paris. Isn't that wonderful?'

'How do you know?'

'I'll give you full details tomorrow. But now . . .' She kisses him, lowering his head to the bed.

Luke casts a wary glance to the window, but soon submits to her unspoken confidence that they are safe, while occasional bursts of laughter from the courtyard serve only to increase the excitement.

An hour later, Rhona slips from the bed, pulls on her white dress, bends over Luke's prone body and says, 'I'll be in the kitchen at six.'

* * *

At the bedside, Eva looks at her watch and realises that it is twelve hours since Barbara last spoke. She wonders if her aunt will speak again.

At 11.30pm a night nurse says to Eva, 'You must get some sleep yourself now.'

Eva kisses Barbara and makes her way to her own room where the sight of her bed makes her aware that she is exhausted through a day of waiting. After undressing, she checks her mobile. There is a text message from Annie: *Checked garden. All OK. X to U & aunt.* There is also an email from Agnes: *Sorry to hear about your aunt. Thinking of you. Luke and Russ safely here. Nothing to report re L and R. Will phone tomorrow. X A.* Too tired to reply to either message, she collapses on her bed.

Shortly after 1am Eva is pulled from sleep by knocking at her door. Opening her eyes, she sees a night nurse silhouetted by the light from the corridor.

'Eva, I think you must come to Barbara's room.'

Eva springs from bed and follows the nurse to her aunt's room. The ward sister is sitting beside her. Eva sits on the other side. Barbara's eyes are intermittently open, but she seems unaware of her surroundings.

'She is breathing, but only just,' the sister says quietly.

'Has she been strong enough to speak?'

'An hour ago she woke briefly. I said a few words to her and she said, "Thank you, thank you." That was all.'

'Is she conscious now?'

'It's difficult to know.'

'Do you think she can hear us?'

The sister comes round to Eva's side of the bed and whispers, 'The hearing is often the last faculty to go.'

Eva bends over the bed. 'Auntie, it's me, Eva. I'm with you.'

The sister returns to the other side of the bed. A nurse brings in Eva's dressing gown. Eva looks at Barbara's face for a response but finds none. A few minutes later she sees her aunt's lips quiver and for a moment thinks it is an attempt at speech, but when Barbara's mouth opens it is only to make a small gasp before the weak breathing resumes.

For another hour she sits beside her. A few minutes later, the sister leans over Barbara and touches her head. She turns to Eva. 'She's slipped away now, darling, God rest her soul. It was as peaceful as we could wish.'

For some time Eva sits motionless until, with great care, she rests a hand on Barbara's forehead. It is still warm. 'Goodbye, you old fighter. I love you.' She kisses her head and feeling tears well up, falls back in her seat.

'Stay with her for a few minutes,' the nurse says. 'We'll bring you a drink.'

Eva remains beside Barbara. The face in front of her seems so peaceful it is difficult to accept she has died. She kisses her aunt's cheek. As soon as her lips touch the frail skin she knows Barbara is dead. Eva looks around the room as if wondering where her aunt has gone.

Through her head play stories of out of body experiences of those seemingly near the moment of death, who, on recovering, tell of looking down at themselves from above. And she is reminded of her own parents' deaths – the car accident, the identification of their bodies, the questions she had never been able to ask them. At least she has been beside Barbara. Her death has somehow atoned for those older regrets.

'I've brought you some tea,' says a nurse. She stays with Eva. 'A fine old lady. We shall all miss her, as I'm sure you will.'

'I'm so glad to have been with her.'

'She was well prepared. The priest called on her Saturday evening – our chaplain, a locum from Limerick.'

'The priest? But Barbara never went near a church in her life. She wasn't even a Catholic.'

'She was received into the Church two months ago.'

'She never told me.'

'She left a list of instructions. I can show it to you.'

'I didn't expect...'

'She was adamant the funeral was to be here in Corofin.'

'A church funeral?'

'That was her wish.'

Eva looks at Barbara's still face. 'You were always inscrutable, one step ahead.' She gives Barbara a final kiss on the forehead, then leaves the room.

In the sister's office, Eva is handed an envelope on which is written her name in Barbara's unmistakable handwriting.

'I had strict orders to give it to you only after she had gone,' says the sister.

Eva opens it.

*Dearest Eva, I have prepared for this day. Since I did not want you rushing about organising things on my account, the church, the funeral director and the pub have already been paid. A funeral mass and burial and a drink for my friends is what I wish. My coffin will rest overnight in the church, but you need not be there when it arrives or keep vigil. The following day will be tiring enough. The solicitors in Limerick will answer any questions you have. A copy of my will is in the drawer of my desk. It is simple. Everything goes to you. All other deserving causes have been attended to in my lifetime. Do not grieve, but live your life to the full as I have tried to. Start now. If I hear you've been mourning for more than a day I shall come back and haunt you. With all my love, Barbara.*

Eva smiles at her aunt's power to be in control, even after death. She looks at her aunt's signature. 'I'll do as you instruct,' she says. 'I shall live life to the full. Like you.'

'How soon can a funeral be arranged?' she asks the sister.

\* \* \*

Luke is woken by the alarm on his mobile, but the sparse furnishings and the light stealing through the shutters tell him that he is in his bedroom at home. When reality breaks through, he thinks of the last occasion he and Eva spent a night there, a few weeks ago, but a time during which his life has irrecoverably changed.

In the kitchen Rhona, in a black dress and sandals, is sitting at the table sipping lemongrass tea. Another cup is waiting for him. Yesterday's flowers have wilted, but retain a scent which, blended with the herbs by the window, lingers in the atmosphere of the sunless room. He bends over her to exchange a silent kiss.

'We'll take my car,' she says when they have finished their tea. 'Happily, it's an easier road than your nightmare drive yesterday.'

At the top of the street, by the bollards at the corner of La Place des Pèlerins, Rhona pulls up. 'If you want some amusement,' she says, pointing, 'look over there.'

La Place des Pèlerins is deserted, but on the bridge over the dried-up stream he sees a curiously contorted figure in white.

'Alden, doing his tai chi,' says Rhona. 'I don't know what time he came to bed last night. One or two, I guess, but that won't let him miss his precious exercises. How he survives on four hours' sleep, I'll never know.'

The figure on the bridge now bends and turns towards the maquis, as if about to confront a creature from the forest. Rhona drives away. 'It always looks faintly absurd,' she says. 'Oh dear, you're not a tai chi addict are you?'

'Gardening's my main exercise.'

'Alden insists on disporting himself in a public place. When we arrived here he took to standing in the middle of the courtyard every afternoon, taking his tiger to the mountain, or whatever it is they do, but the boys started leaning out of their windows to take the mickey, so now he performs on the bridge at 6am before anyone can mock him. And

Friday is his running day, so he'll soon be heading off to the hills. Unless his jogging route takes him up to Louise's bedroom.'

The road out of Santa Marta descends through the maquis, rises again among pine woods and after a few miles meets the main road. With the windows down, the car is suffused with mountain herbs, intensified by the cool, early-morning air.

'A new morning and soon a new life,' she says excitedly. 'Let me tell you about Alden's imminent exit. Yesterday morning, as I entered the kitchen, I saw him hide away a piece of paper in his file of director's notes. I was amicable enough as I made myself tea and he was quite chatty about the play and Lynton. But at lunchtime I sneaked a look in his file and found the paper. It was a very neat hand-written list of his financial assets. Money in the bank – rather more than I expected. Shares and investments – nothing substantial. His share of Saffold Farm – the largest sum – we only have a small mortgage. And the value of his one third share in the business. That took up the left column. The right column was sheer delight. It was the cost of a small flat in London. There were also details of an alternative in Paris. Also – more joy and delight – were details of an interest free loan from his brother-in-law to cover any shortfall.' She shouts, 'Wonderful or what!'

'If you need money to buy his share of the house or business, I'm sure I can help.'

'I'd pay back every penny.'

'You wouldn't have to. When do you think he'll be good enough to tell you he's leaving?'

'After the play I would guess. He wouldn't want to risk ructions beforehand. Not that I would cause any.'

Turning off the road onto a stony track, barely wide enough for a car, she says, 'There's a pool on the Solenzara river which will be deserted this time of day.'

The track ends at the edge of what seems like a slow-flowing river, shallow enough to wade across. Leaving the car among a cluster of low oaks, she leads him along the bank, negotiating large boulders towards a bend in the river where the banks steepen. Here the river is narrower and deeper. Climbing to the edge, she smiles, kicks off her sandals and pulls off her dress, revealing a red swimsuit. Luke strips to his swim shorts.

'Just round the corner,' she says, easing herself into the river. She begins to swim at a slow breaststroke. Luke follows, shocked by the iciness of the water and trying not to think of its possible depth. He is now beside her. They swim against a gentle current.

'I once saw a fisherman on the far bank,' she says.

'I should have brought my trout rod.'

As they round the bend the banks become sheer. Luke, feeling trapped by the rock walls and with the cold sapping his muscles, wonders how much further she intends to go. He is now a few metres behind her.

'Almost there,' she shouts, her voice echoing around the canyon.

Ahead, in the centre of the river, he sees a flat-topped rock and realises that this must be their destination. He catches up with her as they arrive at a submerged platform. Together they wade to its dry upper surface. There is no sunlight but immediately he feels warmer to be out of the water. She sits beside him. He can hear in the distance the sound of a waterfall, but the river surrounding them moves slow and silent.

When they have kissed she says, 'Now, really tell me about yourself.'

'Where shall I start?'

'What was your wife like?'

'Leonie and I were only married two months. She conserved paintings.'

'And you would be able to frame them. A marriage made in heaven.'

'Until a man from hell who owned a smart gallery appeared.'

Rhona places her left arm around him. 'Dear Luke. Were you devastated?'

'For months. And then there was the counselling. And Eva.'

'And you fell in love again.'

'More than I had been with Leonie. But Eva's colleagues discovered and the knives came out. She even got letters from one of them going on about relationships with clients never lasting, and that I had clearly transferred all my feelings to my counsellor but the underlying issues had not been resolved.'

'But you stayed together.'

'Until now. Now . . .' He stares down the length of the canyon.

'What, darling?'

'Perhaps her colleagues were right, and I've lived under an emotional shadow for twenty years. Wasting most of my adult life.'

'Not wasting – waiting. Both of us. And you and Eva never lived together?'

'Not under the same roof. Everything but.'

'I want to live with you. Same roof, same bedroom, same bed. Always.'

'We can. I'll do anything, move anywhere to be with you.'

'Can we make plans? Now.'

'Come and live with me. Or we can buy Alden's share of Saffold Farm and I'll live with you there. Just give me a timetable.'

'Either alternative sounds heaven. As soon as he's packed away his last book and left, we'll toss a coin where to live.' Rhona looks up to the clear sky. 'Luke, I feel free now. We only have a few more days to wait before Alden comes clean and tells me he wants an end to this sham of a marriage.'

'Will you be suitably shocked. Outraged?'

'No. I'm beyond that. And he knows it. The last thing I want is to give him a rough time and make him have second thoughts. God, I was so worried when he and Lou had that spat. I had visions of him slinking back like a tom-cat returning home after an adventure. I should have kicked him out after his first affair not long after we were married. But in those days I was susceptible to his charms. He's got this compelling charisma.'

'I've noticed – I felt it when he was he persuading me to close the shop for a week'

'It's a form of control. At its worst quite scary. Remember that look on his face when he told the story of therapist Neville's suicide? It was bad enough he was glad Neville was dead, but . . .'

'He really believed he had triggered it.'

Rhona shivers. 'Let's swim back. It won't take so long. The current will be with us.'

* * *

Eva leaves her room, aware that ahead of a demanding day she has had no sleep. But through the exhaustion, the pain of loss gives way to thoughts of a new beginning in her life. Guilt that she should feel this way is softened by Barbara's letter, spread open on her bed. It is almost 7.00am. She is ready for a St. Anthony's breakfast, but first she must email Helen. She picks up her mobile but the battery is flat and she places it on recharge. Leaving her room, she goes to the library, a spacious room next to the entrance hall and almost immediately below Barbara's room. Here she is alone, but she detects a lingering whiff of tobacco smoke which brings to mind the cheroots Barbara used to smoke while fishing. Perhaps last night a resident had flouted the strict no smoking rule – or perhaps, Eva thinks, Barbara's spirit, at the very last . . . No, the idea is absurd. She opens a window and enjoys the early morning air until, invigorated, she sits down at a desk in front of one of the two communal PCs. She emails Helen with the news of Barbara's death, telling her not even to think of flying back for the funeral. Next she informs Annie. Lastly she emails Luke, forbidding him to entertain any idea he might have of curtailing his holiday.

Eva again looks out to the garden, knowing that Barbara will never again see these once-familiar lawns and flowerbeds. She feels she is about to cry, but the imperative, *Do not grieve*, makes her look to the future. She turns to thoughts about her own garden and longs to be back there. Soon the sounds of voices and trolleys in the building tell her St. Anthony's is beginning a new day. She thinks of Barbara's body in the room above her and wonders if the doctor has already called and left. Should she go up again? Why? Hasn't she already said goodbye? 'Live life to the full,' she says to herself as she walks to the dining room.

Over breakfast Sister Cyra comes to her table to offer condolences. 'I've had a word with Father – the funeral can be on Monday.'

'So soon?' Eva is astonished.

'We seldom have that long wait you sometimes have in England. I suggest today you register the death at the office in Ennis. Someone can accompany you, if you wish.'

'I must do this alone.'

Later, while Eva waits for a taxi to take her to the register office, her recharged phone rings. It is Agnes.

'Agnes, you really don't need to do this. Please don't phone again.'

'I just wanted to keep you in the loop. How is your aunt?'

'She died last night.'

'Oh Eva, I am so sorry, I shouldn't be phoning you. My condolences. I was only going to tell you . . .'

'I don't want to know. In fact you needn't phone me again.'

'I understand. I only thought I was helping.'

'I'm not sure you are. I've been up half the night with a dying woman. Luke hasn't figured much in my thoughts.'

'So you don't want me to contact you again?'

'No.' Eva pauses, regretting her curtness. 'Perhaps we can meet up when you get back. And as far as Luke and me are concerned . . . There is no Luke and me.'

'Don't let Rhona win.'

'She's welcome to him. I mean it. Goodbye, Agnes.' Eva rings off, knowing for the first time that she has little interest in Luke's future, and is surprised at her lack of concern. In the light of Barbara's death he has drifted to the periphery of her life, and it is in the duteous spirit of contacting a friend that she emails him again: *Funeral Monday. No flowers. E.*

\* \* \*

During the morning rehearsal Luke gives the play no more than superficial interest. He trails Russ's Smee, his mind focused on a life with Rhona. There are no practical difficulties and money is not an obstacle. He finds himself half-heartedly joining the pirates in their *yo ho* chorus. And Rhona is right. He and Eva, as a couple, have never in fact been completely . . .

'Prompt,' shouts Felix.

'Hang on,' says Luke, thumbing through Hook's lines.

'We can't wait on the night,' barks Alden. 'The dress rehearsal's this evening and by now we should at least know the bloody words.'

'Stow that, Starkey . . .' says Russ, giving Felix a nudge.

'Thanks, Russ,' says Luke. He longs to leave and be back with Rhona.

He now gives the rehearsal full attention, remembering his three lines and duly screeching offstage when dispatched by Peter.

By midday a seering sun has made an oven of the courtyard and the rehearsal ends.

'Dress – eight, on the steps. And in costume by half seven,' orders Alden before disappearing to the hotel to talk lighting with Matthew. Most of the others disperse to the café or summer school.

Luke and Russ find Rhona at their side. 'You must meet Lynton and Mathilde,' she says.

Leaving through the cloister gate, they walk up towards the school. Luke is struck by the tranquility of the village, so guarded from the outside world by mountains, maquis and forest, that even the voices from the café and hotel barely disturb it.

Russ notices Agnes and Dan following at a distance. 'I think your employee has found an admirer,' he says

'I would reprimand her for cradle-snatching,' Rhona says, 'but in the circumstances . . .' She gives Luke a gentle punch on the shoulder.

As they enter the summer school's main building Luke is reminded of a village hall, except the walls and floor are stone. Seated in an arc in the centre of the room are nine students at their easels, drawing or painting a woman with long grey hair, wearing a floral print dress and seated on an imposing Italian armchair.

'That's Mathilde,' says Rhona. 'She often sits for them.'

Luke notices, last of all, a small old man in loose blue denim trousers and khaki shirt, carrying a walking stick and bent over a student's work, pointing to an area of the canvas.

'Lynton?' asks Luke.

'Still teaching at eighty-nine,' she says.

They watch him move to another student's work, pause, examine a drawing and at last walk towards them. Luke sees that despite his age he retains most of his hair, white over bushy eyebrows which meet above a long nose, giving the impression of a wary animal peering out from beneath a hedge.

'Rhona,' he says, 'you must introduce me to your guests.'

Rhona introduces Lynton to Russ and Luke who finds the handshake warm but cautious.

'You must join us for lunch,' Lynton says. 'Mathilde will descend from her throne in a few minutes. Go ahead. We'll catch you up. Open some wine, Rhona.'

Rhona, leads them to the house next door, a smaller version of Les Puits. In the courtyard, instead of pots of herbs, there is figurative and abstract sculpture. She shows them into a kitchen, modern, apart from its stone floor. Luke looks at Rhona.

'Yes,' she says, 'Alden had this in mind when he fitted out ours, God help us.' She goes to a fridge. 'Rosé alright?'

When Mathilde and Lynton arrive Rhona helps prepare lunch. Lynton sits with Luke and Russ.

'So you deal in mirrors,' he says. 'And do you frame pictures too?'

'A little,' says Russ, 'when we have to. But mirrors are the core business. We buy, sell and restore them.'

'That's good,' smiles Lynton. 'The professional framer is always an artist *manqué*. A difficult breed.'

'And artists can be difficult too,' says Mathilde, approaching them with an assortment of bread in baskets.

'I won't argue,' says Lynton. 'Those days are over.'

Rhona joins them, bringing salad and cold meats.

'Are you looking forward to *Peter Pan*?' asks Luke.

'I shall enjoy it, yes. A much better choice than a Shakespearian tragedy which ends in death. I'm almost ninety. Do I need reminding of mortality? Now Peter Pan was forever young.' He laughs. 'Like I pretend to be.'

'And you're still painting?' says Russ.

'A few canvases a year. When I was younger I was more prolific. And I would have insisted on a part in the play. A pirate perhaps.' He pauses, as if reminiscing. 'Pretending to fight.' He squeezes his eyes shut and eases himself out of his chair. 'You must excuse me.' He unhooks his stick from the back of the chair. Halfway to the door he turns round. 'Look into my studio before you go.'

'You must forgive him,' says Mathilde. 'As he gets older, thoughts of fighting take him back to the 1930s. He was living in Spain, in Asturia, when the Civil War broke out. As a child he saw unspeakable atrocities. After he and his parents returned to England painting landscapes and portraits was his way of forgetting. But seventy-five years later the nightmares returned. Even by day they haunt him. Until a few years ago he used to hunt boar with his friends. Then the time came when he couldn't handle his gun without trembling with thoughts of old horrors. He'd loved his old rifle, but he gave it away to a friend.'

'Does he ever paint his memories of the Civil War?' asks Luke.

'Never, but he has notebooks full of drawings he did as a boy. Carpet bombing by the Nationalists, the massacre of nuns by the Communists, sketches of nightmares. He seldom allows anyone to look at them.' Mathilde rises from her chair. 'Let's move to the courtyard.'

In the shade of a wisteria arbour, they drink coffee. To Luke's right, standing on a low pedestal is a bronze portrait bust of a young woman.

Mathilde smiles, 'She was a student of Lynton's. Every year he paints or sculpts one or two.'

'The artist's muses,' says Russ.

'Nothing so exotic. The landscape is Lynton's inspiration. Come and look at the other pieces.'

While Russ and Rhona are lingering by a group of small stoneware figures on a low wall, Mathilde says to Luke, 'Go over to the studio.' She points to a door on the far side of the courtyard. 'Catch the old rascal before he goes to sleep.'

Luke pushes open the iron-studded door and is met by the smell of French tobacco. Lynton, cigarette in hand, is sitting on a scuffed leather chair in a room far tidier than Luke's idea of an artist's studio. He glances round. On his right is an easel supporting a canvas placed back to front. Against a wall are two neat stacks of paintings. To one side is a table where artist's equipment is neatly arranged. Shelves either side of the door are arranged with maquettes and other ceramics. Luke's eyes rest on two large maiolica chargers on the wall behind Lynton's chair.

'Savona,' says Lynton. 'I have always promised myself to try my hand at tin glazes, but perhaps now it's too late.'

Luke looks to his left towards the studio's one window, half-open and commanding a view over treetops which seem to stretch to the sea.

'I paint with my back to that window, otherwise I become distracted. Now sit down.' He points to a chrome armchair with black upholstery. 'So what have they told you about me.'

'Alden greatly admires you as an artist. Rhona says you are equally skilled as a teacher.'

'That is very kind of them and diplomatic of you. But neither is true. I am an escapee. Cigarette?' He offers a packet of *Gauloises*.

Luke shakes his head. 'What are you escaping from?'

'My parents escaped with me from Spain in the 1930s, and I escaped from England in the 1950s because I hated the publicity which followed my first exhibition. Not because it was hostile. It wasn't – they loved me. But the adulation felt hollow. I hated it. My work was affected. I wanted to paint unpressured and in peace.' He waves an arm round the room. 'This is my escape from the past.'

'But you still exhibit.'

'Occasionally in Ajaccio or Genoa. London galleries used to bully me to show with them. I always refused.' He cranes his neck with a mischievous glint, 'Alden would like to write my biography, give details of all I saw in Asturia – he has even suggested it would make a great film. But no. It would be more publicity, more intrusion. And I am lucky enough not to need the money.'

'Can I see some of your work?'

Lynton points to the stack of canvases. 'Have a rummage.'

Luke walks over to the paintings and looks at them one by one. The first group are all landscapes. The palette is bright, with some areas – a rock formation, or a branch of a tree – given a subtle degree of greater detail without disturbing the overall balance. The next stack are mainly paintings of the studio in different lights. Some look through the doorway and into the courtyard. One looks through a window. All include a figure, usually Mathilde.

'These are wonderful.' Luke points to the easel. 'What are you working on at the moment?'

'The Girl with Red Hair. Every artist must paint her. Have a look.'

Luke moves to the easel and turns the painting round. He sees Cassie, older than her years, more serious, more attractive, in a pale blue dress, seated by the studio table on which stands a seventeenth-century vase. The purple lustre of its glaze plays with the colour of Cassie's hair and dress.

'She is very lucky to have been painted by you.'

'I am not sure if she likes it. 'Do I really look *that* old?' she asked me.'

'Perhaps you saw into her future – how she will look a few years ahead.' Luke walks over to the shelves and examines some small pottery figures. At the end of the shelf is a small jade brush rest. He lifts it up and studies it. 'This is quite valuable, I think.'

'I forget where it came from – a present perhaps.'

Luke strokes the surface with his fingers. Some green pigment rubs off on his palm. He looks at the mark. 'I see you do watercolours.'

'No, no. It must have been used by a student. Now you must excuse me. I have work to do.'

Luke goes to the door. 'Thanks for the . . .'

Lynton waves a dismissive hand.

In the courtyard the others have been joined by Agnes.

'You were there a long time,' says Mathilde. 'Visitors are normally given a minute, then thrown out.'

'He made it quite clear when it was time to leave.'

As they sit and chat Luke longs to be alone again with Rhona. The presence of Agnes is disturbing. He feels he is being assessed and found wanting. Meanwhile, Russ amuses them with stories of a holiday to Portugal which Luke has heard many times before. He looks around the courtyard. With Rhona-like stealth, Lynton has appeared and is now sitting between them and the studio door, a drawing pad on his lap, and a cigarette in his mouth, but by the time they leave he has once again retreated to his studio.

Outside, Agnes slips away to the summer school while Russ, mumbling an excuse, heads for the hotel. Rhona picks a flower from a bourgainvillea near the front door and drops it into her bag. 'We each seem to have lost our chaperones,' she says.

Back at Les Puits Rhona says, 'I need a short siesta, then I want to take you for a walk.'

Alone in his room Luke lies on his bed and looks up at the uneven ceiling. Running his eyes over the cracks in its old plaster which spread from each side like an irregular web, he remembers he has not checked his messages. He reads the email from Eva and for a moment wishes he were with her, sharing in her bereavement. He tries to phone her but the number is unavailable. He settles for an email, sending his love and sympathies and ends with a row of guilty kisses which he deletes, replacing them with a single one before sending the message. Wondering whether he should ignore her instructions and make an effort to fly to Shannon as soon as the play is over, he falls asleep.

* * *

On Friday afternoon, with the arrangements for the funeral made, Eva moves out of her guest room to Barbara's flat. To be among the familiar furnishings and to sleep here until the funeral will be both a farewell and an opportunity to sort through the contents. A phone call to Barbara's solicitor had confirmed that all her aunt's affairs are in order and that everything in the flat may be disposed of as Eva wishes. But the task, envisaged to occupy the weekend, is completed within two hours. Having often counselled the bereaved that handling and sorting through a loved one's possessions can be a harrowing and at the same time a helpful part of mourning, she is surprised how easy she finds it. Of course, she tells herself, the full force of bereavement can take months to strike home, and initial sadness is often absorbed through the business of funeral arrangements. And yet, as she sifts through papers and old post cards, she finds the presence of Barbara so real and her encouragement not to be sad so strong, that she has doubts whether there will come a time when she will wake to feelings of desolation.

Of the furniture she decides she will keep only Barbara's mahogany desk and its chair. Of smaller items she sets aside the paper weights and a dozen books, mainly scarce editions relating to angling. These she places in a box, along with two albums of photographs. And she will keep Barbara's jewellery – a modest group of old pieces in a small leather box which can be taken home on the plane with her. Two brooches are damaged, and the bands of the rings are worn down almost to threads of gold. From among them she chooses a Victorian amethyst and pearl ring to wear at the funeral; it had been one of Barbara's favourites.

It is the sight of a rail of Barbara's clothes in the Victorian wardrobe which bring tears to her eyes. Each dress and skirt recalls a day when the two of them were together – shopping in Limerick, at a restaurant in Galway, or fishing from a lakeside or boat. To touch a sleeve or hem is to relive those moments. She strokes the green tweed cloth of a jacket, takes it from its rail and shaking it releases into the air a trace of her aunt's perfume. Cautiously, she places one arm in a sleeve, then the other, and straightens the collar. To her surprise it fits. She looks into the mirrored door of the wardrobe and for a moment sees Barbara staring at her. Quickly, she turns away and removes the jacket.

She is wondering how best to dispose of other clothing when the flat bell rings. Opening the door, she sees the St. Anthony's gardener.

'I was so sorry to hear about Miss McKelvey. She was a grand old lady.'

Eva invites him into the flat. 'I apologise for the chaos,' she says. 'My aunt always loved the garden here.'

'And I often used to lean on my spade and talk roses with her.' The gardener looks around the flat. 'If you need any help with any of this furniture, I can have a word with my cousin – it's his line of business.'

For an instant Eva is aware that this is a situation Luke would handle better than she. But she smiles and says, 'How soon could he come round?'

At 4pm the cousin arrives. Eva makes him tea and aware that the tactics of negotiation are required, steers the conversation to the weather, fishing, the economic climate and any subject except the business in hand; lessons from Barbara and Luke have served her well.

At last the dealer says, 'Now might you be thinking of selling a piece or two of the dear lady's?'

After the mutually-expected haggling, Eva agrees on a price for everything she does not wish to retain, and is delighted to discover that the dealer's son will be attending a fair in the Midlands in a few days' time: he might be persuaded to make a detour and deliver the desk and chair to her, but he would have to collect them tomorrow. After some further discussion about the price of this extra work and the cost of clearing all residual contents, they shake hands on the deal.

'And of course I shall be at the funeral,' he says on leaving.

As Eva closes the door she realises that she has been imagining an empty church on Monday morning – herself, the priest, the funeral director, perhaps the matron from St. Anthony's. But the gardener had already said he would be there, and now his cousin too. She feels a spotlight on herself as chief mourner in a filling church and wonders what she should wear. At first she regrets that in her haste to leave for Ireland she had not packed the black dress she had worn for the dinner at Saffold Farm. But on reflection, would she want to wear it, if she had it with her? Wasn't it bought in an atmosphere of uncertainty and under the shadow of Rhona, a presence unwelcome at a celebration of Barbara's life? She empties the case of clothes she has brought with her onto the bed, wondering what among them she could wear. Dismissing them all as too casual, she turns her eyes to the wardrobe.

She runs her hand along the rail of dresses. The act, reminding her of the encounter with Agnes two weeks' ago at the discount store, prompts further thoughts about Luke, but today all anxiety with the pain of suspicion has gone. He now has his own life, she hers. Dismissing three black dresses as too sombre, she unhooks a midnight blue dress with a narrow broderie anglaise collar, which had previously escaped her notice. Trying it on, she finds that it is a near-perfect fit. She changes into a pair of her own dark shoes and stands in front of the mirror, appreciating a further advantage of the dress: she cannot remember Barbara wearing it.

\* \* \*

Luke is woken by Rhona's gentle tap on his shoulder. She has changed into a simple brown linen dress.

'I've heard from Eva,' he tells her. 'Her aunt died in the night. I sent my condolences.'

'Luke, dearest, I'm so sorry.' She hugs him. 'Did you know her well?'

'We visited her every year. She and Eva were very close.'

'Do you think you should join her?'

'She was adamant I stay here.'

'I had an idea for this afternoon, but if you prefer . . .'

'No, whatever you've planned.'

Carrying a denim shoulder bag with a bottle of water, she leads him from the rear of the house along a path in gentle ascent towards the mountains. They walk in silence between olive trees, Luke enjoying the mystery of their destination. After a few minutes the path divides. In the centre of the left hand fork is a large notice: *DANGER ACCES INTERDIT*.

'That goes to the ravine,' says Rhona. 'Even climbers and potholers avoid it. We turn right.'

Their path climbs higher among the shrubs and low oaks of the maquis. In the late afternoon, in places where they are not shaded by trees or the mountain side, it remains fiercely hot. Several times they stop to drink. After negotiating a particularly steep rise, Luke is about to turn round to see how far they have come, but Rhona says, 'Don't look back until I tell you.'

Further on, the oaks give way to pines, but soon they are ascending between sheer rocks where vegetation is scant. Here the shade is welcome, but after two hundred metres the path twists as the rock face on their right gives way to a wide shelf. Halfway along is a low, flat rock. 'We can sit down here,' she says. 'Now you can look back.'

Luke turns his head and gasps at the view over the treetops, across the roofs of the village and the church tower towards the sea. He looks for the coast road but it is lost in the forest. 'It's even more spectacular than yesterday's view, driving over the mountains.'

'That's because today you have walked and earned it.'

She closes her eyes and inhales deeply. 'And being on a remote footpath makes us part of the landscape.'

Luke watches the rise and fall of her linen dress as she breathes the mountain air. He sees that the path continues ahead and knows that this is only a short break in a longer walk. He closes his eyes. A distant dog bark deepens the silence.

After a minute Rhona says in his ear, 'Not far now, but you have to do the next stretch without thinking.'

They continue along the shelf until it becomes no more than a narrow ledge. Luke, seeing a precipitous drop to their right, quickly looks away and follows Rhona, hoping to assume some of her nerveless confidence. After about a hundred metres the path meets a fissure in the rock almost a foot wide. Without pausing or looking down Rhona steps over the chasm. Luke does the same. After another bend the path widens.

Rhona looks back and smiles. 'The last stretch is easy.'

It is now wide enough to allow them to walk side by side. The drop on their right is less sheer, and to their left are deep crevices in the rocks in which are nestled small shrubs, whose presence, by softening the path's starkness, makes it seem safer. A final bend and gentle slope bring them to an isolated group of low pines taking advantage of a small hollow in a hostile environment. Beyond, the mountain towers in an impenetrable wall. The path cannot possibly go further. Rhona leads Luke through the trees to the far side.

Ahead Luke sees a rock face scarred by a vertical crack, the bottom of which is darkened by damp and in parts green with algae. It seems like a dried-up spring. However, as they approach, he notices that every few seconds a drop falls towards the ground where a low, semi-circular, man-made stone wall surrounds what he assumes is a pool. Coming closer, he sees that there is only an area of damp earth beyond the wall. Rhona steps over the wall and beckoning, leads him towards the foot of the rock face where she holds out a palm. Soon a large drop strikes her hand. She licks the wetness and offers her hand to Luke who does the same. It is ice cold with a metallic taste.

'It's called *La Font des Fleurs*,' she says. 'The spring is believed to bring luck to lovers. Now we have tasted the water we have to leave a gift.'

Luke notices some dried stalks on one end of the wall and more on the ground, clearly the gifts of other visitors. Rhona reaches into her bag and produces the bougainvillea flower. She lays it where the ground is dampest.

'It never completely dries,' she says, 'even in the hottest summer. But Mathilde says in winter the pool overflows and it's dangerous even to attempt to come here.'

Luke studies the semi-circular wall. 'I would have liked to have seen this being built – it's been done with such care. Look, each of the stones is slightly curved.' He takes Rhona's right hand and places it on the inner surface of the wall. 'They must have been shaped elsewhere and carried up here. The spring clearly meant a great deal to them.'

'A labour of love. I adore this place.'

Rhona sits on the wall and looks towards the damp rock face. Luke sits beside her. He is hot and cannot understand why he is shivering.

'Do you believe in sacred springs?' she says.

'In the past I've always been sceptical about them. And I've rather joked at Russ when he rushes to the holy well at Walsingham for a cupful before his annual medical.'

'But now?'

'There is an atmosphere here . . . I've never felt it before. It's very powerful.'

Rhona places an arm round him. 'I knew you would sense it. Alden calls this place a superstition not worth the climb, but then he has no soul.'

The return walk is less daunting. Even the fissure seems to have shrunk in size. When they arrive at the place where the path runs between pine trees they pause to rest in the shade, listening to the sounds of insects and the occasional far-off voice from the direction of the village. Luke feels he has known Rhona a lifetime.

Before the dress rehearsal, Luke watches some of the summer school students erect the simplest of scenery on the steps in front of the former church. A cubist pirate ship is positioned to one side, the lost boys' underground home on the other. The alleys either side of the building have been curtained off to provide additional entries and exits. Meanwhile Matthew is testing wires and lighting, including two floods sited in the upstairs windows of Lynton's house. Russ is a more than willing assistant, darting about as if personally responsible for the whole set. At one point he appears on the balustraded balcony above the old church's main door, from which a large screen has already been suspended, and busies himself with ropes and fixings.

At 7.00pm Luke joins the others in the gallery converted from the church's ruined interior. It is a simple rectangular space, its walls covered by the unframed canvases of students. There is an atmosphere of quiet professionalism. Rhona and Agnes are busy with costumes. When Luke is in costume, Rhona appears at his side and without eye contact adjusts his pirate headdress. 'You'll do,' she says, brusque, unemotional. Through a gentle nudge between his shoulder-blades he feels another message.

Soon everyone is in costume and standing in small groups, talking quietly. In a corner, Louise in fairy costume goes through a strenuous routine of stretching exercises before moving to the three mermaids, topless and with wigs of long golden tresses. She gives them some final instructions. By the far wall of the gallery, Russ stands by himself, deep in thought and looking up, as if imagining the building's lost baroque interior.

Luke, Russ and the other pirates assemble in one of the alleys awaiting their appearance in the second act. Through a gap Luke sees a growing group of inquisitive villagers and holidaymakers at the foot of the steps. More are attracted as the song of the mermaids begins to play. From his vantage point he can hear but see nothing of the first act, performed on the balcony, but he cranes his neck to watch the flight to Never Land, a descent by ropes, apart from Louise's Tinkerbell who, when the others have safely landed, makes a rotating fall on aerial silk to the applause of the uninvited audience.

Luke assists his fellow pirates in dragging Hook on his raft to centre stage, but in doing so feels a seam in his coat split. From the corner of an eye he is able to appreciate the full extent of Matthew's technical wizardry: a frozen river projected on the screen slowly changes to woodland by a tropical lagoon. He ignores his torn coat and attempts to be part of the drama, but he is self-conscious, out of place; unlike Russ, he is a stranger to acting. He is also disturbed to be on-stage with fellow-pirate Alden – joined with him in a world of pretence and make-believe, knowing that offstage both are conspirators in real deceptions. He is glad when the act ends. Again there is applause.

In the gallery, between acts, Rhona appears at his side with safety pins. 'It was because you weren't relaxed,' she says. 'Now sit down.' She points to a chair and produces a can of beer. As he drinks it, they listen again to the haunting mermaids' song which heralds the third act.

When they hear Alden speak Starkey's lines, he sees Rhona wince. 'Why does he overact?' she says. 'Dear old Russ makes him look like a pitiful amateur.'

Unrequired until the end of Act Four, Luke stands behind the screen, script in hand, following the cast's word-perfect lines. Once or twice Rhona appears beside him in silent encouragement.

The rehearsal continues without mishap or the need for prompts. At the end of the play prolonged applause encourages the cast to take an unscheduled bow. As they return to change in the gallery's cool interior Russ tells Luke, 'Matthew has invited me to dinner tonight at the hotel. Apologies to Alden and the others if my absence is noted.'

'Enjoy yourself.'

'Well, it is a holiday,' says Russ with an ambiguous grin.

As Luke is removing his torn coat, Rhona says, 'Go ahead with the gang. Agnes and I have some clearing up to do here. Another swim tomorrow morning?'

'As early as you like.'

'We'll go to the sea.'

'You can throw away your prompter's book,' says Felix as they stroll back to Les Puits.

'That might invite bad luck,' says Luke, surprised at his own superstitiousness.

Later, at a candlelit table, Luke watches Rhona and Agnes arrive. They sit at the far end of the table. Rhona's head is framed by the lower branches of the vine. Agnes sits on her right and is chattering non-stop. Rhona listens attentively, but Luke is certain she is alert to every word elsewhere at the table and that if a leaf from the vine behind her dared to fall, she would hear the sound as it touched the flagstones.

Alden is the last to enter the courtyard. As soon as he appears Cassie begins clapping. The others join with ironic cheers.

'To the director. A great dress,' says Josh.

'It wasn't fault-free,' admonishes Alden, taking a chair next to Luke.

'Pretty damn good though,' says Cassie.

'It can still be sharpened up. And of course starting at eight-thirty tomorrow, it will be darker.'

'You're scared of success,' says Cassie. 'Or do you believe that a perfect dress means a hell-awful first night?'

'Fortunately, the dress was not perfect.'

Cassie turns to Louise on her right and in a stage whisper says, 'From what I've been told, an Alden first night is always a disappointment.'

After this, conversation at dinner is restrained. Luke, alienated, wishes Russ were sitting next to him babbling familiar nonsense. He looks towards the end of the table. Rhona catches his eye with a look which he interprets as, 'I'm glad you're next to Alden: it's good to keep things civilised while it remains possible.'

'I enjoyed meeting Mathilde and Lynton,' Luke tells Alden.

'He's lost some of his verve. Ten years ago he'd be sitting with us now, holding forth.'

'He's not bad for almost ninety. I admire his entrenched independence.'

'Too entrenched sometimes.' Alden empties his wine glass.

'But he's only entrenched against the art establishment, surely. Not against the world. Otherwise he wouldn't be so keen on teaching.'

'I think he has more to offer a wider public. I've been planning a biography but he's dug his heels in.'

'It seems to me that he hates public exposure.'

'He does, but he has so many paintings and drawings which have barely seen the light of day, let alone been on the market. They deserve to be published, hung and enjoyed.'

'His Civil War drawings?'

'Almost no-one has ever seen them. I was lucky enough to have a glimpse years ago and they are phenomenal. Not just because they were done by a ten year old, but as works of art in their own right. And he has stacks of other stuff which should be known about.'

'Perhaps they are too personal for public consumption. Loads of artists destroy their own work.'

'I've told him he can trust me to publish them sensitively, but he's very recalcitrant. Mathilde wants him to. In fact she tried to produce a book about him herself years ago but it came to nothing. I simply want his work recorded for posterity. Who would believe it could be so hard?'

'You mean you've ambitions to be his agent?' says Cassie.

'I've no ambitions, only an aspiration, but not as his agent. I've simply offered my services as his biographer.'

'There's nothing wrong in having an ambition to get your name on a book,' says Felix.

'It will be about Lynton, not me,' Alden says.

'Yeah, yeah, we believe you, Alden,' laughs Cassie.

'It will happen one day – I hope before Lynton dies,' says Alden.

'What makes you so certain?' asks Luke.

'Instinct. I had a Cumbrian grandmother with the gift of second sight. I've been told I'm like her.'

Luke wonders whether the claimed insight stretches to the relationship between him and Rhona.

'More wine?' Alden asks Luke.

'No thanks, I must get some sleep. I'm still adjusting to this Mediterranean heat.'

As Luke gets to his feet, Alden grasps his arm, 'It's so good to have you here,' he says.

Luke leaves the table to a chorus of 'Sleep well,' among which Rhona's is the only voice he can hear. Once in his room, he realises that his excuse of tiredness is in fact the reality. He kicks off his sandals and lies on top of his bed. He cannot undress until he has composed his thoughts.

# 19

When Luke wakes it is dark. He is surprised to find himself dressed. He looks at his watch, still on his wrist. It is 4.30am. He is so wide awake that the few hours he has slept feel like twelve. What to do? It is too early to go to the kitchen and wait for Rhona, but the best time for practical thoughts about the future. The major decisions of life – asking Eva out to dinner that first time, moving from London, the purchase of his shop and house, acquiring the barns – have all been planned around dawn. He has always relished this time of quiet, without interruptions and with the strangely assuring thought that all the people whose lives touch his are lost in a sleep where any conscious powers of thought transference cannot influence him. His rational self tells him that this idea is absurd, but early in the morning it has always felt true. He stands by the window, looking out through the darkness towards the mountains, slowly delineated as the minutes pass.

When and how to tell Eva? As soon as possible on his return. He is certain of that. But how? Be as straightforward as possible. Wouldn't it be gross ignorance on his part to assume that she knows nothing about him and Rhona? Yesterday he had suspected it; now, he is in no doubt. He is certain that he has done everything to conceal the affair, but a thousand miles from home, in the still of a Mediterranean village before dawn, he is equally certain that Eva, through intuition or professional insight, is aware of it. Her knowledge does not mean that when he tells her she will not be hurt or angry, but the break-up will be so much easier than the split of partners, married or otherwise, who have been living together. There are no legal implications. Neither he nor Eva will be financially damaged. 'We can still remain friends,' he finds himself saying, then groans at having recited the desperate mantra of the newly-separated. No, there is little chance we shall remain friends. Keep in touch, perhaps, in a neighbourly sort of way. But not friends.

In the increasing light he sees a flock of small yellow-streaked birds, perhaps finches, descend to an ancient oleander below the window. No, he cannot be certain of Eva's reaction. Nor his own on telling her? There would be things missed, companionship, fishing, holidays – he half wants to add sex but thoughts of Rhona preclude it.

Practical matters. Rhona wants to live with me, but in which house? I've told her she can move in to 7 Back Lane, or I'll buy Alden's share of Saffold Farm and live with her there. What could be easier? If we take that course, I shall retain my house, perhaps rent it out or use it for storage. My business would be unaffected. I shall continue my allotment, even if I am living at the farm which has space for a vegetable garden. What have I overlooked? Luke moves from the window and drops onto the hard-seated rustic chair, watching the first light cast dull shadows on the room's uneven white walls. On his neck he feels a slight breeze from the window. He draws a deep breath. The air is heavy with the scent of pines and herbs. Sweet, like the future. He feels thirsty.

In the kitchen he makes tea for himself and waits for Rhona. It is colder here, the dampness of the stone floor blending with the smell of the pots of marjoram on the window sill. He cannot see how the room could possibly look more lovely in its simplicity. Even the cracked blue and white tiles above the sink have a charm which no modernisation could improve. His mauve towel on the table is an intruder. He folds it over the back of his chair where he cannot see it.

It is not long before Rhona appears, wearing a black track suit and red espadrilles. Elated, she kisses him. 'This morning I feel free for the first time in years,' she says. 'Let's go to the sea.' She pours herself half a cup of hot water from the kettle, adds some cold, drinks it quickly, and beckons him to the door.

In the car Rhona starts the engine and turns on the radio, changing stations at random until finding some heavy metal. As soon as they are away from the village she turns up the volume, smiles at Luke and squeezes his hand.

At some speed she drives down the twisting road towards Solenzara where she takes the coast road heading south. After a few miles she turns off down a minor road whose surface rapidly deteriorates until, among trees, it becomes a sandy track which ends at a rough parking area among rocks. She stops the car and the music. There is no other vehicle in sight.

'Freedom,' she says. 'Come on.' Taking Luke's hand, she leads him down to a crescent-shaped beach, bordered by pines. It is totally secluded, but the restless slate sea is forbidding. Rhona points to the far end of a rocky outcrop stretching into the sea like a natural breakwater. 'That's where we swim to,' she says.

When they have walked to the water's edge Luke looks at the distance between them and the rocks and feels uncertain of his ability to swim that far. Rhona also stares out to sea, but Luke knows her thoughts are not about swimming. Suddenly she throws off her tracksuit and runs naked to the water. Up to her waist in the waves she turns round and with both arms beckons him. He pulls off his clothes and follows. She is already surging ahead with a breaststroke much stronger than yesterday's gentle swim in the river. When at last she slows, he is able to catch up and swim at her side, but as they move towards the outcrop the sea becomes rougher. He tries to breathe slowly, to swim with a rhythm unaffected by the waves. It demands great effort. Several times, in troughs, he loses sight of her. He steels himself not to panic. For some time he cannot see the rocks to which he hopes they are swimming. Again she is ahead of him. As the outcrop comes into his view he sees her pulling herself out of the sea. Turning, she stretches a hand to him, as if she can lift him out over an expanse of twenty metres. The act gives him the confidence to negotiate the final stretch, the worst of which is near the edge of the rocks where the waves are more aggressive.

Out of the water and breathless, he sits beside her, looking across the bay towards the cliffs on the far side. Luke takes her hand. For all her confidence in the water, surpassing his own, she seems vulnerable. He looks at fresh scratches on her nail varnish caused by the clamber up the rocks.

She nestles her head on Luke's shoulder. He kisses its warm saltiness.

'Your bruises have almost disappeared,' he says.

'Good. Ditto my husband.' She looks to the far side of the bay. 'This could be one of the lagoons in the play,' she says. 'Thankfully, no pirate ship.'

'But I do see an almost mermaid.'

She smiles, crosses her legs, arranges her hair so it falls in front of her, combs it with her fingers, and says, 'Unlike the mermaids in the play this one doesn't mind being caught.' Suddenly she stands, pulls Luke to his feet and points to their left. 'That's north, isn't it?'

'Almost exactly,' Luke says, looking inland towards the mountains, their rocky promontories changing from brown to mottled pink in the ascending sun.

'Somewhere over there,' she says, 'is the mainland and beyond that home, and a little further on I can see you and me. Alden has disappeared with Lou. I wish them every happiness. But I could almost feel sorry for her – I'm sure she won't be the last victim of his hair-brained world.' She turns from the horizon. 'Luke, I'm very hungry.' She takes his hand and walks to the edge of the outcrop.

Luke looks to the shore where he can see her espadrilles, like two red eyes staring at them. Again he wonders if he can swim such a distance.

Rhona drops his hand, lowers herself into the water and swims at the slowest pace until she and Luke are side by side. He finds the return swim effortless, enjoying her proximity in the rise and fall of the waves and is sad when their feet touch the pebbles.

When they have walked to their clothes, he offers her his towel.

'You dry me,' she says.

The request is more intimate than that first 'make love to me.' He dries her body from forehead to ankles, while she runs her fingers through her matted hair. When she has pulled on her tracksuit she dries his upper body, smiles and hands back his towel.

'I know the perfect place to eat,' she says as they walk back to the car. 'It has many points in its favour. It's an ugly building, Alden hates it and it does one hell of a breakfast.'

'Will it be open? It's not yet eight.'

'The English couple who run it will have the frying pan sizzling hot already.'

On the outskirts of Solenzara Luke sees a white building festooned with the flags of European nations.

'That's it,' shouts Rhona. 'The first sign of civilisation in two days.'

She drives past a huge sign, *Les Drapes*, and parks near two other cars on a dusty patch of gravel with barely any demarcation before the concrete eating area where three other couples are already eating English breakfasts complete with teapots. The smell of bacon hits them before they arrive at a red plastic table in the shade of a vine by the wall of the café. They sit on white plastic chairs already heated by the sun.

The breakfast is as good as Rhona promised. A delivery van pulls into the car park, adding the fumes of diesel to the smell of frying bacon and eggs, a combination which surprises Luke with the comfort of the familiar. He looks at the white-painted, rendered wall beside them where two rows of ants, one climbing, one descending, stretch from the ground up to the branches of the vine where he can see them moving backwards and forwards along the leafy awning's wood and wire framework.

'This is more my world than smart-arse table talk in the courtyard,' he says.

'And it's always Alden's court,' she says opening a second sachet of brown sauce and squeezing it on her plate. She slices into a sausage. 'How he insists on shopping in markets and buying local meat and produce.'

'Don't forget I grow my own veg.'

'That's different. Alden just likes the idea of it all. He'd never get his hands dirty. Even washing the lettuces ends up being done by Agnes or me. And some of the meat he buys is disgusting.' She forks a piece of sausage into her mouth. 'If I'm going to eat rubbish, I like it to be familiar rubbish. When I'm shot of Alden, can I live with you in your wonderful house?'

'Of course. What will you do with Saffold Farm?'

'I could find a tenant.'

'Or make it into offices and storage for your business. Your studio seemed very cramped.'

'A tempting idea.'

Luke feels the sun on his face through a gap in the vine where the ants are still pursuing their two-way journey, undeterred by a can of insect spray on a windowsill. He lifts the foil from a marmalade sachet and spreads a thick coat on a slice of buttered toast, pleased that one of his dawn questions has been answered. He takes a large bite. 'I'm glad you found this place,' he says.

'Before you arrived Agnes and I came here every day.'

'I hope I haven't deprived her of breakfast.'

'Heavens no. Right now she'll be wandering up to the school for muffins and hot chocolate. Unless she spent the night there with Dan.'

Rhona orders more tea. 'We needn't rush back,' she says. 'Come up with me to the school later on this morning. I want to see if Mathilde needs any help with the post-production barbecue.'

'If there's anything I can do ...'

'Call in to see Lynton again. He must like you to have let you stay so long in his studio yesterday. Alden was surprised when I told him.' She leans across the table and kisses him passionately.

* * *

On Saturday morning, after breakfast in the main dining room, Eva returns to her aunt's flat aware that there is no more she can do before Tuesday's funeral. A dozen white roses have been ordered for Barbara's coffin. Instructions have been given for no other flowers, but donations may be sent to St. Anthony's. Again she tries on Barbara's dark blue dress and slips the amethyst ring on a finger. She is about to change back to her own clothes when the flat bell rings. Opening the door, she sees the chaplain.

'My condolences,' he says. 'I'm sorry I couldn't come to see you yesterday.'

Eva invites him in, removes the box of books from an armchair and points the priest to it, taking Barbara's desk chair for herself.

'I gather you rushed over from Norfolk,' he says.

'I'm her nearest, almost her only, relative.'

Eva describes to the priest her close relationship with Barbara.

'She often talked about you,' he says.

Eva thinks he is about to say more but he remains silent. 'Can I make you a coffee?' she asks.

'That would be kind,' he says.

In the small kitchen of the flat Eva is uneasy: now is not the time to express her aversion to Catholicism, its unfounded certainties and ethical rigidity, yet somehow she must make her views clear, but with a polite firmness, not least out of respect for Barbara.

When he has sipped his coffee the priest says, 'Your aunt had already received the last rites.'

'I only learned yesterday that she had become a Catholic. It was a surprise. Our family has never followed any religion.'

'So your aunt told me. She surprised me too. Some converts can be very triumphalist about their change of direction. She was the complete opposite. Low key, you might say. But she requested a funeral mass.'

'Can it be a simple service? I certainly wouldn't want a eulogy, nor would she. And I've no idea if she had a favourite piece of music, but I do know she never liked hymns. And nor do I.'

'That's so refreshing to hear. We're under such pressure for a funeral to be a musical biography that it's wonderful to find a non-Catholic not wanting one. And a requiem says more than a thousand renditions of *I Did it My Way*.'

Eva smiles, wanting to add that Barbara always did things her own way, but has no wish to enter into a discussion about Catholic and secular funeral practices.

'Now, Monday's funeral,' he says. 'Are you familiar with the church service and the committal at the grave?'

'The funeral director has explained everything. I'm sure I know all I need to know.'

The priest seems content with her answer and stands to leave.

Eva shows him to the door, surprised the visit has been so short. It is not the pastoral visit she was expecting, and light years from bereavement counselling. But another part of her is grateful for its brevity; the last thing she needs is unrequested advice from a minister of religion. As she watches him leave and head for the main building, she thinks, off he goes for more last rites, and realises that she is angry. She needs to get away for a few hours. She changes into jeans.

On a bike borrowed from one of the kitchen staff, she cycles down the Kilnaboy road, with half an idea of visiting the graveyard where Barbara will be buried. But exhilarated at being away from St. Anthony's and with a welcome breeze in her face, she cycles past, giving no more than a glance towards the ruined church. Further on she passes the guest house where she and Luke had stayed on their visit to Barbara in the spring. They had talked of returning. Now this would not happen. She speeds up, forcing the pedals as hard as the old bike will allow.

Heading towards the wildness of the Burren, she remembers the many walks enjoyed here with Barbara, and later with Luke whom she had introduced to the landscape. On one trip they had listed the different orchids they had seen, and last April they had searched for other rarities.

Near the Burren, she chains the bicycle to a gate and retraces their footsteps. It had been a damp day, but the weather had not deterred them from walking across the moonscape of limestone ridges and peering into the deep crevices to be surprised by the plants, and attempting to identify them. She does so again, marvelling at the botanical resilience in such a seemingly hostile terrain. After an hour of stooped investigation, her back aching, she walks towards the dolmen where she and Luke had sheltered during a heavy shower. Approaching it, she tries to recall the exact place where they had stood beneath the massive upper stone.

Looking across the Burren she hears Barbara's words about Luke, 'the stick to beat Mark with for leaving'. Surely not. Wasn't her split with Mark as amicable as any divorce can be? Luke was not a weapon against her former husband and his partner. Luke and she had fallen in love. She closes her eyes and tries to focus on the time when Luke moved from being a client to the man she loved. Yes, I was newly-divorced, but how hurt was I?

Struggling to recapture the emotions of twenty years earlier, she finds herself saying the words she said to Agnes in the pub, 'It was too long ago. A different life.' Again she hears guffaws from the bar, but now they are directed to her. Shivering, she opens her eyes and looks around as if the inebriated jokers are close at hand, ridiculing her inability to know herself. But she sees only the dolmen and the limestone terrain stretching out silent in front of her. She wishes Barbara had lived longer – their last conversations had been too brief. Less than three weeks ago when Stella had suggested returning to the past, she had resisted – the prospect of travelling back so many years had been too painful. Perhaps at a future meeting she should allow Stella to guide her there.

She moves about, touching the uprights, their antiquity speaking through the weathered surfaces and making her own life – Barbara's too – seem brief and transitory. Slowly, she walks back to the gate where she turns round for a final view of the dolmen which has become less a prehistoric monument than a memorial to her past, to her life with Luke. Cycling back to Corofin she wonders if the exercise has worked off her anger. And if that anger had been directed to the priest or to herself. Tomorrow she will pass the day reading, undisturbed in the library at St. Anthony's, in preparation for Monday.

* * *

At 11.30am on Saturday Luke knocks on the door of the studio.

'Come in, come in,' Lynton calls.

As soon as Luke enters Lynton points to an old armchair and says, 'I owe you an apology. I have been disingenuous.'

'Surely not.'

Lynton settles himself in his own chair. 'I misled you yesterday. No, I lied. I told you I didn't do watercolours but you, with your dealer's eye, you saw my brush rest had been recently used.'

'It doesn't matter.'

'It does matter. Will you have some coffee? I make my own here.' Lynton stands and turns to a side table. 'Mathilde gave me one of these new machines, and even I can work it.'

Lynton drops a capsule into the coffee maker and presses the start button, pours some milk into the adjacent frother and switches it on. 'You see, Luke, visitors all want part of me. A painting, a preliminary drawing, a scrap of paper with a charcoal scribble. They don't care. Some offer money, others want it for nothing. It's all the same. They want me for whatever they can take. Perhaps prostitutes feel the same. Luke, as early as I can remember there was always a pencil in my hand. Sometimes I would give my drawings a colourwash or a few highlights, but usually not. Now I'm near the end of my life I've dug a few of them out and am giving them the colour which was always intended. It's a private task. You're the first person who knows.' He removes the cup from the machine. 'You have milk? Look, the other gadget has frothed it for you.' He spoons some milk into Luke's cup and hands it to him.

Lynton lowers himself into his chair again. 'I lied to protect myself, but I feel I can trust you. You deal but you don't deal in paintings and I can tell you're not like the others.' Lynton points to his desk, 'So, by way of apology,' Lynton points to the desk, 'I want you to have those. Take a look.'

Luke walks over to the desk and sees a drawing of a line of refugees weighed down with baggage and driving animals on a mountain road. There are a few washes of colour. It is initialled and dated 1937. He turns it over and sees a portrait of a small boy making a clenched fist salute.

'Me at eleven. Already a hardened Republican. That was done by a school friend. He died in a refugee camp in France. Now look at the other one.'

Underneath the drawing is a second, more mature, watercolour. It is a view of a mountain ridge at sunset. The dark contours of the horizon, lit behind from the falling light, form curious shapes, like silhouettes of people and animals.

Luke turns to Lynton. 'The ridge has become a line of travellers, refugees,' he says. 'The two drawings relate to each other.'

Lynton smiles and slowly nods.

Luke sees tears in his eyes. He looks back at the watercolour. 'These are the mountains here on the island. Through this landscape you have come to terms...'

'You understand straight away. I will send these to you, along with some others. I burnt most of my work from the '30s. It is too painful. ' He waves a hand in front of his mouth. 'But don't...'

'I shan't tell anyone.'

'Alden would love to get hold of them. He is a friend and has many fine qualities but...' he shrugs. 'He would like to turn Santa Marta into a venue for a summer arts festival. As if good art need festivals.'

As Luke leaves the studio Lynton says, 'You must visit us one spring – the atmosphere is less...' He hesitates, giving Luke a knowing smile, '... less effervescent – more congenial.' The look and tone inform Luke that the old man is aware of the tensions and social interactions of his summer visitors.

With a lingering handshake Lynton says, 'Look after yourself.'

For Luke the three words are not so much a farewell as a caution. He finds Rhona, now in a long-sleeved navy shirt, in the kitchen with Mathilde, marinating chicken joints.

'You look tired,' Mathilde tells him. 'It is usually Lynton who is worn out by visitors, not the other way round.'

'I woke too early this morning.'

'And I made him swim in a rough sea,' laughs Rhona.

'You should have a siesta before the play,' says Mathilde. 'Now have some bread and cheese with us. Get your strength up for tonight.'

'Mine's only a small part. I'm mainly an unrequired prompter.'

'Even prompters must eat. Now tell me about your shop.'

Luke describes his business, certain that Rhona has already given a full account to Mathilde. He is also sure that Mathilde is Rhona's confidante in personal matters. When Lynton joins them for a light lunch, Alden is hardly mentioned in the conversation. Luke feels that he is among allies. After lunch, Luke, a borrowed straw hat on his head, walks back to Les Puits. In the courtyard Josh and Felix are in a shaded corner going through their lines. By the well Cassie is reading hers.

'Come and cue me in, Luke,' she calls 'I need one more run through to be certain.'

He joins her, cues and shares a beer. When she feels confident, he goes to his room where he closes the shutters, undresses and slips under a sheet. Looking towards the window he watches the play of light through the louvres and is reminded of his bedroom at home. He remembers the last time he and Eva slept there together and her suggestion he should redecorate. Eyes closed, he hears voices from another part of the house, and wondering whose they are falls into a heavy sleep.

He dreams of being back home on his allotment, carrying his watering can up and down between rows of chard and French beans. Sinking to the ground, he rests with his back to the tall brick wall at the far end, enjoying the smell of wet earth. Maurice walks up to him, nestling a warm head beside his.

He wakes to find Rhona beside him, licking his ear. 'I thought you'd never wake up,' she says. 'It's after six.'

Luke lifts his head. 'Should I be getting changed?'

She strokes his hair. 'No, make-up's not till seven. Kick-off's at eight-thirty. Plenty of time.'

Luke looks towards the door.

'Don't worry, I bolted it,' she says.

# 20

Leaving his room Luke finds Les Puits has burst to life with shouts from all directions, as bodies rush backwards and forwards in various states of undress between bedrooms and the only shower. Having had a shower himself, he follows the sound of voices and finds they have all congregated in the kitchen, along with some of the cast from the school. In the animated chatter of mutual encouragement, they are standing around the table, ignoring three bowls of salad and a basket of bread.

A glance tells Luke that Rhona is not here, nor is Agnes.

'Guarding the costumes at the back of the church,' says Russ quietly.

Matthew too is absent. Luke turns to Russ.

'Guarding his hi-tech magic and a mile of cable.'

Luke notices that Louise has her back to Alden as she talks to Thérèse. Alden is sharing a joke with Cassie, but breaks away and announces, 'We may not be hungry but we must get some water down us. There's more up at the gallery. We can't act if we're dehydrated.'

'I'm not sure if I can act, even hydrated,' mumbles Russ.

Alden fills glasses and mugs with well water.

Luke takes two glasses and passes one to Russ. 'Have you and Matthew got the technical side primed and ready?'

'It should be better than last night.'

'Looked faultless to me.'

'There were one or two timing hiccups, but I think we've cured them. We're not a bad team.'

Alden claps his hands. 'We ought to get up there, guys.'

'No pep talk?' Josh asks.

'Do we need one?' asks Alden.

'Oh, come on,' says Felix placing arms round the shoulders of Cassie and Josh. 'Let's have a huddle.'

Arms round one other's necks they form a circle in the kitchen.

'Don't forget the play's for Lynton,' urges Alden.

'Let's go kick pirate ass,' says Josh.

Alden forces a smile. 'Break your legs,' he says and is first out of the door.

As the others leave, Luke feels Russ's hand holding him back. 'A pity to let all this go to waste,' he says, grabbing some lettuce leaves.

Luke tears off a piece of bread and dips it into the dressing. Russ shoots his head round the kitchen door to make sure no-one is lingering in the hallway. Closing the door he says, 'Bugger the water. I can't face the night without a proper drink.' He goes to the cupboard, reaches behind some saucepans on the bottom shelf and produces a bottle of whisky, uncorks it and pours generous measures in their glasses. 'Bonne santé,' he says and drinks deeply.

Luke sips with caution. Russ quickly knocks back the rest of his glass, exhales with satisfaction and looks up at the ceiling. 'Now I can face the vulgar multitude,' he says.

'The audience or the rest of the cast?'

'The whole lot of them.'

Luke downs his own drink as Russ returns the bottle to its hidey hole.

'You're very well organised, Russ.'

'Let's call it experience.'

Luke and Russ walk up to the church across La Place des Pèlerins where the day's heat radiates from the stone flags in the fading light. At the hotel and café a larger than usual number of outdoor tables are packed with chattering diners. Kitchen smells drift up towards the steps, in front of which rows of chairs and benches have been set out, many carrying reserved notices and cushions. At the top of the steps the pirate ship and Lost Boys' home are being examined by a small group of children. The bollards denying access from the road have now been removed and an ice cream vendor has taken position near the school and is doing good business. To one side stand two policemen, both holding cornets. The sun has now dropped behind the mountains, and Luke, looking up towards the peaks, recalls Lynton's drawings of a mountain ridge, its silhouette morphing into a line of exiles or the baggage train of an ancient army. He follows Russ behind the screen hanging from the tower balcony and enters the gallery.

The atmosphere inside is one of quiet bustle and reverential tones, as if the building had reclaimed its origins and its occupants were preparing for a religious festival. To one side Rhona and two girls from the school are on make-up duty, while Agnes is darting about, ensuring that each cast member has the correct costume. Hurrying towards them, she says to Russ, 'Get a move on. Make-up's got to do your beard.'

Luke looks at the tatty blue velvet frock coat and ragged red trousers waiting for him on a chair labelled with his name, and wonders how he has ended up in a ruined Corsican church, converted to a gallery and now a temporary dressing room for an English play in which he has a part. For Russ, already pulling on Smee's billowy navy shorts, the exercise seems as natural as gilding a mirror. Luke looks over to Rhona. Fan brush in hand, she is making up one of the mermaids. Her adroitness sweeps away the absurdity of his situation. He is here for her, not for this ridiculous production by the fool she will soon be leaving. Encouraged, he puts on the costume.

'Cecco next,' calls Rhona.

The make-up chair brings a new level of excitement: she is out of sight, her presence felt through the touch of sticks and brushes. Wordless he responds to her instructions, 'Head up now' and 'Tighten your lips,' knowing that she, like him, is suppressing other thoughts.

At 8.15pm, when Luke and the other pirates have taken their places in the screened-off alley, the spyhole reveals an eager crowd with every seat taken and as many again standing as far as two coaches parked near the hotel from which emanate the only lights in the dark Place des Pèlerins. Lynton and Mathilde are in the centre of the front row. Above Santa Marta stars glitter the night sky, and in the direction of the sea the half moon hangs over the maquis.

From the cheers when the Darling children appear floodlit on the balcony, it is clear that the audience is determined to revel in every moment of the play. The descent by rope receives prolonged applause, while Tinkerbell's rotating fall is met with gasps which give way to riotous clapping and whistling.

Nervous before his first entrance, Luke waits with the other pirates who all seem supremely confident. But when they walk on to great applause he is transported to a world never experienced during rehearsals. The elation is short-lived. Between scenes, anxiety returns, and he waits dry-mouthed and apprehensive for the second act, uncertain if he will be able to join the others in their singing entry. Now the applause heard from behind the curtain has become less a boost than a threat to his confidence. But as he enters the stage, he finds his faltering voice is encouraged by the gusto of the others, especially by Russ's stentorian *yo hos*. The audience responds with more applause, changing to boos as Hook orders his men to search for the Lost Boys. But stage and audience are silenced by the tick of the crocodile, given such volume by Matthew that the sound reverberates around the village like an apocalyptic time bomb, only relieved by the appearance of the beast and consequent laughter. Luke sees Lynton, spellbound in his chair like a child, a grin never leaving his face – the exile in secondary escape.

Offstage Luke hears the third act begin with more hilarity as the Lost Boys try but fail to catch a mermaid. More boos mark the appearance of the bound Tiger Lily and cheers at her release by Peter. Not required for the scene, Luke hears Russ, audience in his hand, draw laughter from almost every line. With a keyring torch Luke follows the script, fighting the temptation to sneak peeps at the stage or audience.

In the interval he joins the rest of the cast in the gallery, where a buoyant atmosphere is not suppressed by cautions from Alden that the play is not yet finished. But the final two acts sustain the success, the single digression from the script coming when the Darling children should sing the *National Anthem*. In its place they sing the first verse of the *Corsican Anthem* – whether for the sake of the audience or to annoy Alden, Luke is not certain. He remembers his own three lines and, after Cecco's death, exits into the gallery where Rhona greets him with a hug.

'I loved your final scream,' she says. 'It almost had me worried.'

'I want out of this costume.'

'And me out of my marriage. But I must wait and so must you. You have to take your bow with the others before you change.'

Peter and Wendy's final exit gives rise to a standing ovation. Even Lynton eases himself from his chair and claps with his hands above his head. There is wild cheering before the full cast of players emerge. Russ pulls Luke to his feet and he joins them, standing at one end of the line. The cheers and applause increase as they bow. Not lingering, they quickly leave the stage, responding to more cheers with a reappearance. Josh now goes to Alden who, with unconvincing modesty, is pulled to the front for further acclaim. The cast join in until he steps to one side and with an extravagant arm points to them, lastly making gestures towards the screen and lights. From the corner of his eye Luke sees Russ beaming ecstatically as if this, not patching mirrors, is his true destiny.

In the gallery they remove their make-up and quickly change, thoughts only on the party. The girls have brought with them celebratory glad rags, but not the boys, apart from Russ: as soon as his beard and make up is removed he pulls on a Hawaiian shirt printed with hula dancers. As Luke places his doublet and hat in one of the costume boxes, Rhona whispers, 'We must be discrete this evening. I'll stay with Mathilde. Ignore me and dance with any of the girls. Apart from Lou of course – she'll be otherwise occupied. Swim tomorrow?'

'River or sea?'

'River. I love the openness of the sea, but the seclusion of the river has its special magic. Six not too early, is it – after tonight's party?'

When Luke leaves the gallery he finds Matthew loading the sound and lighting equipment into a van. He is being helped by Felix. Russ is by the van door, supervising. The scenery has already disappeared and members of the school are stacking chairs. It seems to Luke that disproportionate energy has been expended on a single night's performance. He looks around La Place des Pèlerins. The café and bar are still bustling, but the coaches and ice cream vendor have gone and Santa Marta is already slipping back to its quieter self. Alden has disappeared. As Luke is helping to remove duct tape and cables from the stone pavement, Agnes and Dan pass by him carrying the costume boxes which they load on the van. Dan places an arm around her as they walk up towards the school.

A few minutes later Rhona appears from the gallery, walks up to Luke and running her fingers through his hair says, 'Take your time. Best if we don't arrive together. I'll see you up there.'

When all the equipment is loaded into the van, the boys go up to the balcony, lower the screen, return, roll it and carry it into the gallery. Matthew now drives to the hotel car park, Russ in the passenger seat. Luke, alone at the foot of the steps, looks up to the west wall of the old church and wonders at the speed of the disappearance of cast, scenery and audience.

In no hurry to get to the party, he strolls to the far side of La Place des

Pèlerins and looks over the maquis, dark and still but alive with the unremitting chatter of cicadas. Struggling to accept that he has been part of a play in this remote village, he turns round and gazes at the empty flight of steps. At that moment a figure appears on the balcony. At first Luke thinks it is Matthew or Russ retrieving a forgotten piece of equipment, but the figure is too tall to be either of them. It is Alden.

Luke remains motionless and watches Alden look down at the steps and towards the area where the audience had sat. It occurs to him that Alden is reliving the applause at the end of the play, an impression confirmed when Alden raises his arms like a footballer who has scored a winning goal and lowers them slowly, gazing the length of La Place des Pèlerins in a way that reminds Luke of a monarch surveying his subjects from a palace window. When Alden has left the balcony Luke walks towards the music and rising voices of the party, but at the foot of the steps he is halted by sounds from the direction of the gallery. He walks up the steps and stations himself by the gallery door.

It is Louise he hears first.

'It was your plan, your idea,' she shouts. 'I never said I would live with you.'

'But you agreed about the flat.' Alden struggles to be restrained. 'And you said it would be great if we . . .'

'Where you buy a flat is up to you,' she screams. 'My work takes me all over the world. I'm not the settling sort.'

'But I'm offering you a base.'

'You're offering me a tie. My base is where my company is next.'

'I understand that.'

'You don't and you can't. You're not a dancer.'

'Actors feel the same way.'

'You're not an actor either. I'm leaving first thing tomorrow. Don't try to follow me.'

'But Lou,' Alden pleads.

Luke hears footsteps and spreads himself against the adjacent wall. Holding his breath, he watches the door open and sees Lou run at great speed down the steps and towards the summer school. Alden follows, attempts to negotiate the steps two at a time, but stumbles near the bottom. Picking himself up, he tries to run, but is clearly in some discomfort. With the desperate hope that Louise will reappear with a change of heart, Luke watches Alden walk towards the party.

Disconsolate, Luke closes the gallery door, his hand trembling on the iron handle. Rhona must be informed of this argument which seems nothing less than a final separation. It can only throw obstacles in their plans. But they will not be insuperable, he tells himself. Rhona and he will be resolute. As he walks up to the school he hears the sounds of '50s jazz echo through Santa Marta. Nervous, he walks up the steps of the terrace where the music merges with a crescendo of excited voices. The smell of a barbecue pervades the night and overpowers even the scent of the maquis.

On the candlelit terrace the cast and members of the summer school have been joined by many others. Some are seated on low walls at the sides of the terrace. Three or four couples are dancing. Others, Alden among them, stand in groups. A few occupy chairs near the door to Lynton's house, including Lynton himself who is seated in a wicker chair and listening to a middle-aged woman Luke has not seen before but who reminds him of Freda Elman. She is vociferously sharing her views about painting, the gutturally-pronounced word 'art' booming above Henri Renaud's jazz. Soon, from Lynton's house Rhona appears with Mathilde and Cassie. Rhona, seeing him, raises an arm in recognition, lowers it quickly and finds a chair for Mathilde. Luke turns and moves to one end of the terrace where a long trestle table is heavy with bottles. He pours himself a glass of rosé. Before he has lifted it to his lips Cassie is at his side.

'Do you like the music?' she says. 'Rhona told me to tell you she chose it specially for you. It's from Mathilde's collection.'

'Tell her that was most thoughtful.'

While Cassie pours three glasses of white wine, Luke says, 'Would you also tell her she and I must talk. Urgently. There's a matter . . .'

'Of course. I understand,' says Cassie, clearly a willing messenger not in need of explanations.

Wondering how much Rhona has said to Cassie, Luke scans the terrace. On the far side Alden is laughing with Felix in a way Luke finds hard to square with the voice of pleading desperation in the gallery. Louise seems absent from the party. Luke looks again towards Rhona. He sees Cassie give her and Mathilde a glass of wine. For a few seconds he loses them among the moving heads of the terrace. When he next sees Rhona she is no longer talking with Mathilde. She catches his eye, raises a hand, points to the door and enters the house. Slowly, glass in hand, Luke moves in that direction, pausing halfway to talk with Josh. Another glance around the terrace shows him that Alden has his back to the house. He walks the last few steps more quickly and slips through the door.

In the kitchen Rhona gives him a hug. 'This is most mysterious,' she says. 'But as you know I adore mysteries.'

'Not this one.'

'What is it?'

As Luke tells her of the overheard conversation he sees her face blanch. At one point she grips his arm, holding it until he has finished his account. When she releases it she drops to a seat at the table. He sits beside her.

Rhona says, 'You're certain it was more than a lover's quarrel?'

'It sounded final. Lou ran away from him and she's not at the party.'

Rhona remains silent for some moments. Suddenly she seizes his hand. 'This will make no difference to us,' she says. 'Instead of him initiating a separation or divorce, I shall do so. It would have been preferable if he had taken the first steps, but the outcome will be the same.' Her white-faced fear gives way to a look of resolution. She stands. 'Meanwhile we have a party to enjoy. But we must be extra-vigilant. We cannot risk annoying Alden – not tonight. For safety's sake we mustn't be seen to be close. I shall be the dutiful, long-suffering partner.' She laughs. 'This will be *my* play. We'll talk more at the river tomorrow.' She points to the door. 'You go ahead. I'll follow at a respectable interval.'

On the other side of the door Luke finds Carrie. 'Have you been keeping guard?' he asks.

'I don't know what you mean,' she says archly as Henri Renaud gives way to slower music. 'This is more my thing. Will you dance with me, Luke?' She drapes her arms around his neck.

'What's the song?' Luke asks.

'*Yellow*. Do you like it?'

'Love it,' says Luke, thinking of the dress Rhona wore on his first visit to Saffold Farm.

Moving with the music, they drift to the centre of the terrace. Over Carrie's shoulder Luke sees Louise standing at one end of the trestle table. Alden is not with her. Luke tenses.

'Relax,' says Carrie.

Luke tries to obey, but Carrie's long red hair swings from side to side obstructing his vision. Gently turning Carrie round, he sees that Louise is wearing the gypsy dress she wore at the dinner party. She is between two men he does not recognise. One offers her a cigarette. The other lights it for her. She holds the cigarette in her right hand and places her left hand arm across her body in a way that would warn off unwelcome advances.

A group of other dancers momentarily restrict his vision. When she comes into view again he sees Alden approach her. He speaks to her – no doubt in an attempt at reconciliation. Alden gestures to the men that he would like a private word. They move away. Alden speaks again, but Louise turns her head to the left, looks up to the night sky and blows smoke over Alden's shoulder. Had she spat in his face, Luke thinks, the gesture could not have been more dismissive. As if responding to her mood, the music stops.

Luke sees Russ seated on the low wall of the terrace overlooking La Place des Pèlerins. Russ waves. Thérèse in a '50s style dress is standing near him. Matthew, his all black clothes now replaced by white shirt and shorts, walks towards them carrying two bottles of champagne and glasses. Carrie and Luke join them.

'I hope they put on some more music,' says Russ. 'I'm feeling light-footed.'

'As long as it's not the mermaids' song,' says Matthew, easing out a cork.

Alden appears at Thérèse's side as the blast of *Blue Suede Shoes* fills the terrace. He grabs her right arm. 'Let's show them how to do it.'

Thérèse freezes. Luke sees the white knuckles of Alden's hand on Thérèse's forearm. He is reminded of the bruises on Rhona's arm and is tempted to intervene. But as he looks up at Alden's emotionless eyes, he sees Russ's hand tap Alden on the shoulder.

'She promised the first jive to me,' says Russ, taking Thérèse's left arm.

Alden opens his mouth, but before a word emerges, Russ and Thérèse are dancing. Luke is astounded at Russ's energy and footwork, unrestrained by the heat. Already perspiring, Russ throws Luke a conspiratorial glance.

'I shall have to keep an eye on you mirror men,' says Alden coldly, struggling to regain his composure.

'If you want a girl to dance with you, it's best not to break her arm,' says Carrie.

Alden looks towards Thérèse and Russ, both dancing like professionals. 'All her limbs look in fine fettle to me.'

Luke notices Rhona approaching. She winks at him.

Carrie scowls at Alden. 'You're not without issues, Alden.'

'That patronising litotes is beneath you.'

'Is the word man getting technical?' asks Rhona. She takes Alden's hand. 'Dance, darling?' she says.

Luke hears an unmistakeable irony in her voice.

'Of course,' says Alden with forced enthusiasm and leads her to the centre of the terrace.

'Champagne?' says Matthew, handing glasses to Luke and Carrie.

They drink and watch Rhona and Alden dance – she with perfect timing and neat steps, he never more than perfunctory, shooting glances around the terrace, but not noticing Louise walk up to the others. Matthew hands her a glass of champagne.

'Shall we risk a dance?' she says mischievously to Luke.

'Thanks, but I'll sit this one out.'

Louise sips her wine and sighs. 'That's a pity. It would be fun to see Alden rip his guts out as he watches the girl who's just dumped him in the arms of his wife's lover.'

'Is it that obvious?'

'To me, yes, but I'm not a hundred per cent certain if Alden knows about the two of you.' She gives him a grim smile. 'I'm sorry for both your sakes that I couldn't stay with him longer, but I couldn't spend another minute with the beast. I don't know how I fell for all the sweet-talking and little poems. And he was illiterate in bed. Oafish. An animal. He should have played the crocodile.' She finishes her glass. 'I'm going to disappear now and leave first thing tomorrow.'

Louise kisses Matthew and Cassie.

'Where are you going?' Cassie asks.

'I'm off to Holland. I'll email you.' Louise kisses Luke. 'Good luck – to both of you.'

'You're always welcome to visit Rhona and me in Norfolk.'

'I might – and we could form a Victims of Alden Society.' Louise slips away in the sea of heads and limbs.

As Elvis fades into the quieter tones of Tracey Chapman, Rhona parts from Alden and walks towards Mathilde. He doesn't follow. Russ and Thérèse return to the wall. Alden trails behind them, his face regaining some bonhomie.

Alden places one arm on Matthew's shoulder, the other on Luke's. 'I don't know about you two, but if the barbecue is as good as it was last year . . .' He guides them through a tangle of jivers towards the smell of sizzling meat. Luke sees Russ, Carrie and Josh are following at a distance, but Thérèse has disappeared.

Alden takes a pair of tongs, fills a roll with steak and turns to Luke. 'Steak for you, mate?' he asks.

'Thanks,' says Luke. 'You're doing us proud.'

'Mathilde does the organising.' Alden places a steak in a roll and hands it to Matthew. 'One of these years we'll take a play to Propriano. You really must work on your contacts. I can envisage an exhibition of Lynton's paintings in the foyer and our play in the theatre. We must do it before he breathes his last.' He turns to get himself a steak.

Behind Alden's back Matthew frowns in despair, looks at Luke and lifts his right palm, as if about to push Alden onto the hot grid.

Luke again looks over to the dancers. The music has now changed to a slower number. He notices Agnes and Dan, arms around each other, but no sign of Rhona.

When Alden turns round, Matthew asks, 'Will the school continue after Lynton's lifetime?'

'He wants it to. He plans to form a trust to secure its future. I've offered to be a trustee. It would be a travesty if everything Lynton's worked for goes for nothing – if all this closed and became some hideous holiday complex. Let's find some beer.'

'I think I'll stick with wine,' says Matthew.

Alden heads for the drinks table, while the others resume their seats on the low wall, eating steak rolls and enjoying Matthew's private supply of champagne. Luke watches Alden find himself a beer, and is relieved to see that he does not rejoin them, but heads for Lynton. The song *Fast Car* begins, but only a few couples are dancing, among them Agnes and Dan lost in their own world. Rhona is still with Mathilde, ignoring the conversation between Alden and Lynton.

A minute later the atmosphere changes when Alden walks over to the music system and cuts the volume. He strides to the centre of the terrace.

'Shame on you,' shouts Felix.

Alden claps his hands to call for silence. 'Guys,' he begins, 'I'm not going to say much, but I would like to thank all of you for tonight's performance. It would be invidious to mention individuals – it was a team effort but ...'

'You'll do so all the same,' shouts Cassie.

Josh turns to Luke, 'He always gives one of these speeches. You'd think it was he, not Lynton and Mathilde, who was entertaining us.'

Luke looks towards Rhona. She is sitting next to Mathilde. Her legs are stretched out in front of her. The posture reminds him of his visits to Saffold Farm – he is seated beside her as they look at anemones, a mirror, a butterfly. Somewhere far away a voice is reciting a register of names.

'. . . and the hotel, restaurant and all in Santa Marta for their cooperation and . . .'

'Mention the costume department,' calls out Cassie.

'If you'll let me continue . . .'

'And don't forget the sound and lighting,' shouts Josh.

Alden holds up his right hand, asking for silence.

'And three cheers for Lynton and Mathilde for all of this,' shouts Felix. 'Hip. Hip.'

Luke joins in the hurrays which follow and watches Mathilde help Lynton to his feet. Lynton raises an arm of thanks and goodnight as he moves to the house, while Alden, finding himself stranded mid-speech, throws a flamboyant wave in return, as if this were the planned ending to his vote of thanks. For an instant he is nonplussed, but his confusion is relieved when a boy from the summer school begins playing a guitar.

Luke notices that Agnes and Dan are now seated on the low wall on the far side of the terrace. Alden walks over and sits next to Dan. A minute later Rhona joins him.

The guitarist is now playing *American Pie*. Alden joins in and encourages everyone to do the same. To Luke's surprise Russ knows all the words. Luke relaxes and tries to become at one with the colours and sounds around him. It is irksome to see Rhona seated next to Alden, but she is not singing but chatting to Agnes and all but ignores Alden. Luke reassures himself that the word man may be prince of the party, but when the coloured lights are switched off he will be disappear like a glow from a filament.

Luke checks his watch. It is just after 2am. The air is cooler, the last drifts of charcoal smoke have been absorbed by the night, giving way to the gentler scent of marijuana. The moon is now above them.

As the guitarist begins singing a slow sea shanty, Luke feels an arm rest on one of his shoulders, followed by another arm from the other side as Cassie and Josh lull him into the swaying rhythm of the music. In return he locks his arms with theirs. Other groups in the circle have done the same, but not all moving in the same direction at once and causing gentle collisions like waves lapping against rocks. Luke can see Rhona, looking bored, linked between Alden and Agnes, and moving in mesmeric rhythm. When Russ and Dan join in the chorus, one by one the others follow until the whole circle is singing:

'Way haul away, we'll haul away together,
Way, haul away, we'll haul away, Joe.'

'At this end of the deck we can't hear you,' calls the guitarist between verses.

This spurs Alden to dominate the circle with an almost operatic tenor.

During the next verse, as Luke watches Rhona's group move to and fro, he hears a mysterious exchange of confidences around him. The conspiracy is revealed in the next chorus when Cassie, Josh, Russ and Matthew sing confident harmonies. Among the impromptu choir Luke sings the melody line, savouring the riposte to Alden's choral supremacy.

After the final chorus, the guitarist responds to wild applause by raising a wine glass to the circle. The gesture heralds a drinks break. Luke, watching Alden open a bottle of beer, sees Rhona stand and exchange a word with Agnes and Alden. Alden appears to say nothing, but gives an indifferent shrug. Without looking in Luke's direction, Rhona walks across the terrace towards the steps leading to La Place des Pèlerins. Luke turns to watch her leave the party. At the foot of the steps, no longer within Alden's vision, she looks up, brings her hands together and rests her head on them to signal sleep, but a second later flings her arms wide and mimes a breast stroke. As the guitarist resumes playing, Luke waves goodnight and watches her walk back to Les Puits.

Luke relaxes into the next shanty, the chorus of which is sung loudly and accompanied by excessive swaying. Further singing and drinking follow, during which Matthew's largesse with champagne seems boundless. But Luke refuses more wine and drinks only water, remaining alert among the ambient drunkenness. In another chorus, an attempt at harmonies by the makeshift choir fails amid laughter, during which Josh slips off the wall, provoking triumphant finger-pointing from Alden on the wall opposite who, despite the bottles at his feet, seems more sober than anyone.

Cassie pulls Josh to his feet. 'Home time,' she says, struggling to steady him.

'I'll join you,' says Luke.

'Sleep well,' say Russ and Matthew together, clearly with no intention of leaving before dawn.

As Luke, Cassie and Josh walk down La Place des Pèlerins towards Les Puits, an encore of *Roll the Old Chariot* fades behind them.

# 21

L uke wakes at 5.30am and walks to the window. He breathes in the cold air and watches the light soften the contours of the mountains At 6.00am he is in the kitchen waiting for Rhona.

He hears footsteps on the staircase but they do not sound like Rhona's. Nor are the steps coming along the hallway. There is an unmistakeable creak as the door of the house opens. He moves to the window and sees Alden in a red T-shirt and white shorts walk to the bridge. Luke watches the tai chi exercises begin and wonders what thoughts pass through Alden's mind with each movement of limb or fist.

He makes himself tea and sits at the table where the white flowers have been replaced by sprigs of rosemary. There are voices and sounds of feet elsewhere in the house – perhaps late night revellers have only now returned. Silence again. Five minutes pass and she has not come down. Has she overslept? He cannot possibly go to her room and wake her. No, she will be here.

At 6.10am Luke goes to the sink, stretches over the pots of herbs on the sill, opens the window and looks out, his worries increasing as he counsels himself: in her time, in her time. A memory surfaces of waiting years ago for another girl outside Turnham Green tube station. She'd told him she wasn't working at the florist's that Saturday. She'd be there at 10.00am. She had never appeared. He had waited for an hour. Miserable, he walked back home via the flower shop. She was at the counter, working as normal. 'They needed me after all,' was her only comment. 'I was going to phone.'

He hears the kitchen door open and turns round. Rhona is standing there. Pale, barefoot, she is wearing only a long dark blue shirt. She opens her mouth but doesn't speak. Nervous, she looks around the room. Luke steps towards her but she rushes to the window. He follows. She is looking towards the bridge where Alden in a crouched position stares forward like a wild beast about to pounce.

She turns to Luke and throws her arms round his neck. Shivering, she begins to sob, quietly at first but soon unrestrained.

'The bastard,' she says. 'The bastard.'

'What's he done to you?'

She looks to the window again.

'You're safe here. He'll be on his bridge for half an hour.'

Rhona sits at the table. She rests her head in her hands, her elbows on the rough pine surface. She closes her eyes. Her fingers claw through her hair.

Luke rests a hand on her arm. 'What happened?'

She looks up and opens her eyes. She brushes away tears. 'He forced himself on me.'

'He raped you?'

'He tried to.' She clutches his arms. 'After the party. I was almost asleep. He sat on the side of my bed – naked, stroking my hair. I told him I was tired, I needed to sleep. He kept talking about the play and touching me. I told him to leave me alone. He took no notice. He lay down beside me. I said, "Get off." He persisted. He almost . . . it was hell. I wanted to scream – I couldn't. I punched him. He didn't care. It seemed to excite him. So I kicked him. Hurt him. He got angry. I managed to get off the bed. He threw himself at me – grabbed my wrist. "I'm leaving you. I want a divorce," I said. Immediately he released me.' She turns again to the window.

'You're safe now.'

She looks at Luke. 'He was suddenly calm – a different person. I was more scared than I had been before. "So you don't want the business," he said. "I'll buy you out," I told him. But he just laughed. "You can't. Moira and I wouldn't sell our shares – even if you went begging to your mirror man for the money. You've only a minority stake. You want to sleep? Sleep on that".'

'So he knows about us.'

'Yes, but I don't care – the break-up's already started. Maybe it was naive to think it would ever be easy. I was so angry with him. He lay down on his own bed as if I wasn't there and he hadn't a care in the world. I said to him – I shouldn't have done but I said, "And all this because you can't run away, sell all you've got, borrow from your darling sister and shack up with your little dancer." This made him give me that fish-eyed look he's got. At first I thought he would attack me again. But he didn't. He just said coldly, "The business could survive without you, you know." That really hit me. Worse than if he'd punched me. I was in shock, angry. I couldn't speak.'

She looks up. 'What's that?'

'Nothing.'

'I heard footsteps.'

'Elsewhere in the house.' Luke goes to the window. 'He's still on the bridge.'

She falls back in her chair. 'As he lay there with his eyes closed, I wanted to kill him. I couldn't be in the same room. I ran down the corridor and went to Russ's room. I knew it would be empty. I shut myself in. I didn't get any sleep. I was frightened. I thought he'd come looking for me. I kept checking the iron bolt and worrying about my safety. About you and me. The business.'

Luke cradles her head in his hands. 'He won't touch you again – I'll make sure of that. And he may be bluffing about him and his sister not wanting to sell their shares. I'll help you buy out one or both of them, whatever you have to pay, so you have control. You can get rid of him.'

'Luke, he wasn't bluffing. He's vindictive. He won't give up his share.'

'You could try and buy his sister out. Everyone has their price.'

'Not Moira. She's married to a multi-millionaire. She has no need of the money. She and Alden have always been close and she'll do what he wants. If he doesn't want her to sell, she won't. For the last few hours it's all been spinning through my head. The bastard's in control and he knows it. He's trying to drive a wedge between you and me. Between me and my business. Between me and my team. He knows how hard it will be for me to leave what it's taken years to build.' She walks to the window. 'Look at him standing there, hands in the air.' Unconsciously she grasps a handful of marjoram from one of the pots.

'I saw him like that last night on the balcony before his bust-up with Lou.'

'I wish she'd crept up behind him and pushed him off. Look – that

260

ridiculous way he stretches his arms. Lord of Santa Marta. Imposing his seigneurial rights on any girl who takes his fancy. And I'm meant to be his submissive lady who colludes with his power trip.'

'Live with me and let him do his worst. Start your business afresh.'

'He's coming back to the house.' She dashes to the door. 'I don't want to face him.'

Luke takes her hand. 'Stay here, I'm not scared of him.'

She pulls herself away and rushes into the hall. Luke follows.

'We'll meet up later,' she says. 'I must sleep.' She looks at her hand, frowns in puzzlement that she is holding the herbs, throws them down and runs up the staircase.

The front door opens. When Luke sees Alden he feels his fingers closing to form fists.

'Luke, glad to have caught you,' Alden smiles. 'Now you and Russ must join us for dinner tonight at the hotel. A small thank you for your help. Seven o'clock?' He rests a hand on Luke's shoulder.

With great effort Luke does not raise his fists.

It seems that Alden is about to go to the kitchen but he pauses, noticing the stalks of marjoram on the floor. In that instant it strikes Luke that Alden not only knows Rhona has been here a minute before, but is also aware of every word she said – perhaps the claimed second sight is true.

Alden looks him in the face. 'Rhona and I sometimes have our differences, but . . .' Luke sees the iciness in Alden's eyes above the smile, '. . . how can I put it? You're my guest. Please don't embarrass yourself.' Alden goes to the kitchen.

Luke looks down at his fists, still clenched. He relaxes and breathes in deeply. Knuckles are not the way to confront Alden. So far, on the surface at least, he has been amicable towards him; that is how it must continue. From the kitchen he hears the sound of running water. Rising anger tells him to go in and knock the hell out of Alden, but again he resists. Instead, he scoops up the stalks of marjoram, pushes them into a pocket, and returns to his room.

Lying on his bed, he is glad there has been no fist fight, that sound sense has restrained him. Nor was there any cowardice on his part. In fact his willpower and restraint have been a sort of victory. Nevertheless, alone in his room, he also feels like a child reprimanded by an adult and sent upstairs as punishment. Perhaps Alden also thinks this is what happened – that a small miscreant has been put in his place, warned off, that a minor threat to his marriage has been brushed away, swotted like an annoying insect. Luke winces at the thought that Alden is enjoying his triumph in every department – husband, holder of the purse strings, controller of people – even master over this village and its inhabitants.

'But you will not win, you will not win,' Luke says aloud. In contempt he repeats Alden's words, 'Please don't embarrass yourself.'

Luke again clenches his fists. He talked to me like a Victorian patriarch and treats Rhona the same way. She has been abused, disabled. She is clearly so terrified of him and what he might do in the future that she is afraid to leave him. Is there nothing I can do? Must I wait until we have returned home? Do I let her accept abuse for a few more days – weeks – ask her to play the long game – wait for her until the position of her company and its shareholders is resolved? No, this is not a game and she is not a commodity whose future is to be negotiated over the medium or long term.

He tightens his grip and squeezes his eyes tight as a simmering fury spreads through his body. After some minutes he opens his eyes and looks at the room and open window. The sparse furnishings around him and the cloudless sky outside settle his mind enough to allow him to pull himself up from the bed. He leaves the room. Along the corridor he looks through a window and down into the courtyard where he sees Alden reading a book. Occasionally he pencils notes in the margin. Once he casts about as if waiting for his wife to appear along with a maid carrying two cups of coffee – like an actor, Luke thinks, in an advert for an exclusive holiday villa. Seeing Alden calmly enjoying the morning sun, it is hard to believe that this is the man who last night attempted to rape a woman who is now in terror of him. Luke digs into his pocket and pulls out the stalks of marjoram to convince himself that his earlier encounters first with Rhona, then with Alden, were real, not a pre-waking dream. He knows he must leave the house.

The walk to the spring seems interminable and it is an age before the twisting path begins to ascend steeply. Further on, he cannot recall a stretch of flattish terrain dotted with scrawny oaks. At intervals the track seems to disappear but he trusts to instinct that he has followed the correct route. He is perspiring and thirsty but has no water.

At the interface between oaks and pines, the path again ascends. The air is cooler and the path leads him between sheer rocks which he clearly remembers, but where before they were tamed by Rhona's presence, now they have become intimidating. As the track opens onto the platform of gnarled pines, he pauses by a low, flat rock. It was here he and Rhona sat side by side and she allowed him for the first time to look down to where their ascent had begun. His legs are heavy but he cannot bring himself to sit here again. Looking at the rock, he can see the two of them, his arm around her, and he can hear her words, 'Now you can look back.' It seems wrong to follow her instruction when she is not here but with some reluctance he finds himself turning and surveying the mountainside beneath him, the position of Santa Marta indicated only by the top of the church tower. In the distance the sea is still and blue, merging on the horizon with a cloudless sky. The silence is broken only by the sound of shouts rising from the village below. After a few minutes they cease.

He follows the path through the pine trees. A startled bird flies out of some low branches. Large and dark – he has no idea which species – it reminds him of the nightjars he and Rhona saw on the heath. He wishes he were back there with her on that evening when the future seemed so certain. It will be again, he tells himself. It will.

The path swings out of the trees and becomes a hazardous track, clinging between the mountain face towering on the left and a steep drop to the right. A minute later he is hit by a wave of vertigo. He stops, forcing himself not to look down. There is no Rhona at his side to encourage him but he can hear her voice, 'Not far now, but you have to do the next stretch without thinking.' When he arrives at the break in the path he steps, undaunted, across the crevice, fear suppressed by the urge to be at the spring. Now he finds himself walking too fast and fights to curb his impetuosity. At last he sees the path bend round the mountainside and widen. But after a few steps he is halted by the sound behind him of falling stones. He looks back and down but sees nothing. Have they fallen from above? Worse, has the path behind him slipped away in a rockfall? He must go on.

As Luke approaches the spring, through the stillness he hears the intermittent fall of water droplets. Perspiring heavily, he finds the sound a comfort, as if calling him to him from the far side of the pines. At the rock-face he places his hands on the streaks of algae either side of the fissure. There is sufficient dampness to wet his palms. A drop of water falls on his face. He wipes it with a hand and tastes its mineral coolness. A glass of well water could not have been more refreshing. Another drop falls on his feet. He turns and sees on the ground a stalk and a few dried petals. He wants to touch it, but a primitive voice tells him that since it was an offering it must not be disturbed. He pulls from his pocket the crumpled stalks of marjoram, now more aromatic through bruising, and lays them besides Rhona's gift. In the pleasure of a task fulfilled he goes to the wall and sits. It is safe here. Here he does not feel belittled by Alden. Here he is protected from Alden's second sight and malevolent charisma. It is not until he places his head in his hands that he is aware he is crying. He looks up. The remote place has an otherness which makes it easy to understand why it has always been considered sacred. He cannot imagine feeling this way in the English countryside. He closes his eyes, and rids his mind of thought by concentrating on the slow, irregular pendulum of falling droplets.

When at last he looks up he does not know how long he has waited there, but is aware of a new strength like an answer to a wordless prayer. Accompanying the strength is the knowledge of what he must now do. It is a course of action, but not of his own devising. It has come to him from outside himself – a phenomenon he has never before experienced. At first he is shocked at the enormity of what has been presented to him and its possible consequences, almost too dreadful to consider. Disturbed, he remains seated for some minutes, rejecting the idea, attempting to rid his mind of such thoughts – of all thought. But the restfulness of the spring induces a profound peace which assures him that all will be well and that he must trust the strategy gifted by this numinous place. He continues to sit. Each minute imparts an inner strength. A gust of wind stirs the leaves around him. He senses that Rhona is again beside him.

Buoyed by a new-found confidence, he stands and turns, ready for the descent. He has no fear now and negotiates the narrow path with ease. There is no sign of a landslip – had he imagined the sounds of falling rocks? – and further on, the break in the path has shrunk to insignificance. Walking through the pine trees, he thinks he hears an animal rooting about ahead of him, but sees nothing. Perhaps it is a wild boar. Or even a wolf. The thought does not worry him, and he recalls reading that in some Mediterranean countries it is considered lucky to see a single wolf.

Exhilarated by the mountain air, he increases his pace. The silence is broken only by the sound of voices from the village below, and as he leaves the pine trees he enjoys the panoramic landscape spread beneath him and gives little thought to his strategy. There is no need. It presented itself by the spring fully-formed in exact detail, as if the drops of water, on their journey through the granite rocks, had devised it for him and he can depend upon it. It is simple and it will be undetected. He is cheerful. He will enjoy today, even dinner with Alden at the hotel this evening

At Les Puits he finds Felix and Josh cooking a massive fry-up. He accepts their offer to join them; the walk has left him famished and he needs to be fortified for the tasks of the afternoon.

After a shower he lies on his bed. There are preparations to be made but the unwritten timetable states that he must not begin them until 4.00pm after he has rested. Not wishing to sleep, he is content to close his eyes and listen to the occasional creak in the old building, the gentle breathing of Les Puits during its own siesta.

When it is time he leaves his room and walks along the corridor to the locked store room. Pausing, he listens for footsteps but hears none. He finds the key in its hiding place above the architrave. Having unlocked the door he enters, closes it behind himself and allows his eyes to adjust to the faint light from the arched shutter. The room is as he had last seen it. He walks over to the wall on the left. The single side of mirror frame remains propped against the wall. He ignores it and steps over the rugs towards the cupboard. He unlocks the door. He glances at the parcel of mirror pieces but his eyes rest on the long, canvas-covered bundle. With one hand he lifts it out. It is heavy. Behind it is a tin box. He unties the leather straps on the canvas cover, lifts the upper flap and reveals the barrel of a rifle. On one of the flaps is some faded writing. He can just make out a name, *Lynton Travers*. Undoing all the straps, he finds himself holding a Lee Enfield .303. He smiles. It is like meeting an old friend, all but ignored three days ago. He does not linger to inspect its condition. That must wait until he is in the seclusion of his room, but instinct assures him the weapon is serviceable. He rewraps it. Opening the box he finds seven rounds of ammunition, a bottle of oil and a small roll of flannelette. All these he places in his pockets. On the cupboard floor is a pile of rags. He stuffs one in a back pocket. Rifle in hand, he makes his way back through the maze of boxes to the door. Here he waits, listens and peers down the corridor. It is silent. He rests the rifle on the floor, locks the door, replaces the key, lifts up the rifle and returns to his room where he locks himself in.

When he has unwrapped the rifle he lays it on the bed, takes off the safety catch, opens the bolt and sees that the chamber is empty. He takes the rounds from his pocket and places them in a row on the bed. Next he removes the rifle bolt and unclips the magazine, pleased that lessons in weapon training have remained engrained in his memory. Lifting the rifle, he aims towards the far side of the room. The barrel is unpitted. With the butt nestled in his shoulder he is transported back through the years to the Surrey ranges where he learned to shoot.

To work. Check condition of rifle. Walnut stock and butt are undamaged – not even scuffed. The surface has a patina almost as deep as the chest in his bedroom at home. Lynton must have cherished this rifle. Perhaps he had told Mathilde he would give it to a friend, but had never been able to bring himself to part with such a cherished possession. Check metalwork. No rust. Weapon has been well maintained. Tear strips of four by two inch flannelette from roll. Lift trap door in butt plate. Good – rope pull-through inside. Clean rifle. Don't forget chamber and bolt. His school cadet force sergeant-major is at his side, checking his every movement. When he has finished, he wipes the rope pull-through and the copper weight at the end. He replaces them in the butt cavity. He wipes the trap, closes it. He replaces the bolt and magazine, takes a round from the bed, opens the bolt, places the round in the chamber, closes the bolt, lifts it again and ejects the round. All works smoothly. He loads and ejects twice more to reassure himself. To do so with live ammunition carries an element of danger. It is a risk he is happy to take.

He wraps the rifle in its canvas cover and places it under his mattress. He looks at the seven rounds on the bed, wondering which bullet will remove Alden from their lives. An unfamiliar rifle requires sighting shots, but an inner voice tells him that these will not be necessary. Alden will be less than a hundred metres away. The sights can be adjusted to their shortest range. He can trust the unwritten plan. And the rifle. He wraps the ammunition in a shirt and places these too under the mattress.

The old rag in a pocket, Luke quietly returns to the store room where he wipes all the surfaces he touched, even the books. He does not forget the pieces of frame in the cupboard and the single piece nearby. Lastly, on returning to the door, he wipes the knob and the surrounding area. On closing the door, he wipes all areas with which he has had contact, finally cleaning the key and the architrave. Satisfied all fingerprints have been removed, he goes back to his room, shakes the rag, folds it and places it under the bed.

At 7.00pm, on nearing the hotel, Luke surveys the crowded outside tables. Among the bright dresses and shirts he cannot find any of his

266

party. Pausing inside the doorway, he looks around the main restaurant area, but again there seems no-one he knows and he is hit by the bewilderment felt when he has entered an auction room during a sale, but has failed to see among the crowd a single familiar face, whether ally or competitor. It is Rhona he notices first. He is surprised – he was half expecting her to avoid the dinner. She is seated with Russ and Matthew at a table by an open window. She is wearing the white linen dress she wore when they arrived at the village. Distracted, she stares down at the table as Matthew and Russ chatter. Luke notices Alden at the bar and hears him talking in French with a waiter. Rhona does not see Luke's approach, but when Russ stands and beckons she lifts a drawn face which brightens as she throws him a guarded wave. Luke again looks across to Alden who continues to talk loudly, his face partly visible above rows of bottles in the mirror behind the bar.

Luke sits opposite Russ, leaving the seat at the end of the table for Alden. Russ is midway through a story about a meal he had once enjoyed in Venice.

Luke says to Rhona, 'It's very brave of you to be here.'

'It may have been a mistake, but with you, Russ and Matthew I feel safe.'

Luke wants to speak further but Alden appears at the table.

'Luke, where have you been hiding all day?' Alden asks. 'You should have joined us for breakfast at Lynton's.'

'I had a stroll in the hills, joined the boys for a fry-up, then slept it off.'

'You're hungry now, I hope.'

'Starving.'

'Excellent.' He points to an adjacent table where a couple are being served by a waiter carrying an enormous dish of mixed seafood. 'It's a dish for two. Why don't you and I share one? I could never manage it on my own. The others are having wild boar.'

'Do let him see the menu,' says Rhona, but without conviction.

'No, I'll go along with Alden's recommendation,' enthuses Luke, thinking, let him choose his last meal.

'Great. Now next year you must bring Eva with you.'

'Thanks. I'm sure she'd love to come here.' Luke catches Russ's eye and looks away towards Rhona who is staring out of the window. She is the only one to refuse hors d'oeuvres.

After their main courses arrive, Luke sees Rhona cutting off small slices of meat but eating almost nothing.

'Next year's play must be set in the present,' says Alden who seems able to eat quickly, talk and drink at the same time. 'Any ideas Matthew? Or should we write something ourselves?'

'I don't write,' says Matthew. 'You're the man for that.'

'But you'll do the lighting?'

'We'll see.'

Alden turns to Luke. 'You and Rhona going for your usual early morning dip tomorrow?'

Luke hesitates, knowing that to say yes might anger Alden, but to say no would be to concede defeat.

Rhona answers for him 'Of course,' she says firmly, but not looking up.

'Will you join us?' Luke asks Alden.

'No, I'm having a working breakfast up at the school with a French lawyer. We're drafting a trust to secure the school's future. How about we all hit the beach tomorrow night?'

'I'm not much of a beach person,' says Matthew.

Unconcerned, Alden looks towards Rhona. 'I forgot to tell you, darling, I skyped Moira this morning and she tells me they'll all be over in October and will be returning from Hong Kong after Christmas. They'll be living in the Kensington house of course, but she still hopes she can get involved in the business again. Isn't that great? And she's been looking at the accounts – we really can't afford to give so much to your waifs and strays in India.' He turns to Luke. 'You would get on well with her – she likes her antiques.'

Luke sees Rhona's pale face whiten further as she grips the side of the table. Her look of hopeless despair strengthens his already iron resolve to eradicate her torturer. Barely restraining his anger, he looks towards Alden, but Alden is on his feet looking towards another group of diners.

'Do excuse me,' Alden says. 'I've just noticed Ignace. We need a word about next year's arrangements. He leaves the table.

'The shit,' Rhona says through her teeth. 'He picks his moments, puts the knife in, then slips away.'

'He can stuff next year's play,' growls Matthew.

Luke wants to add, 'There won't be any more plays,' but contents himself with an exchange of smiles with Rhona and slips a paper napkin into his pocket.

'I shouldn't have come out this evening,' she says. 'I've been with Agnes all day, avoiding him.'

'Safety in numbers,' says Russ.

'Shall we say seven tomorrow morning?' says Luke.

'I'll be there,' she says.

When Alden returns to the table and they all have finished eating, he insists they share a Corsican almond cake with their coffee. Rhona declines and leaves the table. Luke notices that she has left a scarf hanging on the back of her chair.

Alden finishes his glass. 'Local liqueur guys?' He stands and walks to the bar.

Luke worries that Alden may have gone after Rhona, but Alden remains for several minutes by the bar talking with the waiter, and does not seem to notice Rhona's return. When he rejoins them the waiter follows, carrying five glasses and a bottle on a tray.

'You'll love this,' Alden tells them. 'Lynton says it's medicinal – made from myrtle which was sacred in the ancient world.'

'Is that a pro or a con?' asks Russ.

'Just try it,' orders Alden.

Rhona stands. 'I must go and find Agnes. We have business emails to catch up on. You boys carry on drinking.' As she walks past Alden's left shoulder she gives Luke a look which he takes to indicate that he too should remain and that she will be safe for the night.

Having waited long enough to allay any suspicion that he might have wanted to follow her, Luke says to Alden, 'Thanks for dinner. I'm knackered. I've got to turn in.' He stands and shakes Alden's hand. 'A great liqueur.'

'I always buy a few bottles to take home. You must try it again with us.'

'I'll look forward to it. Can I take the empty bottle home as a souvenir?' He takes the bottle from the table, says goodnight to the others and leaves.

Back in his room, Luke bolts the door, removes the rifle and ammunition from under the mattress and places them on the floor. He undresses, lies on the bed and rehearses in his mind each part of tomorrow's plan until he is certain that every detail has been mastered.

## 22

A t exactly 4am Luke wakes. He walks to the window and looks out into thick darkness. He puts on two T-shirts and a green denim shirt, pulls on jeans, unbolts the door and listens. There is no sound. He places the rag and seven rounds in a pocket, along with the used four by two flannelette and the small length remaining from the roll. He takes up the rifle, still wrapped, He carries the empty liqueur bottle with him. At the foot of the stairs he pauses. Again, silence. He enters the kitchen and drinks from the jug of well water. He pours more water into the bottle.

Silently moving through the hallway, he goes to the rear door of the house. Aware that the hinges grate, he opens it with care, steps outside and closes it. In the darkness he allows himself a deep breath of the early morning air. Holding the rifle parallel with his body, he walks round to the side of the house towards the gulley and looks up towards La Place des Pèlerins. A single yellow glow of a light from the hotel softens the darkness. There is no sign of life. He steals over to the gulley, climbs down the bank and walks towards the cover of some bushes among a cluster of rocks. Here he lies prone, the rifle, still wrapped, to his right. He looks towards the bridge, through the darkness just visible, about seventy metres distant. The sharp descent of the gulley between his position and the bridge is in his favour. It will be a near horizontal shot. The bullet will pass through the target – with how much deflection he cannot guess – and be lost forever in the maquis, perhaps a mile away. He moves into full cover and unwraps the rifle. From habit he checks it is still unloaded. Again he assumes the firing position, but this time with the rifle in his hands, its canvas wrapping between the butt and his right shoulder. He feels comfortable. The passage of years has not taken from him the ability to be at one with a weapon. He raises the rear sight, checks its setting and aims above the bridge.

Satisfied no further rehearsal is needed, he returns to cover, sitting on a low rock, the rifle butt down between his legs. It remains unloaded. It will be a long wait; rules of safety apply. By leaning forward a few inches the bridge comes into view. He leans back and lifts his shirt cuff to check his watch. Just after 4.30am. The target may not be in position until 6.00am, but regular checks must be made. And he must stretch his arms and legs every few minutes to avoid cramp. He is glad of the extra T-shirt; it will have another use later. He knows he must not think of the shot he will take. Nor of the target. Not even of Rhona. All preparations have been carried out. He knows each step of the morning's work. Now is the art of waiting for the first grey light of morning. And for Alden. Fishing has been a good teacher of patience. Its lessons will serve him well now. And its memories will help pass the next ninety minutes.

He recalls his first rod, childhood visits to lakes, his first fish – a perch. Hours spent by rivers and canals. His first pike. An Isle of Wight holiday when he caught his first mackerel. Escapes from school to fish the Surrey lakes. The minutes pass, he exercises to maintain circulation, leans forward every few minutes to bring into view the bridge, its stonework becoming lighter as dawn approaches. When his mouth feels dry he takes small swigs from the water bottle.

He familiarises himself with the rocks around him, the pebbles on the floor of the gulley and the branches and leaves of the shrubs – he does not know their names – which shield him from view. This morning all these surroundings are his allies, even the small, industrious insects creeping near the rifle butt.

It is now 5.30am. The insects near his feet are joined by others. There is no breeze. His mind moves to Norfolk and sea fishing, to fly fishing with Eva. So often with Eva. He is unlikely do so again. He thinks of bass fishing from the shore and from a boat above the wrecks off Yarmouth. Now, late-August, its season is underway. His memories are interrupted by two gun shots from the mountains. The echo rings round the village. It is a reassuring sound. He wonders what calibre rifle the hunters are using. He moves to a small loch on the Isle of Skye with the promise of wily brown trout. Eva's cast is so much better than his own. Fly-fishing is best learned young. Like languages. Like shooting. His mind moves quickly to the Tweed near Melrose, not fishing but walking over the footbridge, pausing midway to watch the river flow beneath him. Which year was that? Which flies did they buy from the shop in town?

He hears a sound. He doesn't move. Could it have been the front door? He listens for footsteps. He hears nothing. He waits and edges forward. A figure in khaki shorts and white short-sleeved shirt is on the bridge. It is Alden. He is almost motionless, head facing down, performing a breathing exercise.

No need for haste. Luke pulls out the paper napkin from his pocket, tears off two corners, rolls them into balls and plugs his ears. He removes a round from his pocket and in silence lowers himself to the ground. When comfortable, ignoring the roughness of the gulley floor beneath his left elbow as it takes the weight of the rifle, he opens the bolt, kisses the brass cartridge case, places the round in the chamber, closes the bolt. It makes the expected metallic click, muffled to his ears, but a glance towards the bridge indicates Alden has not heard. He looks down the sights, slowly breathing in, equally slowly exhaling. Alden is now performing movements with his arms, but his body is still.

This shot, despite the interval of time, the shorter range, the different target, is like hundreds of others in his memory. He is at full concentration. His body is relaxed. His right hand is firm but not too tight round the small of the butt. He moves his right index finger so it is touching but putting no pressure on the trigger. Again, he inhales slowly, again aims at Alden's chest, begins to exhale and squeezes the trigger.

He hears the shot as the recoil, more forceful than expected, makes him close his eyes. When he opens them there is no figure on the bridge. The target has vanished with the echo. The gulley is silent. In the undergrowth below the bridge, he sees a patch of white, Alden's shirt. It does not move. An image surfaces in his mind of a dead seagull shot with a .22 rifle by his shooting instructor when it had perched on the school range before target practice. The boys had cheered at their teacher's accuracy, all except for one who thought the shot brutish and sickening.

He moves back into cover, removes the ear plugs and wraps the rifle. He turns and with his back to the bridge edges down the gulley until, beyond a bend, the continuing silence assures him that it is safe to climb the bank. At the top, near the edge of the path to the mountains, he does not pause or look back. The task is not complete. His concentration is now focussed on the next stage. He walks quickly through the olive trees, but where the path forks he walks beyond the danger sign towards the ravine. Five minutes later he arrives at a point where the terrain to his left begins to slope, gently at first, but soon steepening until it becomes sheer as the ravine opens. On the right, the mountainside, its gullies lined with opportunistic pines, towers above him. Eyes fixed ahead, he continues. After about two hundred metres his way is half blocked by a fallen tree. Its base and roots hang over the precipitous drop. He halts. The place is perfect. Crouching, he removes the rag from his pocket, unwraps the rifle and wipes every surface. He removes magazine and bolt, wipes these too. Having laid the rifle down, he removes his denim shirt, takes off a T-shirt and wraps it around his left hand. Rag in his right hand, he lifts the rifle and hurls it away from him over the edge of the ravine. For a moment it seems to hover in front of him before disappearing into silence.

Luke pulls on his shirts again and carries the bolt and magazine wrapped in the canvas cover further along the track. A few minutes later he halts by a pile of fallen stones. Choosing one of sufficient weight, he wraps it in the canvas cover and throws it into the ravine. Next, his hand covered with the rag, he throws away the bolt and magazine, followed by each of the unused rounds. There is some pleasure in consigning a forgotten weapon to an inaccessible abyss. In celebratory mood, he throws away the final round with as much power as he can muster, but slips on the path, breaking his fall with his left hand. He picks himself up and examines a gash on his palm. He presses his fingers over the wound to prevent bleeding. He smiles: it is minor damage in a greater scheme. He dusts himself down and turns back to the village. A little further on he wraps the rag in a stone and consigns this also to the ravine. Thirsty, he drinks the remaining water from the bottle, but does not throw it away. It will be treasured, not as a souvenir but a trophy. Now to forget. Today he woke up, left his room, enjoyed an early walk. That is all. With each step the images of gulley slip away. Only the picture of the dead seagull lingers, a remote memory imposing itself on a morning stroll, a trivial incident from schooldays, too long ago to concern him.

As Luke approaches Les Puits he gives no more than a glance towards the empty bridge. No-one is in sight. He enters the house and goes to the kitchen. Rhona is at the table drinking tea. In surprise she looks up at him.

'Oh, it's you.' She remains seated.

'Rhona, darling.' He walks over and kisses her. 'All set for a swim? I've already been for a walk.' He places the bottle on the table.

'I heard the door and thought it was Alden.'

'I hope you're not disappointed. River, isn't it?'

'Alden said he had to go and see Mathilde after his tai chi, then he was coming back here for a quick coffee before meeting the lawyer. I thought you were him.'

'But our swim?' He puts an arm around her.

'No, Luke.'

'Your car or mine?'

'No.'

'Rhona?'

She shrugs him off. 'Alden and I worked out a load of stuff last night.'

Luke stares at her, unable to speak or move.

She stands and rests her arms on his. 'Please don't be angry.'

'He's got to you. You've been bullied, brain-washed.'

'You've been very sweet, Luke . . .'

He places his hands on her shoulders. 'What's the bastard done to you?'

'It isn't like that. We talked and we've made a decision.'

'But you and I had planned everything.' His arms tighten on her.

She gently places her hands on his wrists and lowers his arms from her body. 'I shall always remember this summer, Luke. I hope we can remain friends.'

'But he hurt you. He's violent. You said you wanted him out of your life. You wished he'd been pushed off the balcony. You wanted him dead.'

'We've all said a lot of things which would have been better unsaid.'

'He bullied you into this. Did he threaten you?'

'Luke, sweetest, do I look bullied?' She smiles at him.

He notices a tone of pink lipstick he has not previously seen her wear. Nor has he ever seen the pale blue dress.

'He's really poisoned you this time.'

'It's not like that. Have some coffee. I'll explain.'

'No, he's infected your mind.' He goes to the sink, pours a glass of water and gulps it.

She follows him. 'Please don't take it badly. I shall always treasure my memories of this summer. Alden likes you too, even despite the thing between you and me. He'll be here in a minute.'

Luke, still holding the glass, in confused pity and anger looks into her eyes. He sees her smile change to suspicion. She steps back.

'You've hurt your hand.'

'It's nothing.'

She frowns.

'On my walk I tripped. I grazed it.'

'Did you see Alden?'

'I went on the mountain path. I saw no-one. Come on, let's go to the river.'

'You *have* seen him.'

'Why should I want to?'

'You didn't fight with him, did you?'

'He's the violent one, not me.'

Two steel blue eyes fix him. 'Don't lie to me, Luke.'

'I love you, Rhona.'

'You mustn't talk like that.'

'I'll do anything for you.'

'Now *you* scare me. Where is he?'

'I've no idea.'

'I'm going up to Mathilde's.'

'I'll come with you.'

'No, go and have your bloody swim.'

He takes her arm.

'Get your hands off me.'

He follows her out to the courtyard and dashes to the door, barring her way. 'Rhona, wait.'

'Let me out, will you.' She pushes him away, opens the door and strides out.

'Rhona,' he shouts.

She turns round. 'Go and drown yourself.' She waves a fist at him.

'Rhona,' he shouts again.

He hears her scream, 'Alden, Alden!' as he watches her break into a run towards Mathilde's. In the centre of La Place des Pèlerins she stops and again screams, 'Alden, Alden!'

Unable to move, Luke stares after her. Perhaps he should change his plan. Forget the swim. Isn't it best to be here when the body is found?

Why not make the discovery himself? No, that was never the plan. Last night three witnesses heard him say he would go for a swim. The plan must not be changed now. He must not allow Alden, even after death, to work on his mind, as he must have worked on Rhona's last night. In the hallway by the back door he meets Josh in trainers and holding a flask of water.

'Hi, Luke, want to join me for a quick run?'

'I thought I'd go to the river for a swim.'

As Josh opens the door a rifle shot echoes from the mountains.

'Sounded a bit close,' says Josh. 'Enjoy your swim.' He runs off.

As Luke walks to his car, another shot echoes around the La Place des Pèlerins.

# 23

As the road climbs away from Santa Marta Luke assures himself that it was Alden's voice talking in the kitchen, not Rhona's. It is not possible that she has rejected him. Whatever Alden-induced anger has infected her, into whatever cauldron of emotion she will be immersed when Alden's body is discovered, in a short time all will give way to the calm knowledge that she is free. Of course, at first she will be sad. A bond will have grown between Alden the captor and her the captive, and which will now be followed by the almost inexplicable feeling of guilt felt by the victim when the tormentor is found dead and the prisoner finds freedom: her own form of Stockholm Syndrome. He will wait until they have returned home before he tells her that it was he, not a stray bullet from the mountains, who removed Alden from her life. There will be a right time; the opportunity will show itself, as naturally as the day she first walked into his shop. And she will understand. Meanwhile, he must wait for her as he has waited before. But a mile from Santa Marta the image of the lifeless seagull again reasserts itself. The tyres of the Peugeot scream into the road surface as he brakes. He clutches the wheel and gasps. Now he remembers. He did not throw away the spent cartridge. He did not even pick it up. It is still in the gulley. In an automatic reaction he had pulled back the bolt, ejected the brass case and without thinking closed the bolt again.

In frantic recall he sees it lying on the baked mud, but distracted by a distant memory, he leaves it there. He remembers that by the ravine he removed the bolt, but there was no cartridge. And further along the track he threw away only live rounds. In desperation he searches his pockets but fails to find it.

He must go back and retrieve it. No, the search party will already have found the body. Already someone will have phoned the police. His heart pounds. His hands shake on the wheel. He imagines someone seeing the brass cartridge case as it catches the sun on the gulley floor. He sees a handkerchief pulled from a pocket. He sees the evidence, covered with his fingerprints and DNA, lifted up. Someone else is shouting, 'Leave it there for the police.' It is too late to return. His mouth is so dry it is sore.

What to do? He cannot turn back. He is finished. There is now no point going to the river. Unless, as Rhona suggested, he drowns himself. Struggling for breath, he starts the car. Unsure where he should go, he drives to the main road and follows the sign to Zonza. A coach from the other direction sounds its horn. He is too close to the centre of the road. For a moment he doesn't care. At the last moment he swerves to avoid it. He must think. He pulls into a passing place. He must not panic. The cartridge may not yet have been found. He must go back. It is his only chance. He should have turned round immediately. It is too narrow to turn here. He drives on a mile without finding a place. He feels sweat pour down his arms. A white car approaches. He wonders if it is a police car – are they already looking for him? He expects it to slow down. They will already know the make and colour of his car. He wishes he had brought his sunglasses with him. The car, an estate with a family inside, passes by. He cannot possibly return to Santa Marta. He is safe, but perhaps only for a short time. He has become a wanted man, a hunted animal. Every second of freedom now is precious, borrowed. Too soon he finds himself in Zonza. A group of people sitting outside a café seem to stare at him. He drives through the town, eyes fixed on the road and follows the signs to the D368.

Having no plan of escape, he knows he is facing a trial followed by years in a French prison. The prospect is unthinkable. He begins to entertain thoughts of suicide which, with each mile, seem better than any alternative. The decision made, he drives slowly, searching for a secluded side road where he can park, find a mountain path, climb and let himself slip. But no side road appears. After some miles he looks at the edge of the road. Parts are not protected by a wall or crash barrier from a sheer drop. There are places where he could drive off the edge. His heart races. No, a fall from a mountain would be preferable to ending life crushed in burning metal. He must find a place to park and begin his final walk.

Several times he sees a promising side road, but on each occasion a car is close behind and the opportunity is lost. For a few minutes there are no other vehicles on the road. A series of sharp bends demands full concentration. There is still no suitable stopping place. Half a mile later, he sees another car approaching. He gasps, recognising a police car. He tries not to look at it, to retain his speed, but cannot help slowing. He is certain it will stop. It passes, disappearing beyond a bend behind him. He drives on, waiting for it to reappear in his rear view mirror but the road behind him remains clear. The urgency to find a turning off the main road increases. He is trapped in this car, a marked man. A mountain path would offer the freedom to do away with himself, but with each mile, as the road descends, the chance of that choice recedes.

The business of negotiating the unfamiliar road diminishes his urge to leave the car. While he is driving, he is protected from his thoughts. To stop would be final, a punctuation mark in his life for which he is not ready. And what of Rhona? However long the prison sentence – fifteen, twenty years, he has no idea – would she stand by him, wait for him? He drives on. The miles between him and Santa Marta now distance the events of the morning, diminish their reality. He tries not to think of them. He passes a lake. He could stop here under the pines and leave the car. He slows and sees two men beside a Mercedes. They have parked under the trees to look at a herd of wild boar. The animals are rooting about at the lakeside, unafraid of the proximity of humans. The men and the associations of the boar urge him to drive on. To ward off destructive thoughts he tries to think of home, of the shop, of his garden where fruit is waiting to be picked, his allotment where there will be so much to harvest. And Eva? He pictures prison visits from her: the thought is unbearable. The road becomes less steep. Passing cars no longer pose a threat. For much of the time he is travelling with the sun in his face. He squints, makes himself breathe steadily, tries to listen to the inner voice. It remains silent. He can do nothing but continue to drive, for snatched seconds pretending he has never visited Santa Marta. The mountains give way to gentler hills. Glimpses of the sea suggest he should drown himself. There is some everyday comfort in signs which point down side roads to villas or holiday complexes until one disturbs him: *La Lezardière* reminds him of the green lizard they saw on the courtyard wall of Les Puits his first evening on the island. It is a lifetime away.

Struggling to maintain equilibrium, he finds himself entering Porto-Vecchio. Here the sight of people is a renewed threat. He suspects that every pedestrian has heard a news flash that a murderer is on the loose, and that a description of his car has already been broadcast. His arrest is inevitable. He turns into a side road. At the end is a rough piece of land, a makeshift car park with no ticket machine. He chooses a space between a skip and a dirt-covered lorry which seems not to have been driven for weeks. It is only when he has cut the engine and sat back in his seat that he realises his shoulders ache with tension and that he is painfully hot. He peels off the denim shirt and two sweat-soaked T-shirts, and sits, bare-chested in hopeless thought.

After half an hour, thoughts of suicide are overcome by an idea to escape the island by ferry. He pulls on the denim shirt, still clammy to the skin. With the germ of a plan, he leaves the car and heads in the direction he guesses will lead him to the harbour. Russ's advice never to be without passport and wallet might prove to be a life-saver.

As he approaches the town centre he regains confidence. Families, couples, groups, mainly French and Italian, are too busy to notice one more holidaymaker among hundreds. Nevertheless, for safety, he enters a tourist shop and buys sunglasses and a straw hat. He pays in cash and picks up a street map from the counter. Leaving the shop he feels he has also bought himself time and now the occasional sight of a gendarme or police car does not worry him. At a food store he buys a bottle of water and drinks it in a doorway. When he arrives at the harbour there is breeze, but the rattle of halyards on masts transports him to childhood holidays on the Isle of Wight, whose memory adds a deep sadness to his alienation. He turns towards the ferry port. Here he discovers that there is a sailing for Marseilles at 6pm, but it occurs to him that the purchase of a ticket might require him to show his passport. He has some recollection that rules have changed and this might no longer be necessary, but can he risk it? It might be as good as giving himself up. And his name, perhaps a photo too, will surely have already been circulated to ports and airports. He is trapped. He must think. He is still free. There must be another way of escape.

He returns to the town centre. In a square, shadowed by a tropical tree, a busker is singing to the accompaniment of an electronic keyboard. He recognises the plangent cadencies of Jacques Brel's *Amsterdam*. A small crowd has gathered round. He slips among them and sits on the ground. Here, attention is not focused on him. He is safe. He can steal time in which to make a decision.

He listens to the song. It is about sailors, life and love in another port. The words suggest escape. Even in the mournful melody there is hope. Perhaps he should risk the ferry.

* * *

Eva, in Barbara's navy dress, sits in the front right pew of St. Colman's, Corofin. She looks at the statues and the hanging lamp in front of her and tries to imagine Barbara standing in this small, unimposing church planning her own funeral. Her conversion and this service, Eva decides, must have been devised as a farewell to the community and landscape she loved in respectful accordance with its religious heritage; she cannot believe it was for any other reason, certainly not because of a late-in-life discovery of faith.

She glances to her left at the coffin on its trestles and remembers her parents' coffins in Worcester crematorium. Barbara had been her one comfort that day: 'At least they lived to see you grow up and give them a granddaughter.' She looks towards the altar, and recalls sitting next to Agnes in another church. She replays their conversation, thinks of Luke. Had Barbara died a few months ago, he would now be seated beside her.

From behind her come the sounds of a growing congregation. She turns her head to see rows of faces she does not recognise. But at that moment she sees, approaching, a nurse from St. Anthony's who smiles and joins her in the front pew.

'I think the whole of Corofin is here,' says Eva.

'She had more friends than we realised,' says the nurse. 'Or news of the pre-payment at the pub has pulled in the crowds.'

'A bit of both perhaps, and Barbara would have known it.'

Eva looks again at the coffin and the white roses, matching the marble communion rail and altar, her sadness eased by the knowledge that she is carrying out Barbara's wishes. Today will not be a day for tears. She looks towards the chancel and up at the circular stained glass window, so different from the vast east windows of Norfolk churches to which her eyes had drifted during concerts. She tries to recall the last occasion she entered Cantisham parish church – perhaps the flower festival a few years ago. And even earlier, when a friend of Helen's staying for Christmas had insisted they all accompany her to a carol service.

Eva stands at the entry of the priest. The service is simple, as promised – no music, no eulogy. But she is ill at ease with the words of the mass, the sprinkling of holy water on the coffin, and the messages of sin, forgiveness and a future life. It is hard to accept that Barbara has requested such a ceremony, and harder still to believe that if her soul survives it will be affected by anything said or done in this building.

After the service Eva follows the coffin out of the church and watches it placed in the hearse. The nurse remains at her side. Eva asks her to join her in the black limousine waiting behind. It is welcome support; to be alone in this large vehicle would be absurd, over-important. They drive from Corofin to the ruined Kilnaboy church. The funeral director had given a long story of how her aunt had somehow acquired or laid claim to a burial plot in the graveyard. She hadn't followed the explanation, but on leaving the limousine, is glad of Barbara's decision; better a burial near a ruined church not far from the lake, than a neat grave in a civic cemetery or the disposal-by-conveyor-belt of a crematorium. A surprisingly large number of the congregation have followed the hearse to attend the committal. Eva is amazed that, despite the request for family floral tributes only, there is a carpet of flowers at the graveside.

As the coffin is lowered, she recalls an afternoon when Barbara drove her to a remote lake. She had parked on a country road and they had walked a quarter of a mile over rough open ground towards the water's edge. 'Watch out for the old peat diggings,' Barbara had warned her, and a moment later had herself disappeared into one, by good fortune landing on her feet on soft turf. With some difficulty Eva had heaved her out. They had both laughed. The memory brings a smile to Eva's face, but she restrains herself; the occasion demands respect. And yet, as the coffin touches the ground and the priest begins to speak, she imagines Barbara smiling too.

When the priest has finished the final prayer and the last mourners have thrown in soil and crossed themselves, she looks at the cards attached to the flowers. Most are from people she has never met, but among those from people she knows is a large wreath of mauve and yellow freesias from St. Anthony's.

Not wanting to linger, Eva walks towards the car. The priest joins her, but says nothing. At the door of the ruined church she looks up at an ancient carving of a naked woman holding her legs apart.

'Sheela na gig,' says the priest. 'A symbol of fertility.'

'Not exactly Christian,' Eva says.

'On the outer edge of the church. A little like your aunt perhaps.'

'Hardly – and my aunt never had any children.'

'I think she looked on you as her daughter. She would be pleased that you've taken to wearing that dress of hers.'

Eva is annoyed at the observation. 'Goodbye, Father, and thank you,' she says and walks to the limoisine, angry with herself at having addressed the priest as if she shared his religion.

In the pub a small table with its own sandwiches has been reserved for her. She sits, uneasy, feeling like a visiting dignitary as she receives a succession of handshakes, each with its own story. Drinks and reminiscences flow in quick succession. Some, she is sure, are true: 'She knew Lough Corrib better than any man.' 'She gave my son his first rod.' 'When my dad was out of work she took him on as a gardener.' Others she doubts: 'In her day Miss McKelvey was the best-dressed lady in Limerick.' But meeting each comment with a smile, she tries to find appropriate replies in the increasing cacophony. Pub talk with strangers was more Luke's territory than hers. It would have helped had he been with her today.

By 2.00pm she decides that justice has been done to Barbara's wishes, and after more handshakes leaves the party. Refusing the offer of a lift she walks back to St. Anthony's, deciding she will make a substantial donation to them for their kindness to Barbara and to herself. Nothing else keeps her here. The taxi to Shannon is booked for 4.00pm; she cannot be away soon enough.

\* \* \*

To applause, the busker stands and begins to pack up. The crowd disperses and Luke, no longer safe, drifts away with them. In a road off La Place de la République he finds a restaurant and chooses an inside table, picking up from a vacated table a copy of *Le Monde*. The prices on the menu seem exorbitant, but he has more than enough cash: why should he at least not enjoy what might be a final meal of freedom? He smiles at his own gallows humour and orders a bottle of Corsican red wine, a starter of local charcuterie followed by lamb. The waiter is unobtrusive and even if he knows his diner is English, makes no attempt to speak in English himself. With the other diners ignoring him, he is safe here. Even so, it is more comfortable to hide his face behind the newspaper.

The Domaine Alzipratu has a strong flavour of fruit. He drinks the first glass before his plate of cold meat arrives, but the alcohol, rather than relaxing him, sets his thoughts to work at a frenetic pace. He forces himself to eat but his appetite has gone with any hope of escape. He begins to accept that all is over. In desperation he looks around the restaurant. On a wall is a photograph of the cliffs at Bonifacio. He considers driving there and throwing himself off the edge, but the act of self-destruction demands a bravery he knows is beyond him. A few days ago he had been daunted by Norfolk cliffs; these limestone heights at the tip of the island, staring white-faced towards Sardinia, terrify him. He orders more wine.

As an excuse to remain at his table he accepts the waiter's suggestion of a chestnut pudding. He forces himself to eat it, and as the waiter removes his plate, is tempted to ask for cognac but changes his mind and orders coffee. It is shortly after 2.30pm when he pays his bill. Not feeling in the least drunk, he steps out into the sunlight and from a shop further down the street buys a bottle of brandy which he carries back to the car, telling himself that if the police are waiting for him, so be it. But the car park is deserted and he entertains the possibility that luck is on his side. Sinking back in the driver's seat he opens the bottle and drinks from it. Again, his head fills with thoughts of the cliffs of Bonifacio. He expels them with more brandy. Now he finds himself overwhelmed with sadness. He wishes Eva, not Rhona were with him, and he pictures himself in her garden. His thoughts wander to his allotment, in spring, before Rhona had appeared in his shop. He cannot blame her for where he is now, only himself – and Alden who is, even now in death, meting out this revenge. And he has failed a responsibility towards Russ. Overcome by melancholy, by alcohol and exhaustion, he watches the sun slip behind the lorry, and drops into sleep.

When he wakes it is almost 6.00pm. Any lingering notion of escape on the ferry fades. The evening is warm but he is shivering, and there is cramp in his left leg. After drinking more brandy he leaves the car, but as soon as he stands upright both legs give way under him. For a minute he crouches on the ground before levering himself upright with his back against the skip. Cautiously he walks up and down the length of the car, one hand on its side, until he feels steady. When he has sufficient confidence he walks away from the car park with the intention of finding a café. The act of walking revives him but also makes him aware of a piercing headache. After a few minutes he realises he has lost his way and that he has left his street map in the car. For some time he wanders through a residential area, lost, desperate and perspiring heavily in the dusty heat, pausing for breath in the shade of doorways. An old woman comes out of a house and he asks for directions to the town centre. She ignores him and hurries away. He wishes he had lost himself in the mountains; urban alienation is worse. At the end of the road he joins a busier street. Walking on, he sees a sign, *GENDARMERIE NATIONALE.* Exhausted, defeated, he staggers through traffic across the road to the entrance.

# PART IV

## 24

Through the cell window Luke watches the sun rise higher. He hears footsteps outside and a noise from his door. A gendarme enters carrying a large plastic mug of water.

'Awake at last,' he says. He hands Luke the mug. 'Drink it all,' he orders. 'For the head.'

His head feels clear, but he obeys.

'Come with me.'

With the firm grip of the gendarme on his elbow Luke is escorted away from his cell and up some stairs towards the sound of shouting from the floor above. At the top of the stairs he is taken along a corridor at the far end of which he sees a group of policemen. A high-ranking officer is haranguing them. He cannot understand what is being said. The uniforms, more militaristic than those of the English police, threaten him. The tone of the irate officer terrifies him. He is led down an adjoining passageway to an interview room. 'Sit down,' says the gendarme, pointing to a chair by a table. 'You will be seen in a few minutes.'

Luke sits, his eyes on the table top, too scared to look around the room or towards the standing gendarme. There is more shouting from the corridor. Luke raises his eyes.

'There was a fight this morning,' the gendarme says. 'The crew of a

Russian yacht were involved. It may become a diplomatic issue. We are in a difficult position. Brigadier-chef Cardini will see you soon.'

Luke stares at the table during an interminable silence.

The door opens. The interviewing officer enters with another gendarme who places a cup of black coffee on the table and stands with the first gendarme by the door. The senior officer sits opposite Luke. He moves the cup towards Luke. 'For you.'

Luke sees the brigadier-chef, uniformed, square-headed, balding, snake-eyed, stare through him as if he knows every thought in his head as clearly as the passport, wallet, belt and restaurant bill laid out in a line on the table between them.

The brigadier-chef opens Luke's passport. 'Mister Brewer. A good name for a drunk. Tell me how you murdered your lover's husband.'

Luke cannot speak.

'You had no difficulty in talking last night.'

Luke begins to mouth a reply, but cannot get beyond, 'I ... I ...'

'Let me remind you. You came here yesterday evening to make a confession.' He picks up the restaurant bill. 'You know the proverb, *in vino veritas*? You chose a good wine for your confession – two bottles of it. But the empty cognac bottle we found in your car – that was a poor choice. Drink your coffee.'

Luke lifts the cup to his lips. His hands tremble. The coffee is bitter. Every sip washes away the mental clarity he had enjoyed in the cell. As he lowers the cup he sees the gendarmes smiling at each other.

'And of course . . .' the brigadier-chef turns to his colleagues, '. . . la mouette morte.'

All three uniforms laugh.

Luke does not understand.

'Isn't there a play about a dead seagull? My niece told me she loved *Peter Pan*. Were you a pirate? I think you are a Lost Boy now.'

Luke again has his eyes on the table. He feels a hand under his chin, raising his head to face his interrogator.

Trembling, Luke says, 'Shall I make my statement?'

The brigadier-chef leans back. 'But you made your statement last night. Of course, you had so much wine and cognac in you, there was very little point in recording it, even if we could have understood your drunk French and prattling English? I did not even waste the overworked doctor's time to take a blood sample.' He looks at his watch. 'And the alcohol will probably still be in your veins. Drink your coffee.'

Luke feels sick but drinks more.

The brigadier-chef winks at his colleagues. 'Il en a eu assez, n'est-ce pas?'

His colleagues nod, then laugh.

The brigadier-chef says, 'This is the first time we have had a person reported missing by a murdered man.' He smiles. The others smile too. 'He and his wife – your lover – and your friends spent most of yesterday looking for you. They called us mid-afternoon. Unfortunately, it took us some time to contact the rental company, but when we did – they have GPS in all their vehicles – we soon found your car. And the empty bottle of bad cognac.' He laughs again. 'But you had disappeared.'

Incredulous, Luke knows he is a victim of some mocking interrogation technique.

The brigadier-chef continues, 'But you kindly appear at our door and save us the trouble of a full-scale manhunt. And I inform my friend Monsieur Travers. He wanted me to order you a taxi, but I said to him, "Which taxi driver would want a passenger vomiting all the way up to the mountains?" And I certainly wasn't going to send you back in one of our cars, even if I had the manpower to transport drunks around the island. I said you could stay here for the night and they could make arrangements to collect you in the morning. But Monsieur Travers changed his mind. Said I was to put you on the next flight to England. Did you get any sleep?'

'I don't know,' says Luke, mistrustful of his recent memory.

One of the men by the door says, 'Eleven hours.'

'Do you feel well enough to leave us?' asks the brigadier-chef. 'Finish your coffee.'

Registering a tone of sympathy, Luke struggles to believe the implications of what he is being told. He has not killed Alden. His shot has missed. He is not even being accused of attempted murder. There is a distant urge to shout, but the shock of reprieve is greater. An inner voice, disturbing, inexplicable, tells him to ask if they have found the bullet case. In terror he looks at the brigadier-chef, convinced he has heard the thought. The brigadier-chef says nothing. His face remains impenetrable. Luke's hands continue to tremble. He can still see Alden's white shirt below the bridge. He suppresses the memory with the foul coffee. Some spills down his chin onto his own shirt. He pushes away the cup, a child hoping for a reward after taking medicine. 'I can go?'

'What can I charge you with? Parking on private property? The owner hasn't complained. Being drunk and disorderly? Drunk but hardly disorderly. Wasting police time? Perhaps, but you are not worth the paperwork. Or fantasising that you have killed your lover's husband? If that were a crime and we could detect it, there would not be enough prisons.' He gets up from his chair. 'Don't forget your passport and wallet. You have a friend waiting outside. Your restorer, I believe. Perhaps he can help restore your head.' He laughs, but his face changes and he says without a smile, 'I have arranged for you to be on this afternoon's flight from Figari. He fixes Luke again with his snake eyes. 'I am sure it is in everyone's interests.'

Luke feels the grip of an iron handshake.

At the door, the brigadier-chef looks back. 'You have time for lunch before you leave. I suggest no cognac.'

In dazed disbelief Luke stands to leave. A gendarme is between him and the door. Luke stares at the uniform, certain the past few minutes have been a joke to humiliate him. They know he is guilty of attempted murder. He will remain in custody.

'You will need that,' says the gendarme, pointing to Luke's belt.

Luke stretches a faltering hand to the belt. He fails to find the loop at the back of his waistband. The gendarme assists him, and when Luke has fastened the buckle gives him an approving slap on the back, a gesture which confirms the reality of release.

By the front desk of the gendarmerie Russ is waiting. Luke wants to hug him, but Russ frowns and points to the door. When they are outside Russ says through his teeth, 'Not a word.'

Parked outside is Mathilde's car. Luke climbs into the passenger seat. He does not finally accept that he is being released until he hears Russ's door close and the engine start. Even so he can still smell the cell on his clothing, while the taste of police coffee lingers bitter in his mouth. For the first few hundred metres he continues to obey Russ's injunction of silence. He does not ask where they are going, every inch of distance between the car and the gendarmerie, every building passed, roundabout negotiated, an increment of freedom. While they wait at traffic lights he watches a group of holidaymakers and two old men cross the road. They do not turn their heads in his direction; they are not a threat. He watches Russ follow signs to the N198 and realises they are heading south. As the outskirts of town slip behind them, they pick up speed on a dual carriageway. Safer now, Luke says. 'I can't believe I'm out of that place.'

'The Police Station or Santa Marta?'

Luke looks out of the window and sees a sign, *Aeroport.* 'All of it.'

'We were going frantic looking for you.'

'I'm sorry I've dragged you through this.'

'Someone said you might have gone off to drown yourself.'

'Rhona?'

'I said, gone to drown your sorrows more like. If not, a long walk in the mountains. Josh said he'd seen you before his jog and you looked fine and were going for a swim. One search party went to the river, then to the coast. I went with Matthew in his van up to Zonza. When you failed to appear we returned to Santa Marta and waited. Later someone phoned the police.'

Luke is desperate to know whether Alden fell from the bridge because he was startled by the rifle shot, whether he was injured by the fall, or whether he was even grazed by the bullet. He is too scared to ask: the atmosphere of suspicion in the gendarmerie has followed him into the car. He sits back and watches other vehicles overtake, averting his eyes from the mountains on the right.

As they pass through Sotta, Russ says, 'I packed your bag. It's in the boot. Your flight's to Paris, Charles de Gaulle. You'll have to change. There may be a wait before the flight to Heathrow. I didn't think you'd mind.'

'I don't care if I spend the night on the floor of departures.'

'I'm treating you to lunch. It's only a glorified truck stop but Mathilde recommended it.' Russ turns his head, frowning 'You might want to change out of that shirt and jeans.'

'I should be treating you. I feel I owe you my life.'

Russ shakes his head. Luke is unsure whether he is being modest or indicating that he prefers to avoid the subjects of life and death.

Russ leaves the main road and stops at a *relais.* In the car park Luke exchanges his dirty clothes for a fresh T-shirt and shorts. To be out of the dirty clothes is some way towards being rid of yesterday. They walk through the fierce late morning heat to the restaurant door, but Luke shivers at the sight of a line of bunting above the outside tables and at the menu boards on the door; it is too similar to the restaurant in Porto-Vecchio.

Russ is already at the door. Luke calls him back. 'Can we eat outside?'

At a shaded table a waiter brings menus.

'Russ, you choose for me,' says Luke.

He hears Russ chatter in bad French to the waiter.

When the waiter has left Russ says, 'He told me the beef ragout with pasta is very good, and I asked him if it wasn't too much for a hot day and he said that the herbs and spices are . . .'

Luke sinks into his chair, hardly listening. When the waiter has brought bread and mineral water Luke says, 'How was Alden?'

'Worried sick about you. We all were.'

'But was he alright? When I left, Rhona couldn't find him.'

Russ looks away and says, 'Well, apparently he fell off the bridge when he was doing his tai chi. He gave his head a bang but staggered along the gulley before heaving himself up the bank. He hardly knew where he was and ended up in the gallery, which is where she found him, dazed, blood all over the floor. But the knock on the head wasn't as bad as the gash on his leg. She was all for rushing him to a doctor but he wouldn't hear of it.' Russ turns to Luke. 'Then you went missing, by which time he was back to himself and wanting to lead a search party.' Russ looks away. 'We were all shocked that he, not Rhona, was more concerned about you. It was no secret you and she had argued. We were worried about your state of mind. Several of the girls, Cassie and Thérèse in particular, were beside themselves.'

'But Alden's OK?'

Russ frowns. 'Apart from a limp.'

'And Rhona?'

Russ raises his eyebrows and looks away. They sit in silence until their food arrives.

It is not until he begins eating that Luke realises how hungry he is. He finishes his ragout quickly and drinks two glasses of water. Now brave enough for the question, he asks, 'Did the police come to Santa Marta?'

'I think a gendarme turned up, but I didn't see him. Luke?'

'Yes.'

'There's something else.'

Luke sits up, instinctively looking over his shoulder.

Russ says, 'No, it's nothing about Alden. Or Rhona. I would like to stay on here longer.'

'Of course. Have an extra week if you wish. You know what business is like in August.'

'Matthew has asked me to stay at his house in Italy.'

'That's fine. Take two or three weeks. Paid of course – you deserve it. Which part?'

'Paestum. It could be . . . much longer than a few weeks.'

'Ah. I see.'

'It's been quite a decision, but . . . we seem to have become very close.'

'That's great Russ.' Luke knows his tone is unconvincing. In silence he looks at Russ. 'You ought to have brought him with you.'

'I was going to. In fact we drove down from Santa Marta together. But I realised I had to tell you this on my own. We're meeting up in Porto-Vecchio later.'

'Russ, this is wonderful news. We should be drinking champagne. Let me order some.'

'I'm sorry I can't give you proper notice.'

'Forget it.' Luke attempts to ignore the dismal prospect of running the shop single-handed. 'We must drink to this. I insist.' He signals to the waiter.

'I'll come home for a few days in October to sort my things and put the house on the market.'

'If I can help in any way . . . I'll certainly make sure you have a farewell party.'

As Luke looks at the wine list Russ says, 'Just a glass for me. It's a long drive back up the mountains and I wouldn't want another visit to the police station.'

Luke shivers at the comment. He is aware that he has not yet left the island. There remains in his mind the possibility that before lunch is ended a police car will appear. Two of those militaristic uniforms will climb out. They will walk up to their table, one of them holding in a plastic bag a small brass, cylindrical object with a creased open end, and a small dent in the other end where the firing pin struck.

When they each have a glass of wine Luke says, 'To you – both of you. Good luck.' He sips, drinking as much to the hope of his own freedom as to Russ's future. The wine tastes repulsive. He leaves the rest.

Over coffee Luke asks, 'Was it the police who suggested I leave?'

'I'm not certain. Mathilde phoned to report you missing. Later Lynton had a prolonged phone call from a brigadier-chef. I don't know exactly what was said but we were mightily relieved you were safe at the police station. Alden wanted you to be brought back by taxi. He also volunteered to drive down immediately to collect you himself. But Rhona was adamant you should be put on the next plane. More I can't say. You wouldn't have wanted to go back, would you?'

'No. Never.'

At Figari Airport, there is a heavy sadness in Russ's handshake, deepened as Luke walks towards the check-in among the couples and families in holiday spirit. It is not until the plane moves along the runway that he accepts that the bullet case remains undiscovered. Glancing down at the mountains as the island shrinks beneath him, he is aware less of escape and freedom than the sadness of loss – of Rhona, of Russ, of Eva and also part of himself.

# 25

In Brick Kiln Cottage, Eva, up since dawn, removes all the drawers and clears out the contents of her desk in readiness for its replacement. It is an opportunity to reorganise papers, to throw away all which is unwanted, to prepare for a new beginning. She is not certain how to dispose of the unwanted desk and its chair. A month ago she would have asked Luke to take it away and place it in an auction.

It is not until early afternoon that she makes a brief inspection of the garden. In less than a fortnight, with heavy crops of fruit on the trees, it has become an autumn garden. She sees that Annie has tended the flowers and vegetables with more care than she might have done herself. Annie has even cut back all the delphiniums to the ground and mulched, in the hope of a second growth and a late show of flowers. And in the greenhouse there are more tomatoes and cucumbers than she will ever be able to eat. When she returns to the house she finds some plums waiting in the tray of the fridge. She eats one and goes to her bedroom to dress. Opening the wardrobe for a hanger for Barbara's dress, she sees that Luke has removed all his shirts. But there is no sadness in the row of empty hangers: before reconstruction, doesn't the old need to be cleared away? But not necessarily discarded, she thinks – perhaps reincorporated in whatever new life is to be built. But then she notices that Luke has also taken away his books on the bedside table. Their absence, the bare rectangle of the pine table top, signals a departure, more definite, irrevocable, than a few removed shirts. It informs her that the possibility that Luke will play some part in her new life is slight. She is surprised to be unmoved by the thought; in the brief period of mourning laid down by Barbara, perhaps she has also accepted this other loss.

Late afternoon, as promised, the dealer's son arrives with Barbara's desk, chair and a box of books. She helps him carry them into the house.

'Do you have plans for the other desk?' he asks.

'It can be yours. I want nothing for it,' says Eva. 'Have it to bring you and your father luck with the other items you bought from me.' She knows Luke would not approve of such generosity; Barbara would have understood.

When the old desk and chair are placed in the van, the dealer says, 'Are you sure I can't give you something for them?'

'Certainly not,' she says. 'But if you do well with them feel free to give a donation to St. Colman's.'

As the van drives away she is annoyed with herself: she had meant to say, St. Anthony's – a confusion, she tells herself, made by her subconscious still struggling to make sense of Barbara's last wishes.

Later, she arranges the residual contents of her discarded desk in the drawers of its replacement. There is a pleasing mustiness about its cedar linings. In front of it she positions Barbara's chair with its old cushion. Stepping back to see if chair and desk suit their new surroundings, she brings her hands together in a single clap of approval. They belong here, and there is a space on the wall to her right where she can hang the painting of the Limerick house. Plumping the chair's Aubusson cushion, she releases some fine dust into the room. Its smell, more comforting than offensive, transports her back to Barbara's flat. She looks down at the chair and pictures Barbara seated there. 'You are still here,' she says aloud. Slowly she sits, leaning over the desk and running her hands across the width of its scuffed and ink-blotched, green leather top. She examines the marks. Some of are like Rorschach inkblots. They call to mind only her aunt. On one side where, she imagines, Barbara's arm must have rested, part of the leather is worn through to the wood below. She moves her own arm to cover the wear, and finds a strength in doing so. For the first time she notices traces of gilt in the tooling around the edge of the leather where it catches light from the window. She lifts her head and looks out into the garden along a line of pink Japanese anemones in the border by the fence. They will soon need dividing, she thinks, and the whole bed needs weeding, but those tasks can wait. And I must plant a tree in Barbara's memory, perhaps a quince, somehow appropriate with the wayward shape of its fruit and what Annie calls the breath of autumn. She relaxes in the chair and feels the upholstered back on her spine. To work here will always be a pleasure.

She places her laptop on the desk. Since Barbara had never owned a computer and the worn surface in front of her had known only pen and paper, it sits as an intruder. The desk, Eva thinks, will have to accept its new companion along with its new owner.

* * *

The following morning Luke, travel-weary and despondent, watches rain darken the red brick walls of his garden. He knows he should go to the shop, if not to open it, at least to collect mail. The plan had been for him and Russ to return tomorrow, Thursday, and to re-open the shop on Friday, but now the exigencies of business belong to a different life; the shop's future, like his own, is uncertain. At the kitchen table he checks his emails in the hope there may be a message from Rhona; perhaps now, after two days of reflection, her anger towards him would have calmed as quickly as it flared up. And how much does she know? How much does Alden know? Does he remember only the crack of a rifle and being startled, falling from the bridge? Or did he at the last moment see the half-concealed weapon pointing towards him? Did he in fact jump? Or – Luke shivers – did the bullet inflict a glancing wound? And how much of what Alden knew, or could remember, did he share with Rhona? There is no email from her.

He hears a sound at the front door. He freezes. Was it a knock? He imagines an English policeman on the step. Has there been contact with the French police? Has further evidence been found? Perhaps he will be hauled in for questioning. Before going to the door, he goes into the front room where, peering through a gap in the shutters, he looks down the street for a police car. There is none. Expecting a second, firmer knock, he goes to the front door. Junk mail is on the floor beneath the letterbox. Suspicious, he opens the door. At the top of the street the postman is on his round. Reprieved, he returns to the kitchen.

Looking out into the garden again, he knows he should brave the wet and pick the last figs. They are being pillaged by blackbirds, others have fallen to the ground; no doubt the wasps are feasting. He thinks of last

299

year's record crop, Eva and he picking more than a hundred, eating them, making fig crumble, giving them away – Russ had had a basketful. Now it hardly matters if they rot. He frowns at the weeds in the borders and the uncut lawn. And he must get down to the allotment. To have neglected so much is unforgiveable. But he has no energy for the work. Overtaken by sadness and inertia he returns to bed.

On Thursday morning, no less despondent, he carries a strong coffee to the seat under the fig tree where, in an attempt to return to diligent husbandry, he removes some fruit from the lower branches. But after picking a dozen he finds the work pointless, and decides the birds and wasps are welcome to the rest. Finishing his drink, he sits and looks towards the rear of his house. Should he close the business and leave here? He ponders his future until disturbed by the ringtone of his landline. Is it Rhona? He rushes to the back door.

The ringing stops before he seizes the handset. He checks for a message. There is one, but it is from Eva: 'I'm back from Ireland. Funeral went as well as it could have. Not sure when you return. Hope the play went OK.'

He cannot bring himself to phone her back.

For the rest of the day and all Friday he doesn't leave the house and seldom moves from the front room where, with shutters closed and curtains drawn, he watches old French films, preferring Jacques Tatti to romantic or violent themes. But on one occasion arguing voices draw him back to the police station. He mutes the sound and watches in silence but the memories replay in his mind, continuing even after he has ejected the DVD. For comfort he looks to his bookshelves and the rows of novels. But their subjects are mainly crime, war and political intrigue. He settles on an anthology which had been a favourite of his mother's. When he was a child, she had often read to him from it. It seems the least innocuous volume on the shelves. At random he opens a page and reads:

> Speak not – whisper not;
> Here bloweth thyme and bergamot;

He quickly closes the book, attempting to suppress memories of Rhona's silence, her whispered confidences, the thyme near the studio door and the pots of herbs at Les Puits. But their images persist, vivid and painful. He drops the anthology on the floor.

Returning to the TV, he searches the channels for an unthreatening distraction. Football alone provides some safety. Watching – it doesn't matter which teams are playing – he becomes part of a crowd of thousands where eyes are focused on the players, not on him, and if he remains still, even the police, staring up into the terraces cannot single him out. Between matches and sometimes during them, he sleeps in an armchair and at odd hours, when hungry, eats the contents of whatever packet or tin comes to hand in the kitchen.

On Saturday the rain returns. Its sound is a palliative; there had been only the remorseless sun on Corsica. At 9.50am, fishing hat pulled down over his head, he walks up to the market place, glad of the wet which will deter any acquaintance from pausing to chat. At the shop, the mundane tasks of unlocking, turning the sign to open, removing mail from the front door mat, are encroachments on Russ's morning routine, while in the workshop Russ's presence remains in every neatly-arranged screwdriver, jar of pigment and paintbrush – even his voice lingers: 'I suppose we'll get our usual crowd of Saturday timewasters.' Luke forces himself to repair an Empire frame. It is not an urgent task, there is no client pressing for its completion, but it occupies hands and time and even if it does not remove thoughts about Rhona, it dilutes their intensity. Surely, despite everything, there is still hope? Surely Rhona will regret her outburst. Her accusation that he had attacked Alden was well-founded, but with Alden alive and well she must now believe she was wrong. She may even wish to apologise for her anger, and perhaps her insistence not to see him back at Santa Marta was to prevent any friction between him and Alden. Surely she was protecting, not rejecting him? By now she will have returned from the heady atmosphere of Santa Marta to workaday East Anglia, from the heat of the maquis to dull skies and wet hedgerows. Alden's powers of persuasion will have waned. She will want to see him again. He hears the shop bell ring and dashes to the door.

He opens it to find Alf, holding a sack.

'Hope you don't mind me calling in, but I saw the open sign. Guessed you've been too busy catching up with work to look at your vegetables. I've bagged you up a few.' Alf stares him hard in the face. 'You look shattered. Now don't worry about your allotment – I'll keep an eye on it until you've sorted yourself out.'

Luke thanks him and carries the sack to the workshop, not giving the contents a glance. Without enthusiasm, he looks at the Empire mirror, turns his back on it and decides to encroach again on Russ's territory and make some coffee. He spoons the last of the Ethiopian coffee into the filter and wonders where Russ purchases fresh supplies. At his desk he watches the sky clear and water vapour rise from the warming pavement. No, he and Rhona are not finished. He has been lucky and luck will bring them together again. He finds a scrap of paper and writes the last reported words about her, and which, every waking hour since Russ spoke them, have played and replayed themselves in his mind: 'Rhona was adamant you should be put on the next plane.' Was it heat-of-the-moment anger, or her need for time to reflect? He cannot accept it was rejection. At lunchtime he buys a pie and eats in the solitary work room, knowing that the days of tablecloth, home-made chutney and gossip are over. He survives in the shop until mid-afternoon and closes early.

At 4.00pm, the sun at an almost Mediterranean fierceness, he parks his van in a lane half a mile from Saffold Farm, with the intention of walking there unseen. On no account does he want her to feel he is pursuing her, trying to force her hand. It is she who has taken the initiative; that is how it must remain. But he must have the assurance that she has returned. Simply to see her car might be enough. A glimpse of her would be a bonus. To have phoned her, caller's number withheld, in the hope that she would answer and he would hear her voice, would have been unthinkable: he could not trust himself to put the phone down on her without a word. Nor, when duplicity had almost been his ruin, could he countenance further deception. But a secret walk to the house is harmless, forgivable. If a car drives up the lane, it will be necessary to hide among the tall willow herb on the uncut verge, but the risk is worth the chance of a single glimpse of her. As he sets out, thoughts of hiding stir recent memories, but, surely, he tells himself, a sly walk in a country lane does not have the same magnitude as events best forgotten.

A hundred metres from Saffold Farm the sound of an approaching vehicle brings him to a halt. About to dive for cover, he realises that the noise is coming from the field on the other side of the lane. Peering through the opposite hedge he sees a tractor and trailer moving over the stubble to collect straw bales. Safe, he moves on until, close to the front garden of the house, he hears voices. Peering through a gap in the hedge he sees her. In a familiar yellow linen dress she is seated at a table with a man he has not seen before. Their voices are quiet, as if they know they are being watched. The man stretches his arm across the table and touches her hand, contact which triggers her to spring up and kiss him passionately. When she has returned to her seat, the two look at each other in silence, seemingly for minutes. Luke remembers how he too had once sat with her in wordless pleasure in this same garden. Now, the few metres between him and her are miles, increasing every second he watches, like a childhood kite – that was yellow too – which the wind had snatched from his hand, leaving him helpless to retrieve it. Mouth agape, he had watched it climb higher and higher, diminishing in size, before it disappeared above distant trees. At last the couple at the table move, turning their heads to the house from which Alden appears carrying a laden tray which he sets down. Alden pulls up a chair, sits, pours tea and cuts a sponge cake, placing a slice on each of the three plates. There is a curious comfort in the sight of Alden alive: to see him in the flesh is to dispel a lingering image of the white shirt motionless on the gulley floor.

From the house Rambo appears and with slow, proprietorial steps walks across the lawn and stares in Luke's direction with a disdainful suspicion which persuades him to retreat from the hedge back to the lane. In his haste, he catches the arm of his shirt on a bramble. Looking back one more time he can makes out the yellow of her dress but cannot see her face. Laughter rings out from the garden, as if they are mocking him. Lowering his eyes, he notices hanging from a branch a torn strand of blue cotton, like the last thread of hope ripped from his body. Emotions numbed, he walks back feeling invisible, unaware of the sound of his own footsteps, a ghost from a remote past. Near the van he sees a rat chewing on a root. Unstartled, it looks towards him. He walks closer, but the rat continues to eat as if no human being is near.

At home, whisky in hand he sinks into an armchair, staring at the poster of *Theodora* in her ecstatic dance and remembering the evening Rhona entered this room and warmed to its eclectic furnishings. The first sip cuts into his tongue, tasting less of single malt than of last week's brandy; even the smell carries with it memories of dusty streets and the police cell. Going to the kitchen to swill his mouth with water, he looks at the phone on the worktop. He cannot delay calling Eva any longer. Not to have done so already is cowardly. Seeing her again will be painful but . . . without further thought he phones the number.

When Eva answers he falters, 'Sorry I couldn't phone earlier, and I was in the shop today . . .'

'Come over for dinner – if you're not busy.'

That evening, on his walk to Brick Kiln Cottage, carrying a box of figs wrapped in tissue paper, every step along the road, every building and tree, tempts him to believe he is falling back into a comfortable routine, but the sight of her house, the privet hedge and the day lilies, faded now, speak of a lost past and inexorable change. He finds himself knocking before furtively using his own key to enter.

Calling 'Hello,' he places his box of figs on the kitchen table where they sit, awkward among the newspapers and magazines, part gift from a friend, part guilt offering from an old lover. He is glad that when she appears from inside the house she does not notice them.

'Luke, welcome back,' she says giving him a hug. 'You've caught the sun. It's not too early for some wine, is it? Go through.'

Remembering how, on evenings as warm as this, they had usually enjoyed drinks in the kitchen or in the garden Luke goes to the sitting room. Only after he has settled himself on the sofa does he recognise the desk from Ireland; it seems as if it has stood in the room for years. He wonders how she could have brought it here so quickly. When Eva comes in she sits in the armchair opposite.

'Cheers,' she says.

'Cheers.' It is hard to be jovial.

After a silence Eva says, 'Was she worth it?'

Luke feels a rush of blood.

The therapeutic smile. 'I could tell from your face.'

'Part of me says I've been stupid – no – totally reckless. Another part of me ...' It is painful to speak of this to Eva.

'If she walked in this room right now, would your face light up?'

He glances to the door. Uncomfortable, he stares into his glass. When he lifts his eyes Eva is looking at him, neither angry nor judgmental. He has slipped back through the years to become once again her client.

'But tell me about the holiday.'

Perhaps, he thinks, she too is finding the resumption of roles difficult. He tries to be matter-of-fact. 'Santa Marta is beautiful, almost too perfect. The play went well and Russ has found himself a partner. They've moved to Italy.'

'That's amazing. Good for him.' In silence she looks at him. Slowly she lifts her glass, drinks and replaces it on the low table next to her. 'Were you very hurt?'

'I dare say I'll . . .' No, she will see through any glibness. Nor is it possible to give her a full account. 'I went through hell on Corsica.'

He half expects Eva to ask him for more details, but she does not press him.

After some moments of silence she says, 'And now?'

'I'll busy myself with the shop.'

Suddenly Eva stands. 'Let's go to the garden. Bring your glass with you. The fruit trees are amazing this year: the Cox's are breaking the branches and I'm picking cooking apples already.'

Helping her pick fruit is so much easier than conversation indoors. Reaching a high bough of a tree, he asks, 'I suppose you knew from the start?'

'Almost, I guess.'

'I'm so sorry. Hurting you is the worst of it.' He continues picking. 'The best fruit seems to be high up,' he says.

'Shall we find a ladder?'

As they walk to the shed, he says, 'I wish someone had warned me.'

'Would you have listened?'

He doesn't answer. At the shed he pulls out an old wooden ladder. 'Does it always go like this? It's totally my fault and it now seems so avoidable.'

'Or inevitable.'

He stops. There was no note of accusation in her two words. He positions the ladder against the tree. 'Do you think, sooner or later, you and me were always going to . . . ?'

He sees her purse her lips. Her eyes are watery. 'Get up that ladder,' she says. 'Here.' She hands him a large basket.

In a few minutes he has filled the basket. 'Ten kilos, I bet,' he says, 'and we've barely started. Picking fruit always reminds me of scrumping as a child.'

'Devious from an early age,' she says. He cannot see the expression on her face.

After he has filled a second basket, moved the ladder and picked as much again, they move to the tree of cooking apples.

As they are picking the lower branches he says, 'Is this what civilised behaviour is like?'

'Yes, you two-timing shite.'

'I deserve worse than that.'

'Stay for dinner and tell me more about Russ.'

In the kitchen he offers to help wash vegetables and peel apples for a crumble. 'Go and read the paper,' she says.

He returns to the sitting room and looks through a newspaper, knowing he has moved from partner to guest. In the financial pages he is surprised to see several shares ringed in biro, and assumes they relate to Barbara's will.

Over pork chops and garden vegetables, his descriptions of Russ and Matthew and *Peter Pan* fill the conversation.

'At least there must have been some pleasure in taking part in the play,' she says.

'Seeing Lynton's delighted face was the most memorable part of it.'

While clearing the table before the crumble, her back to him, she says, 'Rhona is very beautiful. You will miss her.'

'She's already spiralling away on a new adventure.' Attempting to be stoical, he tells her about the afternoon's walk. 'She was in the garden. I was looking towards her and . . .' He chokes on his words, as the earlier shock and its accompanying analgesia give way to the devastating pain of rejection, made worse by the presence of Eva whom he himself has rejected. He cannot continue his description.

'Poor Luke,' she says, spooning crumble into bowls.

He is uncertain whether she is being sympathetic or enjoying his discomfort. Perhaps both. But she looks across the table at him with a concern which hovers between counsellor and friend. He is safe here; with Rhona he was never safe. He shudders. That was part of her irresistibility.

'It must have been fun being with such a young, energetic group,' she says.

He wonders if there is some resentment in her tone and remembers her stories of clients, husbands or wives of middle-aged university staff, worried about a spouse's daily association with students so much younger.

'I daresay I shan't be seeing any of them again, except Matthew perhaps.'

'You look exhausted,' Eva says.

'I came back half dead.'

She raises an eyebrow. He wants to give her every detail of the shooting and the police, but the events are too close. 'One day I'll tell you,' he says. She smiles as if she can guess everything which has happened.

'I found a sweater of yours yesterday,' she says. 'I'll get it for you. I see you've taken your shirts and books from upstairs. There was a pair of your secateurs in the shed. I'll find them.' She leaves the room.

He remembers other articles – phones, his diary, fishing rods – accidentally left with her over the years, and her routine comment: 'You know what Freud said about an object left behind.' And the answer he had learned and each time repeated: 'The unconscious desire to return.' There would be no such joking exchange this evening. But perhaps that was why he had left behind the bullet case: a desire to return, a wish to relive the event but not to pull the trigger, the registering of guilt by the unconscious before he was aware of it. Eva would have some insight to share if he were open with her. But not tonight. He remembers he still has a key to her back door. He removes it from his keyring and lays it on the kitchen table.

When he leaves she gives him a hug. 'Keep in touch, I can't eat all this damn produce on my own.' The light kiss he feels on the cheek is the goodbye not of a lover but of a friend and one he feels he does not deserve.

'And thank you for the figs,' she says at the door.

The walk home is burdened by self-loathing, replaced by deep sadness as he enters a silent house.

# 26

Luke wakes late morning, surprised at having slept through Sunday's church bells. Yesterday evening's pain seems to have receded. To suppress its return he throws himself into activity. Early afternoon he looks at the newly-cut lawn, the trimmed edges and four sacks of weeds, pleased that he has not dwelt on thoughts of Rhona. To remain active, he finds a lump hammer and cold chisel and begins to remove loose pointing at the base of the garden walls. The task will occupy the rest of the day and many evenings; the repointing itself will consume almost every leisure hour until the frosts. But after an hour's work he finds himself recalling her final words with him in the kitchen at Les Puits and wondering what sort of conversation had taken place between her and Alden the night before? What had finally reconciled them?

As he chips away at loose mortar he hears her voice again and again: 'Alden and I worked out a lot of stuff last night.' He tries to imagine their interchange. It must have started acrimoniously. He can imagine Alden insisting, *Run off with your mirror man, but say goodbye to your business.* As he works, he envisages Rhona arguing, fighting to be free of Alden. He sees her, worn down in the early hours of the morning, forced to choose between him and the business she has built up. He pictures her face as she makes the choice and rejects him, decides to continue some sort of life with Alden for the sake of her work and team. Raking out loose mortar with renewed vigour he attempts but fails to come to terms with her decision that despite his offer of a home, money, a studio – everything – she has surrendered to Alden. Tired, he refuses himself a break until, above the noise of hammer and chisel, he imagines another voice, Eva's: *She's used you – you never had more than a walk-on part in her marriage drama – how can you still love her?* Working away at the foot of the wall he has no answer.

The physical labour, the modicum of pleasure gained as yet another course of bricks is raked out, affords a sense of progress, but does nothing to counter an underlying feeling of rejection and lack of worth. On his knees, scraping moss from the base of the wall, he remembers lying next to Rhona on her lawn where together they traced the weeds spreading from the crevices in the brickwork of her house. Suddenly the pain returns, more intense than before. His face contorts. He throws down his chisel, clutches his head in his hands and hears an animal groan which seems to well from the earth beneath him. He feels sick. He cannot move. He is aware of getting colder. After some time – he does not know how long – the more manageable pain of cramp in a leg forces him to his feet and he limps to a garden seat.

That evening when he is indoors again, another sadness overwhelms him. It is the despondency he recognises as the emotion felt during his schooldays on Sunday evenings: loneliness with the promise only of another week of drear. The prospect of a Monday in the shop without Russ is depressing. Perhaps he should look for a new restorer. Or train someone. The thought does not appeal. That night, in bed, he wonders where the rest of the cast are now: Russ and Matthew in Italy, some of them still at the summer school, Lou on her way to Holland, Josh and Felix – they had talked vaguely of travelling but seemed to have had no plans. Eva was right: he had enjoyed their company. But now they had dispersed; whatever new energy he had found with them had gone too. Friends for a week they would be missed for much longer. Perhaps it would be possible to keep in contact with one or two. Russ and Matthew might be able to help.

In the shop on Monday, some of Sunday's enthusiasm in the garden transfers itself to the workshop where the Empire mirror finds life with each new sheet of gold leaf. It is not important that his workmanship is slower, less assured than Russ's; to be home and safe and active is enough, when last Monday the same mind and hands were occupied with . . . events best not recalled. Had it been possible to tell Eva about them, a burden would have been lifted, but to see her again was painful enough without added humiliation.

Customers come and go, he allows a dealer to beat him down to an absurdly low price for a pair of large Watts frames – Russ would have been horrified – he takes in some watercolours for framing in the hope that he will not have lost his skills at wash-lining – another of Russ's domains; it becomes an ordinary working day. He struggles through another hour's gilding but at 4.00pm when he decides to close the shop and walk to the allotment, he cannot find his keys and spends another hour searching for them. He finally finds them thrown carelessly with an unwashed mug in the sink. At his allotment it is an embarrassment to discover that Alf has not only looked after the weeding but has also sown a row of what seems, from the handwriting on the plastic label, to be an unusual variety of spring cabbage. The sweet peas are now over, a few washed-out mauve flowers a reminder of earlier splendour. At the end of a row a single pink *Mrs. Bolton* is resilient with long stem. The colour reminds him of Rhona's nails on that first Wednesday morning.

He turns away, leaving it unpicked.

He cuts a few overlarge courgettes and some leaves of Swiss chard and makes for home with the intention of raking out more joints in the brickwork, a plan thwarted by the absence of his cold chisel from his tool kit. After searching the house, he finds it on the lawn, covered in a film of rust and reproaches himself for this further carelessness. For an hour he attacks another area of loose pointing. Where the mortar is stubborn he imagines it to be the immoveable obstacles between him and Rhona – somehow, against all reason, there must still be a chance they can be reunited. Now he works more energetically. Once the mortar becomes Euan, still the main obstacle. With increased force he strikes the chisel, but the hammer recoils from the blow and sheers off some adjacent brickwork. The recalcitrant mortar remains in place. Rhona seems more distant than ever. Annoyed at his clumsiness he gives up work for the day and retreats to the kitchen for a beer. As he places a leg of lamb in the oven for dinner, he is ruefully aware that he normally would have invited Eva to share it with him. Later, the feeling is deepened as he eats alone in the kitchen. That evening, tired and watching TV, he draws strength from the knowledge that another day has been negotiated, that a routine is establishing itself, that survival has begun. But before dawn he wakes, trembling from a dream which refuses to slip back into unreality. Someone – a policeman perhaps – is in the gulley. The figure bends down, picks up the bullet case and for a long time studies it in the palm of his hand before slowly lifting his head. Luke sits up in bed, looking towards the red lacquer mirror on the far wall where two accusing eyes stare towards him. He tries to blink them away but they remain. Even when, with the first seepage of light through the shutters, they disappear, their presence haunts the room.

Late that morning a brief hour of equilibrium in the shop is disturbed when, looking through the invoice book, he sees Rhona's name above the purchase details of the needlework. Feeling his confidence implode, he forces himself to the workshop where he attempts to drive her away by burnishing the Empire frame. The efforts are futile, at best reminding him of the absence of Russ who would perform the task so much better. He lays down the agate and returns to his desk where thoughts of her bombard his efforts to read the local paper.

The next day, market day, is worse. The bustle of the stalls outside the shop, the faces of visitors, are reminders that it was on a Wednesday, unseen and unheard she had first appeared in the shop. He goes to the door, praying that he will see her moving among the crowd. She is not there, but returning to his desk he remains facing the far wall staring into an overmantel mirror, and clinging to the hopeless belief that in the reflection he will see her enter as silently as on her first visit. At last, dispirited, he turns back to the empty shop. Occasional glances into the market place further sadden him. Near the post office a police car is parked in its customary place. He trembles, wondering if he will ever be able to accept that he is truly free.

Over the next two days the knowledge increases that it is not simply her company, her voice and perfume, her touch, her laugh and making love with her that he misses, but the freedom she gave him to think afresh and, despite the near fatal consequences, to do or risk anything, whatever the danger. She has gone and with her that liberation – vanished, replaced by daily tasks which bind him to a present in which he has no confidence. He has independence, financial security but feels no freedom in possessing them.

At his desk on Friday he wonders if he should seek help. But he is done with that business too. The years with Eva have immunised him against therapy. He thinks of Rhona, buttoning her dress on the heath. He can hear her say, 'Psychotherapy and counselling are minefields best avoided. And for creative people they can be fatal.'

'Have I wasted half my life?' he had asked.

'No, stupid,' she had told him, 'nothing's wasted now that you and I have met.'

Gazing out through the bay windows, he feels that not only has his past been wasted but that all hopes for his future have been destroyed. Yet he cannot regret having met her. She had brought him to life, if only for a few weeks. In the afternoon he thinks he sees her walk into the deli on the far side of the market place. Rushing out, he runs towards the shop and bounds up the steps, but the woman with dark hair looking at loaves is not her. Embarrassed and angry at his stupidity he retreats to his own shop. His memory has recently proved unreliable; now his powers of observation are failing him.

# 27

At the end of August and with the changing season Luke's sadness increases. The year is declining and part of him, alive as never before in summer, is dying also. One evening, guilty that he is exploiting Alf's friendship, he goes to the allotment and weeds for the first time since returning from Corsica. Not that there is much to be done. Alf has cared for everything and must be thanked now that his help is no longer required. On the second Saturday of September, outside the shop door he frowns at his forgetfulness in not having turned the sign round from open to closed when locking up yesterday. Worse, trying to turn the key in the lock he discovers a more serious lapse: yesterday afternoon he failed to lock the door. In panic he walks in and looks around to see if any stock has been stolen.

'Coffee coming up,' calls a voice from the workshop.

Doubting his eyes and sanity he sees Russ appear with two mugs, one of which he sets down on the desk.

'The new coffee was in the top cupboard,' says Russ.

Luke continues to stare in disbelief.

'I'm finishing off the Empire mirror,' Russ says. 'The top rail might want redoing and . . .' He drops onto a chair. 'Italy didn't quite work out.'

'Russ, I'm so sorry.'

'I think I'd like to stay on. If that's alright. Unless you've made other arrangements.'

Luke hugs him. 'Russ, I am so pleased to see you. I'm really sorry about you and Matthew, but . . . of course I've made no plans. It's all I've been able to do to open the shop in the morning. I'd say welcome back, but part of you never seemed to have left.'

'I think that was the problem. I belong here. Paestum was very beautiful and Matthew's friends were very welcoming, but I knew after the first day I didn't belong.' In silence Russ stares into his cup as if divining what future he may have had in Italy.

'We'll have an early lunch today in the pub and drown our . . .'

'Dreams. They were never more than dreams.' Not looking at Luke, he returns to the workshop.

Luke wonders if "dreams" also referred to his own dissipated hopes. There are questions Russ might be able to answer, but they must wait. He sets about the pile of letters on his desk, first checking, contrary to reason, that none is addressed in large, childish handwriting.

Later in the morning a parcel is delivered. Seeing its French stamps and the sender's name and address, he feels a wave of excitement tempered by apprehension. It is from Lynton. Nervous, Luke unwraps three sketchbooks of drawings and watercolours, along with a few loose-leaf works. He wants to call Russ and to share the pleasure of them with him, but after admiring two landscapes he turns to a series of drawings of soldiers with rifles, wounded comrades, bodies. He closes the book and places it with its companions in a drawer of the desk; he is not yet ready for them. A note accompanies the parcel:

*My dear Luke,*

*I am sorry about the imbroglio which made your stay with us shorter than planned. You must return.*

*I so enjoyed our conversations. As promised, here are the three remaining sketch books which I know you will care for. Show them to no-one while I'm alive, but when I am dead feel free to do with them as you wish. My good wishes for your future,*

*Lynton.*

Luke puzzles over the word "imbroglio" – how much of the truth did Lynton know, or, for that matter, the brigadier-chef? He folds the note and places it in his wallet, doubting if he will ever return to Santa Marta. But staring at his desk it occurs to him that he could ignore Lynton's wishes and use the drawings as a way back to Saffold Farm. Alden would be keen see them, however annoyed he might be that Lynton's generosity had been extended to a rival and not to himself. More importantly,

Rhona would love to look at them. The prospect excites him. This small group of drawings, made by a child eighty years ago, might provide the means whereby they could become close again. What better pretext for contacting her? He imagines Rhona and himself in her studio, looking at the drawings one by one as he arranges them on her plan chest. He stares at the phone, repeating the mobile number he could never forget. But after some minutes of painful deliberation, loyalty to Lynton's wishes holds sway and prevents him from dialling. The decision gives him no pleasure.

In the pub Russ looks up from his steak pie and pint. 'The best and worst thing about being involved in a play is that it brings you so very close to people for a short time. But when it's all over you can never recapture that moment, the excitement.'

'Perhaps not until the next play,' says Luke.

'I'm only an amateur dabbler – I'm sure professionals rise above it – but for me every last night is a loss – that sadness when the actors take their final bow. I've often felt it after a play, even as a member of the audience, when I find myself outside on the street, leaving reality behind in the theatre. I always think forests and mists are more real at the Royal Opera House than on any country walk. Once, after Swan Lake, I touched a grimy brick wall in Floral Street to make myself believe this outside world was real. I'm not sure I was convinced. Matthew and I had a trip into the hills last weekend, but whatever I felt when we were working on the play had already gone and I was already missing . . . He looks around the pub towards three girls in unrestrained laughter at a nearby table. 'All this: somehow not quite real, but familiar, comfortable. And of course, the camaraderie of a production is not the same as . . . making a lasting friendship.'

Russ drains his *Guinness*. When Luke returns with another pint Russ says, 'I'm sorry about you and Rhona.'

'Did she ask about me when you got back to Santa Marta?'

'Everybody asked if you were OK, and said I'm to give you my best wishes when I see you next.'

'But nothing especially from Rhona?'

'Not that I remember.'

'Nothing else?'

Russ shakes his head. 'I'm sorry.' He looks away. 'I suppose she and Alden are back here now. You haven't heard . . . ?'

'No.'

They drink in silence until Russ says, 'I don't suppose you've seen Eva.'

'We did meet up, but . . .'

'I guessed as much.'

'Russ, after you took me to the airport there was no more contact with the police, was there?'

'None I heard of. Were you expecting any?'

'No. No, not really.'

'When I found you at the police station, I hardly recognised you – you looked like a ghost.'

'I nearly became one.'

'That reminds me. I'm meant to be doing the scenery for Blithe Spirit in November, unless word got out that I'd moved and they've found someone else. I don't know if Alden will be involved.'

Luke feels a tremor of excitement at the thought that Alden could be part of the play, that Rhona might be in the audience and that there would be an opportunity to see her, to talk to her. But the hope is weakened by the memory of last week's stolen glimpse of her, of another man and worst of all the laughter from which he was excluded – so different from the laughter in the courtyard of Les Puits of which he had been a part as much as any of the others. 'I'll miss the Peter Pan gang,' he says. 'Josh, Cassie, Felix – even Lou.'

'We had our moments of fun,' says Russ.

Luke sees a wistful smile rise and fall on Russ's face.

By 5.00pm when Luke leaves the shop there is a light drizzle. He goes to the grocer's, buys a bottle of Scotch and a card for Alf and walks to the allotments. Alf is not there. He considers walking round to Alf's house, but the rain has become heavier and he has no coat. He leaves the thank-you present hidden behind the primus stove in Alf's shed. With rain now hammering down on the pantile roof, he decides to wait before returning home, and making himself comfortable on Alf's chair, watches the downpour, while at the back of the shed a drip, intermittent at first, then regular as a clock tick, pings into a metal bucket. The gutter above the door soon overflows and spills down the window, blurring the allotments to a watery green; he might be looking down into a lake. A dribble of water moves slowly down the window, reminding him of the gentle flow of the Solenzara river as he and Rhona sat together on the rock. He sighs and closes his eyes, breathing in the atmosphere of seed trays, damp sacking and paraffin. In this

316

other world there is a comfort which cannot be found at home, in the shop or over a beer with Russ.

On waking he sees that the rain has stopped; perhaps it was the cessation of the steady rhythm of drips which woke him. Easing himself from the chair, he reaches forward and with a hand wipes a porthole through the condensation on the window, revealing his allotment where the evening sun is catching the red flowers of his late-crop runner beans. He lowers his eyes to the dark earth and the white plastic plant label marking the end of the newly-sown row of cabbages: Alf has deserved his whisky. At that moment a dog appears, sniffing along the row before defecating. It is not Maurice. It must be a stray.

Springing from his chair, he throws open the shed door releasing a shower of droplets, waves his arms and shouts, 'Get the hell out of here.'

The dog seems not to hear and kicks up earth behind its mess, uprooting a plant.

'Bugger off,' Luke shouts again, running towards it.

The dog, some sort of collie, darts across the row towards the greenhouse and slips through the open door. At that moment Luke sees the back of a figure, presumably the dog's owner, stooped alongside the greenhouse bench and pouring liquid from a bottle into a red watering can.

Luke strides to the door shouting, 'Your bloody animal was shitting on my plot. Don't you know dogs are banned here?' The owner, in a crumpled combat jacket and canvas hat, ignores him and continues pouring, while the dog cowers under the far end of the bench. Luke sees the label on the bottle. 'And glyphosate's forbidden. Don't you know the rules?'

Getting no response, he shouts, 'Who the hell are you?'

Unconcerned, the figure puts down the bottle and screws on the top. 'Maud has passed on her allotment to me.' It is a woman's voice. She unbends and turns to Luke, 'Sorry about the dog. What will you do? Try to shoot it? You'd probably miss.'

'You? . . . You?' Luke stares at Agnes.

'Maud said I'd see you here before long – I'm her new neighbour. She warned me about the organic mafia.'

'What did you mean – try to shoot your dog?'

'Maud says she always hits the bindweed with this stuff. On the quiet, of course.' Agnes shrugs. 'Oh dear, now the secret's out. Apparently its roots can go down over a metre and . . .'

317

'What did you mean – try to shoot it?'

'I know,' she says.

The two words freeze him. He stares at her, his mind in desperate playback. How can you know about the rifle? When and where could you have seen me? At the same time his eyes search hers: are you guessing, bluffing? The questions give way to conflicting imperatives: get out of here, this is my world; stay and tell me about Rhona.

'What exactly do you know?'

'Pretty much everything.' Slowly, she removes her hat and straightens her hair. 'First, the gun you found in the store room and borrowed – or rather stole. How much detail do you want?'

He moves further into the greenhouse, confronting her. 'Who else knows?'

'Only me and Dan, but forget about him.'

'And Rhona?'

'Nothing.'

'What about Alden?'

'He only remembers the crack of a rifle – a boar hunter's gun they all thought. Except me. He recalled falling from the bridge, but only had a vague memory of staggering along the gulley and finding his way up to the gallery.'

Shuddering at her unemotional tone, Luke sinks to the bench and stares at the brick floor.

She sits beside him. 'Oh, don't worry. I've no plans to tell anyone.' She pauses. 'Not yet.'

He shivers, 'So it's money, is it?'

For some seconds Agnes doesn't answer. The dog moves out of hiding and looks in Luke's direction. Agnes says, 'Fifty thousand. A lump sum for my silence. You have three days. But I'll start with a couple of mirrors for my new cottage. And a new car. An Audi I think.'

Luke, looking up and turning his head, is unnerved by her smile. 'You're mad. You can't prove anything.'

'Mad? That's rich from a would-be murderer.' She throws back her head and laughs. 'As for proof, to begin with there's the bullet case you left behind with your fingerprints all over it.' Agnes begins giggling. 'That must be worth at least as much as the price of a house. Fifty grand's cheap.'

Luke feels the dog brush past him as it makes its way to the door where it sits on guard.

Agnes looks towards the dog. 'And for insulting Kirby you can tend my allotment. I'll tell you what to grow and . . .' Scornful laughter almost stifles her voice. '. . . you must keep it well weeded. No creeping thistle, ground elder, bindweed. And don't you . . .' In manic hysteria, eyes squeezed shut, she rocks to and fro, 'And don't you dare use any chemicals.'

Luke sees her turn towards him, open her eyes and pull back her lips in an attempt to suppress a further outburst. As their eyes meet she looks down to the ground. 'Oh, and I've always longed to have some handmade shoes.' She releases a suppressed guffaw.

He is certain she is insane.

When the outburst subsides she throws her arm in Luke's direction. He feels the heel of her hand strike him like a fist on the biceps. Again and again she hits him – he does not resist – but the blows have diminishing force, until he realises she is making fun of him and has no thought of blackmail.

His effort to smile fails. 'Do you spy on people so you can mock them? Or do you report back to Rhona, so you can both laugh?'

Agnes ignores him and stares ahead through the foliage of the tomato plants, 'One, two, three, four, five, six . . .'

Luke thinks she is counting the ripening fruit on a bending truss in front of them – insanity returned.

'. . . maybe seven times,' she says, 'I've seen it happen. Rhona finds a man, sometimes older, sometimes younger, and each one *la grande amour*, each time she has discovered her true destiny and soul mate who makes all previous loves illusions. But it's *always* the man who is deeper in love than she is. *Always* she who breaks it off. Then she returns to Alden. *Always* the other guy who is driven out of his wits by her. There's been the Polish art student, the orthopaedic surgeon, the clarinettist, a dull schoolteacher with a lovely wife. Several others in between. And you.'

Unable to look at her, Luke's eyes remain on the ground.

Agnes continues, 'All that varies are the secret locations – not so secret in your case – and the degree of hurt and violence inflicted on or by the lover, and by Rhona and Alden on each other. This is the first attempted shooting, I think. Congratulations.' She pats him on the back. 'And it always ends with *le grand rapprochement* between her and Alden before the remorseless wheel begins to turn again. Meanwhile, he enjoys little affairs of his own.' She turns to Luke. 'As I know to my cost.'

'You and him?'

'The biggest mistake of my life. I could have killed him myself.' The dog moves from the door and places its head on her lap. 'Some people need alcohol or drugs or regular doses of adulation from Twitter followers. Not Rhona. You should see the designs she did while she was away. Unbelievable. Worth more to her than a few . . . than the odd bullet flying near her husband.'

Luke says nothing. He hears rain on the glass roof, gets up, closes the door of the greenhouse and sits down, surprised that this information about Rhona is bringing with it a feeling of calm, as if his private universe is reclaiming him. It is not clear if Agnes is an interloper, like her detestable dog, or a part of it. 'You should have warned me about them as soon as I arrived at that bloody place.'

'The last one I tried to warn off was Elliot, the clarinettist. He gave me a quiet lecture about envy, ending with, "So sod off." I gave up after that.'

Luke looks over the allotments towards Alf's shed where the door he left open swings back and forth. After a minute he says, 'How did you find out about the gun?'

'I was keeping an eye on you.'

'Spying.'

Agnes sits upright and folds her arms. 'At first I thought nothing about this latest man she was whanging away about, the mirror dealer. But a week or two later I met Eva.'

'Professionally?'

'She was quite helpful – if annoying. At one session I mentioned that my employer was embarking on an affair with some mirror dealer she'd bought a needlework from. At the time I'd no idea what I'd said. It must have shocked the hell out of her but she kept her cool. And later I discovered your name in Rhona's cheque book, and always wanting the low down on her latest victim, I found out the address and drove to your shop. And there you were by the front door, all loved-up with Eva, poor cow. And when I saw her next we exchanged notes.'

'Eva discussed me in a counselling session? I don't believe it.'

'No. Later. Our paths crossed. We were both out shopping. She didn't want to be drawn into a social conversation, but it happened. As you know it can.'

'So you told her all about me and Rhona.'

'She'd already sussed something was going on.'

'But you filled in the details.'

'She was being ripped apart by uncertainty. I know what a killer that can be. I wanted to help her. And for a time I did. But soon she didn't want to know. She'd given up on you. When I phoned her from Corsica, she told me not to bother her again: she'd written you off. She sounded as angry with herself as with you. After that, I . . .' She looks down at her bag. 'Do you want a drink? Tea, not brandy, I'm afraid.' She pulls out a thermos flask and unscrews the stopper. 'Mug or plastic top?'

'The top's fine.'

'Good, I can't stand drinking from plastic.' She pours Luke his tea and hands it to him.

Luke sips. The tea is almost Alf-strength.

She looks at him. 'I like tea I can taste.'

In silence they drink, watching the rain run down the panes of glass.

Not looking at him, she says, 'I saw you go into the store room and linger by the junk near the cupboard.'

'I knew I heard footsteps.'

'Next morning, when you and Rhona were out, I searched the room with a torch. I don't know how you could see anything without one.'

'I've made good money from attics and dark rooms.'

'One was almost your ruin. I suspected you were looking at a broken frame, but I also checked everything else and found the gun. I was tempted to hide it but was too frightened. From then on I was scared shitless and tried to keep tabs on you. My chief worry was that if Rhona dumped you, you'd do away with yourself. Like the surgeon almost did. And when Alden attempted to rape Rhona I feared you might try to kill him. Especially with Rhona feeling trapped and wanting him dead.'

'I thought all this time you were getting off with Dan.'

'Convincing couple, weren't we? There was nothing between Dan and me. I told him I was concerned for your safety and he offered to help. It was from his room we saw you set off on your walk up the mountains. Without a hat or water. Mad or what? He followed you at a distance, even along that lunatic path to the spring. At one point he thought you were looking for a place where you could throw yourself off. Once he almost slipped over the edge himself.'

'The falling stones.'

'Had he died it would have been your fault. For a few hours I thought any crisis had been averted. But Rhona and Alden's sudden kiss-and-forgive routine on the Monday night took me by surprise. I didn't know about it until the following morning when Alden went missing. Rhona was demented, screaming his name in the centre of La Place des Pèlerins. I shouted to her from the courtyard door and rushed out. She was beside herself. "Luke's killed Alden," she told me.'

'She was nearly right.'

'Her feral instincts seldom fail her. She rushed up towards Lynton's house. I went to look for Alden by the bridge. Standing where he did those ridiculous exercises, I saw no trace of him, only a curious glint on the floor of the gulley. I climbed down and found the bullet case. It had an acrid smell like it had been recently fired. The next two minutes were a nightmare. I ran down the gulley, first one way, then the other, expecting to find a body, but all I found were traces of blood on the ground. In panic I scooped up dirt with my hands, covered up the blood and rubbed the earth with the soles of my sandals. It almost disappeared, but there were soon flies on it. I was shaking in fear. I walked further along the gulley. There was no sign of Alden, although once I saw what might have been another drop of blood. I scuffed it away. At any moment I thought I would find him, wounded or dead. But I was more concerned for you than him.'

'I'm sorry I dragged you through this.'

'It was mad enough trying to shoot him, but then to leave evidence behind . . .'

'I only realised it after I'd driven away from the village. I thought Alden was dead. And it was too late to go back.'

'So you drove down to Porto-Vecchio and got pissed. It would have been easier for all of us – and yourself – had you gone to the hotel and drunk yourself silly in the bar.'

'I considered fleeing the country.'

'Had you done so there might have been an investigation. I cannot tell you my relief when having failed to find a body I climbed out of the gulley and saw Rhona helping Alden down the steps. He had staggered up to the gallery where she found him slumped in a chair. I ran up to them on the steps. Even to my inexperienced eye the gash on his forehead didn't look like a bullet wound. In Mathilde's kitchen, as she bathed it, she kept asking, "Did Luke do this? Was it Luke?" "No, I fell," he said. "You were fighting – he pushed you," she insisted. "No I fell, I fell," he told her. "Why cover up for him?" she bullied. "I simply fell," he said. "That's all. I'll be all right." I still don't know whether or not he was protecting you – or rather preventing a police investigation which would cause trouble for Mathilde and Lynton. Eventually Rhona calmed down

322

and insisted he should rest on the couch in Lynton's studio. I went back to the house, leaving her fussing over her injured darling. I was hoping to find the gun – then I'd know you wouldn't shoot yourself with it. First, I tried the store room. It was gone. Next I tried your room. What the hell did you do with it?'

'I threw it into the ravine before I left.'

'And gave me ten hours' torture.'

'I'm sorry.'

'When I found Russ, he assured me you'd never do anything rash. I almost told him about the gun but didn't dare. So I went back to Mathilde's and suggested we search for you. Alden wanted to lead the hunt, but Rhona wouldn't let him. So I borrowed Mathilde's car and me and Dan went to look for you at the river, while Matthew and Russ went to Zonza. After the river we tried that café on the coast road. Then the beach. I was going frantic. Dan and I couldn't tell anyone what we knew. And the bullet case in my pocket felt as if it was burning into me. Back at Lynton's, Alden was off the couch, enjoying being the injured hero and using one of the old man's walking sticks. I stayed in Mathilde's kitchen drinking coffee with Rhona. She didn't want to talk. Just sat there in silence scribbling designs. Late afternoon Mathilde phoned the police. You probably know the rest from Russ.'

Agnes refills her mug and offers the flask to Luke.

He frowns and looks at the roof where rain is seeping through a broken pane. 'When did the police say they'd found me?'

'Early evening. Lynton took the call. A gang of us were with him and Mathilde in the kitchen. My French wasn't good enough to understand what was being said, but I realised you were in custody. There was some reassurance in the fact that Lynton was clearly on friendly terms with the brigadier-chef. At this point Alden interrupted and said you should be sent back to us by taxi. He would pay. Or he would drive down and collect you himself – as if he would have been able. But when I heard the police were suggesting you should stay there overnight, I immediately thought they must have found the gun. It was only Lynton's tone which gave me some grounds for hope. At this point Rhona was insistent – she didn't want to see you again. Alden argued with her, until she left the room in a rage. Then Alden looked at me, hoping for support. I turned to Lynton and quietly said, "Tell the police to put him on the next plane home." He stared at me with those suspicious eyes of his and finally gave me a grim smile. After that there was no more discussion.'

'So it's you I thank.'

'I thought you were better away from there in case they found the gun or any more careless clues.'

'When did the police get to the village?'

'Between seven and eight. It was a gendarme on a motor bike. He spoke at length with Lynton. I don't know everything that was said, but he certainly asked about Alden's fall, and it was me who volunteered to show him where it happened. As we stood together on the bridge he looked up and down the gulley and asked if I knew anything about a firearm. I told him we had a few stage guns and cutlasses – he was welcome to look at them – but nothing dangerous. He seemed satisfied with that. I think he was more interested in getting back to Lynton's for a coffee and a chinwag. Whatever your drunk ramblings in the gendarmerie, the police weren't going to pursue it.'

'What did you do with the cartridge case?'

Agnes reaches into her bag. Unzipping a side pocket, she pulls out a wallet, designed like a small ammunition pouch. It holds three bullet-shaped lipsticks. Two have paste gemstones at one end. 'Vintage *Revlon*,' she says. 'I found them in the stage make-up box. There's *Misty Coral*, *Snow Pink*, and this one in the middle which doesn't quite match and seems to have lost its jewel. Yours I think.' She pulls it out and places it in the palm of his left hand.

He stares at the .303 calibre brass cartridge case, afraid to touch it until, cautiously, with his right thumb and index finger he lifts it and examines its shiny surface, buffed to a high sheen and with a faint red smudge around the creased end which held the bullet.

'Lipstick,' says Agnes. 'I gave it a thorough cleaning after I found it, then I polished it and pushed a *Chanel Rouge* down the end, slipped it into my make-up bag and it passed unquestioned through customs.'

Luke continues to stare at it as the rain rattles the glass roof. 'Thank you,' he says.

'Forget it. I must get home – Kirby needs feeding.' She stands and walks to the door.

In the downpour Luke follows her to the gate. At the road she goes to an old Toyota. She opens a back door and Kirby jumps onto the rear seat. Closing the door, she turns to Luke.

'Get in. I'll drop you off at your house. Back Lane, isn't it?'

He climbs into the passenger seat.

Agnes turns the ignition key, but the car fails to start.

'You should have gone with the blackmail,' Luke says.

'So the gunman has a sense of humour,' she says, turning the ignition again, this time firing the engine.

When they arrive at his house, Luke says, 'Come in for a glass of wine. I owe you that at least.'

'A drink with a failed murderer? One of Rhona's cast-offs on the bounce? What do you take me for? And I'm one of your ex-girlfriend's ex-clients – that would be a whole snake-pit of head stuff.'

'I only said a drink. And I've a lamb bone in the fridge if Kirby is hungry.' Luke turns to the dog lying on the back seat. 'Do you like bones?'

Agnes looks round at Kirby. Suddenly alert, it lets out a plaintive whine. 'Idiot, you've said the *b* word. Now we'll have to come in or he'll howl all the way home.'

As Luke opens the front door Kirby shoots past him, nose to the ground towards the kitchen.

Agnes throws a glance round the hallway. 'This place is a morgue,' she says, closing the door.

'I've plans to redecorate.'

A double bark followed by an impatient yowl echoes through the house, diminishing to a whine when they arrive at the kitchen door to be met by Kirby's expectant face.

# POSTSCRIPT

Now sufficient time has passed, I am able to record the story of that summer. I have relied a little on my own memories, but chiefly on the accounts given by Eva who has remained a friend, and by Luke who has become much more than that.

A.B.

Lightning Source UK Ltd.
Milton Keynes UK
UKHW01f1819140518
322593UK00002B/381/P

9 789492 371690